To: Andi – I hope you and Maisie Grace enjoy reading this.

Always!

Celia Martin

To Challenge Destiny

Celia Martin

KITSAP
PUBLISHING

KITSAP PUBLISHING

To Challenge Destiny
First edition, published 2019

By Celia Martin

Cover Image Courtesy of Ylanite Koppens from Pixabay
Interior Book Layout: Tim Meikle, Reprospace

ISBN-13: 978-1-942661-20-7

Published by Kitsap Publishing
P.O. Box 572
Poulsbo, WA 98370
www.KitsapPublishing.com

This book is dedicated to my loving husband Ken who has supported me in my writing career from day one.

Second is to the members of my writing group. They not only encouraged me, they taught me more than I ever learned in any writing class. They are: Alice Anderson, Cheryl Berger, Mike Donnelly, Dee Eide, Carson Farley, Kathy Kvam, Cynthia Percenti (Penny), and Sue Riddle.

Professional Book Review

"Celia Martin invokes this historical era with feeling and fidelity illustrating that she is, indeed, a student of history and not just a teacher. Martin possesses the literary powers necessary for transforming the texture and tone of 17th century life into dramatic form while still maintaining the aforementioned historical accuracy. Too often such works fall into the trap of populating its fictional landscape with one dimensional character while focusing the bulk of its attention on nailing down details, but Martin avoids such pitfalls with To Challenge Destiny. The novel's four primary characters are rendered in a multi-dimensional fashion and never strain credibility.

The novel's conclusion is powerful and convincing. Overall, To Challenge Destiny more than lives up to its billing as a "romance adventure" and Martin proves throughout the course of the novel that she has the vision and talent to make bygone times come alive for modern readers. The book, as well, has a near ideal length and the pacing keeps readers involved and attentive rather than risking their loss of attention throughout self-indulgent sideshows. Lovers of historical and romance fiction alike will enjoy this novel."

Anne Hollister, Professional Book Reviews

"*If you yearn for a story skillfully told – if you like characters who find a home in your heart – if you enjoy historical accuracy blended masterfully into a story with robust action and enthralling, heart-wrenching romance, then To Challenge Destiny is your new favorite book.*

Being a historian myself, I cannot help but carefully monitor historical works for accurate details, and I am delighted with To Challenge Destiny. The attention to the accurate portrayal of seventeenth century America and the customs of a variety of new-to-America Europeans; the topography of the new colonies; the exactness of the procedures for operating seagoing vessels; and even the plethora of languages and accents, add to the authenticity of the tale.

The characters feel so real, it is as though you can reach out and touch them. The main hero and heroine, with their passions constrained by duty and honor, yearn for each other, but cannot unbind the knots of their lives with which destiny has bound them. Only when fate changes course is their love allowed to burst forth in exquisitely portrayed, intense scenes of passion.

In amazing action sequences: the battles, the escapes, the weather, and, especially, the horrendous villains all play havoc on the characters. Who will survive? Will love triumph?

You will thrill. You will cry. You will love To Challenge Destiny, your new favorite book. To Challenge Destiny is: Masterful story-telling! Exquisite passion and breath-taking action! A historical romance feast!"

A Collection of Romantic Adventures

Follow the romantic adventures of the D'Arcy, Hayward, and Lotterby families and their captivating friends in seventeenth century England and the American colonies. Dive into: To Challenge Destiny and savor the rich tapestry of the alluring past. And be sure to watch for A Bewitching Dilemma when the dashing Captain Garrett D'Arcy sweeps Tempest Winslowe from the gallows where she was to be hanged as a witch, Coming Soon!

Excerpt from
A Bewitching Dilemma
At the end of the book.

As a history teacher, the best thing about teaching is bringing history to life. Of less importance are the dates, the wars, the statesmen and generals; it is the lives of the everyday people that make history fun to experience. Travel in the cramped space of a sailing ship across the vast ocean, struggle to build a home in a new land. What do you eat? What do you wear? What kind of home do you live in and how do you keep warm in winter and survive the heat and insects of summer? History should be exciting and eye opening, and never boring.

Visit my web site at:
cmartinbooks.kitsappublishing.com

Prologue

England September 1651

Adler Hayward slumped in his saddle but kept his eyes glued on the bobbing lantern light far ahead in the dark. His arms ached, his legs ached, his head throbbed, and his parched throat cried out for a drink, a drink of anything. What he, a yeoman farmer, was doing on a damned horse traveling down narrow, poorly maintained country lanes in the middle of this dank dreary night was a question he guessed he would never be able to answer.

He could blame his younger brother Caleb for being so blasted good looking with his dark auburn hair and green, heavy-lidded eyes, he had won the heart and hand of Sir Yardley's older daughter, Sidonie. Or he could blame Sidonie's brothers Cyril and William for being so persuasive they convinced Caleb and then him to join their cavalry troop despite his and his brother's meager riding capabilities and lack of experience with swords or pistols.

"'Tis no matter do you fight on foot with musket and pike or on horseback with sword and sawed-off musket, but fight you must unless you want to live out your life under Roundhead mastery," said Cyril Yardley. "We need ride hard to join up with the King. You cannot cover the miles afoot." The Yardleys provided the Haywards with horses and armaments and off they went, joining up with King Charles in time to share in his defeat at Worcester. Now they made up part of the King's guard as he hit out into the hinterland in a desperate bid to escape capture by Cromwell's victorious forces. Adler had no idea where they headed, he but followed his King.

"Pay heed," his brother said, "look we leave the lane."

Glancing to his right, Adler saw a dim glow appearing to the east.

Soon the sun would peep over the horizon and the country populace would be about their morning chores. The King needed to be hidden away by then, concealed from curious stares. Nudging his tired horse over the low hedge lining the rutted lane and into a field of stubble, Adler followed after his brother. Trotting past a few sheep foraging through the remnants of grain, they headed into a woods. Low hanging branches tugged at hats and coats, and Adler heard curses from his fellow guardsmen. The curses helped guide him, the lantern being difficult to discern through the autumn foliage. Some of the men, due to wounds, weariness, or lame horses, were dropping out, unable to continue the mad march. They would hope to find shelter and sustenance in local cottages. Some might well be betrayed and captured. The thought of prison tore at Adler's gut. He did not know how he would survive such an ordeal. He had too great a love for the outdoors. And too much fear of enclosed places.

Breaking out of the woods, they rode through another field, up a hill, and into less dense woods that soon opened onto a grassy meadow. And so they straggled along, fording streams and urging their horses up more hills and down into valleys until they trotted out of yet another woods onto a rough trail and could see their goal silhouetted against an overcast sky. A manor house or hunting lodge, Adler knew not which nor did he care. The gate to the walled enclosure surrounding a half-timbered house opened, and the King disappeared inside.

Arriving at their destination in the King's wake, Adler slid from his saddle. He had had no order to dismount, but his buttocks told him he had endured enough. Others copied him, including his brother and Cyril Yardley. Leaning his head against his horse's rump, Adler longed for sleep. Never in his twenty-five years had he been so tired; not after days in the field behind a plow, not after a gargantuan struggle to get a stump out of a field his father wanted for an apple orchard, not even after the fight he had with a bear that had wandered out of the woods. The poor creature must have escaped from some show. He had a frayed rope collar about his neck and numerous patches of missing fur. He was hungry and angry, and Adler had the misfortune to stumble across him. Adler bore teeth indentations on his shoulders and claw scars across his chest and back, but he had managed to get his knife into the bear's heart before the big jaws had closed over his head. William Yardley had found him, mauled and bleeding, and carted him home across his shoulders. Adler owed William his life, but he had not been able to return the favor this day. William died at the end of a Roundhead's sword but a few feet from Adler.

A cavalryman named Draye who had recently joined their squadron dispatched the Roundhead, but the fighting had been too fierce to retrieve William's body. Adler knew Cyril was grieving. Telling his family of his brother's death would be difficult, but to know William would have no decent burial would be heartbreaking to those who loved the vibrant, good-natured cavalier. A year younger than Adler, William had been a close friend and confidant. They had attended petty school together then continued their education at the town grammar school. Eventually William and Cyril went on to Oxford and Adler and Caleb continued to work on their father's farm. A prosperous yeoman owning his land outright, their father had encouraged his sons to seek professions other than farming, but both loved their farm and the land. Now that the King had lost his bid to reclaim the throne, Adler wondered what awaited him and Caleb and the other members of their squadron who had escaped out of Worcester. He doubted they would be allowed to pick up their lives, resume their daily routines as though they had not trotted off to war.

Their squadron captain, Nathaniel D'Arcy, had followed King Charles into the house. He emerged as Caleb, eyes drooping, shoulders sagging, handed Adler a dipper of well water. "Best we got for now," his brother said. Adler eagerly accepted the dipper, guzzled down its content, then turned his attention to D'Arcy.

His captain gathered together the men still under his command. "We have been disbanded," he said, removing his hat to swipe his thick dark hair off his brow. "We are to look to ourselves. I head back to Cheshire, though no doubt my brother and I, having broken our paroles, will find we have a price on our heads. Are we captured, prison or worse will be our fate. All the same, we head for home. Any of you who wish to ride with us are welcome. We will do best do we stay off the main roads." He looked out over the faces turned to him, and Adler followed his gaze. His eyes lit on a square-jawed man in the plain garb of a working man, coarse linen shirt, leather doublet, and shapeless brown coat.

Adler recognized the man. Jack Chapman, a former peddler whose sister married above her station and gave her brother a boost. Chapman now owned a small shop in Chester and no longer peddled his ware from town to town or farm to farm. But no one knew the Heart of England countryside better than Chapman. From visits Chapman made to their farm before his rise in fortune, Adler knew him to be a King's man. He and his father had fought as pikemen for King Charles I. Adler had not been surprised to find the peddler in their midst.

"Chapman," D'Arcy called to him. "I can think of no one better suited to guide us home. Will you oblige us? 'Tis a risk. You would have a better chance on your own."

Chapman smiled and nodded. "Aye, I will lead you and anyone who wishes to tag along."

"Good man," D'Arcy said. "All right, those of you coming with us, mount up."

No sleep, no food, nothing to drink but a dipper of well water. And it was starting to rain. Adler swung back up on his tired mount. What a fool he had been to join this hopeless cause. Fool, fool, he chided himself as he steered his horse out the gate and fell into line behind his brother. They had traveled less than a mile when D'Arcy called them to halt and urged them to circle up. Rising in his stirrups and raising his voice, he said, "We need get far enough from White Ladies so we are not apt to give away King Charles, yet we are in need of food and rest, and our horses are in sore need of a respite. Jack knows a farmer not far from here he believes we can trust. We are a large party to be on these back roads. Best we travel at night. Are you fearful of trusting this farmer, feel free to make your own way home. Otherwise, follow us."

No one deserted the party and in short order they trotted up to the farmer's croft. A pail of milk in each hand, wiry black hair poking out from under his hat, the farmer stared at the group of riders entering his yard. His wariness turned to relief when he recognized Chapman.

"Welcome, friend, welcome, oi am afeared you are here because the King has lost." He shook his head. "Is that the case we are naow into a heap of trouble."

Chapman swung down from his horse and greeted the farmer. "Aye,

Goodman Snow, we lost, but the King escaped." He swung his arm behind him, indicating the men with him. "We are desperately in need of rest and food and a place to bide until nightfall. Can you oblige us?"

His pointed nose quivering, the farmer nodded over his shoulder. "You may stable your horses and take your rest in yonder barn. Oi will see you get something to eat, is it naught but bread and cheese and a dram of ale."

"We thank you greatly, Goodman Snow," D'Arcy said, dismounting. "We must need water and feed these tired horses even before we mind our own needs." He reached into his pocket and pulled out a purse. "I will pay you well, but have a care before spending the coins, the Roundheads will be on watch for anyone who suddenly becomes prosperous."

"'Twould be a loi did I sye oi had no fear of the Roundheads, but do they come and are you found, oi will but tell them you forced me at gun point to give you shelter." He bobbed his head. "So naow, sir, tike your horses to the ditch. Oi will but tike this milk into the wife and calm her fears and set her to making you a repast. Then oi will meet you in the barn where you can rest easy until nightfall."

Snow's freehold appeared near as prosperous as Adler's father's. It was a tidy property, and Adler liked Snow. He had an honest face. Tired though he was, Adler would not have agreed to bide with the farmer did he not trust him. His horse watered, Adler entered the small barn. It smelled of hay and dung, but it felt good to be out of the rain. Two cows, four oxen, and several hens occupied the barn. Adding ten men and ten horses made for a squeeze, but could he find a place to stretch out and shut his eyes for a bit, Adler could see no reason to complain.

D'Arcy advised against removing their mounts' saddles. "But loosen the girth. We may need to leave in a hurry," he said. "Let us see can we bunch the horses under the loft. Tired as they are, do we get them fed, they are not apt to start picking on one another."

The horses were soon settled and the farmer and his wife arrived with bread, cheese, sausage, a pail of ale and a couple of mugs the men would have to share. "Brave men you be," said Goody Snow, bobbing her head up and down. "Blessed be the King escaped. Oi will have him in me prayers tonight. Lord knows what will become of us all with

Cromwell in command."

His hunger assuaged, Adler pushed around some hay to pad his body and bunched his coat to make a pillow. In an instant he was asleep and did not awaken until Cyril Yardley shook his shoulder. "Rouse yourself, Adler, 'tis near time to leave. Chapman says we have a long ride ahead of us are we to make our next haven by morning."

With the onslaught of night Chapman led them across fields and meadows and down backcountry lanes and rutted trails. With the sunrise he found them shelter and food. Rest by day travel by night, but by the third night of their trek, Adler began recognizing landmarks that told him they were not far from home.

Cyril rode up beside Adler. His dark brown eyes appearing sunken in his tired face, he said "My house is apt to be watched. We are going to your house. Caleb has volunteered to ride in and see is all clear. He is not covered in blood as are you. He could make a good defense that he is but returning home late from a trip to Chester."

Adler could not like the idea his younger brother was to act as bait, but he recognized the necessity. Was his house being watched, they needed to know that they would not ride into a trap. They had not long to wait. The door was thrown open and Caleb's new bride was in his arms. His father and mother squeezed past the lovers, and his father waved a lantern, a sure sign all was well. Judging by the moon, Adler guessed it was past midnight, but he had the feeling his family had been waiting up as though they had been expecting them.

He no sooner rode into the yard than his mother, her blue eyes glistening with joyous tears, was tugging at his stirrup. He swung down from his saddle to be wrapped in her embrace. "Both my boys home safe. Thank the good lord." He was next grasped by his father, and he saw Sidonie slip from Caleb's arms to hug her brother, Cyril, who had been engulfed in his younger sister's arms, though Adler knew not why Arcadia should be at their house at this time of night.

"William, where is William?" Arcadia demanded. A feminine version of her dark-haired, brown-eyed brother, she twisted to look at the other men who had dismounted.

His shoulders slumped, Cyril shook his head. "Dear ones, William was killed in battle."

"No!" Arcadia cried.

"Dear God," Sidonie whispered. "Oh, how will we tell Mother?"

"I hate to interrupt," said D'Arcy, his commanding voice and tall imposing figure demanding attention. "I think 'tis best do we get these horses hidden. We cannot be too careful."

"Yes, yes, of course you are right," said Adler's father. "Let us get your poor beasts watered and fed, then all of you come in the house." Turning to Adler's mother, he said, "My wife has a fine fare for you. Though we were not expecting so many of you, we can assure you all a hearty meal and a warm bed before the hearth."

"Cyril, you go in the house with your sisters," Adler said. "I will see to your mount." Nodding, Cyril thanked him and with an arm around each sister, he trailed Adler's mother into the house. "Caleb, you too. Father will see to your mount. Your wife needs you." Caleb clasped Adler's shoulder. "Thanks," he said and followed his wife inside.

Horses tended and stomachs fed, plans needed to be made. Her eyes red and bloodshot from crying, Arcadia said, "You cannot go home, Cyril. Cromwell's men are watching the house. They came asking for you and William. Father said you went to Chester, but they doubted his word, and at least two men have been stationed in the barn round the clock. I had a feeling you would be coming home tonight, so I had Cook mix a wee potion of laudanum and honey in a couple of mugs of ale I took out to them. They were mighty grateful for the drinks, and within the hour, they were both asleep. I was able to slip away with their being none the wiser."

"She showed up here around dark time," said Adler's father. "Sure to certain she was you would be coming home tonight. So we all waited up, and sure 'nough, she was right." He wiped a hand over his balding head. "When I was in the field with the plow yester morn, a troop of horsemen came round, militiamen they were, trampling through the field with no thought for a decent man's work. Said they were looking for any man who had fought for...," he paused and looked around at the faces watching him, "well, I will not say what he called our King. I told him I knew of no such men, and they rode on. I have not seen them since."

"They will be back," D'Arcy said. "I have no wish to be taken by them. I have heard well the fate of the poor Scots taken at Dunbar. Those who survived imprisonment were sold into indentured slavery in the colonies. I have no mind to experience their fate."

Adler had no mind to experience imprisonment or servitude.

Green eyes flashing, D'Arcy's younger brother Ranulf spoke up, "I am for making my way home, catching a boat to Ireland, then finding passage on a ship bound for Holland or France and meet up with King Charles. He will have need of his guard."

"You are sure he is going to make it back to the continent?" Draye questioned.

Ranulf looked offended. "He will make it." He shook his head. "But should he not, James will need supporters even more. He has not the same leadership qualities as does Charles."

"I have a better idea," D'Arcy said. "We support the King by staying here in England and helping finance him. His income will be limited. He will need whatever we can send him."

"And where are we to get this income for him?" Cyril asked.

"Why from the Roundheads. We become Robin Hood's merry men. We rob from the rich Puritan merchants and give to our impoverished King."

"You are saying you want us to become thieves or highwaymen?" Caleb demanded.

D'Arcy grinned. "Aye, that is what I am saying."

A general hubbub of voices assaulted D'Arcy's announcement, but Adler was watching Ranulf. Shaking his head, his reddish-blond hair flying about his face, he said, "Nay, I am bound for the continent. However, do you proceed with your inane scheme, you will need a contact on the continent. Someone you can trust to get your nefariously gained funds to King Charles. I will send word to Kenrick where you may send your dispatches." Adler had learned Kenrick D'Arcy, the Earl of Tyneford, eldest of the D'Arcy brothers, had heeded his wife's pleas that he not break his parole. She had feared did he break his oath and join his brothers as they rode off to fight for Charles, was he not killed in battle, he could well be executed as traitor if again taken prisoner. Adler understood her feelings. His mother had begged him and Caleb not to go. How he wished he had listened to her as the Earl had listened to his wife. Had he listened to his mother, he would not now be contemplating leaving with Ranulf for the continent.

"I am with Ranulf," D'Arcy said, his strong chin jutting forward, his gray eyes glowing in the firelight. "I have no mind to have my neck stretched for to see the King has a softer bed. I will serve in his guard, but I will not steal for him."

Cacophony rose again with Adler's parents joining in as well as Caleb's wife who sat clinging to her husband's arm. But Adler had made up his mind. He was bound for the continent. He might well be a coward, running away, but he knew, he could never survive imprisonment. Enclosed, unable to see the light of day – he would go mad. His heart heavy, he stared at his parents and wondered would he ever see them again. His brother had to stay. He could not leave his wife. Adler but hoped Caleb would escape imprisonment, and that he would not join Nathaniel D'Arcy in his perilous scheme. He drew a deep breath through his nose. How to say good-bye to this land he loved so dearly. Land that had been in his family since the time of the Conqueror, or so he had been told. To leave family and friends, to leave a way of life he loved. 'Twas hard. What would be his future he could not say, but his destiny had been sealed the day he rode into battle in support of his King, and he was bound on a new path.

Chapter 1

Dublin, Ireland September 1651

Glynneth Bristow Fortier stood in the shadow of the foc's'le and watched three men stealthily board the *Grishilde*. The ship's captain greeted them and a small but hefty looking pouch changed hands. The captain weighed it in his palm, nodded his head, and pointed to the steps leading down to the 'tween deck where Glynneth's family lay sleeping. She felt no alarm. The men did not appear menacing. She suspected they were Royalists bent on escaping to the continent to avoid imprisonment or worse at the hands of the Puritans. Many an Irishman had done the same thing.

Word had flown across the Irish Sea of King Charles II's defeat by Cromwell. A thousand pound reward was being offered for the King's capture. Everyone was speculating about him. Where could he be hiding? Was he in Wales? Had he escaped to Ireland? Glynneth bore no love for Cromwell. In 1649 her father had died fighting Cromwell at Drogheda. The vibrant, hot-blooded Alaric Bristow, for years chafing under the hostile English yoke, had joined in the Irish rebellion. Glynneth believed had her mother not died of a fever that ravished many a home in 1640, her father would not have become embroiled in the rebellion. Her strong-willed mother would never have allowed her adored, yet overly fervent, husband to enter the fray.

The creaking of the ship and its easy roll as it rested in the Dublin Harbor was soothing. Unable to sleep in the stuffy hold, Glynneth, after seeing her children, husband, and father-in-law were resting peacefully, had slipped up onto the deck for some fresh air. The ship would be departing with the high tide, bound for Holland. She expected never to see Ireland again. Yet she shed no tears. She could not help but think a brighter future awaited her and her family.

The moon came out from behind some clouds and struck a path across the deck. One of the three men who had come aboard stepped from the 'tween deck stairway into the bright path. Still in the shadows, Glynneth watched him. He turned in a full circle, slowly, warily. He went to each side of the ship and looked overboard. Seemingly satisfied, he swept off his hat and wiped his brow with his forearm. His appearance seemed more the farmer than a soldier. His light brown hair, cut short in country fashion, curled about his neck and ears. His wide, loose-skirted breeches hung to just below his knees, and under his plain brown coat, the neck line covered by a squared-ended falling band collar, he wore a buff doublet with pewter buttons. Of medium height and weight, he looked strong. He had broad shoulders and sturdy calves. She could not see his features clearly, but she guessed him to be in his early to mid-twenties.

Curious about her fellow passengers, she stepped from the shadows. "Good evening." She smiled at the man's startled mien as he clutched at his chest. "Sorry did I take you unaware."

The man's initial surprise disappeared, and approaching her with a cautious step, he stopped before her and offered a slight bow. "I had no notion anyone other than the watchman was about." He pointed to a man on the half deck. "Are you with the family that sleeps below?"

"I am. I am Glynneth Fortier. I travel with my husband and children and my in-laws. And you travel with two friends?"

A wariness entered his eyes, blue eyes she thought them, mayhap a bluish green, under questioning brown eyebrows. He was an attractive man, not handsome in the classic sense as was her husband, more a rugged good looks, chiseled jawline, straight nose, firm mouth. As he hesitated, she continued, "I saw the three of you come aboard. You appear to be traveling light." She had noted each man carried but one small canvas draw-string bag. "Is your stay in Holland to be of short duration?"

"You are most observant, Mistress Fortier. I take it you are bound for a longer visit."

He had artfully avoided answering her question, and his evasion made her smile. "Mister, ah, Mister ..." She waited.

"Hayward," he finally answered, "Adler Hayward."

She wondered if he had given her his correct name. It mattered not. Did the weather hold, the trip to Holland should take but three or four days, and then she would never see him again. "Ah, Mister Hayward, pleased to make your acquaintance." She nodded then resumed, "We are not visiting Holland. It is but a stopover for us. We are bound for the Dutch colony of New Netherland in the new world." She laughed. "I see that surprises you. Easy to explain. My father-in-law is a French Huguenot refugee. A merchant, he finds the restrictions the English place on his ventures too demanding. His brother-in-law, also a refugee, has done well in New Netherland. He asked my father-in-law to join him there and help him with his business. And so to the new world we go, my husband, daughter, and baby son, my father-in-law, my brother-in-law, and his wife. 'Twill be quite the adventure, I am thinking."

Her companion smiled for the first time. A winning smile, it softened his features and brought a gleam to his eyes and a dimple to his right cheek. "The new world you say? And to New Netherland. Yet none of you are Dutch. Do you speak Dutch?"

"But a little, though I am working on it. However, I speak French, and so we are told, near as many settlers there speak French as Dutch. The Dutch call the French settlers Walloons. They have been generous with land grants to them in the New Netherlands. My father-in-law's brother-in-law is involved in the fur trade."

Her new acquaintance cocked his head. "The fur trade you say?"

"Yes, Monsieur Chappell, my uncle by marriage, has been most prosperous, but he needs someone he can trust to get the best deals for his furs, and the best items for trade with the Indians. He has been asking my father-in-law for several years to come to his aid. Finally, between the war, the land confiscations, trade restrictions, and the plague, my father-in-law has had enough. We are not Catholic, but Irish Catholics have been so devastated, few can afford to buy the products my father-in-law imports. So we seek a saner place to live. The Dutch, so Monsieur Chappell says, are very open and accepting of all who contribute to their colony. He says even Jews and some Catholics have found a home there."

"You paint an inviting picture of New Netherland. I would hear more."

"My husband and his father can tell you more on the morrow. That is, are we all hale. I fear the seasickness. Do you suffer from the sickness Mister Hayward?"

He shook his head. "I know not, though I had no sickness crossing from England. Truth be, until you mentioned it, I had given it no thought. This sickness, is it bad?"

Tilting her head and narrowing her eyes, Glynneth shrugged. "I but know what I have been told. Some do get dreadfully sick and think death would be a blessing. Others have no problem. My father-in-law says when he came from France, his wife was sick, but he was ne'er sick for even a moment. Did he not feel sorry for his wife, he would have enjoyed the voyage."

"Let us hope we are all like your father-in-law. Fortier did you say is his name?"

"Yes, Curtice Fortier and my husband is Etienne." She started to ask the names of his friends, but at that moment the captain emerged from his cabin and told the watchman to ring the bell to get the crew up. The tide was right. 'Twas time to set sail.

With the clanging of the ship's bell, seaman poured onto the deck. Glynneth, dodging out of the way of a scurrying youth said, "I best go below and see that my children have not been disturbed. Are they yet sleeping, I will come back up that I may bid farewell to my homeland."

Adler nodded. "I shall be at the railing. I am in no hurry to bury myself in the hold."

❊ ❊ ❊ ❊

Shouts of the seamen as they set about their duties relieved the knot tormenting Adler's gut. It would not completely untie until they sailed out of port, but he could breathe more easily with departure underway. Removing himself to the bulwark in an area he hoped would not be in the way, he watched the sails rise then flutter as they caught the late night breeze. The captain shouted directions to the helmsman manning the whipstaff in the shadow of the quarter deck.

Adler knew nothing about ships or sailing, but Ranulf D'Arcy, who had organized their escape from England, knew a great deal. Having

4

grown up on the Wirral Peninsula, Ranulf was well acquainted with many types of ships. He had been pleased they had been able to book passage on the *Grishilde*. "'Tis a Dutch Fluyt," he said. "Squared-rigged with a wide hull and high stern, it needs a minimum crew, but when armed, it can put up a good defense against most pirate ships. It is like to have more comfortable accommodations than might a Dutch Bilander."

Pleased the ship would be able to put up a good defense against pirates if need be, and that the accommodations would be more acceptable than what he endured on the fishing vessel that had carried them from Ranulf's home at Wealdburh on the Wirral Peninsula to Dublin, Adler cared little about the other assets of the ship. The crossing from England to Ireland had been without incident. The sea, according to the vessel's fisherman captain, had been quite calm, and they had seen no English navy ships. Ranulf trusted the fisherman and his crew of three explicitly; had entrusted the fisherman with finding them passage on a ship bound for Holland or France. Adler had been less trusting.

His tension had grown, as hidden aboard the gently rocking fishing vessel, they awaited the return of the fisherman. Even was the captain trustworthy, what of his crew? Might they think to claim a reward for three escaping Royalists. Ranulf laughed at his fears. "I have known these men all my life. Think you they would betray me and then return to confront my brother's wrath." Adler knew Ranulf's brother, the Earl of Tyneford, was well respected in the village of Wealdburh situated below the ancient square keep sitting atop a stony hill overlooking the sea. Yet greed had been known to prevail over sentiment in many a man's heart.

Not until they climbed aboard the Dutch ship had Adler relaxed his guard. He had been prepared with gun and knife to fight to the death ere he would let himself be taken. Prison was not for him. The forward movement of the ship as the wind billowed the sails sent Adler's heart soaring. Then it plummeted. He might be leaving his home forever. Or if he did return, his parents might no longer be among the living. His parting with them had been too sudden and too brief. His weeping mother had clung to him. But before the morning sun crept over the horizon, he, Ranulf, and the trooper he scarcely knew named, Latimer

5

Draye, set off for Wealdburh.

"'Tis nice the moon has come out," said a soft, lilting voice from behind Adler. His nerves still frayed, he started and clutched at a soft leather bag hanging from a tie about his neck and hidden beneath his shirt. Glynneth Fortier laughed, a throaty laugh full of mirth. "I do keep taking you unaware. Again, my apologies," she said, stepping to his side.

With her gaze directed on the receding flickering lights of Dublin, he studied her profile. She was a handsome enough woman, no great beauty, soft jawline, rounded chin, straight little nose. She wore no cap and her wavy brown hair hung loosely down her back. As though she felt his eyes on her she turned to look up at him. Her eyes were arresting, not their color, he could not make out their color, mayhap gray, but they seemed to look into his soul. Why had he not noticed them when he had spoken with her earlier? Because his eyes had been darting hither and yon for any signs of a trap. He had barely looked at Mistress, nay Madame Fortier. But he looked at her now. Her full lips curved upward in a sweet smile, and her teeth gleamed white in the moonlight. No, not a great beauty, but she entranced him.

"I grew up in Dublin," she said, turning back to the shadowy buildings disappearing from view. "My maternal grandmother owns land to the northwest of Dublin. It has been in the family from time immortal, or so Grandmother says. My brother, Nolan, will inherit the land. Although my father fought for the King and died fighting Cromwell, my brother heeded my grandmother's advice and stayed in Dublin, neither helping nor hindering either side." She turned back to Adler, and he was again lost in her eyes. Eyes full of life and good humor. Lustrous, twinkling pools that beckoned him into their depth and soothed his sad and anxious heart.

"My brother is a scholar," she continued in her light, vibrant voice, and Adler tried to concentrate on what she said rather than dive into her eyes. "He attended Oxford then studied law at Gray's Inn in London. Now he is a barrister, but he prefers instructing to pleading cases in court. Because my grandmother favors no specific religion, except perhaps the enhancement of the mind, we shift with the wind, as do the sails of a ship." She looked up at the puffy sails filled with a stiff breeze

6

from the south. "My brother will be an Anglican, a Puritan, or even a Catholic should the Irish Catholics ever retake their homeland, which seems most unlikely. Whatever it takes, Nolan, like Grandmother, like our ancestors stretching back through time, will never let our ancient land slip from his fingers."

"You seem to love the land yet seem to suffer no sorrow at leaving it." Adler wished he could feel the same about leaving his home.

She laughed, that intoxicating laugh that sent a thrill racing up his spine. "Did I not have a brother who is married and has two sons who will inherit the land after him, I suppose I would be more hesitant about leaving. Mayhap I would not leave. But as I need have no fear the land will be lost to our family, I can leave with a willing heart." She shook her head, and though a smile lurked at the corners of her mouth, her voice softened. "I think, mayhap, you are saddened at leaving your home. Mayhap you will be gone from your home longer than you would wish."

"I was not as wise as your grandmother and your brother. I allowed myself to be convinced 'twas right and honorable to join King Charles and fight to win back England from the Puritan usurpers. Now I flee England rather than risk prison or worse." He had not meant to tell anyone he had fought for Charles, not until safe on the continent. He meant to keep his recent past a secret, but he had blurted out everything to her. He turned and let the wind whip his face.

Racing along at a good clip, the ship rolled to and fro, and Adler found he had to brace himself against the bulwark. Madame Fortier, Glynneth, he liked her name, stood with feet spread wide and rode effortlessly up and down with the rise and fall of the ship as it plunged through the sea. Her hair blew about her face, and she shook her head and laughed.

"'Tis grand is it not?" she said.

"'Tis grand to think I will not be feeling a rope about my neck."

She laughed again. Gads, he loved her laugh. "Prison, mayhap," she said "a rope, likely not. Defeated rebels, as Cromwell calls the men fighting for the King, lose their land not their lives, except in battle. Do you leave behind a land you love and could not wish to lose?"

Her voice was soft and caring. He believed she asked out of concern, not curiosity. "Yes, I leave behind land I love. A good farm I have helped work since my earliest memories. I leave behind my mother and my father and a younger brother whom I fear for. He is newly married and would not flee as do I. I pray he will come to no harm."

"Then you leave behind no wife and children?"

"Nay."

"'Tis well. Too many Irish men have fled, leaving their families to fend as best they can. I applaud your brother."

"He is devoted to his wife," Adler said, wondering if Madame Fortier thought him cowardly in deserting his parents. He did not even know the woman, and yet he would hate for her to think ill of him. Mayhap he had been cowardly, but he would not have changed his actions. Rational or not, his fear of prison overrode all his other emotions.

Interrupting his musings, she said, "So Mister Hayward, you go to Holland. What will you do there? Do you speak any Dutch?"

"We plan to join up with King Charles when he returns and act as part of his guard."

"Ah, you seem confident the King will escape the wily Puritans."

"We escaped them," he answered.

She smiled, her eyes dancing in the moonlight. "So you have. Do you wish, on the morrow, I will teach you a few phrases and words in Dutch that may help you in Holland."

"I would be grateful," he said.

"Very well then. Now I bid you a goodnight. My son will soon need his feeding, and do I not get some sleep, I will not wish to rise come the morning."

Adler bid her a goodnight and watched her disappear down the steep stairs to the area in the 'tween deck reserved for passengers. The quarters were tight, and there was little privacy. Naught but blankets strung on ropes separated the Fortier family from him and his two companions. The captain had shown them hammocks that had been hung up for them, and Ranulf and Latimer Draye had immediately crawled into theirs and gone to sleep.

No longer fearful of capture, Adler knew he should retire, but he was loathe to go down into the compact space. Loathe, too, he admitted to go to sleep. He wanted instead to think about Madame Fortier. He had never been so attracted to any woman, but she was married. Married and had two children. And she was bound for the new world – he for the old. Still, for this one brief voyage, he could revel in her eyes, her laughter, her lilting voice. He could pretend for these few short days she was not married. He could pretend she was as attracted to him as he was to her. He could pretend to taste her curving lips, run his fingers through her wavy hair, and let her make him forget his sorrow, his grief at leaving his home and family, mayhap forever.

Chapter 2

Roused from his sleep by the cry of a baby, Adler at first could not remember where he was, then the memory of Glynneth Fortier came flooding back. It was her baby crying. And they were aboard a Dutch ship bound for Holland. He heard Ranulf and Draye stirring, and when they arose, he joined them, scrambling from his hammock to stumble about with the sway and pitch of the ship. Draye, near as wobbly, grinned, and said, "Look ye at Ranulf, steady as a seaman."

"I have sailed more than a few times, and I knew to be prepared for the roll of the ship," Ranulf said in a low voice. "Now afore we wake our neighbors, let us go topside and see will the Captain be so kind as to break his fast with us."

Adler agreed to the suggestion as did Draye, but before they could ascend to the main deck, a tall, slender, white-haired man with a small neatly trimmed beard and mustache emerged from behind the curtain of blankets. "Ah, you are awake," he said, smiling and displaying a near full, if yellowed, set of teeth. "We tried to be quiet so not to awaken you too early. My daughter-in-law says you arrived late last night." He introduced himself as Curtice Fortier, and in a decidedly French accent, invited them to join his family for breakfast.

"Glynneth believes you had not zee time to secure food stuffs for zee voyage. We have plenty. Glynneth saw to zat. A most organized woman eez zee wife of my elder son." Dressed in the plain garb of a merchant, close-fitting buff coat with a high waistline and hip length skirt, the neckline of the coat hidden under a plain falling band collar, and brown breeches tied below the knee with a plain black band, he looked as neat as if greeting visitors in his home.

Adler looked down at his own rumpled clothes. Having now slept untold nights in less than pristine surroundings, he doubted not but what he must also smell. Not a pleasant person to sit down to breakfast

10

with, but Ranulf, after introducing himself, Adler, and Draye, accepted Fortier's kind offer for the three of them.

With Ranulf's instructions, they stashed their meager belongings in their hammocks and after tightly rolling up the hammocks, stowed them out of the way that a trestle table and benches might be set up in their place. The only lighting came from the hatch opening at the top of the stairs until a young man, Adler guessed to be near him in age, emerged from the Fortiers' quarters with a lantern which he hung from a hook centered over the table. Fortier introduced him as his younger son, Gaspard.

Other sounds could be heard from the Fortiers' quarters, then with a giggle and a yelp, a little curly-headed girl burst from behind the curtains. A tall, thin man with arm outstretched followed after her. She eluded his grasp and giggled again. "Shush, Meara, do you wake Noel, you will have to wait even longer for your breakfast," said the man. Adler guessed he must be the girl's father, Glynneth's husband.

The girl dimpled, pursed her little round mouth, and putting a small finger to her lips, scrunched her eyes and pantomimed a shushing sign. She then darted away from her father to slide to a stop in front of Adler. Large brown eyes widening, she looked up at him and said, "I am Meara. Who are you?"

Her grandfather said, "Meara, mind your manners," but before Adler could respond, Draye dropped to one knee, and bowing at his waist, said, "I am Latimer Draye, but you may call me Latty." He nodded at Ranulf. "That tall man with the fiery red hair is Ranulf D'Arcy, and the man with the too serious countenance, he is Adler Hayward. He is sad about leaving his home." He poked a finger at her stomach, and she giggled. "Mayhap you can help cheer him. I find him much the drudge and poor company."

The girl again looked up at Adler. "I dance very prettily. Do you like dancing?"

"Meara," said her father, "do you not remember your mother's request?"

Looking but slightly sheepish, the child answered, "Set out the napkins."

"That is correct," he answered with a nod.

Fortier chuckled. "You have met my granddaughter, Meara, and she you. Now allow me to introduce my elder son, Etienne." The introduction acknowledged, Adler studied Etienne. A handsome man, if too thin, he had a Patrician nose, high cheekbones, and thick dark hair swept back from a high forehead. His dark, wide-set eyes radiated kindness and intelligence. Adler could well understand how any woman would be attracted to him. Unlike his father and younger brother, he was clean shaven but for a neatly trimmed moustache. But he was too pale and his cheeks were too rosy.

Then he coughed, and doubling over a bit, he held a kerchief to his mouth. His father looked at him with concern, but Etienne quickly straightened, offered a glowing smile, and tucked the kerchief back in his pocket. "My pardon," he said.

The man had consumption. Adler recognized it. His young sister and his grandmother had died of it. His heart felt as if a vice had tightened around it. He had but met Etienne, yet he felt drawn to him, could not help but like him. And he was Glynneth's husband, and she loved him. He could not doubt that. His heart ached for her, and for her bright little girl who could not know her father was dying.

He looked away and his gaze rested on Meara. She giggled at something Draye said and playfully swatted his knee. The man seemed to have a way with children. Young and full of good spirits, Draye was unconcerned about leaving England. "What have I in England? No land to call my own," he told Gaspard while ruffling Meara's hair. "Once, before Henry VII won the throne, we Drayes owned the very land that now we serve as stewards. In allying myself with King Charles, I hoped to be on the winning side, unlike my ancestor who fought against Henry Tudor and lost our land. I hoped to be rewarded with a knighthood and a piece of land. I thought no matter how small, it would be mine and I could make it grow. But like my ancestor before me, I chose the losing side." He chuckled. "Now I will see what being an exile may bring me."

Gaspard, a more robust version of Etienne, nodded his handsome mien thoughtfully. "Is land what you crave," he said, "you might give some thought to trying your hand in the colonies. There is land aplenty, so we are told."

Draye, gray eyes alight, stroked the dark stubble of his strong, jutting jaw. "Land aplenty do you say?"

"Yes. We go to New Netherland, a Dutch colony. We have family there to welcome us and provide us with shelter and sustenance, but I have heard they have a shortage of labor, so any man seeking work should have no trouble finding some means of support."

"Most interesting," Draye said before looking down at Meara who tugged on his worn coat skirt.

"Do you go with us to our new home, Latty? Oh, I wish you would. You are funny."

"Meara!" exclaimed a mirthful voice.

Whipping about, Adler saw Glynneth had joined them. Her beguiling gray-blue eyes full of good cheer, she added, "You know better than to address adults in such a fashion. Ask the gentleman's pardon."

Meara obeyed her mother, but added that Draye had given her permission to address him by his given name. To Adler's consternation, Draye was staring at Glynneth with the same besotted gaze he had fixed on her. Her wavy hair hidden under a lappet cap, her gown plain and simple, the bodice coming to a point at the waist, a large square neckerchief tucked into a low décolletage, she was tying on an apron, yet her glowing smile brightened the dingy hold.

"Good morning, Mister Hayward," she said, the lilt of her voice sending a tingle to every nerve in his body. "I trust you and your companions slept well."

"Ah yes, Mister Hayward," said Etienne, "you met my wife last night. But Glynneth, allow me to introduce Mister D'Arcy and Mister Draye. Gentlemen, my wife," he stated proudly.

Ranulf sketched a bow and Draye, shaking his head as if to clear it of unwanted thoughts, found his voice and stumblingly offered his sincere thanks to her for suggesting they be allowed to join her family for breakfast.

"You are, of course, most welcome, Mister Draye. Everyone, please be seated. Etienne and Gaspard, do you serve the ale, I will set out our breakfast." She retreated to their curtained quarters, but soon reappeared with a large pewter tray heaped high with chunks of bread and cheese and small links of sausage.

Gaspard and Etienne set pewter plates and mugs of ale on the table. "I fear you will have to share the mugs," Gaspard said. "We have not enough of them for all of us."

"We have no problem there, Monsieur Fortier," Ranulf said. "We have shared mugs a plenty the past fortnight. Do I not speak the truth, Latty?"

Flashing a winsome smile, and giving a poke to Meara who claimed a spot next to him on the bench, Draye answered with a chuckle. "Not as many as I might wish we had shared. Times I went mighty thirsty and would have traded the boots off my feet for another dram or two."

At that moment, a sailor clattered down the stairs. A small pail in his hand, he said, "Madame Fortier, I have the milk from your goat you did bid me bring at eight bells."

The sailor looked at Glynneth with the same adoring gaze Adler had seen on Draye's face, and that he knew must be on his own. Rising from her seat, Glynneth took the pail and warmly thanked the sailor. He backed away, seemingly loathe to leave her presence. Adler marked his slow march up the steep steps. Glynneth poured some of the milk into a mug for her daughter, added a little ale, mixed it, then said, "Do drink every drop, Meara. 'Tis good for you."

"Yes, Mother," the child said, and holding the mug with both hands began gulping down the milk with a glug-a-de-glug sound.

Her father laughed, "Meara, your manners, where are they?"

Lowering the mug to reveal a white moustache before she wiped the back of her hand across her mouth, she said, "I was thirsty enough to trade my boots."

Her comment brought laughter around the table, but between choked chuckles her mother said, "That is fine dear, but next time use your napkin to wipe your mouth. By the way, thank you for setting out the napkins. You did a very nice job."

Meara beamed at the praise and resumed nibbling a large piece of cheese she had grabbed off the platter. Adler noticed Glynneth shared a plate with her husband, and Gaspard shared one with his father. Meara had her own small plate, and he, Ranulf, and Draye each had their own plate. The Fortiers had given their plates to their guests. He counted heads. How had they one plate extra? Gaspard's wife. She had not

14

joined them.

"Monsieur Fortier," he looked across the table at Gaspard. "Your wife has not joined us. I hope she is not ill."

Gaspard shook his head. "I fear she has the seasickness. Glynneth thinks did she but go topside in the fresh air and get away from the bilge smell we must endure here in the 'tween deck, she might feel better, but Jeanette refuses to rise from her cot."

Glynneth said, "Poor dear, she was fearful of this voyage and now her fears are being born out. I hope she may soon feel better. We have a much longer voyage ahead of us."

Adler pitied the young woman and was glad he seemed to be immune to the ailment. Seemingly the other Fortiers were also immune. At least for the present. What they might encounter out in the middle of the ocean he could not fathom. A wish to protect these kindly people tugged at his innards. Gaspard was strong and healthy, but his father was old, his brother was sick. They were a gentle people. A people used to nice things such as napkins and pewter plates and finely woven woolen clothing. They were used to the civilities of city life. He knew little of the new world. Had never given it much thought, but now he wondered how these kind-spirited Fortiers would fare in the new world wilderness.

❀ ❀ ❀ ❀

Standing beside Glynneth at the bulwark, Adler stared out at the land they sailed past. Scotland the captain had told them. From the distance it looked rugged and stark. Not a place he would want to call home. Glynneth had been telling him about her home in Dublin. "Not a grand home, naught but lodgings a short walk from Etienne's father's home. A home his father shared with Gaspard and his wife, Jeanette." She stopped speaking and became thoughtful, gazing up at an eagle soaring high in the sky. "Do you ever wonder why God did not think to give man wings?" she asked, interrupting his reverie.

Shaking his head, he chuckled, "Nay, I never had such thoughts."

"I do believe wings would have come in quite handy." She turned to look at him, her eyes dancing with merriment. "Do think what it would be like to soar through the air. How fast we could get to our destinations. No twisting and turning along poorly kept trails or plodding up and down hillsides and mountains. Of course, we would have to travel light as you and your friends are doing, but think how glorious 'twould be."

Gazing into her eyes, he felt his soul soaring. He might not actually be flying, but in her company, the ache in his heart for his home dimmed and almost disappeared. She was another man's wife. A man he liked and respected. Yet he knew himself to be in love with Glynneth Fortier. He had never loved before, had never imagined love could be so all enveloping. He felt lighthearted when in her presence, at peace with all the world, and crestfallen, lost when her duties as a wife and mother called her away.

She loved being up on deck, hated the hold as he did. Her daughter and son napping, and her father-in-law keeping an eye on them, she had urged her husband to join them on the main deck. Gaspard brought up a chair for him, and Glynneth tucked a blanket about him and handed him a book. "You are content?" she asked.

Etienne smiled at her. "I am content. Go brace the wind at the bow do you wish, my beloved, or take a turn or two about the deck. Do I need aught, I will call."

And so Adler had rejoiced. Glynneth had been freed to join him at the bulwark. To be in her presence was a delight in itself. To have her to himself with no other distractions was an immeasurable thrill. Draye, immersed in conversation with Gaspard, occasionally cast glances in their direction from the port side of the ship but did not offer to join them. Ranulf was engaged in a game of chess with the captain who had beamed his pleasure at having a chance to match his prowess against a skilled opponent. Poor Jeanette Fortier was still abed with the seasickness. Adler knew these treasured moments could not last, but he would store them in his memory to be conjured up when forced to part from Glynneth.

"I met Etienne in Dublin at a book dealer's shop," Glynneth said, bringing the conversation back down to earth. At her urging, he had briefly told her about his home and family then had urged her to reciprocate. Amidst various asides, she obliged. "I thought Etienne the most

16

beautiful man I had ever seen." She grinned. "According to my grandmother, we O'Briain women have ever been bold and have ever been drawn to handsome men. Grandmother said she could not resist my grandfather despite his Norman blood." She chuckled, her intoxicating laugh infusing him with an exuberance he could scarce keep in check. Her smile still lurking on her lips, she continued, "Our family claims Brian Boru as a direct ancestor. Who knows if 'tis true. But our land is not far from the Hill of Tara."

He must have looked confused for she explained. "'Tis a sacred hill where 'tis claimed Brian Boru was proclaimed high king of all Ireland. 'Twas a short lived kingdom. It died with him. We Irish are forever fighting each other. Had we united, we could have chased the Normans from our land, and the English would never have had a foothold. But that was not to be." Her eyes danced. "I cannot complain. No Normans, no me."

"That would be a loss to the world," Adler said, wishing he had the right to take her hand, to hold her, to do anything to prove he meant the words that sounded so trite.

"You are kind to say so." Cocking her head, she widened her eyes. "Now where was I? I think I was telling you about meeting Etienne. He and I fell to talking and discovered we enjoyed reading many of the same books. The more we talked, the more we found we had in common. It grew late and the shopkeeper wanted to close his shop. We made our purchases, and Etienne walked me home. We saw each other near every day after that.

"My father was what the new English arrivals call the old English, his family having settled in Ireland long before Henry VIII decided to divorce his Spanish queen. Many of the old English swore their loyalty to the King but remained Catholic. My father's father, fearful of losing his land, renounced the Catholic church." She chuckled. "He cared more about his land than his soul, 'twould seem. The land my grandfather was so desirous of keeping is now forfeit, confiscated by Cromwell because my father remained loyal to King Charles. Not even my brother's neutrality could save it."

Her eyes betraying no regret, she shrugged her shoulders. "'Tis of no consequence. 'Tis the past and cannot be undone." Narrowing her eyes, she said, "Lost my thread again." Before Adler could respond, she said, "Oh, yes, neither my grandfather nor my father were good Anglicans. But though not particular about his religion, Father was not partial to the Huguenots, they being followers of Calvin. Still, at my grandmother's urging, he consented to my marriage to Etienne. Grandmother knew well my heart. And, as she reminded my father, my mother's father had not approved of him." A smile again lurked about the corners of her mouth and her luminous eyes exuded a lighthearted glee. "Ah, but then my father was an exceptionally handsome man. Mother could no more resist him, despite his limited interest in anything of an intellectual nature, than Grandmother could resist my grandfather. Though I will say, Grandfather was quite well read, having been educated in France."

"'Twould seem a good education and being well read is of major importance in your family." Adler could imagine what she must think of him. Once he had completed grammar school, despite his father's urgings, he had chosen to work the land rather than continue his education. He had had little time for reading. Not that they had any books in the house to read other than his mother's bible, and he had never found the bible a pleasant read.

Tucking a wisp of hair back under her cap, Glynneth said, "Learning is ecstasy. When you read you can visit distant lands, cross vast oceans, laugh at inane humor, shed a melancholy tear for thwarted lovers, and ponder the wisdom of the ancients. Whole new worlds are opened up to you, old ideas are challenged and new ones reviewed." Her face radiant with her joy, she gazed up a him. "I know, being a woman, I am fortunate to have been reared in a family that values the intellect of a woman as highly as that of a man. And I am fortunate to have found a husband who values my thoughts as he values his own."

"He would be a fool did he not," Adler said. Any man would be a fool not to value Glynneth. He had never known such a merry soul, never known anyone with such a zest for life. Had her love of books made her what she was, then he too valued her quest for knowledge, wished he could share it with her as did Etienne.

"Neither Etienne nor his father have tried to force me to accept the Calvinistic teaching," she continued. "Likewise, I accept 'tis their faith and would not attempt to change them."

"How is it but for the lilt in your voice, your speech would ne'er define you as Irish?"

She laughed, and her eyes sparkled. "As I said, my father was English. He insisted my brother, sister, and I have English nurses and an English tutor. We were trained to be good little English subjects. My mother was fine with his wishes as long as we learned of our Irish heritage at my grandmother's knee."

"What of Etienne and Gaspard?"

"English tutors, then schools in England. Now, enough about me and mine. I did promise to teach you a few phrases in Dutch. Shall we begin?"

Chapter 3

To Adler's thinking, they arrived at Rotterdam much too soon. He had but three days in Glynneth's company when he needed months, years, a lifetime. The thought of never seeing her again tore at his innards, but what could he do? Latimer Draye solved his dilemma for him. They stood together at the bulwark watching the lowering of the skiff that would take them ashore.

"Hayward," Draye said, "I have decided to go to New Netherland with the Fortiers. Seek my fortune." He turned to Adler. "Why do you not come as well? I told Monsieur Fortier I would ask would you consider changing your plans. Do you, he will pay your passage. He says he will feel safer having us along. 'Tis easy to rob an old man, and he carries much merchandise with him. And as you know, one son is young, the other ..." He shook his head. "He is ... not well."

Go to America! Adler could have hugged Draye. Instead, clutching the soft leather bag hidden under his shirt, he stared wide-eyed at Draye. He could stay at Glynneth's side. When she had first mentioned New Netherland, it had intrigued him. He had intended to talk with the Fortier men and learn more about their expectations. He instead found himself bound up in Glynneth. All thoughts other than wrangling ways to be in her company fled his mind. But Draye had spent much of their brief voyage talking with the Fortiers. He had apparently won Monsieur Fortier's confidence.

Concern for Glynneth and her family's safety had plagued Adler, but he had been unable to think how he might help them. He knew he could not afford passage to New Netherland. He had naught but a couple of farthings and a handful of pennies his father had pressed on him. Coins were hard come by, and he had been loath to take them, but his father had insisted, saying, "You may find need to buy your bread and ale before you reach your destination."

Adler fled England to escape possible imprisonment, not because he had a driving desire to serve in the King's guard. He had no wish to live out his life in Holland or France. His silence must have made Draye think he was hesitant and needed additional convincing. "What awaits you here but poverty of mind and spirit?" Draye continued. "Think you the King will miss you? Nay, there is no future here. Come with us. I know Ranulf is too loyal to his King to desert him, but you – you have a'ready given up your home for the King. Is that not enough? There is land to be had in the new world. You could start your life anew. What say you?

"Fortier assures me his brother-in-law will give us work" Draye added. "A fortune can be made in furs. And land can be bought with that fortune." Draye looked away from Adler and out to sea. "My ancestors lost their land. I will not lose mine. There will be no King to take it from me in the new world." He looked back. "Well?"

Clamping a hand on Draye's shoulder, Adler said, "Latty, I am with you. 'Tis to New Netherland we are bound." He knew he was grinning from ear to ear. But was he also floating? Had he taken wing? Life again had meaning. He wanted to run find Glynneth and tell her his news. Somehow he managed to control his exuberance as Draye returned his smile.

"'Tis good," Draye said. "Amidst all the Dutch and Frenchies in New Netherland, I will be glad to have a fellow Englishman I can depend on or confide in." Draye stuck out his hand. "Shake, my comrade. To our new friendship and to our futures."

Adler grasped Draye's hand and held it fast. "To our friendship and our future. May both blossom and bear fruit."

"Now we must tell Ranulf we desert him. I know he will not blame us. All the same, I am grateful to him, as I know you are, for getting us out of England. And for paying our passage from England to Ireland and from Ireland to Holland. We owe him."

Adler looked past Draye to Ranulf. He stood talking to the ship's captain. A handsome man, Ranulf had the blood line, the education, the polished manners of the nobility. Fluent in French, able to read and write Latin. Life would be good to him. Adler could feel no remorse in abandoning Ranulf. He would fare well with his King.

✹ ✹ ✹ ✹

Before he knew it, Adler found himself in the skiff with all the Fortiers except Gaspard. They would stay in lodgings in Rotterdam while awaiting passage to New Netherland. Gaspard and Draye would remain aboard the *Grishilde* until it could dock at the quay and unload the Fortier personal items, supplies, and merchandise.

Adler met Gaspard's wife, Jeanette, for the first time when she appeared on deck shortly before she was to be lowered by swing into the skiff. She had not emerged from her sick bed until they were ready to leave the ship. Was she pretty, he could not discern it. Pale and wane, hair disheveled, gown rumpled, she but nodded vacantly when introduced to him and Draye.

Fortier had been exuberant when informed Adler would be joining them on their voyage to New Netherland. "I cannot tell you my pleasure, Monsieur … er … Mister Hayward that we will have your support on zeez adventure we undertake. Etienne and Glynneth have both told me you are a good man, trustworthy, honorable. Your friend, Mister Draye, he assures me you are brave and competent. I admit to being fearful about our journey. To know my leetle family will not be so alone on zee vast sea calms my soul."

Adler understood his fears. Anything could happen out on the ocean – a greedy captain, a malicious crew member – who would know or tell did one of the Fortiers have an accident or did some of their merchandise go missing. And Glynneth – the way men looked at her – who would defend her virtue? Etienne? Gaspard? No. Adler thanked God the old man had the good sense to recognize the dangers and to ask him and Draye to accompany them and provide protection.

Finding lodging did not prove difficult. Fortier did not lack for funds, and the innkeeper at the Wynkoop was most welcoming. Ranulf D'Arcy took lodging at the same inn. He had been genuinely gracious when Adler and Draye informed him they were heading for the new world instead of joining him as members of the King's guard.

"I can scarce blame you," Ranulf said. "You fought well and bravely for our sovereign, but for now, there is little we can do. That you choose to rebuild your lives is natural. I can do naught but wish you well as I am sure King Charles would also do."

Ranulf stayed in Rotterdam a couple of days then left for Paris, but Adler, Draye, and the Fortiers spent near a month in the city. Adler enjoyed his days in the Dutch city. He found the people lively yet industrious, good-hearted yet thrifty. He liked their food, especially their baked goods, but thought their clothing flamboyant. He found no fault with the women's bright, colorful skirts and aprons nor their love of jewelry, but he thought the men's breeches excessively baggy and their coat tails absurdly long and comical.

Whenever possible, he escorted Glynneth on walks. She loved experiencing the city, and he thrilled to her exuberance. Jeanette had no interest in investigating the city, but she did join Glynneth when she visited some of the local shops, including a dry goods store and a millinery establishment. Recovered from her seasickness, Jeanette proved to be an attractive young woman, blond hair, pale blue eyes, pert little nose, but she was dull in comparison to Glynneth – and sadly lacking in a sense of humor.

Etienne hired a chirpy young woman to mind the children so Glynneth could have the freedom to explore the city. "I cannot thank you enough for escorting my wife about Rotterdam," Etienne said, and Adler could not prevent his conscience from pricking him. "As my illness prohibits my stirring far from our rooms," Etienne added, "Glynneth becomes my eyes and ears. What she sees and hears, she imparts to me in such vivid detail, I feel I have experienced the sights and sounds myself."

"We have hope the ocean air will benefit Etienne," Glynneth confided to Adler on one of their outings. They were making their way back to their lodging after visiting an older section of the city near the dikes. Glynneth had marveled at the land reclamation. "They have reshaped nature. I must hold this in my memory that I can describe it to Etienne."

Though he accompanied Glynneth and saw everything she saw, when with her, he saw things he would never have noticed did she not remark on them. She was near as much his eyes and ears as she was her husband's. She pointed out the purple-colored sky that set off the red brick warehouses making them appear to be on fire. She noted the contrast of the muddy river water with the sparkling blue of the sea on a sunny day. She exclaimed over the canals, and the barges plying the canals carrying goods and people to various destinations. The houses, their gable ends fronting the streets or canals, and their walls extending above the roof in a series of steps fascinated her. She made sketches of the narrow houses of differing size and height with their slate or tile roofing to show to Etienne. Reflections of the houses in the calm waters of the canals beguiled her, and she laughed in delight when a passing barge turned the reflections squiggly and wavering.

She marked the wealthy merchants with their rich clothing and the impoverished laborers often doubled over under immense burdens who followed in their employers' wake. She always had a penny for a beggar or a child, always a smile for anyone or everyone they passed on the street. She enjoyed comparing and contrasting Rotterdam with Dublin. "I would think 'tis important to both ports they are situated on a confluence of rivers," she maintained. "Yet Rotterdam prospers, and much of Dublin is in near decay. The city walls, Dublin Castle, even various churches are crumbling and are a hazard to the populace. At least what is left of the population after the Catholics were kicked out and then the plague that struck last year." For a brief instant her exuberance waned. "'Twas a sad and frightening time." She shook her head as if to shake off the past and brightened again. "Here in Rotterdam most of the buildings are of stone or brick, but in Dublin, most are of timber, and the poor, clustered on the outskirts of the city, live in mud and straw hovels. Of course some brick and stone buildings have been built in Dublin, but naught compared with this thriving Dutch port."

She cocked her head and regarded him out of her lovely eyes. "I do think perhaps 'tis their religious tolerance that helps promote their prosperity," she said. "What say you?"

He laughed. "I say I have no idea. In fact, I cannot say I knew there was any great difference between Rotterdam and Dublin. If you recall, I saw very little of Dublin."

"Very true," she said with a nod and changed the subject. "I cannot believe how the Scots abound here. They seem to be thriving. Their Calvinistic religious beliefs are similar to Etienne's and his family's as well as to that of the Dutch. From what I have seen thus far, though, the Dutch beliefs are less rigid."

24

"Again, I plead ignorance. I know little enough of my Anglican faith, and nothing of the Calvinist beliefs, except, like the Puritan religion, they would take much of the joy out of life. I have ne'er been religious. I was baptized as a babe, but I admit to attending few services past the age of ten. Mother goes regularly, but she seldom insists my father or brother or I accompany her." He chuckled. "Father drives her to church in the cart, but he then visits with friends whose wives, like my mother, are in attendance at the service. Though ale houses are closed on Sundays, they always manage to share a few mugs before 'tis time to fetch their wives home."

Glynneth's throaty laugh gurgled out. "Oh, my grandmother would like you. And your father. As I told you, religion means naught to her. I could not swear does she even believe in God. 'Tis of no moment." She looked at the sky. "The time grows late, we must return ere we will be late for supper. No doubt Noel has been demanding his supper for some time now."

Upon returning to their rooms, they found a delighted Meara running around and around the trestle table that had been set for supper. A pinwheel clasped in her hand, Meara came running to Glynneth. "Oh, Mother, do look what Latty has brought me." She pursed her mouth and blew and the pinwheel whirled. She giggled. "I can blow on it, or I can run, and it will twirl around. 'Tis great fun. He brought the sweetest rattle for Noel. 'Tis shaped like a bear. Noel loves it. He has been chewing on it."

Glynneth stooped to hug her daughter. "What wonderful gifts. You did thank Latty?"

"Of course, Mother," the little girl answered. "Latty also fed Noel his pap. Alva had to leave early."

Slapping her hand to her forehead and rising, Glynneth said, "Oh, dear, I forgot. 'Tis mid-week and 'tis lecture day at her church." She looked over at Draye. Sitting next to the hearth with Noel balanced on his knee, he appeared perfectly comfortable with his young charges. Adler envied Draye his ease with children. He would have had no idea how to care for three year old Meara, let alone six month old Noel.

The baby, recognizing his mother's voice, attempted to turn to her. His new rattle clattering to the floor, he held out his chubby little arms.

Glynneth laughed and hastened to swoop her baby up and give him a hug and a kiss. "Thank you, Latty, for minding Meara and Noel. Where is Etienne?"

"He is resting. He had rather a busy afternoon. He went with us to check out the ship we will be taking to New Netherland."

Glynneth had turned from Draye, but she jerked back around. "A ship has been found to take us to our new home?"

"Aye, the *Alida*. 'Tis a three-mast, square-rigged merchant ship called a fluyt. Like the one we sailed from Dublin on," Draye said. "We will be the only passengers, so we will not be terribly cramped, and there will be plenty of room for your family's supplies and goods."

"How splendid," Glynneth said, her smile brightening Adler's heart. He thanked God he would be going with her to New Netherland. With a minimum crossing of two months, he would have more time to revel in her company.

"Where is Jeanette?" Glynneth asked.

Draye clucked. "She too is resting. News of our imminent departure set her nerves on edge. She fears the seasickness."

"Ah, poor Jeanette. She hates it here, yet she dreads the voyage. I will see to her later."

"Gaspard and Monsieur Fortier are at the warehouse, making arrangements to have your goods sent to the *Alida*," Draye added, "so you are not late for supper. The captain plans to depart with the tide a week from today."

Smiling, Glynneth said, "You have been most informative, Latty. Thank you. Now I will see how Etienne fares and will feed Noel. Did he eat much pap."

"He did!" piped up Meara. "I think he is starting to like it."

Adler's stomach turned over. Pap, naught but bread softened to mush in milk was not appealing. Tasteless, or worse, near like paste. Yet he supposed since the babe had no teeth, beyond his mother's milk, he had little choice in his meals. No doubt when he was a babe, his mother fed him the same disgusting concoction. He had no experience with young children. Their ways, their likes and dislikes were a mystery to him. On the voyage to their new home, he would have a good chance to learn more about the little people.

Feeling useless, Adler said, "I will see does Betje need any water drawn or more coal for her fire." He found the plump Dutch cook stirring a pot of thick pea soup. Professing no need of a man's help in her kitchen, she shooed him out, and he returned to the parlor. Draye was down on the floor with Meara playing a game of knucklebones. Pitching one bone into the air, he scooped another off the floor, then caught the first bone with the same hand before the tossed bone could hit the floor.

"Oh, you are good," exclaimed Meara. "So much better than I am."

Draye chuckled. "That is because my hand is larger. 'Tis easier for me to hold two bones. I see no reason you should not use both hands do you so wish."

"Do you think 'twould not be cheating?"

"Of course not," Draye declared, and Meara beamed.

Absently, fingering the bag next to his heart, Adler heaved a sigh. 'Twas good Draye had a way with children. He would be a help to Glynneth on the voyage. She would have her hands full caring for her husband. Wishing he knew some way to assist Glynneth, Adler settled onto a stool to await the Fortiers' return. Soon they would all be greeting new lives in a new world.

Chapter 4

Glynneth pulled the cloak tighter about her throat and drew in a deep breath. It was a glorious day. Sunbeams danced across the water and sea spray misted her face as the bow of the ship rose and fell on the waves. They had a good stiff breeze, and with all the sails hoisted, seemed to be flying. Their ship's captain told them, did the weather and the wind hold, they could expect to reach New Amsterdam in record time.

Looking back over her shoulder at her husband, Glynneth gave him a little wave. His arms tucked under two blankets, he could do naught but smile and nod. On these sunny days, Glynneth insisted Etienne come up on the deck. "Best to enjoy the fresh air and get away from the bilge smell," she said. She had her children up on deck every morning after breakfast no matter the weather. She believed they not only needed to fill their little lungs with fresh air, but they needed to see the sky, and Meara needed room to run.

Curtice and Gaspard usually came up whenever the weather permitted, and Glynneth had finally convinced Jeanette to leave her sick bed and venture up on deck. "I promise you, Jeanette, you will feel better do you get some fresh air. You are not eating enough. You are getting weaker every day. The smell down here is nauseating. For your husband's sake, do come up with me."

Gaspard near had to carry his wife up from the 'tween deck. She had been sick almost from the instant they left Rotterdam and had been able to keep down little nourishment. Because of the good weather, Glynneth, aided by Adler, had been able to use the cook's brick stove in the forecastle to cook their meals. They had not been forced to rely on nothing but sausages and cheese. Glynneth had been surprised to find Adler skilled at cooking.

"Having no sisters, my brother, Caleb, and I were often wont to help

28

mother with her household chores when father had no special need of us," he said. "Usually naught but fetch the water or build up the fire, or stir the pot. But once Mother was sick for near a month after the loss of a baby. Father hired a neighbor woman to come in to help care for Mother and see to other household chores, but she too needed help. In helping her, I learned much about the basics of preparing a stew, plucking a fowl and stewing it or dressing it for roasting, preparing a fish for stewing or pan frying." He chuckled. "I found I rather liked cooking."

Using the last of the prized eggs, Adler had made a delicate custard that was one of the few foods Jeanette had been able to keep down. "Learned to make it cause it was my favorite," he declared. "Mother said did I collect the eggs, milk the cow, and make the custard, I could have it as often as I wanted. Of course I had to share it with the rest of the family. Good thing else I might have made myself sick on it."

Glynneth enjoyed Adler's company. Having recovered from his sadness at leaving his home and family, he seemed ever cheerful, and ever ready to lend a hand in any capacity he could manage. She enjoyed his humor and his interest in learning. His education had been limited, but by his social status, not by a lack of intelligence. He quickly mastered the elements of chess and spent hours playing the game with Etienne. He eagerly read any books she loaned him and enjoyed discussing them with her or Etienne.

That Etienne enjoyed Adler's company pleased Glynneth. Since he had contracted consumption, Etienne, due to his weakened condition, had become near a recluse. Adler drew him out. Told him stories of his childhood that had Etienne laughing so hard tears came to his eyes. At times the laughter would set Etienne to coughing, but Adler was handy with a mug of ale and a clean handkerchief. Overall the conviviality seemed to revive Etienne's spirits, and his strength seemed to be increasing daily. Was it the laughter, the companionship, or the fresh air, Glynneth knew not. She but knew her husband's health was improving. And that was a miracle.

Did she find any fault with Adler, it was the overwhelming masculinity he exuded. Sometimes when they stood at the ship's railing and their hands touched, or when cooking in the foc's'le galley, their shoulders touched, a tingle raced up her spine. She had experienced no such tremors when he escorted her around Rotterdam, but now in the small confines of the ship, she found she was much too aware of him. Years of heavy farm labor had strengthened him, built up his physic – his broad shoulders, solid chest, and sturdy legs. Though his nearness at times could be troubling, in a way his strength made her feel safe, protected. Few men would want a confrontation with Adler Hayward.

Then there was the way she sometimes caught him looking at her. He would quickly drop his gaze or look away when she looked in his direction, yet she saw something. It was not a look that in anyway frightened her. Was it a look of longing, mayhap a look of love? He never did or said anything improper or insinuating. Surely she must be mistaken.

"Your thoughts seem distant, Glynneth. Is ere wrong?"

Glynneth braced herself against the railing to keep from jumping. She had been so deep in contemplation, she had not heard Adler come up behind her. He moved quietly for a man used to plodding about a farmstead. Forcing a smile, she said, "I was thinking about Etienne and how well he is doing now we are at sea."

Adler nodded. "Aye, to my thinking, his cough seems better, and his appetite has improved. Speaking of improved appetites, Jeanette seems finally to be getting her sea legs. Gaspard informs me this is the second day she has not been sick. He says 'tis all your doing. Getting her to come up on deck to get away from the smells below."

"I do hope she continues to improve. I feared she would starve to death." She glanced over her shoulder. "Look at her. Strolling with Gaspard, smiling as they wobble with the rise and fall of the ship. Let us hope this weather holds that we may continue to come up on deck."

"Aye, 'tis good for all of us. Is there aught you would have me do in preparation for tonight's supper?"

Glynneth shook her head. "Nay. 'Twill be but more of the bean and bacon porridge we had for dinner. 'Tis a shame Father Curtice could not convince any woman to immigrate with us to serve as our cook. Cooking is not my foremost skill."

Adler chuckled. "Monsieur Fortier says the Dutch are too happy in the Netherlands to want to immigrate. He says he should have thought to bring an Irish maid along."

"Yes, so he has said. Thankfully, you know as much about cooking as do I. Together we manage. However, Meara is complaining about the groats porridge we have every morning."

Adler chuckled. "'Tis what we had most mornings of my life. 'Tis hot and 'tis filling. But is the little one tired of the porridge, come morning, I could fry her a flat bread like Betje made for us, do you have some butter 'tis not yet rancid."

"You and Latty are spoiling the girl," Glynneth said with a shake of her head. "But yes, our flour and butter yet hold, so mayhap you can make enough for Etienne and Jeanette as well."

He nodded. "'Twould be a nice treat for them. They both need strengthening. I will go now to fetch what I will need for the morrow."

"Thank you," she said as Adler, swaying with the motion of the ship, made his way to the hatch that led down to the 'tween decks. Their food supplies for the voyage as well as for their first few weeks after arrival at New Amsterdam, along with their home furnishings, extra apparel and bed and table linens, cook and table wear not being used on the voyage, and books, paper and ink were stored in the 'tween deck. Besides their own two goats, two dozen chickens, and two hogs that were quartered there, the various live animals meant for the Captain's table shared the space with but a thin wall as a divider. No matter was the animal waste cleaned daily, the smell was ever present and added to the stench from the bilge water. The ship's food supplies, from biscuits to dried peas, to salted pork and fish, along with casks of water and wine or ale for the crew occupied space in the 'tween decks, as did extra canvas, and various tools and weapons, not to mention eight cannons.

Squeezed in amidst that medley was the passenger living quarters. Glynneth was grateful to Adler and Latty for fashioning platforms with privacy walls to hold the bedding for her family members. Thick downy mattresses piled high with warm blankets and quilts kept the November chill at bay during the night. Curtains afforded them additional privacy. She could not think what else could have been done to insure their comfort on their voyage to their new home.

Adler and Latty continued to sleep in hammocks that had to be stowed each morning, but they made no complaint. When asked were they warm enough at night, they assured her the blankets Monsieur Fortier provided them were indeed sufficient. Smiling, Glynneth thought how different were the two men. Adler was dependable, caring, and humorous. Latty, vibrant, charming to both young and old, male and female, had but one desire, land ownership. Despite their differences, the two men seemed to have formed a bond. She thought that wise. In a land populated mostly by the Dutch, French, and Indians, they might have need of one another.

She wondered how she and her family would adjust to their new surroundings. She prayed Etienne would continue to improve, and that their new home, away from damp, smoky Dublin, would offer him a new life. How happy Etienne's father would be was his older son again able to help him in his business. Gaspard, though but three years younger than Etienne, had not the same business sense, or so said his father. But Gaspard had been the one to supervise the loading of their goods when they left Ireland, tended the goods unloading and storage when they arrived at Rotterdam, and again seen to the loading and storage of goods and supplies when they set sail for New Netherland. She hoped he felt no resentment. She had never noticed such.

The cargo hold below the 'tween deck held the goods Curtice had purchased at his brother-in-law's request for trade with the Indians – blankets, muskets and shot, hatchets, beads, an assortment of pots and pans, needles and thread, cloth of various prints, and knives. Curtice also had items for the chandlery shop he meant to open, as well as for a dry goods shop. He had plans, too, to build a warehouse. In his late-fifties, yet willing to set off on this grand new venture, he showed stamina. Ambitious for his sons and their families, he meant to leave them comfortably situated. Glynneth had little doubt but what he would accomplish his goals. That was good. She need not fear for Meara's or Noel's futures.

At Curtice's direction, Gaspard, with Latty's and Adler's help, had carefully inventoried their cargo. "Not that I fail to trust zee capitaine," Curtice said, "but one cannot be too careful. He carries zee cargo for a number of merchants. I want no error where our goods are concerned." A shrewd businessman was Curtice Fortier.

Looking back out to sea, Glynneth saw the sun had dipped low. 'Twas time she nursed Noel then set about preparing the evening meal. They ate early, before all light coming down through the hatch disappeared. Once supper was ended and the dishes and remains cleared, a precious candle would be lit, and they would sit around the table and talk or play games or tell stories. She would cuddle Noel on her lap and feed him a bowl of pap that would keep his little tummy full that he might sleep through the night. He now had two lower front teeth poking through and was starting to scoot on his belly when freed of his swaddling. She knew his gums caused him grief because he wanted to gnaw on anything and everything, yet he seldom cried. She believed he enjoyed the rocking of the ship. It seemed to soothe him, especially when he lay in his cradle. The motion of the ship kept his cradle continually rocking.

Meara, fortunately, seemed not to mind their cramped quarters. Though she had no children to play with, she always had an adult to keep her entertained. Latty and her grandfather were her favorite playmates, but at times she could be found in Etienne's or Adler's care. Adler at first seemed at a loss as to how to tend the child, but he soon learned Meara was happy to have someone race with her, especially if he let her win. The ship offered scant area for running, but the three year old child needed little deck space to satisfy her demands. Meara's delighted squeals would reverberate around the ship, and Glynneth noted even the seamen could not help but smile at Meara's antics. 'Twas good exercise for man and child.

"Glynneth." Her father-in-law called to her from the hatch. "Noel eez stirring."

She waved and called back, "I will be right there." Taking one last look at the brilliant fusion of sea and sky, she hurried below to tend her baby's needs.

Chapter 5

Latimer blew out the lantern's candle and eased himself onto his hammock. In a matter of moments his eyes adjusted to the dark, and he stared up through the open hatch at the multitude of stars in the sky. He liked these peaceful nights aboard ship. All too soon the voyage would be ended, and he would begin his new life in a new world. He doubted he would ever again know the calm he enjoyed during these quiet nights. Not that the ship had not its own sounds – creaking wood, clanking metal, the tread of the watch. But soon the ears adjusted to those noises, and he almost found them soothing as sleep crept over him.

Adler was not yet asleep. There was no steady pattern to his breathing. What was his friend thinking about? Was he wondering, as Latimer did, what the future held for him. Would he grow wealthy from his labors in the new world? Or mayhap his thoughts were on Glynneth. Could not blame him if they were. Latimer's thoughts were often on Glynneth. He decided he might even be in love with her. He knew Adler was in love with her. He saw it in his eyes every time he looked at Glynneth. But neither he nor Adler would ever hint to Glynneth of their love. They had too much respect for Etienne. Fact was, he and Adler were both genuinely pleased Etienne seemed to be improving. They both liked and admired him.

Knowing Adler, he could be bemoaning the loss of his family. Though he had accepted his fate and was cheerier than he had been when first they left England behind, Adler still had his moments of sadness. Latimer thought mayhap he was the only one who saw his friend's distant gaze or heard his lingering sighs. Adler tried never to show that side of himself to the Fortiers, especially not to Glynneth. He wondered at that. Glynneth would be sympathetic, understanding.

For an instant Latimer's own family sprang to mind, but he quickly pushed such thoughts aside. They were a part of his past, a past that held nothing for him. He was meant for greater things, and by God, he would be humbled by no man. The Drayes had bent their knees and bowed their heads for the last time. That chain ended with him.

He tucked the blankets up tighter around his throat. The weather was growing colder. 'Twas the first of December, and they had been a month at sea. The winds that had filled their sails for over a fortnight had slackened, but they were still making good progress according to the captain. Thus far they had been caught in no great storm. They had sailed with the winds to their aft so had not needed to tact back and forth with an uncooperative wind. The captain doubted their luck would hold. He had sailed this route many a time and knew what to expect, but Latimer resolved to remain optimistic. He was due some good luck after the devastating defeat he had suffered at the King's side.

Adler's rhythmic breathing reached his ears. Whatever had occupied his friend's thoughts had eventually led him into sleep. Latimer decided to let thoughts of Glynneth put him to sleep. He pictured the sunlight nestling in her hair, her smile when watching Meara dance a jig with him, her laughter when Adler told one of his humorous stories about his neighbor's spoiled younger daughter and her willful ways or an anecdote about his life on the farm he loved. Glynneth serving their meals, playing with her baby, kissing her husband. That last thought brought out a silent groan. He should not be thinking about a married woman. 'Twas wrong. Yet, he could not help himself. Glynneth was attractive. Taken feature by feature, maybe not as beautiful as Jeanette, but Glynneth exuded life. Dreariness disappeared when Glynneth was near. No, he could not stop thinking about her, but he would ne'er do aught to cause her or Etienne any grief. Like Adler he would keep his thoughts and longings to himself.

※ ※ ※ ※

Touching her fingertips to her lips, Glynneth roused and drew in a silent sigh. All was dark and quiet but for the creaking of the ship and the even breathing of her family at sleep. Etienne's breathing was slightly labored, but better than it had been before they had set out on this journey. The baby, snug in his cradle, made occasional mews. Meara, snuggled between her and Etienne, exhaled in little puffs. From his bunk, Curtice's snores were mild, not worrisome enough to keep her from going back to sleep. 'Twas the dream that troubled her sleep.

She could feel Adler's kiss on her lips, feel his strong hands gentling fondling her, touching her in places and in ways she had not experienced in well over a year. Not since Noel had been conceived. Etienne's illness sapped his strength. He could not make love to her. They shared a bed, but not marital relations. She missed their love making. Etienne was a tender lover, eager to give her satisfaction before satisfying his own needs. Afterward, they cuddled, and talked. They still cuddled and talked, but that did not satisfy her longings, her needs.

Why she had dreamed of Adler she could not say, but in her sleep, he aroused feelings in her that left her aquiver. In her dream, with his lips on hers, his hands touching her erotically, she had almost reached that long absent peak. What awoke her and deprived her from that release, she did not know, she but felt an intense disappointment. She also felt a certain shame that she had been brought to near fulfillment by dreaming of a man who was not her husband. She hoped she would not find herself blushing when next she saw Adler. No one could know what she had dreamed. She need but act normal. Surely she would not have such a dream again. Yet as she drifted back into sleep, she could not help but place her fingertips to her lips.

※ ※ ※ ※

Craving more warmth, Jeanette cuddled closer to her husband. She both loved and hated the man beside her. Loved him with all her heart and soul. Hated him for taking her away from her family, her safe home, all that she had ever known, to travel to a new land where the people would be different, their tongues and ways strange. Hated him for the days of seasickness she had endured. Sickness so bad at times she had prayed she would die. Fearing she might starve, her husband and Glynneth had forced her to eat. Forced her to go up on the main deck when all she wanted to do was cling to her bunk. They had been right to get her up. With the fresh air, the light wind in her face, she finally adjusted to the motion of the ship. Now she found if she kept food in her stomach, she did not get sick. How strange. When for days the sight or smell of food set her to heaving, food now kept the sickness at bay.

Often, she also hated Glynneth, the perfect daughter-in-law. At least so Gaspard's father termed her. Glynneth the scholar. Glynneth always organized, ever cheerful. Jeanette was sick to death of Glynneth's perennial cheer, her gurgling laughter, and never ending energy. And 'twas not fair Glynneth suffered not even a moment of the seasickness. Truth was Glynneth loved sailing, loved being up on deck with the brisk wind blowing in her face.

Jeanette envied Glynneth her two healthy children. Their grandfather doted on them. Not that she blamed him. They were both adorable. Jeanette longed for her own baby. Married two years, her childlessness had not been from lack of trying. Gaspard was a lusty husband, and she responded to him with fervor. Since she had recovered from the seasickness, they had made love several times. The lack of privacy and cramped space made her less responsive, but Gaspard had been persistent. Each time she had given in to his ardor. She liked knowing he wanted her, needed her. She needed that reassurance. Though she told herself she was being foolish, at times she feared she saw a longing in his eyes when he looked at his sister-in-law. The same longing she saw in other men's eyes when they gazed at Glynneth.

Why men found Glynneth alluring, Jeanette could not hazard. Glynneth was pretty but no great beauty. Jeanette thought herself prettier. Yet men never looked at her the way they looked at Glynneth. Until this upheaval in her life, she had devoted little thought to Glynneth or her children or Etienne. They had their own home, and she normally saw them but once a week. She and Gaspard lived with his father in his large, comfortable home. She had been the lady of the house, and when Glynneth and her family came to dine, she had been the hostess. She liked that.

Enjoying her comfortable life, she paid little heed to her father-in-law's complaints about his business. Her own father, who like the Fortiers, was a Huguenot refugee from France, had voiced similar complaints. Concerns about the disruption in trade with first the Irish rebellion, then the war, then the displacement of the more prosperous Irish. Anger over trade restrictions imposed by the English Parliament. Blissfully unaware of the seriousness of her father-in-law's grievances, she had been shocked when he decided to sell his home and his business and move to the New Netherlands. That her husband chose to move also left her devastated. She had begged her father to intervene, but he said he could not blame Curtice. Was her mother not set against the notion, he would consider migrating with him.

Now here she was, eager for the voyage to end, yet terrified at what she might encounter upon landing. At least she had a strong husband at her side. That was more than Glynneth had.

Chapter 6

Adler watched the clouds massing before them. They were headed into a storm. The captain, his genial, bulging eyes alight, wiped his bulbous nose with a handkerchief, and speaking in his heavy Dutch accent said, "Aye, dat be some dark clouds ahead, but looks more like mere rain clouds dan a vicious storm. De *Alida* is a sturdy ship. She will not fail us whet-her 'tis rain or storm, so you rest easy."

But Adler could not rest easy. He knew soon he and Latty and the Fortiers would be forced to stay below in the 'tween deck, and the hatch would be covered. Locked in they would be. Could he abide it? He wondered. What if he started going crazy, yelling and screaming. He could frighten Meara and maybe Glynneth. All would be dark but for one lantern light. And if 'twas truly a storm, not just rain, advancing on them, they would not have even that light. All flames would need be extinguished so not to risk a fire.

Might he convince the captain to let him stay on the main deck? He wanted to be with Glynneth should she need him. At the same time, he feared he would cause her grief did he stay below. 'Twas his fear of being locked in a prison that had driven him to flee England. His insides crumpled when he thought of being locked in anywhere, no matter how brief the time.

Draye came up beside him. "Seems our luck may have deserted us. I cannot like the looks of those clouds.

Adler nodded, but repeated what the captain had told him.

"I guess the captain knows of what he speaks," Draye said. "Having lived my life on the Sussex coast, I have seen many a storm roll in from the sea. Those clouds look fearsome, but I have seen worse. In any case, the crew will soon be charged with battening down the hatches."

Adler gulped. A pain stabbed his innards and weakened his knees. Clutching the leather bag under his shirt, he said, "I am thinking I will stay above. I could mayhap be of some use."

Draye snorted. "More like be in the seamen's way. Or else you will wash overboard. Nay, Adler, you would be wrong to put an extra burden on the captain. You would not want him to worry about your safety and not tend his duties."

Frowning, Adler looked around at his friend. "Truth be, Latty, I cannot abide being locked in below. 'Twould be like a prison cell."

Pursing his lips thoughtfully, Draye said, "I understand. Best you speak to the captain. Mayhap he will let you stay in his cabin. We can tell the others you mean to stay topside in case an extra hand should be needed. We are not sailing with a large crew. 'Tis feasible."

"Do you think?"

"Aye. Go on. I will make your excuses."

Feeling a weight lifted from his shoulders, Adler slapped Draye on the shoulder. "Thank you, Latty. God keep us all safe," he added before going in search of the captain.

❧ ❧ ❧ ❧

Crooning a little ditty her mother had sung to her, Glynneth cuddled Meara in her arms and stared into the darkness. She could hear the wind howling around the ship, hear the heavy rain pounding the deck. Drops of rain seeped through the above deck, and dampness permeated everything. The animals bleated, squealed, and squawked whenever sudden gusts buffeted the ship and caused it to jump sideways. When the hatch had first been covered, Latty had engaged Etienne and his father in a card game, but in short order the game had to be abandoned as the ship's gyrations grew steadily more intense, and the light in the lantern had to be extinguished. To keep from being flung about the deck, everyone had been forced to settle on blankets on the floor. Head lowered, Jeanette sat with a bucket between her knees. Though she moaned, she had not yet emptied her stomach. Gaspard wrapped an arm around her hunched shoulders to keep her from sliding around the deck.

They had packed away as many objects as they could and had turned the table and benches upside down so they would not fall over on anyone. Glynneth prayed the cannons and other heavy objects in the 'tween decks were properly secured. Curtice had managed to sit on the floor but a short time before his joints began to pain him. Latty helped him to his bunk and tucked his blankets tightly around him to keep him from being tossed out. Noel, cozy in his cradle, seemed to be the only one enjoying the excess rocking. He gurgled happily and chewed on the rattle Latty had given him.

Glynneth knew they all missed Adler. His stories would have helped take their minds off the storm. Latty told them Adler stayed above to help was he needed, the crew being small, but Glynneth suspected Adler stayed above because he feared confined spaces. She had heard about such fears. Some fears manifested themselves after some dreadful or frightening experience. Often soldiers relived the horrors of war. Some could never again engage in battles, others turned hard and cruel and would welcome a fight with anyone. Some people feared heights. Certainly Jeanette feared seasickness, and with good reason, poor dear.

Glynneth wondered if some horrid event had triggered Adler's fear. Other than the first night they met when he spoke of his dread of prison, he had never mentioned his hatred of tight places. She had but observed his reluctance to spend anytime below deck. He came down to eat and to sleep, but often at night, when the others retired, she heard him tread lightly up the steps to the main deck. He would stay up there, no matter the weather, until the need for sleep forced him back to his hammock.

She wondered too what he kept tied about his neck. When startled, he grabbed for it. When thoughtful, he fondled it. Several times she had determined she would ask him then had changed her mind. 'Twould be too forward. 'Twas something very dear to him, of that she was certain. Could the object have anything to do with his fear? 'Twas a puzzle.

"I think mayhap the storm is lessening," Latty said, interrupting Glynneth's thoughts. He cocked his head. "Listen. The patter is much milder. We may be through the worst of it."

"Let us pray you are right, Latty," said Etienne. "I will offer a prayer of thanks to our maker." He bowed his head and closed his eyes. "Oh, Lord in Heaven, …" he began, and Glynneth, resuming her thoughts of Adler, heard but his soft drone in her ears.

She hoped Adler was safe. Surely he would not do anything foolish.

He knew nothing about sailing. He could try to help and end up going overboard. She gave her head a slight shake. Such thoughts were not good. Adler was no dunce. He would take no unnecessary risks. Come morning, she would awaken to find the hatch had been opened, and Adler had prepared their porridge for breakfast. Thinking of food reminded her she would need to feed her family and Latty a supper. Noel was starting to complain. 'Twas past his feeding time. She would need to turn Meara over to Latty or Etienne that she could nurse her son. Then for those whose stomachs would permit it, once they could again light the lantern, she would set out a picnic supper.

🎇 🎇 🎇 🎇

Adler was not afraid of the tossing sea, though he sometimes wondered that he was not as fearful of water as he was confined spaces. He hated being cooped up in the captain's quarters, but at least he was not locked in. Did he wish, he could leave the room at any time. He had peered out at the rain and wave soaked deck several times. Having naught but the captain's terrier to keep him company, he could do little to occupy himself but pace the undulating floor. The crew were at the helm, manning the pumps, or in the foc's'le riding out the storm, which had proven to be more vigorous than the captain had predicted. All the sails, but the foresail, had been furled, and the ropes whipping about in the wind made an eerie sound. He heard thunder rumbling in the distance, but no loud booms cracked overhead. He hoped Glynneth and her family were not frightened. He wished he could have stayed below to comfort them, but he knew he had been wise to convince the captain to let him stay in his cabin.

The captain had been surprisingly understanding. "You are not de first man to fear being imprisoned in 't 'tween deck during a storm. I have known men to veep and beg not to be forced to stay below. I vill not be making you beg. You are velcome to ride out der storm in my cabin."

Adler thought the storm might be abating. The ship no longer darted hither and yon, the thunder seemed more distant, and the patter of the rain against the shuttered windows seemed to have lessened. He had no idea the hour, but he guessed it well past supper time. He was hungry. He had had nothing to eat since breakfast. He imagined Glynneth would be feeding her family and Latty with cheese and sausages and dried fruit of some sort.

A yap from the captain's dog told him the little fellow was also hungry or mayhap thirsty. The dog stood next to a wooden bowl that had flipped over and had been sliding about the cabin during the storm. Everything else in the cabin had also done some traveling – the captain's table with his charts and maps, his chest, his chair when Adler had not been occupying it. Adler could see no reason to attempt to right things until the storm ended.

Another bark. Shaking his head, Adler addressed the dog. "Naught I can do for you or for me. My stomach is rumbling just like yours." The terrier was a friendly little cur, and according to the captain, "As good een mouser as any cat. To see him take de rat by de neck and shake it until it is dead is een sight to see. Loves de challenge of catching de rats I do tink."

The dog had the run of the ship, and almost any time, day or night, his light-weight patter could be heard as he made his rounds. Meara had early on made friends with the little black and white, pointy-eared terrier, and 'twas only the captain's insistence the dog be allowed to do his job that kept Meara from adopting him and keeping him at her side.

Chuckling to himself, Adler recalled Meara's first meeting with her furry friend. "Why has he no name? You but call him 'hond' which Mother says means naught but dog in Dutch," Meara said, her hand resting on the dog's head.

"He is een hond," the captain answered, jovially. "Why should I call him anyting else?"

"But your ship has a name. Why not the dog?" Frowning, Meara gazed up at the captain.

"Een ship is like 'n voman. She must have 'n name. But de hond, why he needs 'n name? He is de only hond on 't ship. I call 'hond', and he comes."

Meara stuck out her lower lip. "Well I intend to give him a name. I shall call him Sir Galahad because he is brave to fight the rats just like knights were brave to fight the dragons."

The robust captain rocked back and forth from toe to heel and said, "Ja, ja. You call him vat you vill. For me, he is but hond."

Each time the captain said 'hond', the dog wagged his tail. He seemingly had no problem with his lack of name, but within a week, he had also learned to answer to Sir Galahad. A few choice tidbits from a tiny hand seemed to help him learn. The crew, too, seemed fond of the dog. Any and all had a pat for the little guy. Why should they not. They could have no love of the rats that accompanied any voyage.

"Oh, Meara, do release the dog and let him do his job!" Jeanette had once demanded. "I know I heard a rat scampering around our quarters last night. I cannot abide the creatures." Meara had been playing a game of tug-a-war with Sir Galahad. She looked up in surprise at her aunt's proclamation, but Jeanette had turned to Glynneth. "You should have some concern for Noel, Glynneth. I have heard stories of rats going after babies in cribs."

"Oh, no," spoke up Meara. "Sir Galahad would never let any rat near Noel."

"Well, a rat was here last night," Jeanette snapped, "so let that dog go find it and kill it."

"Your Aunt Jeanette is right, Meara. Send Sir Galahad on his way. You have monopolized enough of his time. Mayhap Adler will tell you one of his stories, or Latty will play a game with you, either cup and ball, or get your peg board for a game of *Fox and Geese*."

Meara, after sending Sir Galahad on his way with a stern admonition to, "get that rat!", opted for one of Adler's stories. "Tell me a story about Arcadia. I like her stories."

"You would," he said with a chuckle as she climbed up on his lap. "You are much like her. Just as headstrong and determined to have your own way," he said as she squiggled around until comfortable. "I shall tell you about Arcadia and the black kitten."

Adler had never thought of himself as a story teller before joining the Fortiers' voyage to New Netherland. He had always enjoyed his mother's and father's stories when the family had settled around the hearth on dark winter evenings. Stories of the long ago past. Stories about the family's history, real or myth, but intriguing either way. Some of the stories he had repeated to the Fortiers to help pass the time. Upon learning they enjoyed his tales, he had expanded his narratives to tales involving him and his brother and their neighbors, the Yardleys. Meara found Arcadia, the youngest Yardley and a bit of a hoyden, a captivating character.

His musings interrupted by the sound of heavy footsteps, Adler turned to find the captain had returned. Stepping through the portal, he hailed Adler. "Ah, Mister Hayvard, I see you have survived de storm."

"Indeed, sir. Would you say it is over."

"De vorst is over. My mate is on de deck, and I mean to get some rest as soon as Cook sends me some-ting to eat. You vish to join me, I vould velcome your company. You can tell me how you come to be in 't company of de Fortiers. Aftervards, you may bed down vit de crew in 't foc's'le until de morning. By den, de rain should be ended."

Adler accepted the captain's invitation and helped him set his cabin to rights. By the time the cabin boy arrived with two bowls of cold gruel, sausages, cheese, and mugs of ale, all was back to normal. Adler recounted his history with the Fortiers, but chose not to tell the captain the reason for his flight. Better the captain think Adler and Latty fled poverty and lack of land than he think there might be a price on their heads worth claiming.

The meal finished, Adler excused himself, and gripping the life line that stretched from fore to aft, he made his way to the foc's'le. The deck was still awash with rain, but the wind and waves had calmed, and the seamen were raising the main and mizzen sails. "Vee vould not vant to remain becalmed and have der storm vash back over us," one seaman told him.

Given a hammock, Adler crawled into it. He might not have attended many church services, but he still believed in God, and he offered up his thanks that they had made it through the storm with no real signs of wreckage to the ship. He prayed that in the morning he would find Glynneth and her family were safe and had fared as well as he had.

Chapter 7

"Take a long deep sniff," Adler told Glynneth. "The captain says we can smell the land even before we can see it. He says the forests are so thick, their scent floats on the air for miles."

Glynneth tilted back her head and inhaled deeply. Yes, she could smell an earthy scent like that of damp soil and fallen leaves, but also a sweet scent as of pine and cedar. The sharp chill that had been with them for several days and had forced them to keep below wrapped in blankets had dissipated, and the sun, bright in a blue winter sky, brought everyone up on deck. Her father-in-law, Jeanette, and Etienne sat on chairs with blankets tucked about them. Noel dozed in his cradle, Latty entertained Meara with a game of cup and ball, and Gaspard prowled the deck, stretching his legs, he said.

Blankets and linens, even the woolen mattresses and some clothing items that had not completely dried out after the storm, had been brought up and spread out on the decking along with the ship's crew's meager coverings. Glynneth, with Adler and Latty helping her, had washed down their quarters with vinegar. It helped disperse the musty smell that had been accumulating over the weeks of the voyage.

Standing at the bow of the ship, Glynneth loved the brace of the wind in her face. They were moving at a good clip again. After the storm, as the cold had set in, the wind had died. They had not been becalmed, but there progress had been slowed. "'Tis good to be whipping along," she said. "I have enjoyed the voyage, enjoyed watching the sea and the sky both during the day and at night. What wondrous sights. Yet I confess I am now ready to reach our destination."

Adler nodded thoughtfully and fondled the object hidden beneath his shirt. He saw her watching him, and dropped his hand. Then he smiled. "You are wondering what I have tucked under my shirt, are you not?"

She blushed. "I admit I am curious. I have noted since our first meeting that your hand goes to it whenever you are thoughtful or worried."

"Were you curious, you might have asked."

"I would not so presume," she said, looking back out over the water at the twinkling sunrays dancing on the waves.

"Let me show you," he said, and she turned back as he drew a soft, worn leather bag from beneath his shirt. The bag was attached to a strong leather thong tied about his neck. Opening the bag, he pulled out a curved object and held it out to her.

Taking it in her hand, she felt its weight and examined its dull yellowish color. It appeared to be half a circle of intricately twisted wires. One end had been cut, the other had a small round nob with a hole in it. "Is this gold?" she asked.

"Mayhap. I could not say, but 'tis possible."

"How did you come by it?"

He frowned. "My father insisted I take it with me. It has been handed down in our family to the eldest son for untold generations. It, along with a ring with the emblem of a hawk on it. I was against taking it. Afraid I might lose it, but I am the eldest son, and my father pressed it on me. He was afraid did the Puritans search our home, they might confiscate it. The ring stayed with my brother. That way, does anything happen to one or the other of us, at least one of the heirlooms will remain with our family."

Cocking his head he looked out to sea. "Do I survive this new world adventure, and do I someday have a son, this will be his. Does Caleb have a son, the ring will be his."

An odd pain pricked Glynneth at the thought of Adler marrying and having children. But why should he not, she chided herself. "'Tis wise. My grandmother has heirlooms that will be passed on to my brother, Nolan. But this," she said, holding it up to catch the sunlight, "this I do think ..." She shook her head. "I could be wrong, but I do believe this is half a torque."

"Half a what," he asked, his brow creased.

"A torque. 'Tis a type of necklace, a relic of the Celts."

"The who?"

"The Celts, ancestors of the Welsh and the Irish."

"Oh," he nodded. "My family has ever lived right on the border of

47

England and Wales. Many Welsh live in the local village, and there is much trade back and forth across the border."

"That could explain why you have this torque, or half of one. Mayhap you have a Welsh ancestor in your distant past."

He nodded. "Could be, but I wonder why 'tis but a half. Who has the other half?"

"'Tis an interesting mystery. I would guess years ago your ancestors would have known," she said, smiling and handing the relic back to him.

He carefully replaced it in its bag and tucked the bag back under his shirt. "My father says the tale, handed down over the years, claims our ancestors, before the Conqueror, were great landholders. He says these family relics are proof we are the true owners of some vast estate." He chuckled. "Where that estate may be located has long since been forgotten. Many Saxon and Welsh lords were displaced when William defeated Harold. However, even did we discover the lost estate, I cannot see how this half a torque as you did call it and a ring could prove our land had been usurped, and I was the rightful heir."

She brushed a wisp of hair from her eye and joined in his mirth. "No, I cannot think the relics would prove much. I would like to show the half torque to Etienne, did you not mind. To see does he think I am correct in my assessment. But not until this evening, when we are below and away from prying eyes. For you that is a prized heirloom. For others ..., well, better you not show it to any of the crew."

"Agreed. We will let Etienne examine it after supper, after the little one is abed, then best we not mention it again."

"Speaking of my little one, I best go see how she fares. Latty will have her spoiled beyond redemption ere this voyage is over."

"I will go with you. 'Tis time Latty, Gaspard, and I get the bedding below. The sun and fresh air have no doubt benefited them greatly."

As she had so often on the voyage, Glynneth wondered how her family would have managed without Latty and Adler. Was there a God, the two men had certainly been a God send.

※　※　※　※

"No question about it. 'Tis most definitely half a torque," said Etienne after examining Adler's relic. "You must take great care of it. Its historical value is of more worth than the gold. Not that many men would recognize that fact. They would think but to melt it down. I have seen torques on statues in museums, and I saw a nicely preserved torque in a case, as well. This is but half, but I would say it once belonged to a prominent chieftain or warrior."

"As 'twas once whole," said Latty, "mayhap at one time your family found itself in need. Rather than destroy the whole torque, as Etienne does call it, they cut it in half and used the other half to pay off a debt or buy land."

Adler twisted his mouth and nodded. "'Tis possible. A distant branch of our family were the village smiths. They died out or moved on, I know not which. Never thought to ask. But I would say this has been cut by someone who knew what he was doing. No rough edges.

"So could have been a smith cut it. For that matter, could be that branch of the family kept the other half," Latty said.

"Why yes," said Glynneth. "That could well be the answer. All the same, best put it away. I almost wish I had never seen it. Now I will be worried you may somehow lose it."

Adler liked Glynneth's concern. He had been pleased to show her the heirloom. That Glynneth was impressed by its ancient value made it more special to him. He would need to take even greater care of it.

"Were I you," said Latty, "I would stop grasping it so often. You give the impression you wear something of value. And in this case you do. The fewer men observe this the better."

"I agree," said Etienne. "In the future, you might wish to be more circumspect."

"Especially as you often choose to wander alone on the deck at night," Latty added. "'Twould be too easy for a member of the crew to knock you over the head, take the torque, and toss you overboard."

"Oh, Latty, you must not say such things," said Glynneth, her eyes wide. "But indeed, Adler, heed these warnings and do think to be careful."

"I will," Adler promised, treasuring the fretful timbre in her voice and the apprehension he saw in the depth of her eyes. Foolishly, it mattered that she cared. It warmed his soul.

"I think now 'tis time we all turn in," said Gaspard. "Our candle grows short, as does our supply of them. We used a great many of them these days when we could not go up on deck."

"Most wise, brother," said Etienne. "Let us pray this fine weather will hold until we reach our destination."

"May that be soon," snapped Jeanette. "I am sick to death of this hold. I am sick of the smells, the dampness, the near intolerable food. I am sick of being sick." She put her hand to her stomach. "Did I go even one day without a queasy stomach, I would count myself blessed."

Gaspard put an arm around his wife. "Come, dear, 'tis late, and you are tired. Let us to bed. Soon, very soon we will reach New Netherland, and you will no longer be sick."

Her pale blue eyes rose to meet his dark eyes. "Why do you say such? What have you heard? Do say 'tis true."

Tightening his grip on her shoulders and urging her toward their bunk, he said. "The captain says we may well see land tomorrow. After that, a day, two, three at the most and we should make landing."

"In truth?" asked Glynneth.

Gaspard looked over his wife's head and smiled at Glynneth. "In truth."

"What glad tidings," she said, clapping her hands. "Now I can scarce wait for the morrow. Come Etienne, let us to bed so morning will come all the sooner."

He laughed, but rose and joined her. "To bed," he said, but he looked back at Adler. "You or Latty will put out the candle?"

"Aye," Adler said, masterfully controlling the envy in his voice. Soon the voyage would end as would his days with Glynneth. What would the new world offer him in her place?

Chapter 8

"That is New Amsterdam!" cried Jeanette.

Standing at the bow of the ship beside her sister-in-law, Glynneth could have echoed her consternation. New Amsterdam consisted of naught but a wooden palisade fort, a few brick buildings, and a hodge-podge of wooden houses scattered along dirt tracks. This wilderness was to be their new home. Etienne slipped his arm around her. He must have sensed her apprehension. "'Tis a great deal different than we might have expected," he said. "But I have no doubt we will soon adjust to this simpler form of life."

Clutching Noel in her arms, Glynneth cuddled closer to Etienne. "Does it improve your health, my love, it matters not what else we may find." Clucking sadly, she added, "I think we will not find any libraries. I hope the books we packed survived the voyage and were not destroyed by moisture."

He smiled down at her. "Aye, but if not, we will send for more."

"Look, Adler, look," came her daughter's voice, "'tis our new home."

Adler had hoisted Meara onto his shoulder that she could have a clear view of the port as they drew near. "Aye," he answered the child. "Let us see can you determine which house will be yours."

"Oh, that is easy," Meara said. "'Tis the one with the shingle roof."

Laughing, he tickled her, and her ensuing giggles brought a smile to Glynneth's lips. Adler had become much more comfortable with the children. Someday when he had children of his own, he would make a good father.

"Little minx," Adler teased Meara, "near all have shingle roofs."

Still giggling, Meara stated, "Aye, and so does ours," and she burst into more giggles.

"I can see nothing to laugh at," said Jeanette. She turned to her husband standing beside her at the railing. "Look at what you have brought us to. A pig squalor."

"I admit 'tis rustic, but it gives us all the more opportunity to build, to improve ..."

Jeanette interrupted him. "To build what, another squalid house?" She burst into tears. "Oh, to think what I have endured to come to this."

Gaspard attempted to put his arms around her, but she pushed him away and ran off. He watched her until she disappeared down the hatch to the tween deck that had been their home for the past eight weeks. Glynneth touched his hand, and he looked around at her.

"She will be all right," she said. "This voyage has been very trying for her. Once we are settled, and she has recovered from the seasickness, she will be her old self again."

Smiling wanly, he said, "I hope you may be right. But I, too, admit this is not what I expected. I had not expected anything on a par with Dublin, but this ..." He swept his arm out and around. "'Tis so crude."

His father clamped his hand on his shoulder. "Wee, Gaspard, eet is crude, but as you tried to tell Jeanette, eet gives much opportunity to build. And so we will build." He inhaled deeply. "Zee air eez fresh and zee land eez young and ripe. We will grow rich here." He reached over and chucked Noel under the chin. "My grandson will someday own warehouses and wharfs. He will live in a brick house and dine off fine silver plate. Wee, zat eez what awaits us here."

Laughing, Glynneth gave her father-in-law a hug. "You make all seem right Father Curtice. As you say, we will build a new grand life here. Lord knows there are enough trees we can build whatever we may wish." She had never dreamed so many trees existed in the world. When they had first spotted the coast, she had been able to do little but stare at the unending trees that lined the shore. "A true wilderness," Adler had called it."

Soon the anchor was dropped, the sails furled, and the ship shuddered to a halt. A few other ships rocked gently in the massive bay, and several small boats were being propelled across the water to greet the *Alida*. A man in the smallest boat, and the first to reach them called up in halting Dutch, "Have you a Monsieur Curtice Fortier aboard your vessel?" At least that was what Adler thought the man asked. His comprehension of the Dutch tongue yet being very poor.

52

"Wee," cried Curtice. "I am he."

The man switched to French, and Adler asked, "What does he say?"

Glynneth smiled and translated. "He welcomes us. He says Monsieur Chappell has been expecting us. He is going to return to port to let him know we have at last arrived. He will send a large boat to transport us to shore."

Curtice nodded and thanked the man who set to his oars. He then turned to his family. "We must gather up our zings." He looked at Gaspard. "My son, you must again stay with our goods." His gaze sought Latty. "You will stay with him, wee?"

Latty bobbed his head up and down. "Aye, I will stay."

Glynneth was pleased with the arrangement. Adler would be there to help her family settle. He was so gentle with Etienne and with her aged father-in-law. He would see everyone securely settled in the long boat. Latty would be as diligent in his help to Gaspard. She was going to miss these two men who had so benefited her family.

※ ※ ※ ※

New Amsterdam might not be what she had expected, but Glynneth hoped adjusting to the new life style would not prove onerous. After speaking mostly English for Adler's and Latty's benefit during the past eight weeks, she caught her tongue tripping over some of the Dutch words she had prided herself on knowing so well. The Chappells spoke French and Dutch, but they knew no English. A growing number in the colony spoke English, but Adler and Latty would need to become more proficient in both French and Dutch were they to prosper in their new home. In the meantime, Glynneth and Etienne did their best to translate for them. Glynneth wished she had been more insistent about teaching her two friends the languages during the voyage. The long dark evenings would have been the perfect time for lessons, but listening to Adler's tales or enjoying various games had occupied their time instead.

Glynneth found her husband's cousin, Armand Chappell, charming. He was the perfect host, and his wife, Capucine, was kind and welcoming. The couple made room in their home for her, Etienne, and their children, and for Adler and Latty. Glynneth was delighted Adler and Latty would not be immediately separated from her family. They were given cots in the loft. Glynneth and her family were given the Chappells' daughters' room, and cots were set up for their girls, nine year old, Jolie, and thirteen year old, Raissa, in the family room. The Chappells' young sons, five year old, Guyon, and one year old, Pierre slept in a trundle bed in their parents' bedchamber. The house was not large, having but the two bedchambers, the family room, and the loft, but it was cozy and warm, at least during the day when the fire was kept burning.

Glynneth appreciated the warming fire in the hearth and the heavy woolen blankets on the bed. New Amsterdam was bitter cold compared to Dublin. The first morning she found the water in her pitcher frozen, she had scrambled back into bed. 'Twas too cold to be about. Not until Capucine tapped on the door did she force herself to rise and face the day. She would not let Etienne or Meara rise, though, until she had warmed their clothes by the fire in the family room.

Her blue eyes dancing, Capucine laughed. "Soon you will adjust." She spoke in French, it being her native tongue, but a smattering of Dutch occasionally crept into her speech. "You will learn to wear extra stockings and petticoats – mayhap a pair of your husband's breeches under the petticoats. You will sleep in two woolen shifts, and when it is truly cold, you will forgo modesty and sleep with your bedchamber door open so the heat from the family room can circulate into your room."

Glynneth wondered how Gaspard, Jeanette, and her father-in-law fared in their new environs. She had been so busy putting her own world to rights, she had visited them but once. Jeanette had done naught but cry and complain despite their tidy abode. Curtice's brother-in- law, Jacques Chappell, having decided to spend the winter at Fort Orange, had left his house at the ready for his in-laws. Two slaves, a woman to care for the house, to cook and clean, and a man to attend to the fire-wood, draw the day's water, and feed the goats, chickens, and pigs that nearly every family had in the yards behind their homes, had been left to assist the Fortiers.

Every morning, Armand, a robust man with a hearty laugh, a wide-

54

mouth grin, and genial brown eyes similar to Etienne's, took Adler and Latty off with him. "Training them to be woodsmen," he proclaimed.

"What does he teach you?" Glynneth asked Adler one evening when they were the last ones still sitting before the hearth.

"We have much to learn it seems," he said, stretching his feet out toward the low glowing fire that he would soon bank when they headed to their beds. "Walking seems to be more important than near everything else?"

She giggled. "Walking? Are you not already walking?"

"I thought so, but it seems this method of walking, which is near like falling forward, allows a man to cover a vast distance in a day without tiring. I knew a chapman back home did walk like that. Where we will be going to trade with the various Indian tribes, few trails allow for travel by horse. We might have a pack horse or mule to carry our trade goods and to return with the furs, but we will be traveling by foot if not by water. We are also learning to paddle a canoe."

He took a puff on the pipe he held in his hand then coughed. Grinning he said, "I never took to tobacco, though many I knew smoked. Seems the smoking can be ceremonial with the Indians, so I must learn to smoke it without all this coughing."

Glynneth screwed up her mouth and harrumphed. "I could wish Armand would not smoke in the evenings. Between his smoke and the smoke from the fire in this tight house, 'tis not good for Etienne."

Adler nodded. "How does Etienne? Is this cold afflicting him?"

She shrugged. "Some mayhap. But when we go outside, the air is so fresh. So different from the pall that hangs over Dublin. We walk to the edge of the village and take deep gulps of the fragrant air. We also look about at various sites to determine where we want to build our house. Do we want to build at the edge of town? Is it safe, if we did build there?"

"'Tis good he can walk with you. He seldom went out when we were in Rotterdam."

"True, but the air there was much as it is in Dublin." She stared into the fire for a moment, remembering the walks she had taken around the thriving seaport with Adler. He was a good companion. Easy to talk to. Shaking herself, she looked back at him. "Is Armand teaching you anything besides how to walk?"

He chuckled. "Aye, we are learning the various qualities of the furs, premium, good, and poor. We are learning how to blaze a trail – er – that means how to mark a trail. How to look for distinguishing features so we will not get lost. He says we are but beginning. We will have much more to learn once we reach Fort Orange and actually begin working."

"When do you leave for the fort?" She had been pleased Adler and Latty were sharing the Chappells' home with them. She had thought once they landed in New Amsterdam, she might not see her friends on any regular basis. Of course, she knew their time in New Amsterdam was limited. Their work would take them far up the North River. She determined she would enjoy their company while she could.

"We will not leave until spring when the river thaws," he answered before taking another draw on the pipe.

"Ah, yes, I guess I knew that." She changed the subject. "Do you ever get frightened when you are out there in the woods?"

He shook his head. "Nay, but then I trust Armand. Was I alone, mayhap." He shrugged. "Armand says do we ever get lost, we should try to find a brook and follow it downstream. It will almost always lead to a river or to some sort of civilization. Plus it will keep us from going in circles. He says too often people who get lost in the woods just keep walking in circles."

"Why would they do that?"

"They cannot help it. They get disoriented or some such."

"You and Latty must learn your lessons well that you will not get lost and go in circles. You must be doing better with your French if you can understand what Armand is teaching you."

"Latty is doing better, and he translates for me. I seem to have an easier time with the Dutch tongue. The words are more similar to English, and I find them easier to pronounce."

"'Tis good you two have each other. You can translate for one another." She rubbed her hands on her shoulders and glanced at the fire. "The fire grows low. Time we turn in."

"Aye. You go ahead. I will sit here a bit longer before I bank the fire."

"Very well. Pleasant dreams good friend," she said, rising and wondering again as she had so often, what made him so dread tight quarters he would put off his sleep.

Looking up at her, his blue-green eyes bright in the last glow of the fire, he smiled. "Same to you, Glynneth."

Away from the fire, she grew chilled and hurried to her bed. Slipping out of her bodice, skirt, and multiple woolen petticoats, she pulled her night shift over her day shift. She would leave her stockings on, too. Before blowing out the candle on the table beside the bed, she checked on her little family. Meara lay next to Etienne, her arms cuddled around Noel. Glynneth had decided the cold was too intense to leave Noel in his crib or Meara in a trundle bed. They would all stay warmer tucked into the same bed. Children could fall into such deep sleep, did Etienne begin coughing, he likely would not awaken them.

They all looked so peaceful. Etienne's breathing was steady and easy. Their walk in the sun had been good for him. She prayed the morrow would be sunny. This New Amsterdam was good for her husband. Every day he grew stronger. She was grateful to Capucine's daughter, Raissa, for taking care of Noel and Meara that she and Etienne could have their outings. Raissa was a pretty girl with her light brown hair and soft brown eyes. She looked nothing like her blond haired, blue-eyed mother. Her sister, Jolie, though, was the image of her mother, right down to her short, thin, upward tilting nose, straight jawline, and wide-set eyes. She was a true beauty, and her laughter was infectious. For one so young, she had an amusing sense of humor.

Raissa was more sedate, and Glynneth feared the girl had formed a tender for Latty. Not that she blamed her. Latty was jovial and fun loving, and he teased Raissa and Jolie about the hearts they would someday break when they grew older. He treated them like young adults, never like irrelevant children. Despite his jutting jaw, he was a handsome man, with his bright smile and laughing gray eyes. She doubted not that he would break many a woman's heart. Not on purpose, just by being so charming.

Adler, on the other hand, though generally cheerful, was more earnest. He could tell wonderful stories, and he had become much more at ease with the children, yet he could often be distant. At times, the way he looked at her, as he had looked at her this evening when he bid her good night, set her heart to racing. Sometimes she could not keep herself from wondering what it would be like to kiss him. For such a strong man, he was ever gentle, and his concern for Etienne was heartfelt, that she knew. She wondered at the attraction she felt for Adler. She never for an instant doubted her love for her husband. And yet ...

Burying under the blankets, she cuddled close to her children. Etienne stirred, but did not wake. She reached across the children and touched his arm. Dear husband, she prayed, please, get well, please, please. Do you get well, this whole adventure will be worth every hardship.

Chapter 9

As one day flowed into another, Glynneth fell into a routine. Help Capucine with the household tasks – from cleaning to washing to cooking to shopping, even to feeding the animals and collecting eggs – then enjoy an outing with her husband or her children. Despite the numbing cold, she needed her daily walks. She had learned to wear more clothes, and she insisted Etienne and the children do the same. Etienne laughed at her, but obeyed her wishes. He had grown strong enough to go to the warehouse to help his father and Gaspard, and her joy in his improvement had her more lighthearted than she had been in well over a year.

The first thing Curtice had done upon arrival was to have a new warehouse built. He proclaimed the one his brother-in-law had was far too small. He had more goods on order, plus he had his own house furnishings to store until he could have his new home constructed. He and Gaspard stayed busy, first supervising the construction of the warehouse then setting up their office. From the numerous workers they employed, they selected several permanent hirelings. With all in place, Etienne settled into a warm office and resumed his duties as his father's accountant, freeing Gaspard and his father to engage in organizing and inventorying the stock, including the goods they had brought with them and the furs waiting to be sold.

That Etienne enjoyed being useful, Glynneth well knew. His Calvinistic upbringing made him feel guilty was he not contributing to his family's support. But she, too, needed to keep busy. Fortunately, there was much that needed doing in the Chappell household. She had returned from the market with two large cod for their dinner when Capucine beckoned to her.

"Come join me in a hot tisane." Pulling a clean cap down over her blond braids, she invited Glynneth to sit. "The chores will still be here when we are rested. I do hate wash day in the winter. My hands get so numb, and they chap and crack. Can be painful at times." She held up her sturdy hands for a moment before turning to the hearth to pull the kettle off its hook and fill two wooden noggins with the steaming water. "I have washed Pierre's napkins, and the children's clothes. They dirty them so quickly. And I thought, as I am doing that, I might as well wash a couple of Armand's shirts and my bodices. Now I am done. I suppose you will want to wash some things as well, especially your babe's napkins. There is yet room on the fence for hanging whatever you may choose to wash."

"Thank you. I know I must wash a number of items. It is never pleasant work, but as you said this morning, we must take advantage of this sunny day. At least it is easier than washing the napkins aboard ship. I had to wash them in sea water, then rise them in vinegar water. Poor babe, his bottom was often raw. I had to coat him in grease to soothe him." She chuckled. "Oh, he did have a strange smell then."

"You are lucky you and yours fared so well on the crossing. I remember well the horrors of life aboard the ship. And I had no children to tend then." While she talked, Capucine took an herbal mixture from a box and dropped several large pinches into each noggin. "The hardest part of the wash day is getting and heating the water. Luckily we have Noam to haul the water."

Noam was Jacques Chappell's slave, but he also did chores for Armand's family. "For close to two years, before I married Armand," Capucine said, "taking in laundry was how I supported myself and the girls." Glynneth had learned Raissa and Jolie were Capucine's children by her first husband.

"You were very brave," Glynneth said. "How did your husband die?" She feared someday she too would be left a widow, but at least she and her children would not know hunger and want. She would never have to take in laundry.

Capucine took a spoon and slowly stirred the two brews. "He and our two sons were killed in an attack by the Lenape Indians in forty-three."

Glynneth had been watching Capucine's deliberate stirring, but she jerked up in her seat, exclaiming, "Killed by Indians!" She looked from Capucine to Meara who was happily playing cup and ball with Guyon. Pierre and Noel were asleep in their cribs near the hearth. Raissa and

Jolie had gone off with friends after hanging out their mother's morning wash.

"My husband and my sons were working in the field when the Lenape struck. They had no chance to escape," Capucine said. "My daughters and I hid in a tiny cellar under the house" she continued. "The Lenape tried to burn down the house, but a heavy rain started and doused the fire. Otherwise, I think the smoke would have killed us, too."

Glynneth's heart pounded in her chest. "I cannot think how you … you can now … sit here so calmly," she said haltingly. "I think I would still be living in a state of terror."

Capucine gave her a crooked little smile. "Sometimes the memories come back at night and haunt me. I cry out, and Armand knows to wake me. I never sleep alone. Is Armand away, I have the girls sleep with me. The dreams are too real, too terrifying." Her eyes glazed over and she turned to look at the fire. "I know not how long we stayed down in that cellar. I was afraid to leave it. The roof had burned away, and the rain dripped down through the floor slats. We sat in the mud, huddled together. Hunger drove me to try the trap door. I pushed it slowly up. Night had fallen. It was so dark, I could see nothing. I listened for a long time. I heard nothing but the patter of the rain. I climbed out and pulled the girls up. They were but one and five at the time. My sons were ten and eight when they were killed."

Glynneth thought of her own dear children. How could she bear to lose them.

"Some of the house had burned, mostly the roof, but we found shelter." Capucine turned back to her tisane and took a sip before continuing. "I dared not light a fire in the hearth. We were wet and cold and hungry. Fumbling around in the dark, I found some carrots the Lenape had not taken. That was our supper. I must have dosed some. Morning took forever arriving. I longed for the dawn, and yet I feared it. What would I find. Would the Lenape still be around? I knew my husband was dead, I had seen him killed. My sons, too.

"Finally morning came. A neighbor arrived to see how we fared. The Lenape had struck his farm, but he and his sons had been able to drive them off. He helped me bury my husband and sons then took us home with him. His wife, fearing another attack, insisted we return to the fort. For the next two years, I took in washing and made beer and managed to keep a roof over our heads and food in our stomachs. I could have married many times over. There is a shortage of women in New Amsterdam, but until I met Armand, I could not take another man to my bed." Her voice took on a sweeter tone, and the light returned to her eyes when she spoke of Armand.

"We lived with his father until we could build this house. We had to borrow from the West Indian Company. We could not sell my farmland because of the trouble with the Indians. No one was brave enough to settle far from the fort. Not until the spring of forty-seven when the new Director General, Peter Stuyvesant, arrived and took over the reins of the government did things improve. The first thing he did was make peace with the Lenape. That meant we could sell a portion of my farm and pay off our debt to the company. We kept half the land and lease it to the family who bought the other half."

Glynneth shook her head. "You have lived through such horror. I wonder that you are willing to leave your home here to go to Fort Orange and live so near the Indians. Do you not hate them, fear them?" Glynneth had been surprised to learn her new friend would be going up river with her husband when the ice thawed. She would miss her.

Capucine smiled. "Was I not married to Armand, yes, I would hate them, hate them all. And at first I did, but Armand knows the natives. They are not all the same any more than the Irish are identical to the English or the English to French or the French to the Dutch. And from Armand, I learned of the horrors committed by a platoon of Dutch soldiers under the orders of the former Director General, Willem Kieft. The Lenape know nothing of taxes, but because they would not pay the taxes Kieft levied on them, he sent his soldiers to butcher them, men, women, even children. The soldiers destroyed two villages ..." she turned her head away and swallowed hard. "And they ... they brought the severed heads back to New Amsterdam."

She looked again at Glynneth. "We knew nothing of this atrocity. We were not a party to it. Yet the Lenape struck back, and my husband and sons paid for Kieft's brutal butchery. So yes, I hate, but it is Kieft I hate." A small smile lit her face. "There are those who struggle under Stuyvesant's strict rules, but I like him and his rules. He has nine armed men who patrol the streets at night to keep New Amsterdam safe. He has banned drinking on the Sabbath, public brawling, and driving wagons too fast. Like Kieft, he has little sympathy for the Indians, but since his arrival, trade is prospering and windmills have been built to grind the grain the farmers bring in. I will miss New Amsterdam, but I want to live at my husband's side, and now that his uncle and cousins are here, he will serve our family better helping his father at Fort Orange. That is where nearly all the fur trade goes on.

"Come summer, you may wish to come up river," Capucine said. "It gets hot and humid here during the summer, and often the sweating sickness strikes. And is the wind blowing in the wrong direction, horrid little biting flies make life for people and animals miserable."

"You are not making it sound very pleasurable. We must endure this dreadful cold of winter only to endure a dreadful heat in the summer?"

Chuckling Capucine rose and set a large kettle of water onto a trivet over the smoldering fire. "I will start the water heating for your wash. It will be warm by the time we finish our tisanes." She sat back down. "You are correct, the winters are cold, the summers are hot, but spring and autumn are incredibly beautiful. You will see soon when the new growth starts poking up out of the earth. Already the trees are budding. Yes, it is glorious."

"I look forward to it. I know my poor sister-in-law, Jeanette, will be happy when spring arrives. She has barely set foot out of her house. Did she not have the two servants, Noam and Heloise to tend her needs, she and her family would starve."

Capucine frowned. "Call them what they are, Glynneth. They are slaves. They have no choice but to serve. They will never be free. I cannot say I approve of slavery, but with such a labor shortage in New Amsterdam, many have decided owning slaves is respectable. Jacques bought Heloise when Simone, his young wife, got with child and could no longer perform the arduous household tasks. The following year he bought Noam, and the year after that, Arno, the youth he took with him to Fort Orange. At the fort, there are Indian women to help Simone with her chores. They are not slaves, but most are treated poorly by the men at the fort. When the women tire of the abuse, they disappear into the forest and return to their own people."

Capucine rose again to test the water. She looked over her shoulder at Glynneth. "You are not used to hard work, though you have learned much since you arrived. Still, I fear you may never be a good cook. Your husband may find he needs to buy a slave to help you with your chores. Especially if you again get with child."

Before Glynneth could form an answer to this observation – she did not take it as criticism – Capucine said, "The water is hot. I will help you pour it into the tub."

The confidences were at an end. Glynneth turned to the clothes she had collected for washing, and Capucine set about preparing the dinner. The men would soon be home, expecting their noon time meal to be on the table. As she scrubbed the food stains on Meara's dress, Glynneth pondered Capucine's observation. Her friend was most likely correct. Glynneth knew how to run a household, but she had always had servants. The chores she now performed, she could not say she enjoyed. When Capucine and her family left in the spring with Adler and Latty, she would need help to manage the household. She doubted she would ever be able to prepare fish for cooking or kill and clean a chicken.

And she hated doing the laundering. Kneeling on the hard floor hurt her knees and the soap stung the cut on her hand from her morning tussle with the uncooperative goat. She hated milking the silly animals. All the animals would be in her care when the Chappells left. No, she must have help. She would have to speak to Etienne about it this very evening. She sighed and continued washing. More scrubbing and wringing, then she beat the gown on a large clean stone slab as she had seen Capucine do. Two more gowns, twenty baby napkins, four shifts, and two shirts to go. She had no intention of washing her skirts or Etienne's breeches. Did they have to wear their garments until they were dirty enough they could stand up on their own, then so be it.

Capucine said she had kept a roof over her head by doing laundry. Surely with all the men in this town, someone did their laundry. She would speak to Etienne about finding a laundress as well. She hated to complain, but she had not been bred to this kind of labor. She had to have help. She would prefer a good Irish girl like had served her in Dublin, but that she knew to be impossible. She supposed she would

64

have to settle for one of the African slaves. Noam and Heloise both seemed nice. Jeanette made no complaint about them. And was anyone going to complain, it would be Jeanette. Still, the idea of enslaving humans seemed wrong.

Glynneth glanced over at Capucine. She found her a remarkable woman. To think what Capucine had endured, yet to still be such a caring person. And so competent. Chuckling, Glynneth thought how often Curtice had called her his competent daughter-in-law. Could he see her now, sopping wet, her hair falling out from under her cap, he would not think her so competent. Well, she would get this wash done, and get it hung out to dry in the crisp winter air, but she could not help but hope this would be the last time she had to do the laundry. She would be the competent daughter-in-law Curtice thought her to be by finding a laundress, even did she have to pay her a small fortune.

� ※ ※ ※ ※

Was it only this morning she had thought she could not be more miserable, Jeanette wondered. Gaspard had promised her she would no longer be sick once they were again on dry land, yet every morning for well over a month she had been sick. And she hated the cold, the unbearable cold. Would she ever feel warm again? She sat in front of the hearth until one side of her roasted, then turned and roasted the other side, then turned back.

The house was hideous, cold air whistled in around the door and shuttered windows. It had naught but two bedrooms, a family room, and a loft. The serving girl, Heloise – no, the slave – slept on a cot in the family room. Noam slept in the loft. At first frightened by the big man, Jeanette had begged Gaspard not to leave her alone with him, but he had laughed at her and told her she was being foolish. Said he had work to do. In time, she learned that Noam was not a threat. He was courteous, deferential, ever ready to do whatever she might ask of him. He always had a big bright smile, and he never got too close. He seemed to recognize her fear of him.

Heloise, on the other hand, never smiled. She, too, did whatever she was bid, but she never looked happy like Noam. Jeanette supposed she could not blame her. Was she a slave, she would not be happy either. But then people had to accept the station in life that God granted them. To do otherwise was to be blasphemous.

She wished Glynneth would visit more often. She was lonely, and Glynneth was better than no one. Today, after dinner, Glynneth did come by for a short visit. She brought Capucine with her. Jeanette could not care for the woman. She was a peasant, a farmer's wife. How Gaspard's cousin had chosen to marry such a woman had been a mystery to her until she learned there were many fewer women in New Amsterdam than men. Some desperate men had even taken Indian women to wife. At least Armand had not stooped that low.

But Capucine's visit had been a blessing. Jeanette had barely started to complain of her aching back and constant sickness in the mornings, and Capucine had recognized her symptoms. "Most likely you are with child," she said with a chuckle. "In another month or two, the sickness should fade, but then the cravings will begin."

Jeanette stared at Capucine for a moment then cried, "Oh! You think I am with child?"

"Of course you are with child," chimed in Glynneth. "I should have realized it. I have been so busy, I gave it no thought." She looked to Capucine. "You recognized the cause of her laments immediately. I am so glad you came with me today." She turned back to Jeanette. "You will make your husband a proud and happy man. Congratulations," she said and hugged Jeanette.

Jeanette numbly accepted the hug. Her head spinning, her heart beating a happy little tattoo, she could scarce believe she was finally with child. She was not barren as she had feared. Maybe now Gaspard would show more concern for her. Maybe now his father would find her as estimable as Glynneth.

Long after Glynneth and Capucine left, she sat staring into the fire. So intent was she, she bolted upright in surprise when Heloise addressed her. "Madame wishes me to start the evening meal? I have finished churning the milk. It is rich, creamy butter. I have mended the sheets as you requested. The sky is now starting to darken, so I put the chickens back in their hen house."

Jeanette looked up at Heloise's somber black face. Her dark eyes were unreadable, her full lips, set in a straight line, offered no warming smile. Jeanette nodded. "Yes, do start the meal, but I want it to be special, not just another soup and that dreadful cornbread." Smiling brightly, she said, "I have a wonderful announcement to make this evening."

"Yes, Madame," Heloise answered, but she showed no interest in Jeanette's announcement. "We have some corned beef. I could make you a red flannel hash with turnips and beets. Then dried apple dumplings for your dessert, if there is enough flour."

"That will do nicely," Jeanette said, springing up from her chair. "My, my, I must ready myself." She put a hand to her hair. How long since she had washed it? Well it was too late to try to wash it now. She would tuck it up under a clean cap. She started to her bed chamber but looked back over her shoulder. "Heloise, do put a clean cloth and napkins on the table."

"Yes, Madame," Heloise answered, before turning to add wood to the fire.

The woman seemed to have no curiosity, Jeanette thought with a shake of her head. Not that socializing with servants was ever a good idea, but she was bubbling over in her joy. She wanted to share her good news with everyone. She still hated New Amsterdam, but she finally had something to brighten her horrid existence.

Chapter 10

The spring thaw came too early to suit Adler. Saying good-bye to Glynneth had been the hardest thing he ever had to do. It had been even harder than leaving his parents and home in England. Yet he had no choice. He had to earn his living, and his job was taking him upriver. He knew not for how long. 'Twas for the best. He knew that. At times his love for Glynneth near drove him mad. He wanted so desperately to hold her in his arms, to taste her lips. To hide his love was a constant effort. But hide it he would. Forever if need be. Never would Etienne be subjected to the knowledge that Adler coveted his wife.

Adler counted Etienne a treasured friend. He had learned much from him. Etienne had helped him with the nuances of the French tongue as well as its grammar and vocabulary. Etienne made a better teacher than Glynneth because Adler need not fight his emotions while struggling to learn the language. When near Glynneth, he was so aware of her scent, her eyes, her body, he could scarce concentrate.

Time spent in Etienne's company was always an enjoyable experience. Etienne was knowledgeable in so many areas. He helped both Adler and Latty with their arithmetic. "You want to make sure you receive the appropriate pay for your services," Etienne told them. "Good book keeping is important. It becomes even more important when you have saved up enough to buy land or launch a new business. You must know how to figure your costs, your initial and continuing investments, savings needed for unexpected disasters."

Adler wished he had paid more heed to ciphering in grammar school. He had hated being closed up in the classroom every day. Had longed to be outdoors in the fresh air. He had loved being out in his father's fields, yet now he did not see himself returning to farming. What his future held for him, he could not guess. He preferred not to think of the future, he would live in the present, live day by day and let happen whatever would happen. He wondered if the world Etienne had exposed him to had changed his thinking. Mayhap. Learning about the past, about previous civilizations, and about countries near to England and those clear around the world fascinated him. As did the history of torques. His curiosity about his own past was piqued. How had his family come by such a strange and ancient object.

Not knowing what he would encounter in the wilds to the north, he asked Glynneth and Etienne to keep the half torque for him. "Should anything happen to me, you will know how to return it to my brother."

"Let nothing happen to you," Etienne said. "But have no fear for your torque. It will be safe with us. We will keep it locked in the chest where we keep our own valuables."

"Is there a God in his heaven, may He keep you and Latty safe," Glynneth said holding out her hand to Latty and then to Adler. Treasuring the touch, Adler gazed into her eyes one last time, and then he and Latty departed for the ship taking them to Fort Orange.

They were sailing into a head wind which meant the ship had to tack back and forth, but the tide was with them, and it would help push them up river. Due to the amount of trade goods Curtice had brought for his brother-in-law, they sailed on a fluit rather than the smaller ketch. That meant more comfort for Armand's family. Adler was glad the Chappells would be settling at Fort Orange. Having familiar faces around would ease the strangeness of his new home.

Armand had told them they would have another month of training, then they would be sent into the wilds with an Indian guide and interpreter. Adler hoped he learned his lessons well. Trekking through the dense woods, down meandering paths with a heavy pack of trade goods on his back, would test his stamina. He wished he could walk with the same fluid motion Latty had mastered. The man never tired. His body in a forward lean, his legs straight and swinging from his hips, his arms moving in rhythm with his legs, he never even worked up a sweat. He could cover more ground in a day than a horse. Adler hoped he could keep up with his friend. Though he had learned much about survival in the wild, he had no wish to test his skills on his own.

The ship tacked sharply to the left, the motion was accompanied by a shriek and a giggle. The two Chappell girls, Raissa and Jolie, clung to each other as they fought to stabilize their footing. Adler smiled at them and at Latty. As usual, Latty was surrounded by the children. He had the one year old Pierre balanced in one arm, and he was using his other arm in a mock sword fight. Five year old Guyon was his opponent. Raissa and Jolie shouted encouragements. Latty drew children to him like a piper. Mayhap because he was as light hearted as any child. They recognized one of their own. Full of mirth, he always had time for play.

"What a good father you are going to make," said Capucine, coming up from below deck. "We need but find you the right woman."

She spoke in a mixture of French and Dutch, and Latty guffawed, then answered in the same, but a more halting mix. "Do you find me a wealthy widow with vast lands, then I am your man." He slanted his eyes at Capucine. "Now could we get rid of that husband of yours, you would be the perfect bride."

Laughing, she cuffed him on the shoulder. "Silly boy, I am much too old for you. You need a young wife to keep your blood boiling."

"Yes," said Armand. "Enough flirting with my wife. You are handsome enough. Couple of years in the fur trade, you can buy a little farm and settle down with a pretty young wife."

"No, I must have a widow with lots of land. I want much more than a farm. I want a dukedom. I will settle for no less." He bounced Pierre on his arm and nodding his head said, "What say you, Pierre, am I not right."

The little boy, his dark eyes shining, had no idea what Latty said, but he nodded in agreement, and everyone laughed.

Raissa, a wisp of her light brown hair blowing across her cheek, her large brown eyes glued to Latty's face, said, "Oh, Latty, you cannot be serious."

He tweaked her chin. "Well, maybe only if I can find a widow as pretty as you." Chuckling and turning to Adler, he added, "Or one with so much land, it matters not what she looks like. What say you, friend?"

Proud he could understand most of what everyone had said, he answered in his fumbling Dutch, "I say I will make no commitments of any kind at this point. For now, I but want to survive my first trek into these forbidding woods." He looked out over the water to the shore, dark with a thick green forest.

"You will have no trouble," said Armand. "You have a keen sense of direction and good observation. You and Latty make a good team. I expect you to do well. I look forward to introducing you to Father. He will see your merit immediately."

Adler appreciated Armand's praise. And he hoped his confidence in him was accurate.

※ ※ ※ ※

Jacques Chappell was nothing like Adler had imagined. In his early to mid-fifties, he was not robust like his son. He was thin, wiry, and somehow a cross between a woodsman and a successful merchant. His attire bespoke a man of wealth – a high-waisted, loose-fitting doublet over a shirt with a falling lace collar, his breeches though full, were not as extreme as the Dutch preferred. His boots were of a fine leather, and his wide-brimmed hat was trimmed with an eagle feather. Despite his debonair dress, he was no milksop. His face was weathered, his hands hard and strong, not soft like the hands of a man who had never known real labor.

Adler liked him instantly. He could understand how he had won the heart of his much younger bride. Simone, petite and lively, with black twinkling eyes, welcomed Adler and Latty into her home. "You will stay with us until you can find housing in the fort. This time of year, it is never easy. But the trappers and traders come and go, so something will open up."

The Chappell home was outside the fort in the small but growing village of Beverwyck. The house was no larger than their home in New Amsterdam, but as Simone said, "What need have we for a larger home. It would but mean more work for me, and I have enough to do caring for Jacques and Ignace."

Ignace was their seven year old son. He had his mother's black eyes, his father's wiry frame, and a wide-eyed stare that seemed to miss nothing. He took an immediate liking to Latty and was at his side whenever in his presence. The boy spoke Dutch as fluently as French, and when he heard Adler and Latty speaking English to each other, he begged to be taught their tongue. Adler liked the idea. Having someone else who spoke English appealed to him. He had improved in French, and could understand what people said if they spoke slowly enough, but often, the speech was too rapid for him to comprehend. He always had to ask the speaker to repeat the sentence more slowly. It seemed to take so many more words to say something in French than in English, and native speakers rattled it off so rapidly. Fortunately, Latty had become quite proficient in the language. He would do much of their bargaining.

A number of Englishmen from the New England and Virginia colonies had moved to New Amsterdam or nearby villages when the Dutch West Indian Company abandoned its monopoly on trade in 1638, and then in 1640 opened trade to all friendly merchants. But in the first week in his new home, Adler met no English speakers in the Fort Orange area. He learned much about the history of the region, though, from Jacques.

"The merchants have to pay the company a ten percent import duty and fifteen percent export duty," Jacques said, "but the trade has been lucrative enough to make it worth the fees. At least until this past year when the English passed their Navigation Act requiring all trade with their colonies be done in English ships. That has hurt some merchants who own their own ships, but as I continue to use Company ships, it has not hurt me exorbitantly. Now, when I trade with the English, I use their ships. I am more pleased than ever that Curtice has come. He speaks English, he is used to trading with the English, he will stand us in good stead. And the goods he brought with him will be well liked by our Mohawk trading partners. You wait and see. Copper kettles, steel knives, sewing needles, blankets, and best, the mirrors. You should be well received on your first venture."

Adler prayed his patron was right. He had seen a number of Indians in and around New Amsterdam, and they had seemed harmless enough, but the ones coming and going in Fort Orange had a different look to them. Noble, he would say. Yes, they looked fierce and noble. Naught but three more weeks of training, and he and Latty would be confronting these Indians in their own homes. He hoped his knees would not knock the first time he entered one of their villages. And he hoped they would be as pleased to see him and his goods as Jacques assured him they would be.

※ ※ ※ ※

Eager to begin amassing his fortune, Latimer felt he and Adler were more than ready to set off on their trading venture. The constant training Armand put them through was trying. So Adler was not the best of shots, he would improve with time. And neither he nor Adler objected to living on pemmican, the dried meat and berry mix the traders had adopted from the Indians. Light, easy to carry, filling enough. Were they unable to bring down a deer, they could always set a rabbit trap. Hunting hares or deer or wild boar might be the prerogative of the nobles or wealthy gentry in England, but he and Adler both had experience in trapping rabbits. Rabbits and dove were the yeoman's game.

He had been rather amazed at how readily Adler took to the woods. In no time he had learned to distinguish the scat of the various animals and birds of the forest. His sense of direction was unerring. As many times as Armand tried to confuse them and get them lost, Adler could always find his way back to the fort. He could follow any trail, might lose it for a bit, but could back track and pick it up again. He had impressed both Armand and Jacques. He had trouble with the easy going tinker's stride that Latimer had quickly mastered, but Adler had perseverance and would press on even when bone weary.

"Until I went to fight for the King, I doubt I had ever been more than twenty miles away from home," Adler said one evening when they sat before the Chappells' hearth. "I went to petty school and grammar school in Aldford, not four miles from our farm. My brother and I rode to school each day with the Yardleys' in their pony cart, driven by one of their father's servants until William was old enough to drive it. When I walked anywhere, it was generally behind a pair of oxen, back and forth across our fields. I knew tinkers and chapmen walked many miles to sell their wares, but I cannot say I ever paid heed to their manner of walking. As a youth, I ran races, played chase, and other sports, but I can remember no walking games."

"Never fear," said Jacques, "you will learn. Once you master the stride, you will not forget it. Believe me, it is much easier than riding a horse. Now the Indians have their own mode of travel, a sort of jog, toes pointing inward. They can move through the woods so quietly, a whole string of them, often stepping in each other's footsteps. No one hears them, no one knows how many are on the trail. Admirable people in many ways."

Latimer, and Adler, too, had been surprised to learn Simone was one half Lenape Indian. Her father had come over on the same ship that brought Jacques and Armand to New Netherland in 1624. Jacques's first wife, Aida, had died in child birth aboard the ship. Jacques had had no interest in remarrying until he met Simone near fifteen years after Aida's death.

"Armand was but five when we arrived," Jacques said. "And no mother to care for him. I was so busy, he practically had to raise himself."

"He did a good job of raising himself," said Latimer.

"Yes, I am proud of him. And of Ignace." Jacques reached over and tousled his younger son's hair. "Ignace has a mother to care for him, to give him love, but Simone will not spoil him. We live in the wilds here. He must know how to cope with the elements. He is already learning a woodsman's skills."

"He is quick," agreed Adler. "When he went with us the other day, he spotted the deer scat before any of us, even Armand."

Ignace beamed at the praise. "Someday I will be the best hunter in New Netherland."

"Someday you will be the brightest scholar in New Netherland," said Simone, and Ignace frowned. "Ah, Mother."

Jacques laughed. "Simone's mother was a Lenape, yes, but her father was a highly educated man. Like me, like Curtice, he fled France to escape religious persecution. He should have been teaching at a university. Instead, again like me, he went to work for the Dutch West Indies Company. He was a clerk. He kept track of transactions, the fur trade primarily. He was well paid and invested wisely. He owned three houses in New Amsterdam, including ours, the one Curtice is now living in. And, like me, he lost his wife." He looked over at Simone. "When Simone was but ten her mother and younger brother both died of the measles. Simone almost died. But my love is a fighter." He patted Simone's knee. "Are you not my wife?"

Simone took his hand in hers and held it to her cheek. "Truth is, I have little memory of my illness. I think I have tried to shut the memory away. The loss of my mother and brother was so painful. I became responsible for keeping the home running smoothly. Father worked long hours. But in the evenings, he always found time to give me my lessons."

"Not only does she speak, read, and write French and Dutch," Jacques stated proudly, "but she knows Latin and a smattering of Greek."

"With my limited skills, I try to teach Ignace," Simone said. "I want him to be more than a woodsman, more than a trader. Was my father still alive, he could teach him."

"The Company sent her father to the West Indies for a year," Jacques said. "He caught the sweating sickness and died not more than six months after he arrived in those disease ridden islands. Now I must attend his properties and investments until Ignace comes of age. He will someday be a man of some wealth, does the colony continue to prosper."

"I would rather be a woodsman like Armand and Latty and Adler," said Ignace. "I find all the studies mother gives me boring."

Adler chuckled. "I felt the same at your age. I have since learned how much I missed by not paying heed to the schooling offered me. Since meeting Etienne and Glynneth, I have discovered a whole new world. They see things I never saw before, they know things I never knew existed. I found learning can be exciting."

Latimer watched Adler as he espoused his new love of learning. His eyes lit up, his voice took on a rich resonance. He envied Adler his interest in renewing his studies, but he had no such interest himself. His goal was to amass a vast tract of land, and he would let nothing interfere with that goal.

"I look forward to meeting all of my husband's in-laws," Simone said. "Capucine has told them they should come here when the sultry summer heat breeds the ague in New Amsterdam. We will arrange to have a house for them."

Latimer glanced again at Adler. He was trying to hide his elation, but Latimer could tell by the joy that leapt to his eyes that Adler relished the possibility of getting to see Glynneth, if only for a few treasured moments. Latimer understood his feeling. He had the same desire. No woman had ever affected him as did Glynneth. She aroused a passion in him that could keep him awake at night – the way she glanced upward out of the corners of her lustrous gray-blue eyes, the way her light-hearted laughter burbled up out of her, the way she walked with a natural grace, a slight sway to her hips. Her figure was enticing, full breasts, rounded hips, trim ankles. But it was her vitality, her exuberance, her love of life and of all God's creatures that most attracted him to her. With a woman like Glynneth at his side, a man's life would never be dull, never be humdrum. He hoped they would be back from their first expedition in time to see Glynneth, did she and her family come up river in the summer.

Chapter 11

Adler dipped his paddle into the murky river water in rhythm with his Mohawk guide. He was glad the first part of their trek was by water, even though it meant paddling up stream and portaging around the falls at the mouth of the Mohawk River. He liked being on the water, liked the soft sound of the paddles plying through the water and pushing the canoe forward with each stroke. He and Latty had each gained quick command of canoe navigation.

"Far superior to rowing a dingy," Latty proclaimed. "Having to look over your shoulder to see where you are going is a constant hazard. I like facing forward and seeing what is ahead of me. Paddling is easier on the back, too."

Adler agreed with his friend. He had no experience rowing a boat, but he liked the canoes. He knew Latty had been more than ready to set off on their adventure, but he was still leery. Jacques and Armand assured him that he and Latty could trust their guides, but he would feel better if he understood their language. His guide, Otetiani, meaning He Is Prepared, spoke Dutch about as well as he did, which was not great. Latty's guide spoke so little Dutch, that most of the time, the two guides communicated in their own language. Neither guide spoke French. Adler got nervous when they spoke in their tongue then laughed and glanced at him or Latty.

The two canoes were piled high with various goods from pots and pans to combs and knives to guns and shot. Armand expected Adler and Latty to trade most of their goods at their first stop, the Mohawk town located at the confluence of the Mohawk River and a smaller tributary. Their trades made, Latty's guide, with the assistance of local tribal members, would return to Fort Orange with the furs. Adler's guide would lead them on to smaller villages further north. They would then be carrying their trade goods in packs on their backs. Once trades were made, they would have to carry the furs they bargained for back in the same manner.

The dense forests, the trees overhanging the water, the call of birds, the scent of spring filled him with an awe he had never known. No, not even out on the vast, seemingly endless ocean. Majestic, that was what he would call this country, majestic. Most Europeans called it a wilderness, yet numerous tribes of natives lived in these woods, along the rivers and streams, down meandering paths. They had their homes, their families, their own cultures and religions deep in this so called untamed land. He tried to open his eyes and mind to see things as Glynneth would see them. He wanted to be able to describe things in detail to her, and to Etienne.

One day drifted into another, paddle while the sun gave them light, find a place to tie up at night. He and Latty would secure the canoes and set up camp, and their guides would go hunting. The guides always returned with something, a couple of squirrels, a rabbit, once they brought back a turkey. Adler had been surprised to find turkeys were a wild bird in the new world. The birds often traveled in small flocks and had no trouble flying up into trees to roost at night. In writing to his family, he enjoyed describing his incredible new home. He hoped his letters would reach his family. He had written his parents from Holland, telling them of his change of plans, and had written again upon arrival in New Amsterdam, but when they might receive his letters, or when he might receive a letter in return, he could not guess.

He and Latty had received a letter from Etienne and Glynneth a week past, urging them to take care and return home safely. All was well in New Amsterdam. Curtice and Gaspard had selected a lot for their new home, and the building had started. The home would be toward the edge of town and would be made of bricks. Glynneth and Etienne had decided not to build, but to continue renting Armand's home. They liked the small size. It was easy to care for. They had acquired a servant to help Glynneth with the household chores – a young slave from the West Indies. She spoke French with a lovely sing, song cadence. They were paying her a decent wage, and she could use a portion of it to make payments to buy her freedom. Neither Glynneth nor Etienne were comfortable with the concept of slavery. Adler agreed with them.

Owning another human seemed somehow immoral, even if the Bible condoned the practice.

The smell of smoke and the muted sound of barking dogs brought Adler's thoughts back to the present. Soon they were paddling past fields of sprouting corn. Stunned by the size of the Mohawk town that came into view, Adler momentarily stopped paddling. He had not imagined the town could be so large. It dwarfed New Amsterdam. He guessed it housed at least a couple thousand residents. Fields radiated out from the town, and more fields across the river fanned out along the riverside. Numerous canoes of varying sizes lined the water's edge. As they approached the town, barking dogs raced down the embankment and pranced about in and out of the water. The dogs were followed first by children, then by men and a smattering of women.

"Something is wrong," Otetiani said in his halting Dutch. "No smiles."

Adler's heart thudded against his chest. He looked at the faces of the Mohawk braves. They did not appear welcoming. If they turned around now, could they race back down the river? Would the Mohawk jump in their canoes and chase after them? He glanced at Latty. His friend had his usual bright smile spread across his face. If he sensed any danger, he did not show it.

Several of the men came forward to pull the canoes up onto shore as they struck ground. Both guides hopped quickly out. Adler followed more slowly, his gaze searching the faces of the men nearest him. One man, who looked to be a man of authority, was talking to the guides. Latty moved to stand beside Adler. "Not an auspicious welcoming," he said, reverting to English so none of the Mohawks would understand what he said.

"Aye," Adler agreed. "My guide did say something seemed wrong."

Adler's guide turned to him. Speaking slowly and struggling with the Dutch words, he said, "Not three days past, other traders were here. Dutch traders, Bold Crow says. They traded guns, but the guns will not fire. They gave the men a strong drink that made some go crazy. We have told him you are not Dutch, but Bold Crow knows you have come from the Dutch fort."

Though he spoke to Otetiani, Adler looked at Bold Crow. "Tell him we have brought many items for trade, including some guns, but no strong drink. Such drink is forbidden by the Dutch governing body. The guns are good. He may try the guns before we do any trading. Tell him the man we work for, Jacques Chappell, has never been one to cheat the Mohawk."

Before the guide could deliver Adler's message, Latty spoke. "Tell him we will buy the guns that fail to work and take them back to the fort that we may confront those who would try to cheat the Mohawk."

Brilliant, Adler thought. Trading for the non-working guns could well make a hefty dent in their profit, but it might save their lives.

Otetiani delivered their message, and Bold Crow turned to talk to several other braves. A couple still seemed angry, their speech hard and guttural. Others looked less angry, even seemed to be nodding amicably. Adler's stomach was in knots. His throat felt parched, and he could not swallow. At last the debate ended. Bold Crow stepped away from the braves and addressed the crowd that had gathered. To Adler's frayed nerves the crowd's responses seemed menacing. Bold Crow turned back to the guides. He spoke briefly to them and pointed to Adler and Latty.

Otetiani had trouble meeting Adler's eyes. "Many are still angry" he said. "They say they cannot trust you. Some think they should kill you as an example to those who would trade with the Kanien'kehake to show how they deal with those who would cheat them."

Adler's knees wobbled. His heart pounded in his ears. He had heard how the Indians tortured people. Dying at their hands would not come easy. But what had he missed? His guide had continued speaking. Had they been offered a reprieve? He heard Latty saying, "We accept the combat." What combat? What had they accepted?

The villagers started talking and shouting. They began moving away from the river and Adler found he and Latty were being swept along with the crowd. Again reverting to English, Latty said, "Shall you or I take on their challenger? To be honest, I have been in few fights. Have you? You are a bit stronger built than I am. Could be an advantage."

"Latty, I have no idea what you are saying. What are we doing?"

Latty looked at him in some surprise. "We are fighting for our lives. At least one of us is. I thought 'twas better than facing their gauntlet.

I remember too well Armand's description of such. A one on one fight seemed sounder. Do we win, we are back in good favor. Do we lose, 'tis our last day on this green earth."

Comprehension slowly dawned on Adler. "I am to fight one of these braves?" he asked. "And do I defeat him, we have proven ourselves worthy of their trust?"

Latty nodded. "That is about the size of it. Do I take it you mean to be our champion?"

Adler started removing his coat. "Aye. That is right." Adler was relieved Latty had been paying attention to the guide while he had been quaking in his bones. He was glad Latty had chosen a one on one competition. Fighting he knew. He was good at it. He had bested his brother, the Yardleys, and any number of neighbors in competitions at the annual fairs. Like Latty, he had no wish to face a gauntlet. Stripped naked and running down a stretch between two lines of angry braves who would beat him with clubs, attempt to trip him and set upon him if he fell seemed the height of folly. He preferred the alternate choice.

His coat removed, he started unbuttoning his waistcoat. He glanced at Latty. "I have had many a fight, but ne'er one I was more determined to win than this one." His waistcoat off, he untied the bow at his throat, and prepared to slip off his shirt. All around him the Indians were chattering. His gaze floated over them. Though they all had dark hair and eyes, they were dressed in a variety of manner. Some wore skins, others wore shirts, skirts, and hats that might have been sported by any European man or woman. They all looked excited, eager for the entertainment he and their champion would offer them.

Otetiani stepped over to him and pointed to a brave on the other side of a large ring of stones. Speaking slowly, he said, "You are to fight Kills Many. He has never lost a fight."

Adler looked at the man he had to master. Bare chested, Kills Many – what a name, he thought – wore naught but a breech clout and a bear tooth necklace. His dark eyes staring back at Adler, he dipped his hand into a bag a brave held for him. He removed a glob of something from the bag and started rubbing it on his body. He grinned, knowing Adler realized what he was doing. He was greasing himself up, making himself harder to grab and hold. So he meant to fight dirty did he? Adler returned his grin. He had a few tricks of his own.

Slipping his shirt off, he tossed it to Latty. He heard his guide gasp and begin blathering and pointing at him. What now he wondered. Bold Crow stepped forward and touched Adler's shoulder, then his back. Oh, they had noted his scars from his fight with a poor suffering bear those many years ago.

In halting, poorly pronounced Dutch, Bold Crow asked, "You have fought the bear?"

Adler nodded. "Yes, I was forced to kill him. It was him or me. But he left his mark on me." He swiped his hair back from his forehead. "He aimed for my head."

Bold Crow touched the scar hidden at Adler's hairline. He stepped back and spoke to the villagers. A hushed murmur rose from numerous throats. Wary, Adler looked around. All eyes were on him. Had he somehow offended them? Was killing a bear a malefaction? Would he no longer be allowed to fight for his life?

His challenger strode purposely across the circle. He lifted the necklace from his chest, selected one claw, and traced it lightly down one of the scars on Adler's chest. "Brother," he said, and pointed to his own chest. Adler looked at his combatant's glistening coppery skin. The same thick puckered scars were in evidence.

Kills Many said something in his own tongue. When he finished speaking, Otetiani told Adler, "He says he cannot fight you. You are his brother. Like him, you have defeated the bear in hand to hand combat. You have shown your courage. He believes we should trust you."

Bold Crow, Kills Many, and several other braves again huddled. Adler looked at Latty. "I near died from that bear attack. Had William Yardley not found me and carted me home, I would have bled to death. Now it seems that bear may have saved our lives."

"I was beginning to worry when I saw your new brother greasing himself up," Latty said. "Do you think you could have taken him?"

"Aye. I had no choice. I am not yet ready to leave this world."

Bold Crow turned back to the guide and gave him instructions which Otetiani repeated to Adler and Latty. "You are to go with Kills Many. He will help us take your trade goods to his lodgings. You are to be his guests. Tonight there will be a feast in your honor. Tomorrow, you may

82

begin to trade your goods for the furs and skins."

Kills Many stepped forward and clasped Adler's forearm. "Brothers," he said.

Adler nodded. "Brothers," he repeated.

Before he could don his clothing, several Indian women came up to him. Looking at him at first shyly and then more brazenly, they reached out and touched the scars on his chest and back. They were all smiling. Kills Many laughed, and in the Dutch tongue, said haltingly, "The women like you."

"They are kind," Adler answered, not knowing what else to say.

"We should get our trade goods," said Latty.

Adler agreed, and with the guides and Kills Many helping them, they soon had their goods safely deposited in Kills Many's lodge. All the lodges looked similar. All were long and made of a framework of poles covered over by sheets of tree bark. Adler guessed most to be three or four hundred feet long. Apparently a number of families lived in each longhouse. Kills Many's compartment was to the middle of the lodge. Each compartment was divided in half with one family on one side, another on the other side of a ten foot wide center aisle. A fire pit in the center of the aisle provided heat for both families and in inclement weather, they could cook their meals indoors. The ceilings were high and the smoke drifted upward and out a small hole which could be covered over if it rained. The walls and lower benches were covered in various furs and skins – fox, bear, beaver, and deer. Higher shelving held numerous objects from cookware, to baskets, to weaponry.

"You will sleep here," Adler's guide said, indicating a bench piled high with furs. "But now, you will have a sweat bath."

Adler looked at Latty. They had been told they might be offered a sweat bath, and they should by all means accept. Not to do so would be the height of rudeness.

"Besides," Armand had told them, "to the Indians, we smell. They bathe much more often than we do. To us, they smell, not because they are not considerably cleaner, but because they use various greases on their skin to keep the insects at bay. If not enough sunflower seed oil is available, I have been known to use a bit of bear or goose grease myself come late spring, early summer when the insects are at their worse.

And yes, I have learned to appreciate the sweat bath. So is it offered, enjoy it."

They were lead to the outskirts of the village where a small round hut of rushes and reeds sat next to the stream. Kills Many informed them his wife had heated the stones in the hut. She was scraping out the remains of the fire when they arrived. The stones were doused with water, and Adler and Latty were told to strip and enter the hut. With a number of women standing around watching them, Adler was slow to disrobe, but Latty copied Kills Many and the guides, and in an instant stood in the buff before slipping inside the hut.

Kills Many looked questioningly at Adler, and Adler, fearing he might be offending his new brother, hastened to shed his garments and follow Latty into the sweat bath. Wondering how long he was to remain in this enclosed hut, he clenched his fists and tried to calm himself. His eyes met Latty's. He saw the sympathy and concern in his friend's eyes. Latty knew he could not abide tight confines. Drawing in deep breaths, he turned his mind to Glynneth. He pictured her aboard the ship with her hair blowing out behind her. He saw her in the glowing light of the hearth's fire as she helped Capucine with the evening meal; sitting cross-legged on the floor playing with Noel and Capucine's young son, Pierre; brushing Etienne's hair back that she might plant a kiss on his furrowed brow and draw him from his book that he might come to the table. No matter how great his desire for Glynneth, he could never be envious of her love for her husband. She was a dedicated wife and mother, and he honored her for it.

When he had arrived in the Mohawk village, he had feared he might never see Glynneth again. Might never again know the touch of her hand on his. Never again see her eyes so full of the love of life. Never hear her lilting laughter or thrill to her magical voice.

His breathing became more labored. Again his eyes sought Latty's. "I cannot do this," he said, hearing a desperate rasp in his voice. "I will go mad and start screaming."

Kills Many said something to Otetiani and the guide looked at Adler. "Kills Many wishes to know what is this tongue you speak. It is not French or Dutch. He has never heard it."

"Anglais," Latty answered. "It is our native tongue."

84

"It sounds much like Dutch," Kills Many said.

Eager to find anything to take his mind off his growing panic. Adler shifted his gaze to Kills Many. "Yes, it does. That is why it is easier for me to speak Dutch than French."

Kills Many smiled, his teeth white in the dark hut. "That is good. I wish to talk with my new brother. After we smoke the pipe of peace, you will tell me of yourself."

"Yes," Adler agreed. "I will tell you of my home far across the great sea."

That is if he did not go mad first. The walls started closing in. He was down in the cold well, clinging to the wooden bucket. He was sweating, yet chilled to the bone. His eyes again sought Latty's. His friend's gray eyes became the patch of gray sky that he had watched hour on end. Someone would come. He would be missed. He should cry out again. Mayhap someone would hear him this time. But no, he must conserve his voice. He was already hoarse. But did he not cry out, how would his father find him? He opened his mouth, but the gray eyes swam before him. He blinked. Latty was shaking his head. No. No, he must not cry out.

When he thought he could bear no more, Kills Many touched his arm. "We go now. Time we cool off in the stream."

Adler needed no second invitation to leave the sweat lodge, he was out the door in an instant. His nakedness forgotten, all he cared about was the wide open sky above him. "This way," said Kills Many, again touching his arm.

Adler, with Latty behind him, followed Kills Many into the stream. The cool water felt like satin on his skin. Kills Many scooped up sand off the bottom of the creek bed and scrubbed himself. The guides did the same, so Adler and Latty copied them.

"You did well," Latty told him in an aside. "My guess is you would have rather had that fight than sit in that sweat lodge."

"Happen you would be right there, my friend. I but hope this is not an everyday ritual."

Latty chuckled. "To my knowledge, 'tis not. But you must admit, 'tis refreshing."

Adler admitted nothing. He but scrubbed himself until his skin tingled. He could not remember when he last felt so clean, but he knew one way or another, he had to avoid another sweat bath – and hopefully not offend his new brother in the process.

Chapter 12

The peace pipe smoked – Adler was proud both he and Latty had managed to take several good puffs and not cough – and the feast completed, it seemed it was time for the entertainment. The drums started and a number of the younger men and women got up and started dancing around a blazing fire in the center of the ring where earlier he had almost fought a fight to the death. He could determine no set pattern to the dance. Each dancer seemed to weave his or her own way around the circle in their own chosen pattern. Each seemed to be singing some sort of song. They all seemed happy.

A young woman came up to Adler and indicated she would like him to dance. He looked at Kills Many. If he refused, was he offending the woman?

"She is single," Kills Many said. "She may choose any man she wishes to dance with and to share her bed." Chuckling, he slanted his eyes. "Or more likely a hideaway in the woods."

Relieved he and Kills Many could communicate in Dutch, if somewhat haltingly, Adler asked, "Will I offend her do I not dance with her?"

Kills Many smiled. "You have a preference for the men? We have those men who have chosen to be women."

Adler put up his hands, and shaking his head, said, "No, no. I want no man or woman. I have a woman I love. I have no desire for any other." He could not hold another woman in his arms, touch her as he longed to touch Glynneth, kiss surrendering lips when his whole being wanted naught but to be one with Glynneth.

Kills Many nodded. "I will tell her." When he finished speaking, Adler's suitor looked disappointed but not angry. She was an attractive young woman with neatly braided hair, bright eyes, full lips, and an appreciatively developing body. Adler guessed her to be in her late teens. Even had he not been in love with Glynneth, he thought the girl too young for him.

"I feel the same way about my wife," Kills Many said. "I want no other. You say in your culture, once you marry, you must stay married whether happy or unhappy. In our culture, does either partner become unhappy, they may separate. The woman tells the man to leave or he chooses to leave and return to his mother's home. Because of this, the couple works hard to keep each other happy. The man proves himself a good hunter. The woman decorates his clothes." He showed off the decorative quill work on his leather shirt, and Adler suitably admired it. "The woman gives her man a grand welcome whenever he comes back from the hunt or from battle. As long as a couple is married, they remain true to each other. It is right to be that way."

Adler heartily agreed. He was not married, but he could not help but be true to Glynneth. He smiled, noting Latty had no compunction against joining in the dancing. He followed behind an attractive young woman in an intricately decorated doeskin skirt and a bright blue man's waistcoat over a man's shirt. Despite her incongruent dress, she looked svelte and sensuous. Adler doubted not but what Latty would have a pleasant romp with the young woman. He had been known to enjoy the company of other uninhibited women when given the opportunity.

Adler and Kills Many were joined by Bold Crow. The three of them talked long into the night. Adler told of his home and family, his part in his King's losing battle, his flight, and then his crossing of the ocean. His new friends marveled at his stories and asked many questions. Bold Crow shook his head as Adler tried to explain the religious differences. "You mean all the white men have the same God, but because they worship this God differently, they kill each other in battle?"

Adler nodded. "Men have killed often in the name of God, yes. But in my homeland, they also fight because some believe the King was not using his power justly. They believe he was not listening enough to the elected representatives of the people."

Bold Crow pursed his lips and nodded. "This I understand. If the selected members of the council fail to pay heed to the wishes of the women, they will be removed from the council."

As astounded as were Bold Crow and Kills Many by the things Adler

88

told them, he was astounded that the women of the tribe had so much power. The women owned the houses and everything in them except for the men's clothing and weapons. The women selected the men who would sit in council and lead their clan and tribe. The children stayed with the women did a couple separate. The women were the farmers, they provided and prepared the daily fare but for the meat the men might provide. They made the clothes, the baskets, and they raised the children. The men did naught but hunt and fight. Occasionally they had to clear new fields when the soil became less fertile and the tribe had to move, and they had to build new houses, but the women ruled those houses.

Adler would be joining Kills Many, his wife, and two children in their compartment for the night. He hoped the high ceiling and smoke hole open to the sky would keep his demons at bay. He was tired. Could he go quickly to sleep, he should have no problem. A miasma of smells assaulted him upon entry to the house; smoke, drying herbs, grease, babies, not much different from the smells of any home. He found them soothing, and in no time, he slept.

🌿 🌿 🌿 🌿

"'Tis the powder causing the problem," Latty said.

In inspecting one of the defective guns, Latty had poured powder from his own horn into the muzzle. To everyone's amazement the gun fired. Latty examined the powder. "'Tis obvious it is missing an ingredient, or something has been added that should not have been added."

"Mayhap it got wet," Adler said. "Let me see it." Scooping a handful of the black powder from the small keg sealed with pitch, he brought it up to his nose and smelled it. He rubbed it around in his palm and shook his head. Switching to Dutch, he held up his palm to Kills Many. "Look at the size of these grains. This powder is most likely still good, but it needs to be dried and reground. The grains are too large. They must be finer. These grains are near large enough to use with a small caliber cannon."

That the guns were sound saved them having to take a loss. Adler, though not particularly competent with a firearm, had learned enough about black powder to show the Mohawks how to dry and regrind their powder. The help he and Latty gave the Indians increased their bond, and the trade negotiations proceeded profitably. Beaver was becoming more scarce. The Iroquois had to range farther from home to bring in the pelts, but they also had fox, bear, otter, and mink furs and deer and elk skins for trade. The canoes Latty's guide and a couple of the Mohawks were taking back to Fort Orange were bulging, but going downstream with the flow would be a quicker process than navigating up the river. Adler expected Jacques to be pleased with his and Latty's first transaction.

As he, Latty, and Otetiani, their packs upon their backs, set off through the woods, Adler prayed they would not encounter any life threatening problems at the next village they were set to visit. His thoughts turning to Glynneth, he wondered was she enjoying the warmer weather? Had she made new friends? Had she adjusted to her more rugged existence in New Amsterdam? Did she miss her home in Ireland? Did she miss him, ever think of him? He knew it was wrong, but he hoped she some-times thought of him. But mostly, he hoped she was happy.

🌿 🌿 🌿 🌿

Glynneth could not begin to express her delight to have spring burst-ing upon them. The severe cold of the winter had been wearing on her spirits. Too many days had been too cold for her walks, and she hated being cooped up in the house. Even though the spring thaw had taken Adler and Latty and Capucine and her family away, she had welcomed the budding trees, the colorful flowers, and warming sun. Melting snow and spring rains made for muddy streets, but that seldom hindered her. She slipped on her cape and pattens, helped Meara with hers, bundled Noel up in a warm blanket, stuck him on her hip, and off she went.

She enjoyed walking about the burgeoning town. She liked the vi-tality. Something new seemed to be happening every day. Houses and shops were being built. A defensive wall stretching from one side of the island to the other was a work in progress. Ships arrived with cargoes needing to be unloaded. Ships at anchor preparing for departure were being loaded with raw materials from the colony; timber, furs, skins, and grains. Fresh produce from nearby farms, a welcome addition after the dried fruits and salt pork they had been eating for much of the winter, was hawked from carts and shop fronts. With her new serving girl to care for the household chores, Glynneth took over the shopping for the family. The merchants were always very courteous to her, and the African slaves always stepped back to let her make her purchases first, even when she indicated she was willing to wait her turn.

Glynneth wished she could be more comfortable with slave ownership, but she found it troubling. She and Etienne had discussed the merits and defects of slavery, and despite knowing it had been in existence since the dawn of civilization, they could not like it. Yet Glynneth knew she needed help about the house. Reared in a wealthy home, she had never known labor. Her days had been spent in furthering her education, visiting with friends, attending entertainments, shopping, and taking long invigorating walks. Never had she been expected to wash clothes, prepare a meal, or feed and care for farm animals.

Fortunately, the new serving girl, Dominique, knew how to cook, clean, and care for the few animals Capucine and Armand had left with them. Etienne had paid an exorbitant sum for Dominique, but Glynneth believed the girl to be worth every guilder. In her early twenties, Dominique was cheerful, hardworking, and eager to please her new owners. She had not liked her former owner, a fat, balding Dutchman who had thought to have his way with her. Unable to force her into submission, he reluctantly sold her.

Upon being informed she would, over time, be allowed to buy her freedom, Dominique had been even more eager to impress her new owners. "Your kindness will not be misplaced, Madame," she trilled in impeccable French, her dark eyes shining. "You will see. I will take good care of your home and your family."

Tall and shapely, with black skin, hair, and eyes, Dominique looked striking in the colorful Dutch clothing she enjoyed wearing. Glynneth liked that Dominique took pride in her appearance and delighted in the compliments she received. And Dominique was good with the children. That was helpful as Meara and Noel not only missed their playmates, Guyon and Pierre, but they had been genuinely desolated by Adler's and Latty's departure. She could not blame the children. She, too, missed the two lighted hearted men who had made their lives so much easier on the long crossing from Holland to New Amsterdam.

Glynneth had little doubt that Jeanette wished she could trade her slave, Heloise, for Dominique. Ever sullen, Heloise made no attempt to brighten a day with a smile. Not that Glynneth could blame her. Being a slave was bad enough, being an unappreciated slave had to be even worse. Glynneth had yet to hear Jeanette thank her servant for anything – and as her pregnancy advanced, Jeanette became more demanding. To be fair, Gaspard and Jeanette could not offer to allow Heloise to buy her freedom as both Noam and Heloise belonged to Jacques Chappell.

Glynneth found Etienne's uncle an intriguing man. Once the river thawed and Armand had been able to journey to Fort Orange to manage their trade with the Indians, Jacques paid a brief visit to New Amsterdam to welcome his brother-in-law and insure his needs were being met. Though dressed in Dutch costume, he looked nothing like a Dutchman. Thin-faced and sinewy, his tanned ruggedness gave the appearance he had been born in the wilds, yet his address was as cultured as Curtice's. He spoke French and Dutch equally well, using whichever best suited his needs at the time. In the years since he had come to New Amsterdam to work for the Dutch West Indian Company, he had accomplished much. Now a prosperous merchant with a thriving trade, a couple of warehouses, and a home in New Amsterdam and one in Beverwyck, he was well respected throughout the colony.

"I look forward to meeting your wife," Glynneth told him one evening as the family sat around a glowing fire. The spring evenings still held a chill.

Jacques's smile in the firelight brightened his bronzed face. "She will be pleased to meet all of you," he answered. "Like her father, she is a scholar, and she will appreciate talking with people who share her interest in literature, art, and matters other than furs and trade. Come summer, you must remove to Beverwyck. You will not wish to expose your children to the risk of the sweating sickness that can often strike in the hot sultry months. We will have a house for you, must we vacate ours and move in with Armand."

"We could not ask that of you," Etienne said.

His eyes resting gently on his nephew, Jacques said, "It will be no imposition. That I promise you. As I said, it will be a treat for Simone."

Glynneth hoped they would be able to go to Beverwyck. She wanted to see more of the colony, and she hoped to see Adler and Latty. She knew her children would dearly love to see the two men who had entertained them for so many months, had been like family to them. Her concern was Jeanette. Her sister-in-law's time would be near. Was Jeanette unwilling to travel up river, unwilling to board another sailing vessel, Glynneth felt she could not leave her to bear her child with no one but Heloise to attend her. Jeanette had made no attempt to meet other women in New Amsterdam. With spring upon them, mayhap she would be more willing to get out of the house, take a few strolls, visit some of the shops, make some friends.

Well, Glynneth shrugged, she would not worry about the future with the present so pleasant. Her home, if not luxurious, was comfortable. Fresh foods were now plentiful. She and her beloved family were healthy, and best of all, Etienne was healthier than he had been in over two years. Healthy enough they could again make love. And how beautiful their first renewed love making had been. A gentle, caring lover was Etienne. She was a fortunate woman. A most fortunate woman.

Chapter 13

Carefully shifting his weight so not rock the canoe, Adler eased backwards to rest his buttocks against the bundle of furs behind him and take pressure off his knees. He, Latty, and Otetiani were paddling down river to Fort Orange, their canoes bulging with furs and skins. He had no doubt Jacques Chappell would be pleased with their accomplishments. In each village they visited, Otetiani had introduced him as the new brother of Kills Many. Obviously impressed, the villagers had made them welcome and had eagerly traded with them. Furs and skins had been delivered to Bold Crow's village to await transport to Fort Orange. Adler had been both pleased and amazed that the Indians could be trusted to keep their end of the bargain even when he and Latty moved on to yet another village. He doubted many white men could be trusted so implicitly. That lack of trust in mankind was the primary reason Curtice Fortier had asked him and Latty to accompany them to New Amsterdam.

He wondered if he might find Glynneth at Fort Orange. He longed to see her, to hear her voice, her laughter. He had had many opportunities to find comfort in the arms of native women, but his love for Glynneth always stopped him. Latty had known a couple of women, and Adler could not blame him. The women's and the men's clothing was far more revealing than was the European dress, and the women were appealing with their dark hair and eyes and slim coppery arms and legs. Adler did not know if Latty was curious why he never availed himself of the sweet fruit offered him, but Latty never questioned him.

Paddling closer, Latty interrupted Adler's thoughts. "Look over your shoulder," he said.

Adler did as told and saw two canoes moving away from shore and headed down river. The canoes appeared to be empty except for two men in each one. "I cannot say I like the looks of them," he said. They had been warned to watch for river pirates. Men who waited to prey upon Indians and traders heading to Fort Orange with their furs. Latty was an excellent shot, but shooting from a loaded canoe could be tricky. The kick from the musket or spark from the charge could cause havoc. Still, they might have little choice. The two canoes were gaining on them.

"Oohoo there," called one of the men, waving an arm. "Are you heading to Fort Orange?" He spoke in Dutch, but with an accent Adler could not discern. New Netherland was awash with men from many different nations.

"Watch their hands," Latty said. "Do they draw much closer, they could fire on us at any time. Get your gun ready. We will slow a little." Calling in Dutch to Otetiani, he cried, "You paddle on ahead." Turning back to Adler, he said, "Do they think one of us might escape and later identify them, they may show their colors sooner. Better we know are they friend or foe."

Otetiani began a more rapid stroke. His canoe shot out ahead of them. Adler heard shouting from the two approaching canoes then saw a musket raised. Damn!

"Steady my canoe," Latty said, raising his musket and twisting to his left.

Adler obeyed as two shots rang out. He saw the puffs of smoke rise from the guns in the advancing canoes, but the shots fell short. The men now had to reload.

"We have an advantage," Latty said, positioning his musket on his shoulder. "They must hit us. Do we turn our bodies sideways, we make a smaller target. They dare not hit our canoes and risk our precious furs sinking to the bottom of the river. The furs being what they are after."

Adler could not see Latty's face, but he knew his friend was smiling. "We on the other hand," Latty continued, "have easy targets. We can put large holes in their canoes. Now hold me steady, soon they will be close enough."

"They are near ready to fire again," Adler said, watching the two front men at work reloading their muskets.

"Yep," Latty said. "I am but waiting for him to raise … his gun … and…"

Adler saw Latty squeeze the trigger. The shot exploded in his ears, jolting him, but he held both canoes steady. Latty's shot was dead on. A gaping hole below the surface of the river had water rushing into the forward canoe. Adler guessed the musket ball must have hit the forward man as well for the man had yelped and dropped his gun into the river. Both men were now shouting – the man in the rear began paddling rapidly toward shore, the injured forward man was using his hat to shovel water out of the canoe.

"Hand me your musket," Latty said.

Adler obliged, but he was not certain why Latty wanted it. The second canoe had given up the chase and was following the damaged canoe to shore. Its occupants were no longer a threat, yet Latty was setting his sights on them. The man in the bow was waving his arms and shouting, "No, no." But Latty fired, hitting the canoe in the exact center. The man in the aft started paddling even harder and the bowman grabbed up a paddle and joined him. In but moments, it was obvious neither canoe would make it to shore.

"Hope they can swim," Latty said with a chuckle, and turning back to Adler handed him his musket. "We will go a bit further downstream then reload. Want to get away from here."

Adler nodded. Lifting his paddle, he said, "Why did you waste shot shooting the second canoe. They had given up."

"Would you be wanting to see them again on our next trip?" Latty cocked his head. "I want everyone on this river to know we are not an easy target. Do they know we will take revenge, they will think twice about attacking us."

"I can see you are right. 'Tis hard for me to wish drowning on any man, though." He looked back over his shoulder. Both canoes were sinking into the river. The four men were floundering in the water. He turned back around. Did they drown, he would rather not know.

Otetiani waited up ahead for them. "All is well?" he asked.

"All is well," Latty answered him. "Let us see if we can make Fort Orange before nightfall. I am hungry."

Adler knew he and Latty made a good combination. Latty's skill with a musket was uncanny. He never missed what he aimed at. But Latty's tracking skills were not keen. "You fail to concentrate," Armand chided him. "Forget for a bit this future estate you intend to have, this great land you mean to acquire, and watch for the little things that are all around you."

"As long as I have Adler at my side, I will not get lost," Latty answered with his usual chuckle. "However, to please you, I will attempt to pay closer heed."

Latty had improved Adler thought, but he was such a jolly soul, his attention often wandered. His lively nature made him popular with the Indians. Always grinning, eager to lend a hand to anyone. Adler had never suspected his jovial friend could be so cold and calculating as when he took aim on the pirates. Yet Latty was right. No doubt those men would have killed him, Latty, and Otetiani for their furs with no regrets. He hoped the men would survive. If for no other reason than to warn other would be pirates they had best not pick on Latimer Draye.

❀ ❀ ❀ ❀

Jeanette could not believe she was again aboard a ship, a small Dutch flute, bound for Beverwyck. Her father-in-law had insisted, despite her condition, that she go up river to escape the ague that often struck coastal areas in the late summer and early autumn. Children and pregnant women were known to be most at risk, but Jeanette believed Curtice was more concerned about Etienne than he was her.

Etienne was healthier than he had been in a long time, but did he get the sweating sickness, he would not survive it, that everyone knew. Etienne's father wanted him up river where the dreaded disease would be less likely to strike. Etienne would not go without Glynneth, and Glynneth insisted she would not leave Jeanette. Consequently, Jeanette found herself leaving her husband behind for at least two months. When her baby was born, Gaspard would not know for several days was his first child a boy or a girl.

She prayed her baby would be a boy. She wanted to see her husband's eyes glow with delight when he looked upon his son. She wanted Curtice to praise her as he was forever praising Glynneth, wanted him to bounce her son on his knee as he did Noel and call him a fine little man. She wanted Gaspard's eyes to follow her about the room as they too often followed Glynneth. She doubted her husband even knew his gaze held such longing for his brother's wife. Did he know, he would try better to disguise it.

Nor would he forever be complimenting Glynneth. "Glynneth, that frock becomes you. Glynneth, your reading was very moving this evening. Your observation was profound, that chess move was inspired, good to see the bounce back in your step. I can see you are enjoying spring." Any time he was in Glynneth's company, he had some form of compliment for her.

She wondered if Glynneth knew Gaspard was enamored of her. If she did, she gave no indication. She treated him like a brother. Jeanette frowned. That did not make her feel any better. She was still jealous of Glynneth. She knew jealousy was a sin, but she could not help it. All would be better once her baby was born. She would have proven herself a fruitful wife. She would get her figure back. Her husband would be proud of her and would no longer hunger after Glynneth. She but had to endure another month, month and a half at most, and her ordeal would be ended. She would hold a pink, cuddly baby in her arms, and her joy would be boundless.

She was glad she would have Glynneth and Glynneth's servant, Dominique, with her when her time came. She did not trust Heloise. She had asked Gaspard to find her a new servant, one like Dominique for when they moved into their new home. It should be ready when she returned from Beverwyck. Its completion was one of the carrots Curtice held out to her while cracking the whip over her head to get her to overcome her fear and board the ship.

"You will see, my dear," Curtice said in his cultured French that she so admired, and that was so like her father's. Her father, so far away in Ireland. How she missed him, missed her mother, missed her lovely, gracious home. "When Gaspard is not worried about you," Curtice continued, "he will have much more time to devote to the new house. I give you my word. It will be ready for you and the baby when you return." He held up his hand and nodded his head when she asked about the servants. "Yes, yes, I will do my best to get you your own maid, and a nurse to tend to the baby. Now make haste, the tide is coming in. You must board."

So she had boarded the flute. Gaspard had given her a sweet kiss and told her to take good care of herself. "And mind what Glynneth tells you to do. She has had two babies. She will know what is best for you."

Such parting words of endearment, she thought. Mind what Glynneth tells me. Well, she would. Some women died giving birth. She did not intend to be one of those women. If Glynneth could have two healthy babies, so could she. And she would.

❀ ❀ ❀ ❀

How vast was this country they now called home, Glenneth thought. Standing at the bow of the flute, she stared out at the thickly wooded land they were passing. Finally she had some time to herself. The children, Etienne, and Jeanette were all down for their naps, and Dominique was watching over them. At first, Glynneth did naught but enjoy her moments of peace, but eventually her thoughts shifted to Adler. Would she see him, or would he be off in the wilderness trading the numerous items Curtice had brought from the old country for furs and beaver pelts.

She was confused about her feelings for Adler. She liked him. Liked him a lot. In many ways he was much like Etienne. Not in appearance. Not in education. And he had not been born to wealth or station. But he was kind, caring, and sincere. All characteristics that had attracted her to Etienne. He had an enthusiasm for learning, and she enjoyed the spark in his eyes when he learned some new historic fact or listened to a moving poetic verse.

Had she met Adler before she met Etienne, might she have fallen in love with him? She shook her head. Probably not. An uneducated farmer would hardly have caught her attention. She would have had no way of knowing his potential for learning, his zest for life that lay hidden beneath his rugged exterior. How strange was the fate that had brought them together. Now he invaded her dreams, disturbed her conscience. She loved her husband with an intensity that still left her breathless, yet she could not deny her attraction to Adler. She could sympathize with Guinevere, torn between Arthur and Lancelot.

She knew Adler was attracted to her. She could see it in his eyes, hear it in his voice, but he would never make his feelings known. Would never infringe upon her trust or Etienne's. She believed Latty had also formed a tender for her, but though she found him handsome and amusing, she was not drawn to him as she was to Adler. She rather pitied any woman who might fall in love with Latty. He had but one goal – accumulate land. His soul, rankled by the loss of his ancient heritage, would know no peace until his objective was achieved. What love could compete with that?

"You seem deep in thought, my dear. Do I disturb you?"

Glenneth turned at the sound of her husband's voice. She greeted him with a smile, but asked, "Should you not be resting?"

"I found I had no wish to miss any part of our trip. I want to see and experience as much of this glorious land as I can. These past two years, I have missed so much of life. Now that I am feeling stronger, I want to taste all I can."

Putting her arms around Etienne's neck, Glenneth kissed him and said, "I feel the same. Life sometimes seems so fleeting. It seems only yesterday that we first met. Yet we now have two wonderful children, and we have journeyed across a vast ocean to this new and thrilling world. I want to treasure every moment. I feel I dare not let any new experience slip away without fully relishing it."

He laughed. "Sometimes I feel our souls are interlocked. You express so well the feelings that overwhelm me." Growing more serious, he added, "Could any man have so dear a wife, so competent a helpmate. I would be lost without you, my sweet love."

She touched her palm to his check. "And I without you. You give meaning to my life. Yes, our souls are bound together in a bond that can never be broken. Forged of the strongest steel. It will endure through eternity."

Chapter 14

Glynneth's gaze searched the shore. Who would be meeting them? Ah, there was Armand, and Capucine – she had Guyon and Pierre with her. There was Jacques. She shaded her eyes against the bright sun. If Adler was at Fort Orange, he would be there to meet their boat, she knew he would. Ahhh, she sighed softly. There he was. And there was Latty. The two dear men. "Look, Meara, Noel, look, Adler and Latty are awaiting you as are Guyon and Pierre."

"Where, Mother, where," asked Meara, standing on tiptoe to see over the ship's railing.

Glynneth squatted beside her daughter, and pointing, she first indicated Adler and Latty, then her children's playmates next to their mother. "Do you see them?"

"I do," Meara cried and started waving. Adler and Latty returned her wave. Her daughter was thrilled to see her friends. Glynneth was, too. Her heart beat faster as the flute glided effortlessly up to a dock, and her gaze momentarily locked with Adler's. She wished she could understand what feelings she had for the man. She could not love Adler, for she loved Etienne, loved him with a depth that at times left her breathless. At the same time, she could not deny the currents of attraction that passed between her and Adler. She thanked God, was there a God to thank, Adler never attempted to act on that attraction. Never attempted to start a flame with the sparks that flew back and forth between them.

"Madame," said Dominique, "do you wish me to see to Madame Jeanette?"

Standing at Glynneth's side, Dominique was holding Noel. Nodding, Glynneth took Noel into her arms. "Yes, please help her up and see if she needs anything before we disembark." Jeanette had spent most of the voyage up the river in her bunk. She would need Dominique to help

101

her dress her hair and straighten her gown.

Jacques had written that they had a new house for them for their summer sojourn in Beverwyck. The owner's wife had been too fearful of the constant parade of Indians in and out of Fort Orange to adjust to her new home and had insisted they return to New Amsterdam. Glynneth hoped no one would mention the woman's fear to Jeanette. She did not want her sister-in-law's imagination to run away with her. Jeanette could easily decide they would all be killed in their beds. Glynneth prayed all would go smoothly with Jeanette's delivery, and that the baby would be healthy. The poor woman needed something to rouse her from her melancholy.

"Ah, Glynneth, Etienne, how glad we are to see you." Armand, having boarded the flute before all the ropes had been tied, embraced first Glynneth and Noel, then Etienne, before swooping up Meara in his arms and proclaiming, "I have two little boys who are most eager to be reunited with you and Noel."

Meara bounced in Armand's strong arms. "Oh, let us hurry. I can scarce wait to see them. And Latty and Adler, too."

Glynneth laughed. "She has barely been able to contain herself since we came in view of the fort." She glanced over her shoulder. "Here comes Jeanette. We can now disembark."

A firm grip on Jeanette's elbow, Dominique steadied her as they advanced across the deck to be greeted by Armand. He glanced at Jeanette's rounded stomach and chuckled. "Ah, soon you will be making Gaspard a proud man."

Jeanette beamed at his praise and let him take her other arm and help her over to the ramp which had been secured to the boat and the dock. Jacques met her there and carefully escorted her down the slight incline. Dominique was free to again take Noel into her arms. Having handed an eager Meara over to Latty who tweaked her curls and called her his little sweetheart, Armand escorted Dominique with Noel off the boat.

Adler, jovially greeting Etienne and Glynneth, offered to escort them down the ramp. "Can be a bit tricky," he said. "Especially as you still have your sea legs." His eyes meeting Glynneth's, he extended his hand. The heat of his touch nearly made her pull her hand back. Her breath momentarily caught in her throat. This reaction to Adler was not good. But in an instant, he had her standing safely on the dock and had retraced his steps to help Etienne.

"Dear Adler, 'tis so good to see you and Latty," Etienne said, joining Glynneth on the wharf. "We have missed your companionship more than you know."

"And we have missed yours," asserted Latty, a bubbly Meara still in his arms. "Young miss here is eager to greet Guyon. May I set her down?"

"Of course," said Glynneth. Guyon, clutching Capucine's hand and bouncing up and down on his toes was obviously eager to greet his playmate. No sooner was Meara on her feet than the two children were wrapped in each other's arms.

"He has talked of nothing but Meara for the past week," said Capucine, stepping forward to give Glynneth a half hug. She had Pierre balanced on one hip.

"Noel, want Noel," the little boy cried, stretching his baby arms toward Noel.

Still holding Noel, Dominique looked to Glynneth. "Do I set him down, Madame?"

"By all means," Glynneth said, "let them greet each other. They see Guyon and Meara hugging. They naturally wish to copy them."

"Better we leave the wharf first," Jacques said. "It is much too crowded and noisy. Simone awaits you at your home. She has a cool drink for you and a hot stew warming on the fire. Raissa and Jolie, and my son, Ignace, also await you at your home. I felt we had enough people greeting you here on the dock."

Glynneth agreed. She could tell Jeanette felt overwhelmed. So much noise and bustle. But she knew the two little boys would soon be screaming did they not get to greet one another. "Best we let them hug, Uncle Jacques, or we will know no peace." No sooner did the two youngest members of the group exchange delighted greetings in a gibberish of words only they seemed to understand, than Capucine and Dominique scooped them up to follow after Jacques. Armand took Jeanette's arm, and amidst much praise for her endurance, promised her she would not need to walk far. Glynneth took Meara's hand and

Etienne took Guyon's and they brought up the rear of the procession.

Adler and Latty stayed behind to collect their sundries. Glynneth was relieved they would not be accompanying them. She needed time away from Adler. Seeing him after the months of separation had been surprisingly overwhelming. She needed time to regain her composure.

"You are tired, my dear?" Etienne asked.

Smiling wanly, she looked up at him and nodded. "I do think I am. Too much excitement I suppose." Looking down at the two children who trotted along between them, she said, "These two seem to have formed a fast friendship."

Etienne nodded. "So it would seem. They may have boundless energy, but I am glad we will soon be able to settle into our home. Perhaps a nap will do us all some good."

"I think I would like that," Glynneth said, and she meant it. She needed a quiet time to arrange her thoughts and sort through her turbulent emotions. She would feel better after a meal, a cool drink, and a nap. Surely she would.

⚜ ⚜ ⚜ ⚜

The tavern being quiet, Adler, slowly sipping on his mug of ale, let his thoughts swirl randomly about in a multitude of directions. His first sighting of Glynneth. His eyes meeting hers. His hand touching hers. He had wondered if his feelings for her might have lessened after being separated from her for over four months – but no – if anything, his love for her had intensified. He wanted to be near her, wanted to gaze at her, to bask in the brilliance of her presence. Thoughts of her kept him sane when the deep forest seemed to close in around him. He desperately needed to replenish those images. At the same time, he feared the intensity of his need for her, his desire for her.

What if he could not control his passion, his ardor? Did he lose control, gaze too lovingly, hold her hand too long, speak too caressingly, what might she think? What might Etienne think? He could not bear to read hurt or contempt in their eyes. He could not bear to lose their trust. Yet how could he be around her and not give himself away?

By the time he and Latty arrived at Glynneth's home, the Chappells had taken their leave, and the Fortiers had settled down to nap. Only their slave, Dominique, had been up to greet them and help them unload the cart and deposit the belongings in the family room. He hoped Glynneth would be happy in her temporary abode. Besides the main room, the house had two bedchambers and a storage loft. Newly built, it was clean and still smelled of new cut lumber. Cooking smells had not yet settled into the walls, and the chimney stones were not blackened with soot. He could imagine sitting by the hearth watching Glynneth sew or give Meara her lessons. Or he might just listen to her lilting voice when she read from one of her favorite books or discussed some aspect of history that he had never known but found fascinating.

Every moment he could spend with her was precious, but fraught with peril. He must be sure he was never alone with her. Was he alone with her, he knew he would be unable to resist sweeping her into his arms. His lips longed to claim hers, to taste her sweetness, but he would never know that delight, never know that incomprehensible thrill. Yet his love for her was far more than just a physical need. His love for her demanded he move mountains if necessary to secure her happiness. He could never be whole or content was anything amiss in her life.

He could not explain this overwhelming love he had for Glynneth. He but knew from the moment he looked into her eyes, she had given him a peace, a branch to grasp when waters of despair were flowing all around him, threatening to drown him. Leaving his home and family had ripped him into a multitude of pieces, and somehow, she had found those pieces and bound them back together. She had given him back his life, and he had given her his undying love.

"You drink late," a familiar voice broke in on his reverie.

Adler glanced up to find Latty standing over him. Where Latty had been he could but guess. Most likely a visit to one of the Indian women who satisfied the carnal needs of the single men living in and around Fort Orange. He hoped his friend was being careful. Such amorous encounters could lead to the dreaded pox.

"You are usually to bed afore I return of an evening. What keeps you at the table?" Latty spoke in English. The two men liked to use their native tongue. Few people understood or spoke English so it allowed them to converse without threat of eavesdroppers. In addition, they could express their thoughts more simply and succinctly.

"My thoughts are scattered," Adler said. "Jacques says he wants us to head back out within the week with the trade items that came in on the ship today. I could use a tad longer to rejuvenate my soul. I am not certain I am ready to face the wilderness again so soon."

Latty sat down on the bench across the table from Adler. Rocking and nodding, he pursed his lips before saying, "Mmmm, I feel much the same. Yet our share of the proceeds are substantial. The sooner we return to our trade, the sooner we will accumulative more funds, and the sooner we can begin to direct our own futures. You know well my plans, Adler, but you have never spoken of your dreams. Have you none?"

Adler realized with a start that he really had no dreams. He could not return home. His love for Glynneth could not be reciprocated. What did the future hold for him? He certainly had no desire to live out his days traveling from one Indian village to another. Frowning, he shook his head. "I was a farmer. I loved our land, yet I cannot see myself farming again. I seem to have lost my interest in laboring on the land. I enjoy the freedom of rising in the morning and having no need to feed the animals or look to the sky to see if the rain comes too soon or too late. Your dream of building a grandiose estate holds no appeal to me. Yet, I will not end my days roaming this vast wilderness – that I do know."

Latty chuckled. "Nor will I. But I will build my manor here on this foreign soil, and I will have a son who will pass it on to his son, and so on down through the generations."

"So have you had any luck finding that rich widow you seek?"

Chuckling again, Latty said, "Nay, but find her I will. In the meantime, we must prepare ourselves to resume our trade with the natives."

"I know you are right, though I could wish otherwise." Yawning, Adler stretched his arms over his head. "I am off to bed now."

"I am with you," Latty said, rising as he spoke. The two men had accommodations in the Fort Orange barracks. Their bunk space was sparse, but as their needs and belongings were meager, they had no complaints. Adler, with Latty following, left the tavern and headed for his barracks room and his bed.

Chapter 15

Latimer tossed the giggling Meara up in the air, then catching her, clasped her against his chest. She wrapped her arms around his neck and hugged him tight. "Oh, Latty, I have missed you so. I am so happy you are with us again."

"I am as happy as you are, little one," Latimer said, glancing around the Fortiers' temporary home. Clean and comfortable. That was good. He wanted things right for Glynneth. She and her serving girl had been busy since their arrival. Already the abode looked neat and cheery. "I wish we could stay all summer," he added, poking Meara in the rib with his finger.

The girl pulled back to look into his eyes. "Why will you not stay all summer?"

He frowned. "Because I have not found myself a rich widow to marry so I must continue to work until I find one."

"Now, Latty, I say again, you know you cannot mean that," said Capucine, and Latimer smiled at Armand's pretty blue-eyed wife. Capucine always chastised him for making such statements. She thought he joked, but he was sincere. Could he find a wealthy widow, be she as comely as Capucine or not, he meant to marry her. He meant to be a man of substance, a propertied man who could pass his land on to his descendants. And this time no king would take his land from him or his descendants.

"You are right, Mother," said Raissa. "Latty likes to tease is all."

Latimer chuckled and set Meara down on the floor so she could resume play with Guyon. He liked Capucine's young daughters, the quiet Raissa, with her solemn brown eyes and the joyful Jolie, so full of mirth. He enjoyed teasing them. He liked how Raissa brightened and how Jolie preened. But neither of them realized, though he intended to marry, and marry well, he cared not whom he married. He had given his heart to Glynneth and doubted he could love another. He would never be able to claim Glynneth as his own, but he would ever love her.

He shrugged. It would do him no good to cry after something he could never have. Planting a grin on his face, he tweaked Raissa's chin before turning to Glynneth. "I am off to stretch my legs this bright sunny day. But have no fear, I shall return 'ere dinner is served."

As he exited, he heard Capucine huff. "Stretch his legs. Humph. He is off to browbeat my husband again."

She was right, he thought with a chuckle. He and Adler were the ones risking their lives in the wilds. They had brought back a handsome profit to the Chappells, and he wanted a larger share of the profit. He wanted to start buying his estate. His future was in land, not love.

❀ ❀ ❀ ❀

When Capucine and her children departed, Adler and Etienne settled down to a game of chess. Adler willed himself to concentrate on his game and not let his eyes follow Glynneth as she moved about the room, seeing to her children, helping Dominique with the meal preparation, or setting the table. He and Latty were to join the Fortiers for dinner as Etienne had bid them do every day until they need depart into the wilderness. Having but a minimum of days to collect the memories that must sustain him through the long months when he would have no contact with Glynneth, Adler cherished each moment in her presence.

"Come now, Adler," said Etienne, "do you really mean to move your Bishop there?"

Adler frowned. "Nay, I fear my mind wandered. Still, the move is made."

Etienne laughed. "Fear not, I am willing to let you try again. You are still learning. It would not be fair did I take advantage of my more extensive years of play. Do make your move again."

Adler thanked Etienne and spent more time surveying the board. He enjoyed the game of chess. It challenged his mind, and he reveled in the challenge, though he could not say why. Since meeting the Fortiers, a whole new world had opened up to him. He could never again be content to be a farmer. He wondered that he should have changed so much. Or had this quest for knowledge always been a part of him? Had he buried it, knowing in his previous life it would but make him discontent? Etienne insisted he had ancestors who must have been royalty.

"No other way to explain that half a torque," Etienne said. "It is pure gold. I shined it up, and it is as fine a specimen as any I have seen in any museum. Father has it safely secured in his brick vault. It is too precious to risk losing. You could not have such a treasure, such an heirloom passed down through generations was it not once a part of your lineage."

Laughing, Adler shook his head. "Was it ever a part of my lineage, 'tis of a lineage long since forgotten. The torque is naught but a prized keepsake, and I thank you and your father for keeping it safe for me." But might Etienne be right? Might his family once have been meant for greater things than plowing fields and threshing grain? Could that long lost past account for his new aspirations? He supposed he would never know. Best he concentrate on the game and not be dreaming he was of noble birth.

He chuckled softly at his foolishness, and Glynneth stopped at his chair. "Have you a jest to share?" she asked, her voice falling sweet upon his ear.

Fearing to look at her should his love show in his eyes, he looked across the board at Etienne. "I was thinking of our earlier discussion of my torque and consequently my lineage. Soon, Etienne, you will have me believing I should be a king or at least a prince."

"Nay," laughed Etienne. "More like a Celtic chieftain."

"Yes," agreed Glynneth. "A Welsh prince or chieftain. Coming from the borderlands as you do. It is too bad the story that goes with the torque was lost to your family."

Stealing himself to keep his face passive, Adler raised his gaze to meet Glynneth's. "My mother always said 'twas distant Welsh blood that accounts for the red hair that abounds in my family. There is no knowledge, though, of any Welsh union so it must be distant."

Glynneth patted his shoulder, and her touch scorched him through his coat. He longed to reach up and grasp her hand in his and bring her fingertips to his lips. Knotting his hands into fists in his lap, he controlled the urge and managed a smile when she said, "Mayhap someday the pieces may all fit together."

"Mayhap," he answered as she moved away to attend Noel. The little boy had fallen and was admitting a mournful screech.

"There, there," he heard her console her son, scooping him up in her arms. He saw her dry the tears on Noel's cheeks with her apron then cuddle him close. He would have continued to watch her had Etienne not drawn his attention back to the board.

"Do you need more time for your move, Adler?" Etienne asked, his head cocked.

"Aye, but I promise I shall concentrate." He moved his knight closer to Etienne's queen. A pawn in the queen's path protected his knight. The queen which had been advancing on his king would have to flee or risk being taken by his knight.

"Good move," said Etienne, studying the board. "Now you have put me on defense rather than offense. Most astute."

While Etienne debated his next move, Adler glanced briefly at Glynneth. He dare not stare, but just a glimpse of her ever so often gave him little memories he could store away like he had once stored tidbits in his pocket to have surprise treats for the family cat. He would relish those memories as much as ever the cat relished her treats.

※ ※ ※ ※

While stirring up corn meal, milk, eggs, and molasses to make a boiled pudding, Glynneth's thoughts drifted back to the previous day's dinner at Jacques and Simone's house. She had learned of Adler's and Latty's near fatal episode in the first village they had visited. When listening to Adler's account of their adventure, her heart had stopped, her breath caught in her throat, her fingernails dug into her palms. Had Adler not borne the scars of a fight with a bear, both her friends might now be dead. The thought that she might never have seen Adler's dear face again, seen his smile, gazed into his blue-green eyes horrified her. At that instant, she realized, did she not love Etienne so deeply, she could fall in love with Adler Hayward. She had been fighting her attraction to him since their time together on the ship to New Netherland. Her feelings for him left her confused and wary.

She dreaded the day Adler and Latty were to leave. At the same time, she knew having Adler close to hand was dangerous. She had come to realize his attraction to her was as great as hers for him. She could not understand or explain the attraction, all the same, it was there. There between them whenever their eyes met or their hands touched. No longer did she dare spend time alone with him as she had done in Rotterdam. Yet part of what made Adler so endearing was knowing he would never take advantage of her weakness.

She could name numerous things about Adler that she admired; his gentleness, his eagerness to learn, to become more educated, his calm reassuring presence coupled with the knowledge he was always reliable. His humor and his captivating stories that held adults and children in suspense and brought a lightheartedness to sometimes stressful situations. Most of all, she liked the friendship that had developed between Adler and Etienne. Adler awakened a joyfulness in Etienne that she had not seen since the consumption attacked him. With Adler's encouragement, Etienne, when his cough was under control, was becoming an accomplished story teller. His tales of Greek or Roman myths or past heroic deeds never failed to intrigue his listeners. Adler, in particular, seemed to relish every nuance, every detail.

These traits that made Adler so engaging, did not in themselves cause her heart to skip beats or her skin to tingle. It was the entirety of his essence – the combination of his physical attributes, his integrity, and his vitality. When in his presence, his strength gave her a sense of security. At times, she longed to be shielded from the new world turmoil in the shelter of his arms. Often in her dreams, she would lose herself in his loving gaze, let him take her cares and worries onto his strong shoulders. The dreams were so real, she could almost feel his sturdy chest pressed against her breasts, hear the thud of his heartbeat, taste his lips in a lingering kiss. But she was never to know him as she knew her husband. She always awoke before such intimacy occurred. The dreams were indecent, she knew, yet they continued, especially when Etienne's health took a turn for the worse or when some other happenstance made her wish she had never left Ireland.

Glancing at Adler from under her eyelashes, she wondered that he now made sure he was never alone with her. Always Etienne or the children or Capucine were near to hand. Was he concerned about his self-control or hers? She did not know. She but trusted him to protect them both from their heated ardor. Amusingly, Latty was just as circumspect. He need not have been concerned. She liked Latty as a friend, but she was not attracted to him. She pitied the woman who gave her heart to Latty. He had but one love. Land. Sadly, was she not mistaken, Capucine's young daughter, Raissa, had fallen in love with Latty. Poor child. Still, Raissa was but thirteen. No doubt she would soon outgrow the attraction.

Sighing, Glynneth wished she could outgrow her attraction to Adler.

❈ ❈ ❈ ❈

"Check mate," said Etienne.

Adler laughed. "Well, you must admit, I gave you more of a challenge this time."

Etienne smiled and nodded. "You get better all the time. Soon you will defeat me. Did you have the time to play as often as I play, you could become a master. You are astute, your tactics are sound. I would say you have an innate knack of stratagem."

Adler flushed, embarrassed by the praise, yet pleased. When with the Fortiers, he saw life in astonishing new ways. Life had more color, more beauty, more gentleness, more graciousness. Life was more than a day to day existence. Before he had ridden off to fight for his King, his life had a sameness to it. Rise in the morning, see to the animals, breakfast, then go to the fields – plow, weed, harvest, according to the seasons, shear the sheep, thrash the grain, mend the fences. The list of mundane tasks seemed endless yet ever the same. The occasional holiday, feast, wedding, or funeral was all that enlivened the farmer's existence. What did he know of the wonders the world had to offer. Did he know of Homer or Gilgamesh or the pharaohs or Marco Polo? Did he know of Paris or Rome or Athens?

He had loved his life as a yeoman farmer. Had chosen that life rather than continue his schooling. Never had he suspected what doors he had closed or never chosen to open. The Yardleys had continued their education, but to his knowledge, they had not gleaned from it what Glynneth and Etienne had found. The Chappells, leastwise Jacques and Simone, enjoyed discussions about the Greek and Roman civilizations and their eventual demise, or the merits of poetry verses prose, or innumerable other subjects that challenged the mind. And like Glynneth and Etienne, the Chappells were happy to answer his questions and encourage his curiosity, but their discussions often lacked the vibrancy and scintillating conviviality he savored when Glynneth and Etienne communed.

His thoughts were interrupted by Latty's return. Rising from his seat, he placed his chair at the table as Glynneth said, "You are just in time, Latty. Etienne and Adler have finished their game and dinner is ready to be served. Wash up then have a seat," she added, nodding toward a bowl of water on a stand near the door.

All became a bustle, but soon, dinner was on the table, everyone was seated, and Etienne bowed his head to give thanks. Adler's gaze met Glynneth's. Her lovely eyes glowing, she smiled. One more cherished memory to tuck away he thought with a silent prayer.

Chapter 16

The two weeks rest Jacques granted Adler and Latty before sending them on another trading mission had sped by. Before Glynneth knew it, her two friends were again off to the wilds. She feared for them. So many dangers in the untamed wilderness. At times she felt overwhelmed by the vastness and the extremes of her new home. Forests that seemed to go on forever, biting flies, stinging wasps, poisonous snakes, the struggle to keep warm in the winter and to find some relief from the heat in the summer. Snow too deep to walk through, torrential rain storms, constant fires raging through the town, drunken brawls at all hours of the day and night. No book stores, so no new books, no theater, naught but constant, never ending chores.

Dominique did the washing, the cooking, and tended the animals. Glynneth helped where she could, but she had duties of her own. She did the marketing, took Etienne and her children for a daily walk, gave Meara her lessons, mended sheets and clothing, though her patching was not very good, and helped with the making of soap and candles. She had welcomed the sojourn in Beverwyck. It was even more rustic than New Amsterdam, but it was a change in the routine.

She was happy to renew her friendship with Capucine, but in Simone Chappell, she found a kindred spirit. From the moment Simone greeted them in their new home, her gentle speech and lively eyes had intrigued Glynneth. Simone had shown them about their small but comfortable home, offered them mugs of cool cider, and fed them a hardy stew. She and a silent, but watchful, Indian woman in a colorful skirt had made up their beds, and Simone urged them to rest after their long journey.

"Especially the children will need their naps," Simone said. "So much excitement will tire them, and they could become cranky." Turning to Guyon when he protested, she added, "Yes, I know my dear grandson, you are eager to play with the adorable Meara, and Ignace is

114

eager to become better acquainted with his cousins, but you will have the entire summer to play with them. Now you must be courteous and let them rest."

Meara had appeared ready to join in Guyon's protests but had been quieted by Simone's soft but firm admonition. Glynneth stifled a snicker. She wished she could as easily silence her spirited daughter. Over the next few days, as she became better acquainted with Etienne's uncle's wife, Glynneth discovered she and Simone had much in common. Separated in age by naught but a year, they had both suffered the loss of their mothers and fathers as well as other loved family members. They had both found reading and immersing themselves in other worlds brought them solace. And they had found not just love, but companionship in the men they married. They were treated as equals, and their mental astuteness was respected, not challenged or denigrated.

Other than her grandmother and her younger sister, Glynneth had never known another woman with an intellectual background to match her own. She often found herself at Simone's snug little home enjoying a tisane and a chat. "My father's mother was English," Simone said. "Her father was an ambassador or something to France. I have no idea how they met, but meet and fall in love they did. She was highly educated, and according to my father, she valued education above even God." She chuckled. "He always whispered that, as if he was afraid God might hear and be offended. He was considerably more religious than I am. Jacques, too can be devout, but he tells me he is less devout than when he set sail from France with his first wife and Armand to escape persecution."

"I believe this land can make one see things differently," Glynneth said. "Myself, I was raised without any religious beliefs, yet somehow, since coming here, I cannot help but feel God's presence. My grandmother would disown me did she hear me admit to such."

Simone laughed. "My mother accepted my father's God when she agreed to marry him, but I believe she secretly continued to pray to the gods of her youth." She cocked her head. "I wish I could remember her better. Father I can still see clearly, but my memories of my mother and my brother are blurred."

"I am fortunate, memories of both my parents are still very vivid,"

Glynneth said. "It would be difficult to forget either one of them. They were both so vibrant. My Meara reminds me greatly of my mother. Meara has no fear of anything, which scares me at times, and like mother, she is very headstrong," she smiled and added, "though very loving."

"How did your mother die?" Simone asked, her dark eyes gentle and caring.

"A virulent fever that attacked many people throughout Ireland. Mother was always helping the poor. She wore herself down tending them. When the fever struck her, she was too tired to fight it off."

"I am sorry. She sounds like a remarkable women."

Glynneth half smiled. "I suppose we all think our mothers are re-markable."

Simone nodded. "Yes, I feel that way about mine."

"Etienne's mother died of consumption," Glynneth said. "She lasted but a short while before the consumption took her, but she had been an invalid ever since Gaspard's birth. I never knew her, but Etienne's father was devoted to her. Etienne has survived the consumption three years now, and he seems to be getting stronger here in New Netherland. I do think the clean air does him good. No pall of smoke hangs over everything as it does in Dublin."

Placing her hands around her cup, Simone said, "He does appear vi-brant and lively, and he is almost as good at telling stories as is Adler. Ignace is fascinated by the Greek myths." She gave a light humph at the back of her throat. "He enjoys stories of heroic deeds. He wants to be a woodsman. I want him to be a scholar."

Sighing, Simone shook her head. "Was my father still alive, I could send Ignace to New Amsterdam to study under his tutelage. Get him away from these wild influences."

Glynneth nodded sympathetically, but at the same time she was for-mulating a plan. Was Etienne willing, could not Ignace come to live with them and study under Etienne's tutelage? She would talk to Eti-enne that very night.

Draining her cup, she set it back on the table. "I suppose I had best return and check on Jeanette. I cannot get her to leave the house. She says it is too hot to go out. I also need to take Meara and Noel off Capucine's hands. She is so good about watching them so I can enjoy some time away from my chores."

"Capucine is a dear. Armand was lucky to find her."

"He was indeed," Glynneth said. "I cannot think how I would have managed when we first arrived in New Amsterdam without her help. I am so glad she will be handy when Jeanette is finally ready to have that baby."

"Do remember, I will mind all the children. Best they are not around when the screaming starts. Could frighten them."

"I agree, and thank you."

❦ ❦ ❦ ❦

Glynneth crooned softly to the little bundle in her arms. "Hush little baby, close your eyes. While your mother sleeps, I will sing you a lullaby." The song was one she could remember her father singing to her. Her father had loved to sing, and what a grand voice he had had. Yet he could sing soft and sweet when holding his tearful little daughter in his arms. Though she had been but three, she could still remember her fear that her mother was dying.

"Nay, little one," her father had said, scooping her up in his arms. "Your mother has but given birth to your new baby sister, Una. Now you must be quiet that your mother may sleep. She had to work very hard to bring your sister into this world. When your mother awakes, you may see her and your new sister."

"When your mother awakes, little Lothair," Glynneth told the baby, "you will get your first feeding." Thank goodness you are a boy, Glynneth thought. Jeanette had been determined to have a son. Her birth pains had lasted most of the day, but as the evening advanced, Capucine had tickled Jeanette's nose with a feather and with the ensuing sneeze, out came Lothair. Glynneth was grateful to Capucine for helping with the delivery. Simone had kept all the children for the day, and Etienne had promised to help entertain them. He might not be able to play games with the children the way Latty and Adler did, but the children did love to listen to his stories. His expressive voice could hold them spellbound as they waited breathlessly to hear how Aladdin escaped the treacherous Sultan, or Robin Hood bested the Sheriff of Nottingham.

"I have the sheets and towels washed up, Madame," said Dominique, "and hug out to dry in the warm night air. Would you have me start the supper now?"

"Yes, Dominique, and thank you. But would you first peak in on Madame Jeanette. I hope she will soon be stirring. I do believe this little fellow is beginning to get hungry. Poor babe is making mewing sounds."

Dominique stopped to look down at the newborn. "He is certainly a red-faced little baby. Hardy looking, though. And what a mass of hair he has."

"He takes after his father," Glynneth said, slightly jiggling the baby. He was hungry. She wanted to let Jeanette sleep, recoup her strength, but she feared she would have to awaken her. "Does she stir?" she asked Dominique.

"No, Madame. Would you have me wake her?"

Glynneth shook her head. "No, you go ahead with supper. Etienne will soon be bringing the children home. I think it best I attend Madame Jeanette."

Jeanette at first grumbled when awakened, but when learning her son needed feeding, her whole being changed. "Oh, give him to me. The little dear. He is perfect, is he not?"

Glynneth laughed. "Yes, he is perfect," she said, helping Jeanette settle the baby at her breast. "And hungry," she added, watching the baby eagerly begin suckling his first meal. "I will leave you for now, but I will return soon to put Lothair in his cradle."

Jeanette looked up at Glynneth. "Thank you. Thank you for helping me birth my baby."

Glynneth wondered if that might be the first time Jeanette had ever thanked her for anything. She smiled down at her sister-in-law. "You are very welcome. Enjoy your son."

Softly closing the door behind her, Glynneth returned to the main room as Etienne arrived with Noel on his shoulders and Meara tagging along behind him. A frown on her face, Meara snipped, "Cousin Capucine said I might have supper with them, and that Cousin Armand

118

would bring me home, but father said no. He said I must come home to see the new baby."

Glynneth scooped Noel from Etienne's shoulders, gave him a kiss, and set him on the floor before addressing her daughter. "You should want to see your new cousin. Think how hurt your Aunt Jeanette would feel did she believe you had no wish to see Lothair."

"I see him," said Noel, his dark round eyes glowing in the last light of day that poured through the open doorway. What a dear he is, Glynneth thought. He was in every way the image of his father. Not quite two but so caring, so bright.

"Did you have fun playing with Pierre today?" she asked her son, leading him over to the basin to wash his face and hands.

"Fun! My pie best!" Beaming with pride, he stuck out his little chin.

"Raissa and Jolie helped us make mud pies," said Meara. "Aunt Simone judged his pie the best pie of the lot."

"Did she now?" Glynneth said with a chuckle.

"That is because Raissa helped him," said Meara.

Noel's lower lip trembled, and he pointed to himself. "I make. I make."

"Of course you did," Glynneth said, taking a swipe with her rag behind her son's ear. "Meara is but jealous – and disappointed she had to come home. Pay her no mind."

Meara giggled guiltily. "Am I being cross, Mother? I am sorry. But I was having so much fun with Guyon. I like living here in Beverwyck. Might we live here forever?"

"There Noel, you are all done. Try to stay clean until supper." She beckoned to Meara. Her daughter was a constant source of joy and amusement to her. Ever cheerful, never able to stay cranky for more than a few minutes, she had a love of life that was invigorating and contagious. "Come here, dear, and let me get you cleaned up." Picking up a clean rag and soaking it in the basin, she said, "I am afraid we cannot stay here. Your grandfather misses us. And he needs your father to help him with his work. When the weather cools, we must return to New Amsterdam. But I have some good news. Ignace will be coming with us."

Meara clapped her hands. "Oh, might Guyon come, also?"

Glynneth shook her head. "No, dear, at least not this year. Mayhap next year. You see, Ignace will be studying Latin and Greek with your father. And arithmetic, that he may be prepared in his education to take over the properties his grandfather left to him and his mother."

"I like Ignace, but I like Guyon better," Meara said. "Does Guyon have properties like Ignace? Will he have to learn Latin and Greek?"

"Guyon, no doubt, will follow in his father and his grandfather's business, but Uncle Jacques would like his grandsons to learn to read the classics. Your great uncle Jacques studied them in his youth when he lived in France. But Cousin Armand never had a chance to learn them. Uncle Jacques was too busy with his fur trade to have time to teach him. But as Uncle Jacques and Cousin Armand have prospered – well, Guyon and Pierre can have opportunities not afforded their father."

"Is it fun to learn Latin and Greek?"

Chuckling, Etienne sank onto a nearby stool and joined the conversation. "Some find it vastly amusing. Some find it boring. I enjoyed it. It opened new doors to me."

Meara turned to him. "What kind of doors?"

He laughed again. "Doors of knowledge, adventure, reason – but not a door like the door to this house. No – I speak of doors of the mind."

"Might I learn Latin and Greek?"

"If you wish," said Glynneth, drying her daughter's face and hands. "Enough questions for now. Go see if Dominique needs help. She might be ready for you to set the table."

"Yes, Mother."

As Meara scampered over to Dominique, Etienne, his eyes following his daughter said, "What children we have produced, my dear wife."

"They never cease to amaze me," Glynneth answered, rising. "Let me see if Jeanette has finished feeding the baby. If so, you and the children may see her and Lothair before we eat."

Glynneth found Jeanette with the baby sleeping in the crook of her arm. Gazing down at her son, a sweet smile on her face, the new mother looked beautifully content. "Might Etienne and the children come in to see you and the baby?" Glynneth asked.

Jeanette looked up. Her eyes glowing, she nodded. "Yes, but they must be quiet. Then if you would put Lothair in his crib."

Etienne, Meara, and Noel were suitably impressed. Meara wanted to hold Lothair, but Glynneth told her she must wait. "Mayhap on the morrow. Now off with you while I tuck him in his crib. He will do little but sleep and eat for the next few weeks."

Eager for the long day to be over, Glynneth herded her family through supper. Afterward, she got Jeanette to eat some venison broth. She mixed Etienne a posset to keep his cough under control during the night when it would most often erupt. With kisses and hugs, she tucked her own two little ones into their cots then saw Dominique settled on a pallet in Jeanette's room that she might be near to help with the baby. Finally, she checked that the fire in the hearth had been banked before wearily dropping into bed beside Etienne. They shared a good-night kiss, and within moments, she heard her husband's soft steady breathing. She had thought she would drop off immediately into sleep, but she found she was too buoyed up. Sleep would not come. Instead her thoughts went to Adler.

She had enjoyed his company but for two short weeks, then Jacques had sent him and Latty back out with more trade goods. "They have already surpassed all my other tradesmen," Jacques said. "With these new trade items, they should have furs pouring into the fort."

Armand explained that they were encouraging the Indians to bring their furs and skins into the fort to trade. The water ways were getting too dangerous for his tradesmen to bring back large quantities of furs all at one time. Adler and Latty had been attacked on their return trip. Better the individual Indians brought in their own furs to trade for the specific items they wanted. Adler and Latty carried samples and gifts and some items of trade, but their mission was to penetrate deep into the Iroquois territory to show off the goods the Indians could purchase.

"That Adler is an adopted brother to Kills Many is a great asset," Armand said. "That relationship gives him safe conduct throughout the Iroquois nation."

Staring up into the darkness, Glynneth wondered if Adler might be thinking of her at this moment. Might his sleep be troubled? Might he be tossing restlessly? Did he wonder how it would feel to have his arms around her? Did he wonder what was this attraction between them? How foolish she was. She adored Etienne. She could never have asked for a better husband. And yet – and yet? What? She did not know.

Soon she and her family would be headed back to New Amsterdam. Months would pass before she would again see Adler. Mayhap even a year did he and Latty not return to Fort Orange before the river froze over. She prayed Adler and Latty would be safe. "God, if you are real," she silently whispered, "do watch over them." She did not want to imagine a world without Adler in it.

Chapter 17

Adler had only one thought – soon, very soon he would see Glynneth. Shivering, he pulled the woolen blanket closer around him. The fire in the pit he had dug did little to warm him. And the pemmican did little to stop his stomach from gnawing on itself. Winters in this new land were far colder and harsher than any winters he experienced in England. He and Latty had been fools to set off on foot in this weather. Yet they both wanted to return to New Amsterdam for at least a portion of the winter. Winter at Fort Orange was too dreary. New Amsterdam offered more entertainment to help wile away shortened days and long nights. And, both he and Latty admitted to missing the Fortiers.

Since they had last seen the Fortiers in Beverwyck, he and Latty had traveled deep into Iroquois territory, had seen sights that left them astounded, witnessed some events Adler wished he could put from his mind. The Iroquois were a strong nation. There was much he admired about them – but they could be immeasurably cruel. They could also be extremely kind and accepting of individuals they adopted into their tribe. They took care of widows, orphans, and the old. No one was left to starve or freeze in the cold as were people in England. They had no beggars, no paupers.

By the time he and Latty returned to Fort Orange, winter was upon them. The Hudson was not yet frozen over, but floating chunks of ice made river travel dangerous. A thin layer of snow that had coated the ground had melted into slush, making travel by foot tedious. All the same, against Chappell's advice, he and Latty headed south. They encountered a few straggling Mohican villages and were made welcome. But they had been forced to spend a couple of nights hunkered down in whatever shelter they could find or contrive. A fallen tree was their only shelter this star studded night. They took turns staying awake to keep the fire going. They placed stones warmed in the fire at their feet to keep frost bite at bay. Dried leaves scraped out from under the tree gave them some padding so they were not sitting or lying directly on the cold ground. The tree blocked the light breeze that swept down from the north.

Adler sighed and wished for the dawn. Once they were up and moving, they would warm up. Was he not mistaken, they should reach some of the outer settlements around New Amsterdam by mid-afternoon. They could be in the village by nightfall. He imagined the welcome they would receive when they arrived at the Fortiers' door. They would be hustled over to the warming fire, hot mugs of ale or cider would be offered, a stew would be hastily prepared. The slave, Dominique, would ready their beds in the loft. Bone weary, they would promise to tell of their adventures the next morning. Then amidst joyful exclamations, they would go to bed.

But he would not sleep immediately. His thoughts would be of Glynneth. He would record every smile, every glance, every tantalizing laugh to be replayed when once again he set off for the wilderness. The images warmed him as he stared toward the horizon and watched for the morning sunrise.

※ ※ ※ ※

Jeanette gazed down at her son at her breast. He was so strong and healthy – robust, she would say. Just like her husband. She smiled thinking how Gaspard doted on his son. From the day she had come home from Fort Orange with Lothair in her arms, she had reveled in the glow of pride she saw in Gaspard's eyes when he looked at his son.

Lothair was six months old this very day. The painful memory of his birth receded with each passing day, but the smothering heat of that long day stayed in her memory. How relieved she had been when the cooler days of autumn allowed them to return to New Amsterdam. She had returned to the new house Curtice had promised her. A brick house, it was as large as the house they left behind in Ireland. Downstairs, it had a nice sized hall and a small parlor, large and small dining chambers. Upstairs were four bedchambers and a nursery. The kitchen was separate from the house. Curtice said it was for fire safety sake and to keep the kitchen smells from permeating the house – she liked that, even if the dinner was sometimes cold. The servants quarters were off the kitchen.

Behind the house, in the courtyard, was an herb and vegetable garden, and beyond that, housing for the chickens, pigs, sheep, and a goat. Since coming to this new and wild land, she had learned that keeping animals was a must. The choices in the market could be scarce, or equally bad, limited to venison or turkey – both items she found barely palatable. And did one want cheese or milk or butter, a cow or at least a goat was a necessity.

She admitted to being happier in her new home than she had expected to be. The furnishings were sparse, being naught but what they had been able to bring with them when they left Ireland, but Curtice had ordered furniture from Holland that he expected to arrive before many more weeks. He had also paid a vast sum for two women slaves from the Dutch Indies. Lina, a young gracile charcoal black woman with wild curly hair that she kept contained under a colorful scarf, helped with Lothair and did the lighter household chores. Gusta, a hefty woman with brownish colored skin and a gap-toothed smile, did the cooking and heavier chores. A skinny Swedish youth and his wizened grandfather tended the garden and saw to the care and feeding of the animals. Unlike the two slaves, they were day help and did not live on the grounds. Jeanette was pleased she was no longer served by the solemn-faced Heloise.

Looking out the diamond paned window at the dawning sky, Jeanette considered her plans for the day. Etienne and Glynneth and their children would be coming for dinner. She liked being the hostess and sitting at the end of the table, calling for the various dishes to be served. She wondered if Glynneth envied her. She liked not having to see Glynneth more than once a week. She had thought once she produced a son for Gaspard, he would not continue to gaze longingly at Glynneth. But his eyes still followed her, he still paid heed to her every utterance. She also thought her father-in-law would be as thrilled with Lothair as he was with Glynneth's son, but no. The old man acted as though Noel made the tide rise and fall. He might give Lothair a little tweak on the cheek when she brought him down in the evenings before Lina put him to bed, but he never raved about him, never predicted he would have a bright future. Curtice was near as enraptured by Meara, and what a little harridan was that child. Glynneth seldom curbed the girl's antics. Why, Meara even felt she could join in on adults' conversations. And Curtice would listen to her as though she spoke words of wisdom.

Jeanette frowned. When she complained to Gaspard about Meara's deportment, he made excuses for the child – she was precocious, spirited, and blithesome. Surely Jeanette could not wish to dampen or blight the girl's vivacity, her zest for life. With a silent humph, Jeanette thought she would indeed like to subdue the little minx. Were she her daughter, she would soon learn to deport herself like a lady. Well, at least she only had to endure Glynneth and her children one day a week.

🌼 🌼 🌼 🌼

"Must you rise so early?" Glynneth asked Etienne. "'Tis terribly cold out. Could you not wait until the sun is higher in the sky?"

Etienne snuggled back under the quilts and drew her into his arms. He brushed his cold nose against hers and softly kissed her lips. "You make it very tempting to stay abed my love, but a new shipment is to be unloaded today. This load might even contain the furniture for Father's house. I have not seen the manifest yet. 'Twas late when the ship dropped anchor and the captain sent word he would come ashore this morning. I mean to be there to check the bill of lading. You have no need to rise until the room is warmer. I will stir up the fire in the hearth, and I hear Dominique bustling about. No doubt she will have a mug of warm cider readied for me."

Glynneth clung to him. How thin he seemed. Yet, he was eating enough. The cold, the long hours at work, the recurring cough that left him exhausted, all worked together to weaken his constitution. "Try to come home early. We are due to dine with your father today."

Etienne thunked the heel of his palm to his forehead. "I completely forgot this is Thursday. No doubt Father is also eager to learn if his furniture has arrived. Am I late for dinner, it will be his doing. He and Gaspard will be late as well."

"Ah, poor Jeanette, she will have the dinner all prepared, the table set, the baby fed and down for a nap. Still, does the ship bring the new furniture, she may forgive her menfolk for their tardy arrival. Mayhap I will go early to ease her wait time."

Etienne gave her another kiss. "You have a good heart, my love. Now I must rise." He slipped from the bed, and stirring up the fire in the hearth, added more wood.

In the dim light, Glynneth saw him shiver. He was the one with the good heart, she thought. He always praised her, but she knew he was a far kinder person, and she treasured him. Watching him dress, she wished she could convince him he need not work such long hours. Yet he seemed to enjoy being helpful to his father and Gaspard. Today he would work tirelessly through the morning, pushing himself to accomplish whatever goals he set for himself. He would then hurry home to ready himself for dinner at his father's. When at last they returned home after a long afternoon of socializing, he would find the time to check the lessons he had assigned to Ignace. Etienne enjoyed teaching the boy, and Glynneth was glad Ignace's mother had wanted him to return to New Amsterdam with them. Etienne would answer any questions Ignace might have concerning his lessons, then give him several new assignments. Finally, a cough shaking his fragile body, Etienne would retire for the night. Dominique would have used the warming pan between the sheets, and Etienne would remark on the coziness.

Glynneth sighed. 'Twas routine. Her last act before retiring would be to bank the fire so they would have embers in the morning. She would snuggle in next to Etienne. He would take her in his arms, kiss her, but they would not make love. He would be too tired. A cough would rack him, he would apologize, as though he could keep the cough at bay did he choose. They would say good night and soon he would be asleep, sleeping the sleep of the truly weary. At some point during the night she would touch him and find he had either a fever or night sweats. Most likely a coughing spell would attack him. She would pretend to sleep through it. He would know she pretended, but he would accept her ruse.

Life had become predictable, monotonous. She missed Ireland. Missed her family, especially her grandmother. She missed Dublin's bustle, missed the book stores, the theater, the pageants and firework displays, the various festivals and their traditional celebrations. She missed the minstrels and puppet shows, the sporting and recreational events from bowling to horse racing. Here, more so in these dreaded winter months, one day followed after the other with very little change.

She had been spoiled all of her life. She knew that. For so many people, life was a constant struggle to survive. She had never lacked for anything. She had no right to complain now. Yet her soul was complaining, aching for more excitement, entertainment. She who had everything was not content. She wanted more. Springing from the bed, she chided herself. Did she seek a more interesting existence, she must take responsibility for finding new forms of entertainment. She must stop letting the cold keep her indoors. She added more wood to the fire, stirred it up to get a good blaze going, then hurriedly dressed.

Dominique tapped on the door and entered. "I heard you up, Madame. Would you have me make you a mug of cider?" The pretty maid had quickly learned English and enjoyed using it. "That I may become more accomplished in your speech," she had told Etienne when he asked why she was favoring English over French.

"Yes, some cider would be lovely. Thank you," Glynneth said, then asked, "Are the children up yet?"

"Ignace is up, but Meara and Noel are still abed."

"Well, tell them to get up and to dress warmly. After we breakfast, we are going out."

Dominique looked surprised by her pronouncement, but said, "Yes, Madame."

Glynneth was not certain what her morning's outing would accomplish, but that was good. At least it would not be the same dull routine.

�™ ☞ ☞ ☞

"Good morning, Madame Fortier."

Glynneth nodded to the plump, pretty Dutch woman who greeted her with a bright dimpling smile. Despite the chill wind that blew in off the river, Glynneth, feeling confident in her Dutch, decided to stop and chat. Shifting Noel from one hip to the other, she said, "Good morning to you, Mevrouw Kerstan. This winter seems even colder than last year, and I have been house bound. Today I felt the need to get out despite the hint of snow in the air." Glynneth wondered if she would ever adjust to the bitter cold and intense heat of this new world. The glorious days of autumn had flown by and winter weather had come all too soon.

Mevrouw Kerstan nodded. "Yes. I have ventured out only when necessary. Today I must market." She indicated a basket in the crook of her arm. "My son, Gerhard, offered to accompany me." She put her other arm around the blond, blue-eyed boy at her side. "I believe he has hopes of stopping by Meneer Vogel's bakery for a gingerbread man."

"Hmmm, that sounds good." Glynneth looked down at Ignace. "If we stop at the bakery, will that make up for my taking you away from your studies."

Ignace's eyes gleamed, but before he could answer, Meara said, "Oh, Mother, do go by the bakery. I would love a gingerbread man and so would Noel. Would you not?" she asked her brother, who nodded vigorously.

"Indeed," Ignace seconded Meara, and Glynneth laughed, her breath coming out in white puffs. "I would say it is unanimous. The bakery will be our destination for this day's outing. Do you and Gerhard accompany us, Mevrouw Kerstan?"

"Why, yes, we will. Fact is I have wished to speak with you," Mevrouw Kerstan said, falling into step beside Glynneth.

"Oh?" Glynneth said, cocking her head to look at her companion.

Mevr. Kerstan's narrow gray eyes, so different from her son's large round blue eyes, gazed unblinkingly back at Glynneth. "I have heard your husband gives Ignace lessons in Latin and Greek as well as arithmetic and geography. I wonder if Gerd might also take lessons from him. Gerd turned seven this past month. Neither my husband nor I have advanced educations, but we have prospered since coming here to New Netherland." She raised her chin. "My husband builds the finest boats in the colony," she stated before returning her attention to her son. "I taught Gerd his numbers and his letters, and the minister is teaching him to read and write, but there is an extra fee if he is to teach him ciphering and other skills. To take his place in better society, Gerd needs to have a superior education. Better than he is getting from the minister."

Though unprepared for such a request, Glynneth could understand Gerhard's mother wanting a more promising future for him. She knew how much the Dutch valued education. Thinning her lips, she nodded. "I appreciate your desire to see your son advance in the world. A good education is an important means to achieving such a goal. However, my husband is busy at his father's office most days. He has not the time to do more than check Ignace's work, and on Sundays, examine him. Etienne, of course, designs the lessons for Ignace, but at present, I am teaching him. My background is not equal to Etienne's, but it is sufficient for this stage in his lessons." Stopping, she switched Noel to her opposite hip and said, "Now, if you would like Gerhard to study with me, I would be willing to teach him. He could do his assignments in the mornings then come for his lessons in the afternoon."

"Oh, Madame Fortier, I would be ever so grateful. I never dreamed you would have such an advanced education. Mayhap when my daughter is older, she too will have an opportunity to study with you. My husband and I believe a girl should also have a good education."

Glynneth was not surprised Mevr. Kerstan would want her daughter to receive a good education. Since coming to New Netherland, she had learned Dutch women, for the most part, were better educated, and had far more freedom and legal rights than women under English rule. "I agree," she said. "A girl's education should not be neglected. Meara already knows her letters and numbers, and I started her reading." She looked down at Mevr. Kerstan's son. "As Gerhard has not yet had any lessons in Latin or Greek, he will be studying different lessons to Ignace's, but I think it will help Ignace learn if he helps Gerhard. If you wish, Gerhard can start his first lesson tomorrow afternoon."

Mevr. Kerstan's face spread in a wide grin. "Thank you, thank you. I will have him at your house at two of the clock if that is satisfactory."

"That will be fine. We normally dine at noon, Etienne has his nap, and heads back to work at two. He can meet Gerhard before he goes. Meeting your son should help my husband in planning his lessons."

"What a fortunate day this is," said Mevr. Kerstan.

Yes, it is, thought Glynneth as they resumed their walk. She had wanted something to change her routine. Well, having another student would give her a new challenge. And maybe some of the other mothers

130

in New Amsterdam might want their children to learn more than the basic reading and writing. She could end up with several students. She smiled. She would like that. Teaching was far more entertaining than mending sheets or stockings. Besides, her sewing was poor. Maybe she could trade lessons for domestic help. She had been right to brave the cold this January morning. Life was looking brighter again.

Chapter 18

Adler knew his disappointment showed on his face. He and Latty arrived at Glynneth's home to find she and her family were dining at Etienne's father's home. Dominique graciously invited them in and gave them mugs of warm frothy ale, but the welcoming scene Adler had been envisioning since setting off on the journey to New Amsterdam had come to naught.

While they sat down to a simple meal of peas-porridge and ham hock, Dominique went up to the loft to make up cots for them. "I think my toes are finally warm," said Latty, drawing his feet away from the fire and tucking them under his chair. "I feared frost bite."

"Aye," answered Adler, "we made better time getting here than I expected. I think 'twas your pushing us that kept our feet from freezing."

Latty chuckled. "I do believe you finally have the hang of the fall forward pace. You seemed to have no trouble keeping up with me."

Adler frowned. "Took me long enough to learn. I think I always felt I would fall flat on my face did I trip on anything, and lord knows we encounter enough roots and rocks and fallen branches in the paths we traverse that 'twould be easy enough to do. When walking upright, you at least have a chance to regain your balance."

"True enough. Fortunately, whenever I have tripped, I have managed to catch myself."

"Your beds are ready," Dominique said. She had come down the ladder so quietly, Adler had not heard her. "Perhaps after your long walk, you wish to rest before the family returns."

"That would be a good idea," Adler said, though he doubted he would be able to sleep. He would be listening for Glynneth's return. Surely they would not be much longer. The sun was low in the sky. Soon it would be dark.

"I will put warmed bricks at the foot of your beds," Dominique said in her light, vibrant voice. "Should keep your feet warm."

"Thank you," Latty said with a grin. "You are a pearl, Dominique."

Her dark eyes dancing, a smile playing at the corners of her mouth, Dominique answered, "You need not try to flatter me, Monsieur Latty. I am well aware how you charm the women. Do not think I will be one of your conquests."

Latty guffawed. "Oh, indeed, I am right, you are a pearl. When you have paid off your debt and have your freedom, Madame Fortier will feel your loss." He stood. "By the by, I compliment you on your English. You learn fast. I wish I was as good in the French and Adler as good in Dutch."

Dominique thanked him and started to pick up two bricks wrapped in rags, but Latty said, "Now you hand me those bricks and I will take them up with me. No reason to put you to extra trouble." He look down at Adler. "Coming?"

Adler nodded and rose. "Aye. I am coming." He had wondered if Latty had seduced Dominique when she had been with the Fortiers in Beverwyck. He was glad to know he had not. Glad Dominique knew better than to be beguiled by Latty. He was glad Glynneth had a servant so dependable and industrious. Indeed, Dominique was a pearl.

※   ※   ※   ※

"Latty and Adler are here!" Adler heard Meara's piping voice from below. The Fortiers were home. Glynneth was home.

He heard Glynneth's voice, that sweet lilt that set his heart to thumping. "No, you may not go up to the loft. Dominique can awaken them. You stay there by the fire and warm up. It was a cold walk home."

The cot next to Adler's creaked and in the dim light, he saw Latty rise.

"No need to send anyone up," Latty said in a raised voice. "Adler and I are awake. How could we be sleeping with that little trumpeter spouting off."

Rising, Adler heard Meara giggle and say, "Oh, hurry, hurry down!"

The greeting they received when they descended made up for the earlier disappointment. Laughter and hugs, squeals of delight from Meara when Latty presented her with a shell necklace. "Made especially for you," he told her, "by Chief Bold Crow's only daughter."

"It is lovely," Meara said. "Why did she make it for me?"

Latty squatted and pulled the little girl closer. "Because I admired her necklace and told her I would dearly love to buy it for you. When I told her how old you are and that you are my dear friend, she insisted she would make a necklace just for you."

"You will tell the Chief's daughter thank you for Meara, will you not, Latty?" said Glynneth. "That is a rather exceptional gift for a little girl."

Latty rose and turned to Glynneth. "I will convey Meara's every reaction and every word," he said. He then turned to Noel. "For you young Master Noel, I have a whistle." He pulled a small white tube from the pouch he had slung over his shoulder. "This whistle is made from the wing bone of an eagle. When you blow it, it makes the shrill sound like an eagle makes."

"Oh," the little boy said, his eyes round as he took the whistle, held it to his lips, and blew. A shrill call emitted from the whistle, and he gasped with pleasure.

"Ignace," Latty said, "I also have this flute for you." The wooden flute had six holes and was decorated with two red stripes and an eagle feather.

The slim, dark-eyed boy took it reverently into his hands. "Thank you, Latty. I will strive diligently to learn to play it."

Adler had brought naught for the children but a number of new tales – some of his and Latty's experiences, some of Iroquois legends and myths. But for Glynneth, he had a lovely rabbit pelt he hoped could be made into a warm muff for her. For Etienne, a pair of deerskin moccasins. He would wait for Latty's presentation to end before bringing out his gifts.

Latty next produced a small intricately beaded bag which he handed to Etienne. "I thought you might enjoy the skill that went into making the design," Latty said. The round bag had a red maple leaf on a golden moon.

Seated close to the fire, Etienne smiled and nodded. "It is exquisite, I will treasure it." he said. Adler thought his voice sounded weak and raspy. He did not like the way he looked either. His eyes were too bright, his skin too pale, his cheeks too rosy. And he saw him shiver as he caressed the beads and fingered the design of his gift.

Latty had turned to Glynneth, and Adler did not think he noticed Etienne's appearance. "For you," Latty said, handing Glynneth a round, lidded basket decorated with colorful porcupine quills.

"It is lovely," she said with a bright smile. "Thank you."

He returned her smile, and said, "One more gift. I have not forgotten you, Dominique."

Standing in the shadows, watching the family she served, the Fortiers' slave jerked to attention. "For me. You have a gift for me."

"Part of the household, are you not?" Latty said, holding out a beaded tiara. The red, blue, and gold beads that decorated the headdress glowed in the flickering firelight. "I know well what help you are to the family. I also know you like colorful things."

"It is dazzling," she said, taking it from Latty and holding it to her brow. "Thank you."

Adler felt shamed. He had not thought to bring anything for Dominique. Hopefully she would enjoy the tales as would the children. With Latty's gift giving ended, Adler presented his gifts to Glynneth and Etienne. Both gifts were accepted with fervent thanks. "I feel these moccasins will be most comfortable around the house," Etienne asserted, and Glynneth said, "I can scarce wait to have the rabbit skin made into a muff.

"What did you bring Noel and me?" Meara asked.

After Glynneth chastised her daughter for her impertinence, Adler said "I brought you many new stories. In fact, I will tell you one this very evening if you would like."

"Oh, yes, we would. We do miss your stories, Adler."

"The story will have to wait for a little while," Glynneth said. "We want to hear how Adler and Latty got here. We know it was not by canoe or boat. The river is near frozen."

"That is a story in itself," Latty said. "I will let Adler tell it. He will tell it better."

Glynneth turned to Dominique. "If you will stir up the fire and put on another log first, please. It is bitter cold this evening." She looked to her husband. "Etienne, it has been a long day for you. Much as I know you wish to enjoy some time with Adler and Latty, I wonder if you should retire. You look exhausted."

Addressing Adler and Latty with a half-smile, she explained, "My father-in-law's long awaited furniture arrived today. Etienne had to check the manifest, consult with the duty magistrate, and then hurry home to ready himself for our weekly dinner at Father Curtice's house. Dinner ran long because of the excitement over the furniture arrival. Jeanette is near beside herself."

"I can imagine she is," said Latty. "And how is her baby? We heard she was delivered of a healthy boy."

"Lothair is a little delight. We saw him for but a moment today before his nurse took him away to bed. I fear he has little contact with other children, only Meara and Noel. And they seldom see him. He is sitting up now and will soon be crawling. I do hope Jeannette will let him have more contact with other children once the weather warms."

Adler heard the concern in Glynneth's voice. For Gaspard and Jeanette's sake, he hoped their son would stay healthy and vibrant. For the baby's sake, he hoped he would have his father's personality, not his mother's.

"I am warm and comfortable in my chair," said Etienne, returning Adler's thoughts and gaze to Glynneth's husband. "I believe I will listen to Adler's tale err I retire."

"As you wish, my dear," Glynneth said, "but we will get those boots off you and your new moccasins on before Adler begins his tale." She looked at her daughter. "You, too, Meara. Off with the boots and get your warm slippers on. Dominique, will you help Noel."

Dominique turned from the fire she had built up into a crackling blaze. "Yes, Madame, I will attend him immediately."

Glynneth insisted they all have some warm spiced cider before they were finally settled around the hearth, and Adler could tell them of his and Latty's trek from Fort Orange to New Amsterdam. Meara snuggled onto his lap, and Noel climbed up on Latty's. Glynneth sat opposite Adler. He could watch her, watch the expressions flicker across her face. She sat next to Etienne, her hand on his arm, her head resting against his shoulder. How much in love the two of them looked. Sigh-

136

ing, he began his tale.

☙ ☙ ☙ ☙

Latimer lay awake, staring into the dark. He could tell Adler was also awake, no rhythmic breathing yet. No doubt, like him, Adler was thinking about Glynneth. How lovely she had looked in the glow of the firelight, her loosened hair floating about her shoulders, her eyes bright with the joy of their arrival. For him it had been a perfect evening – basking in Glynneth's presence. But his gaze had occasionally sought out Dominique. She was a comely woman, and smart. How strange that a person of so much wit and character should be a slave. Until he met Dominique, he had never given slavery a thought. It existed. That was all.

He wondered what Dominique had planned for her future. What would she do when she earned her freedom? What would Glynneth do? Would she be able to find another slave that could in anyway match Dominique? He doubted it, but he could not know for certain. In truth, he did not really know any other slaves. Maybe they were all bright and witty. Few were as appealing as Dominique. He was attracted to her. Not the way he was attracted to Glynneth. None of the women he bedded were anything more than a physical release for him. Had he not fallen in love with Glynneth, he might meet a woman who could make him forget his desire to marry for wealth? Perhaps, but he rather thought not. Land meant too much to him.

He heard a sound below, someone was stirring, then Glynneth was calling, "Adler, Latty, come quickly. Oh, do hurry."

Adler and he were off their cots, into their boots, and down the ladder before Dominique had a candle lit. "What, Glynneth, what is amiss?" cried Adler.

Glynneth grasped Adler's hands. "'Tis Etienne. He is burning up, and he is delirious."

Adler grabbed the candle from Dominique and hurried into the bed-chamber. Glynneth followed him, and Latty followed on their heels. Dominique must have hastily lit another candle for before Latimer knew what she was doing, she thrust the holder into his hands and returned to the hearth to stir up the fire. Adler handed his candle to Glynneth then placed both his palms on Etienne's face. "Lord," he said.

Etienne, his breath coming in ragged gasps, opened sightless eyes and murmured something. He rolled his head from side to side then a raking cough shook his body.

"My poor, dear husband," Glynneth said, the candle shaking in her hands. "You cannot die, you cannot."

Adler turned to Latimer. "Set that candle down and help me get him into a sitting position. He cannot breathe. There is fluid on his lungs. We must get him upright."

Latimer did as directed, setting the candle on a table beside the bed. Reaching across the bed, he helped Adler lift Etienne into a sitting position.

"He will be cold," said Glynneth. "We must get the quilts up around him."

Adler stopped her. "Nay, we need to bring down his fever. He is too hot. We must cool him off. I saw my mother do this once when my father had a high fever. We need to bathe him in cool water."

"Surely not," Glynneth said, fear in her eyes as she looked at her husband.

Adler gripped her arms and forced her to look up at him. "You must trust me, Glynneth. Do we not bring down his fever, he...will...die."

She must have seen something in his eyes that convinced her for she nodded. "All right," she said and turned to the door. "Dominique, fetch us some cold water."

"Yes, Madame," Dominique said though Latimer heard the question in her voice. He hoped for Adler's sake, as much as for Etienne's, that Adler knew what he was doing. Did his treatment fail, and Etienne die, Adler would never forgive himself. Glynneth would not blame him, but Adler would blame himself.

Shivering, Latimer looked down at his bare legs. He and Adler were a pair in naught but their shirts and boots, their bare bums barely covered. He imagined when he had leaned across the bed to help Adler with Etienne, he had exposed his bum to Dominique.

"What is happening? Is Father sick?"

Whipping around to find Meara standing in the doorway, Latimer's worry about his lack of dress fled. Meara had a quilt wrapped about her shoulders, but being barefoot, she was dancing back and forth from one foot to the other on the cold flooring. He hurried to scoop her up in his arms. "Do you not know to put slippers on your feet, little one? You will catch a cold like your father. Here now, let me tuck you back into bed. Is your brother or Ignace awake?"

"Nay. But what of Father?"

"Your father will be fine. You are not to worry." Cuddling her close against his chest, he prayed he was not lying to the child. "Your mother and Adler are looking after him." While tucking her back into her bed, he glanced at her soundly sleeping brother and cousin in the next bed. During these bitter cold nights, having another person in bed for body warmth was a good idea. Dominique had been sleeping with Meara, but now she was needed to help with Etienne.

Latimer hoped Meara would be warm enough without her bed companion. Dominique had stirred up the hearth fire, and the door to the bedchamber stood open. That should help. He started to snug the quilts tight about Meara but changed his mind. "Best let me warm up your toes first," he whispered. Taking first one little foot and then the other, he rubbed them until they felt warm to his touch. "That better?" he asked, pulling the quilts up around her neck.

"My toes are all tingly, now. Thank you, Latty," she said in a hushed voice.

"Will you be warm enough without Dominique in bed with you?"

"Yes, but could you tell me a wee story? I fear I am wide awake."

Latimer could not see her eyes. She was naught but a shadow. The only light in the room came from the hearth fire in the family room. She might or might not be wide awake, but he could hear a little tremble in her voice. Whether from cold or fear, he could not tell, but he would do his best to help her go back to sleep. "You know little missy, I cannot tell tales like Adler."

"No one tells tales like Adler," she answered, "not even Father, but that is all right."

Latimer chuckled then caught himself and again looked at Noel and Ignace. Both boys continued to breathe evenly. "Very well," he said, keeping his voice low. "How about I tell you of the only time I met

139

Arcadia Yardley. You always seem to like tales about her."

"Oh, yes, do tell me about her. Is she truly as pretty as Adler says?"

"Yes, she is pretty. She has very dark hair and dark brown eyes and a little turned up nose, but I pity the man who will someday marry her."

"Oh! Why? Why do you pity the man who marries her?"

Latimer heard the surprise and curiosity in Meara's voice. The tremble was gone. "Because she is too much like you. Willful, spirited, and conniving."

"Conniving?"

"Yes, have you not managed to get me to tell you a tale when you should be sleeping?"

She giggled. "Well tell the tale, and I promise I will go back to sleep."

Latimer began by telling about the fearful ride back to the Haywards' house. The worry that Cromwell's militiamen might find them out at any moment. Then their arrival at Adler's home and his first glimpse of Arcadia. His mind was only half on the events he recounted. He was listening for any sounds from the other room. He heard Dominique return with the well water, but he could tell nothing else. He was not a praying man. He had never given much thought to God, but now he prayed. Dear Lord, please let Etienne live.

Chapter 19

All through the night, Adler worked with Glynneth, Latty, and Dominique to keep Etienne alive. When chills shook Etienne's weakened body, they bundled him up. Several times Adler had Glynneth climb in next to Etienne to add her warmth to his shivering body. The chills would stop and the sweating would resume. Again they would sponge him off with cool water. The candles burned to nubs and Dominique replaced them. She kept the fire going in both hearths and had hot cider ready for anyone who needed it.

Adler slipped off to the loft long enough to don more clothes as did Latty. When morning came, they each took time to break their fast with some bread and cheese, but Glynneth never left her husband's side. She followed whatever instructions Adler gave her, but the frightened look never left her face. Her eyes bloodshot, her hair disheveled, she paced the small room whenever she was not needed to help with Etienne.

"You should get some rest," Adler said. "Soon the children will be up, and you must explain to them the necessity of being quiet and keeping out of mischief."

She stopped her pacing and looked to the door. "Yes, yes," she said. "I should go to them while they are yet abed and have a talk with them. I must not frighten them. Their father will not die." She looked back at Adler. "You will call me if you need me?"

He nodded. "I will. It is a good sign that he is sleeping and his breathing is less raspy."

Her gaze went to her husband. "Yes, he is better. I am certain of it."

When she left the room, Latty said, "'Twould be good could you get her to crawl into bed with Etienne. She is so exhausted, she might fall asleep. It would do her good."

Adler agreed, "Good idea. Does she grow too weakened, she could come down with the ague, and that would do no one any good. Speaking of rest, you look like you are ready to drop." Latty, a quilt draped around him, was seated in a chair brought in from the parlor. "While Etienne is sleeping, you should catch a nod or two."

Latty stood. "I think I will take your advice. But what of you? You, too, must be tired."

"Aye, I am, but I want to watch over Etienne for a while yet. When you have rested, I will take my turn at a wink or two."

"So be it," Latty said and left the room.

Adler turned to his patient. He thanked God Etienne had made it through the night. Etienne still had trouble breathing, and he still had a fever, but the fever was more mild, and the breathing less labored. Sleep was a great healer Adler's mother always said, and she was right about so many things. Thoughts of her saddened him. He would never see her again. He recalled the tears in her eyes when he left with D'Arcy and Latty. She could never have imagined the life he now lived. Nor could he. Never would he have dreamed he would be desperately in love with a married woman, nor that the woman's husband would be a beloved friend. How he had changed – from a farmer to a woodsman. And what would he be next? He sighed. It mattered not – as long as he could continue to have occasional visits with Glynneth. He would be content.

Adler affirmed his approval when Glynneth arranged for Dominique to take the children to stay with Jeanette so they would not be underfoot. The slave was then to take a message about Etienne to Curtice and Gaspard at the warehouse office. Once Dominique left with the children, Adler insisted Glynneth get some sleep. "You will be right beside your husband. I will be right here on this chair. Should his condition change, I will wake you. You will be no good to Etienne do you collapse from exhaustion."

Ultimately she agreed and was soon cuddled up next to her husband. When Curtice and Gaspard, their brows furrowed with fear, arrived with Dominique, they discovered to their relief Etienne and Glynneth were both sleeping. "Sleep is good. It strengthens the body," Adler said.

Curtice nodded, "Wee, but what can we do to help?" For Adler's sake, he spoke in English, though after more than a year in New Netherland, Adler had become comfortable to a certain extent with French. At least he could come close to understanding French, even if his tongue and mouth could never master French pronunciations. Curtice was little better with Dutch, but fortunately for his business, his two sons had mastered the language.

"You can do nothing here for now. But could you help make sure the children are not frightened, that would relieve Glynneth. She is most concerned about them."

Turning to Gaspard, Curtice said, "You go back to zee office. I will go home and help Jeanette entertain zee children." He looked again at Adler. "I will return before dinner to see how my son does and to see do you need anyzing. And I zank you for all you have done."

"I did what I could," Adler said. "Now we can do naught but wait and watch."

❆ ❆ ❆ ❆

"Oh, my, how horrid!" Adler awoke to voices speaking in Dutch. When Latty had risen from his nap, Adler had stretched out and fallen instantly asleep on a cot Dominique set up in the family room. Opening his eyes to mere slits, he saw Glynneth talking to a plump attractive woman in the colorful Dutch garb. A young boy stood at the woman's side. "You must not apologize that you failed to send us word that Gerd would not begin his lessons today. I, of course, understand. But please, let me send Gerd home, and I will stay and help you. I have dealt with these fevers in the past. You must make sure your husband keeps liquids in him. And nourishment. He should have mulled cider, and I could make him a switzel tonic. I need but honey, cider vinegar, and water for that. A mustard plaster for his chest would also be good. As would an onion poultice. Best would be a feverwort tincture if the apothecary has some of the dried herb. I failed to take the time to go to the country to gather some this fall. The local natives taught us about the feverwort herb. It has many uses, but it is best used to help lung congestion."

Adler rose from the cot with the woman's last words. "If this fever-wort will help, I will go now to the apothecary."

"Oh, Adler, I meant not to wake you," said Glynneth.

"Nay, I am glad I heard you talking. Will this herb help with Etienne's congestion, we must have it," he said, pulling on his boots.

Latty came from Etienne's room. "What is all the bustle?"

"I go to the apothecary," Adler said. "Mevrouw …?" He paused and looked at Glynneth.

"Excuse me," Glynneth said with a nervous flutter and a shake of her head. "Where are my manners? Mevr. Kerstan, let me present Adler Hayward and Latimer Draye." She nodded first to Adler then to Latty. "And this is Mevr. Kerstan and her son, Gerhard. Gerhard was to start lessons with me today, but of course now his lessons will have to wait."

"Mevr. Kerstan has said an herb called feverwort can help with congestion," Adler told Latty. "I go now to get some."

"I could go," Latty offered.

"Nay, I am stiff, the walk will do me good," Adler answered, heading for the door.

Mevr. Kerstan stopped him. "As you go to the apothecary, may Gerd walk with you. I would feel better if he had an escort. And you could bring back some of my cider vinegar. My servant girl will know where it is."

"I will do as you ask." Adler looked down at Gerhard and said, "Let us go, boy."

The air was cold, but the threat of snow had disappeared and the sun shone brightly. Adler welcomed the fresh air. He hated being cooped up inside. This errand was a blessing, as was Mevr. Kerstan. No doubt she had better skills than he did for dealing with Etienne's illness. He could not help but be relieved to have Etienne's treatment rest on someone else's shoulders.

"Lead on," he told the boy, matching his steps to the boy's shorter stride.

"I hope Monsieur Fortier will soon be well," Gerhard said. "My father was very pleased I was to take lessons from him and Madame Fortier. He says he wants more for me than he will ever be." He slowed his pace and looked up at Adler. "I am not sure what it is he wants for me. I think my father is a fine man. He is the best boat builder in New Amsterdam. Everyone says so."

"Do they now. Well then, do I ever need a boat, I will remember his name. Kerstan, correct?" he asked smiling down at the boy.

Gerhard looked up again, his large blue eyes clear and honest. "Bonifacius Kerstan," he said. "His shop is behind our house if you would wish to meet him."

"Perhaps another time. Now I must get the cider and hurry on to the apothecary."

"Oh, yes, the feverwort. Mother made my sister the tincture last year when she had the croup. She was soon well. I hope it will work as well for Monsieur Fortier."

"I do, too," Adler said. "I do, too." Please, God, let it work he prayed. Etienne must live, he must. Not just for himself, but for Glynneth.

"There is my house," Gerhard said. "I will tell Mina to get you the cider," he added, hurrying ahead and calling, "Mina, Mina," as soon as he opened the door.

Adler followed after Gerhard who left the door to his home open. It was a neat, yellow-brick, two-story home with black shutters and the typical stepped stoop that the Dutch loved. Stopping at the threshold, Adler peered into the semi-dark interior. A fire burned in the hall hearth, and a young girl he thought to be around sixteen was stirring a large cauldron. Pushing a fly-away strand of golden blond hair off her forehead, she looked up from the pot when Gerhard told her he needed the cider for Meneer Hayward.

Before the girl could answer, a male voice said, "Gerd, why are you home? And why have you left the door open?"

Surprised by the voice, Adler, blinked his eyes. Not yet accustomed to the dark room after the bright outdoors, he had not observed the man concealed in the shadows until he spoke and rose from a low, three-legged stool. Gerhard had apparently not seen him either for he looked startled before saying, "Ah, Father, I thought you in your shop."

"I came in to comfort your sister. The rooster spurred her. He will not do that again. He will be dinner tonight. Even now Mina scalds him to remove his feathers." He looked down at a little girl Adler had not noticed. "No more tears, Skyla. Be a big girl." He turned back to

Gerhard. "Now, you, Gerd, again, why are you home, and where is your mother?"

The boy pointed to Adler, and his father, shielding his eyes against the bright sunlight coming in the door, saw Adler. "Meneer Hayward is here to get Mother's cider for Monsieur Fortier. He is ill and Mother stays there to help Madame Fortier. I will have no lessons until Monsieur Fortier is well."

Kerstan stepped toward the door, his hand outstretched and welcoming. "Come inside Meneer Hayward. Warm yourself by the fire while Mina fetches the cider. I am Bonifacius Kerstan. Tell me, is Monsieur Fortier very ill?"

Adler entered the room, happy to accept Kerstan's open hospitality. He noted the cleanliness of the room. A green cloth covered the table and four well-made chairs were drawn up to it. The floor appeared to have been scrubbed, and neat cupboards held red clay dishes and dried food items. "I fear Monsieur Fortier is yet very ill," he said, bringing his attention back to Kerstan, "but I hope your wife can help him. She sends me for feverwort."

"Ah, the feverwort," Kerstan said, nodding. "It is good for many ailments, especially the fever. Monsieur Fortier has the fever?"

Rubbing his chilled hands by the fire, Adler looked over his shoulder at Kerstan. The man had certainly marked his son. Both man and boy had large, round blue eyes, golden blond hair, and strong firm chins. "Aye," he said, "he has the fever. It was bad last night, but he is some better today. He was sleeping when I left."

"That is good," Kerstan answered thoughtfully. "You will let me know if I can do more," he added as Mina handed Adler a jug of cider.

Adler thanked the girl, thanked Kerstan, and hurried on to the apothecary's shop. He was eager to get back to Etienne, to Glynneth.

Chapter 20

Glynneth brushed her husband's thick dark hair off his brow. No fever. For the first time in a week, his brow was cool. His dark eyes were again clear and cognizant. "My dear husband, what a trial you have been," she teased with a smile. "Scaring us as you have done. Certainly a poor way to welcome Adler and Latty back into our home."

He returned her smile. "Have I been such a dreadful boor, my love?"

Kneeling beside the bed, she took his hand in hers and raised it to her cheek. "You will be forgiven, do you promise never to frighten me so again."

A sweet smile still on his lips, his eyes met hers. "I promise I will do my best. But now tell me, are Adler and Latty still with us?"

Rising, she tucked his hand back under the quilts. "Oh, yes, they will be here until the ice on the river thaws. They have been marvelous. Every night they took turns sitting with you that I might get some sleep. During the day, Mevr. Kerstan helped me care for you. She has so much more experience than I. I am not sure how we would have managed without her."

Tilting his head to one side, Etienne said, "Yes, though in and out of muddled sleep, I remember clearly a kind-faced woman often about. You must thank her for me."

"You may thank her yourself. She will be here later today. When your fever broke right before she left last evening, I told her she need not come in this morning." She walked to the foot of his bed. "The children have been worried about you. I have been sending them to your father's, but this morning I let them stay home so they could come in and see for themselves how much better you are. Your father has been wonderful, by the way. He stayed home every day to help care for the children rather than leave them to Jeanette's ministrations. And he saw we had plenty of wood and food. Gaspard called every day before he went to work and then on his way home. Dominique has been a Trojan. Every day she has washed your sheets and shirts. Fortunately, though cold, the days have been bright and sunny, so everything dried quickly. It being so cold out, her hands are raw and cracked, poor dear, so Latty and Adler started helping her ring out the sheets and hang them to dry."

"It seems I truly have been a strain on everyone," Etienne said with a sigh.

Glynneth hurried back around to the side of the bed to give him a hug. "Oh, dear husband, I told you of all the wonderful things our friends and family have done for us so you would know how much you are loved. I meant not to make you feel you were a travail for that is not the case. That you have survived and will now get well is all anyone wants."

She kissed him. "Now, let me bring in Meara and Noel. They have been waiting so patiently for you to awaken. After you have seen them, your father is also here."

He smiled. "Thank you, my dear love. Do send in the children."

Nodding, Glynneth went to the door. She hesitated for a moment, then squaring her shoulders and lifting her chin, she opened the door. Her husband was going to live.

❧ ❧ ❧ ❧

Jeanette whirled around the parlor, her arms outstretched. Except for the servants and her baby, she had the house to herself. It was wonderful. No noisy, fussing children. Had her father-in-law not decided to stay home every day, she would have had Meara and Noel behaving properly, or despite the cold, they would have found themselves locked in the woodshed. But Curtice spoiled them, coddled them. Worst, he insisted Lothair be allowed to play with them. Her precious baby, exposed to their hoydenishness. She wrinkled her nose. How Lothair had laughed his little, tinkling chuckle at his cousins' silly antics. His little laugh that delighted her, warmed her heart, and was meant for her, not Glynneth's miscreants.

She had thought Etienne would die. In his weakened condition, he should have died, but early in the morning, Latimer Draye arrived with news Etienne's fever had broken, he was sleeping peacefully, and the children would be staying home. She was pleased not to have the children again, but disappointed Etienne had survived the ague. Not that she had anything against Etienne. He was a kind man, but if he died, surely Glynneth would return to Ireland. Jeanette knew Glynneth missed her home and family. With Glynneth and her children gone, Jeanette believed she and Lothair would become Curtice's beloved ones. And Gaspard would no longer look with longing eyes at Glynneth. He would come to appreciate the wife who adored him.

❊ ❊ ❊ ❊

Eyeing the woman asleep beside him, Latimer frowned. She had satisfied a carnal lust, but nothing more. She was the tavern keeper's hefty wife and was known to offer herself to anyone with the coin to buy her wares. Her husband knew of her dalliances. For all Latimer knew, approved of them – it meant an extra income, and the man was known to be penny-pinching. She was the first white woman Latimer had bedded since coming to New Netherland. A scarcity of women in the colony meant few women remained unmarried once they came of age or were widowed. The prostitutes he encountered had all been Indian women. Most were far more appealing than the plump, pasty-skinned woman, gape-mouthed and snoring, on the prickly cornhusk mattress they shared.

She had ooed and awed over his physique when leading him up to the bedchamber, had rubbed her ponderous breast up and down against his arm, and had reached down with her beefy hand to cup his crotch and cackle. "Ho, not yet ready? Never fear," she said pushing open the door to the ramshackle chamber. "Mahault knows what to do." Dingy curtains on a small window allowed the only light into the room which held naught but a bed and a wash stand with a chipped bowl on it.

When he extracted his sheath and donned it, she again cackled. "Now what would that be that you have tied so prettily on your manhood." Having never seen a protective sheath before, she was at first intrigued, then wary. "Take it off," she demanded. "You have no need for it. I have not the pox." But when he started to draw up his breeches, and she saw she would not be getting the promised coin, she relented, and pulling up her skirt and whipping her breasts out from her low cut shift, she proclaimed she was ready for him.

He quickly found his release, but to his surprise his partner, finding her pleasure at the same time, wrapped her meaty arms about him and pressed him fast to her voluminous breasts. When she stopped shuddering and loosened her hold, he hastily rolled away from her.

"That was most pleasant," she said, her eyes slits in her pudgy face. "I will have that coin, though." She held out her hand, and he dropped a Spanish reales into it. Biting the coin, she smiled. "Now we have a little nap, huh? Maybe we will have another go at it when we awake."

Latimer had no desire for another coupling with Mevrouw Smedt. With her contentedly snoring, he quietly rose, dragged up his breeches, donned his shoes, and slunk out the door. He wondered that Adler never seemed to have the need to copulate with a woman. Of course, Adler could be using his hand. Latimer often resorted to self-manipulation himself, but after a while, the hand could not take the place of a woman.

Adler, like him, was in love with Glynneth. It would seem Adler's love was so intense, he could remain celibate. In a way, Latimer envied Adler his deep devotion. Coupling with Mevr. Smedt had been a disgusting experience and enough to turn a man in a priestly direction. Her vulgarity, her stain splattered clothing, and her unwashed smell – he could see the dirt in the folds of her skin – did little to stimulate passion. Still, was he feeling the need, and she was the only option, he would again avail himself of her favors – that he knew, as depraved as it seemed.

He would far prefer a tryst with Dominique, but the woman made it plain she would not be granting him her favors. She would laugh and joke with him, and she appreciated his help with various household chores, but she never gave him the least indication or encouragement that she might enjoy intimate relations with him. He supposed it was for the best. A relationship with the Fortiers' slave could get complicated. He would not want anything to come between him and his dear friends. They and Adler were his family.

A dearer family than the one he left behind in England. The only members of his family that he could say he ever cared for were his sister and his father's younger brother who had died the summer of 1645 at Naseby fighting for his King who suffered a crushing defeat by the Parliamentarians.

Latimer's father had not even been saddened. "Bond was ever a fool," his father declared. "Always hoping for quick riches. Never settling down to steady employment."

"Not settling down to drudgery, you mean," Latimer stated and received a box to his ear for his effrontery. Latimer remembered well the day his happy, carefree Uncle Bond had marched off to join the Royalists forces. When he left, never to return, life at Drayehurst grew more bleak with each passing year. His uncle had been Latimer's friend, his confidant, his advisor. Shortly after Latimer's twelfth birthday, his uncle had introduced him to his first seductress. A woman, he assured Latimer, who would teach him ways to pleasure himself as well as his partner.

He also gave Latimer his first sheath. "Wear this, and you will have less chance of contracting the French pox. But do you ever get the pox, take the cure early. A little mercury ointment on the first chancre you find in your nether region, and you will soon be back to normal. At least so I am told, but I think 'tis best do you avoid the pox from the get-go. Never hurts to examine the woman before you have relations. Never be so lost to desire that you have not the time for a quick peek." Latimer's uncle cocked his head and smiled. "I have known me fair share o' the ladies for many a year now and ne'er had cause to regret my trifling."

Since his first unparalleled sexual experience, Latimer had been ever ready for a quick tumble or, did time allow, a night of vigorous passion. He enjoyed women. He liked to tease and flirt, and make women smile and feel good about themselves. Women were kinder and more caring and certainly more beautiful than men. To him, a woman's body was more beautiful than any mountain, or sunset, or satin raiment. In his eyes, of all God's creatures, women came the closest to perfection. And Glynneth topped the list.

Thankful Etienne seemed on the mend, Latimer considered his frolic with Mevr. Smedt his way of celebrating. A week of close contact with Glynneth and her pretty slave had him more than a little ruttish. Feeling rejuvenated despite the baseness of the sexual encounter, Latimer left the tavern and sauntered down toward the wharfs. He knew Gaspard would be busy off-loading the long awaited furniture, and he thought he might be of some service. He liked Gaspard. The two of them had worked closely together whenever the Fortier goods had been transferred on or off the ships that took them to Rotterdam and then to New Amsterdam. A sort of bond had evolved between them. Renewing that friendship would be a good way to spend the remainder of this bright, sunny, wind free day.

Adler looked around Bonifacius Kerstan's boat building shop. He was impressed. The brick building, though not large, was surprisingly neat. A nearly completed boat was up on a cradle, and two lanterns hanging above it afforded light for Kerstan's work. To one side of the room a fire in a large hearth blazed offering warmth as the large double doors were open to let in the day's rays. To the other side of the room was a sturdy work bench with an orderly arrangement of tools. The man had a remarkable number of tools. "They were my father's and his father's before him," Kerstan stated when Adler commented on them. "For as long as anyone can remember, the Kerstans have been boat builders," he added, his round blue eyes full of pride.

"After so many years in your trade, what made you decide to move here? Am I not impertinent for asking," Adler said.

Kerstan frowned. "A property dispute. We had a fire. It burned down much of the house. My father borrowed to rebuild, but he died before the debt was repaid. The goldsmith who loaned him the money, wanted the property more than he wanted the debt repaid." He snorted. "The miser said the deal he made was with my father, not me. He said my youth made me a poor risk. I had not the boat building skills of my father. He said he wanted the loan repaid immediately or he wanted the house. I could not pay him, but I was determined he would not get my father's house. So I sold it, paid off the loan, to the wrath of the goldsmith, and we came here to New Netherland to start our lives anew."

"Ah," Adler said, nodding. "Goldsmiths. I suppose some must have hearts, but I have been told most have naught but lead where the heart should be. Fortunately, I never had dealings with any goldsmiths. Never needed any loans, so I cannot say.

"But I have another question for you. You are proud of your work and your heritage, and I know your son is proud of you. It does seem strange to me that your son will not be carrying on your trade. Certainly there is a need for boat builders here."

Kerstan did not answer immediately. He busied himself applying hot tar pitch to the oakum calking he had packed into the seams between the planks of the boat. Adler decided he had been too forward and regretted his question. He was trying to think of a new subject to switch to when Kerstan straightened from his work and said, "My wife and I decided we want more for our son and daughter and any other children we may have." He held out his hands. "You see my fingers – blackened with pitch, black under the nails that no amount of scrubbing removes, swollen knuckles, callouses so rough they hurt my wife when I touch her."

He shook his head. "This is not for Gerd. I have an apprentice. Dirk Cuyler. He has worked with me for two years now. A bright, eager youth. Better had he started with me when he was younger, but he learns fast. Even now, I trust him to bring back the wood I specified and not let Devoss, the lumberman, foist any shoddy oak off on him." He smiled. "Am I not mistaken, I think Dirk and our servant girl, Mina, who is more family than servant, will make a match when they come of age. Mina, poor little one, lost her parents on the voyage over. We took her in and have promised her a dowry when she chooses to wed."

"You and your wife are good people," Adler said. "Etienne might not now be alive and recovering if not for your wife's generous help."

"She was glad she could be of help," Kerstan said, turning to again apply the pitch to his boat. "She has developed a fondness for Madame Fortier and expects their friendship to continue as Gerd begins his lessons."

"That would be good for Madame Fortier. She has missed Madame Chappell since she went with her husband to Fort Orange. Though they may be returning after the summer. Armand says he and his father are not both needed at the fort, and he wants to personally supervise the transport of the furs downriver and the trade goods up. Their inventory has had some discrepancies on both ends. And too, Guyon, Armand's older son, will be ready to start his lessons. No doubt Armand will want Etienne to prescribe his study course."

Kerstan chuckled. "Monsieur Fortier will soon be so busy with students, he will have no time to continue his work at the warehouse."

Nodding, Adler agreed. He thanked God Etienne was on the mend and would be able to design lessons for his young students.

Deciding he was keeping Kerstan from his work, Adler ended his visit. "Thank you for your time Meneer Kerstan. I was intrigued by your young son's description of your shop and wanted to see it. I am sorry if I intruded on your work."

"I am pleased you stopped by, Meneer Hayward. Come again anytime. The occasional interlude is always welcome. Do give my regards to Monsieur Fortier."

"I will do that," Adler said with a wave of his hand. As he strode through the Kerstans' courtyard out to the street, a plan was beginning to form. Latty had asked him what he meant to do with his life. What would his future entail? Latty meant to invest in land – as much of it as he could. Adler was thinking he might invest in a business. Perhaps a boat building business. He would have months wandering down narrow forest trails to formulate his ideas.

He had had enough of the wilds. He wanted to return to civilization. Well, to the white man's civilization. He could not call the Indians he had grown to know uncivilized. They were excellent farmers, they were good to their children and to the old and orphaned. Their leaders were elected not determined by birth. They had no royalty. Yes, their brand of civilization had much to be admired. Yet, it was not the manner in which he wanted to live.

And yes, he had to admit it. He wanted to be near Glynneth. To see her, to hear her voice, her laughter. To watch her with her children. To feel the occasional touch of her hand. He wanted to be handy should she need him. What if he had not been there the night Etienne came down with that intense fever. Etienne might have died. No, this could well be the last year he would traipse off into the woods. Jacques Chappell

154

would not be happy when he informed him of his future plans. Chappell considered him and Latty his best agents, especially as Adler was a blood brother to Kills Many. That relationship had assured them of a welcome at any Iroquois village no matter how far afield they traveled.

Adler realized he would also have to bid a final farewell to Kills Many. Despite their different cultures, he had found they had much in common. An abiding concern for those they loved, a respect for honesty and loyalty, a deep interest in learning new things, and a love of laughter. They both enjoyed a good joke and looked for the humor in everyday occurrences. Because of these shared values, Adler knew Kills Many would understand the need he had to be near the one he loved. Funny that Kills Many was the only one he had told of his love for Glynneth. He doubted he would have told his own brother. Kills Many understood Adler's love for another man's wife. But Adler knew his own culture would condemn him, no matter how chaste that love might be. Strange world, he thought.

Chapter 21

Saying good-bye to Adler and Latty was harder this time than any other time, Glynneth thought. Standing at the wharf, her cloak tight about her throat to keep the chill March wind at bay, she waved until her arm ached as her two friends disappeared behind the billowing sails of the serviceable little flute that sailed away up the river. The two had been such a tremendous help, she wondered how she would now manage without them. Etienne had been a long time recovering from the ague, and had been confined first to his bed, then to the house. His father had refused to allow him to resume work until his strength returned. Adler and Latty had born him company, kept him entertained. They had undertaken some of Gaspard's duties at the warehouses while Gaspard assumed Etienne's work with the accounts and invoices. They had continued to help Dominique with various burdensome chores, and had amused and diverted the children with games and stories. And they had done all these kind offices with cheerful zeal. But too soon, the ice on the river melted, and they were again off to the wilds.

Once Etienne felt well enough to leave his bed, he resumed Ignace's lessons and began a program for Gerhard Kerstan. Mevr. Kerstan, Hendrika – Glynneth was now on a first name basis with the cheery Dutch woman – continued to check in on Etienne each day when she walked her son to the house. She and Glynneth would then sit and have a tisane and talk quietly while the boys did their lessons. Knowing she had not the knowledge or experience to treat life threatening illnesses, Glynneth was ever so grateful to Hendrika for her help with Etienne. Glynneth's life had been too sheltered, still was. There had always been servants to take care of everything. Her childhood nurse had been the one to care for any illnesses.

Thankfully Adler had known what to do for Etienne's raging fever. She had no doubt he had saved her husband's life. When she profusely thanked him, he had blushed, told her he but did what he could, and changed the subject. Backing away from her, he avoided the touch of her hand on his arm. He swallowed hard, and his hand went involuntarily to the spot where her hand had briefly rested. She knew how he felt. She felt the same tingle of excitement, the same passionate thrill that came anytime they touched. Despite the fact they both loved Etienne, she had to acknowledge there was a magnetic attraction between them. As he had done at Fort Orange, Adler never allowed himself the opportunity to be alone with her. She wondered what would have happened if he had.

"Should we go home now, Mother," Meara broke in on Glynneth's thoughts. "I am cold and so are Noel, and Lady Ann."

Lady Ann was the children's new dog. Adler had come home with the little yellow puppy tucked into his coat pocket. "Paid but three stuivers for her," he said in a whisper so the children who were playing with a whirligig Latty had made them would not hear him or see the dog. "She was the last of the litter," he continued, "but the old woman selling the pups said if you should not want a dog, she had another possible buyer."

How dear Adler had looked. She could see the hope in his eyes. Had he done something good, or something wrong? She had laughed and said, "By all means, we will keep the puppy. You may present her to the children."

Squeals of delight greeted his gift, but Dominique looked up from the stew she was stirring and said, "Best let me give that dog a bath. Most likely it has the flees. You would not be wanting them on the children or in the house. We work hard enough now to keep things clean."

"Dominique is right, children," Glynneth said, and amidst woeful cries, she handed the little dog over to receive the thorough cleaning she knew Dominique would give it. It short order, the dog became part of the family. It followed Meara everywhere, was ever at her side, and whined inconsolably if Meara left the house without her. Consequently, Lady Ann was at the wharf with Meara to see Adler and Latty off.

Feeling melancholy, Glynneth decided to stop by the bakery on the way home. She would get some ginger bread men to have after their dinner. Mayhap she would get some for Hendrika and her family as well. A visit with her friend might cheer her. At home, Dominique would be busy with her chores, and Ignace would be studying. Despite its small size, the house would seem empty with Etienne again at work and Adler and Latty gone for who knew how long. How much they would be missed.

Adler had taken her hand at parting, looked into her eyes, and at her indrawn breath, seemed to offer her his soul before bidding her take care and stay well. Then with a wrenching sigh, he released her and hurried up the plank to the deck of the ship. From the railing he waved to them as did Latty. They were sailing up river with numerous trade items; blankets, iron and copper pots and skillets, steal knives and hatchets, linen and woolen fabric and thread, colorful beads and ribbons, sugar, pepper and various spices, gunpowder and guns, and a variety of other goods Curtice had imported for trade with the Indians.

Curtice and Gaspard had also been there to see them off, but Curtice had forbidden Etienne to go to the wharf on this bright, but windy morning. Etienne had made his farewell at the office. He again thanked Adler and Latty for all they had done to care for him while he was ill and for all they had done to help his family. They in turn thanked him for again sharing his home with them. "Careful of that cough," Latty said. "Be sure to try the brandy I suggested."

Etienne had regained much of his strength, but the persistent cough that had been his companion when they lived in Dublin had returned. He tried to hide it, especially from his father, but Curtice was no fool. He often wore a worried frown when he looked at Etienne. Glynneth understood her father-in-law's fears. She faced the same fears. Etienne had not regained the weight he had lost. The night sweats continued, and sometimes he coughed up blood. That worried her the most. She longed for warmer weather that she might again take him on walks. Cooped up in the smoky house or office could not be good for him, but neither was the cold. He seemed so fragile, yet he wanted to work. He also wanted to teach Ignace and Gerhard. At night after supper, he would plan out lessons in advance and then go over them with her. She now had a year's worth of lessons written out.

One evening as he sat bent over the table, his pen making scratching sounds on the parchment, she laughed and wrapped her arms around him from behind. "Enough my dear husband. Enough. Time for bed.

Put down your pen, close up your ink well. You need not work so late into the night."

He looked up at her and smiled, that smile that warmed her heart. "You are right, my dear. We will go over this tomorrow evening to make sure you understand it. Now we will go to bed. I do say, I am pleased with the progress the boys are making. Both are bright boys."

She laughed. "They are, but they both have hard task masters. I never allow Ignace out for a romp until he has memorized his lesson. Hendrika is the same with Gerd."

Etienne started to say something, but a cough took him, and he grabbed for his kerchief before doubling over. Glynneth's hand rested on his back. How she wished she could help him.

Shaking the memory from her mind, she stopped in front of the bakery. She did love Dutch bakeries. She found their breads and pastries far superior to anything she had eaten in Ireland. Fact was, she was too fond of the pastries. Was she not careful, she would find herself unable to fit into her clothes, and she had not the access to seamstresses that she had had in Dublin. She was in need of a seamstress. The children were outgrowing their clothes. She and Etienne, and Dominique, needed new work clothes and shifts. One of her skirts had so many patches it near looked like a quilt. Jeanette's maid, Lina, could do some sewing, but her skills were limited. Hendrika made most of her own and her families clothes, but Glynneth could not feel right asking her to sew for them, even as payment for Gerhard's lessons. Mayhap her friend would know someone handy with a needle and in need of extra income.

Having made her selections of bread and gingerbread men with help from Meara and Noel, Glynneth set out for the Kerstans.

❅ ❅ ❅ ❅

"Ah, Glynneth! Come in," said Hendrika, welcoming Glynneth and her children into her home. "You have seen off Meneer Hayward and Draye have you not? You must be chilled."

Glynneth nodded, and Meara piped up, "We waved until we could no longer see them." She looked down at her dog. "Lady Ann will miss them, and so will I."

"No doubt you will," Hendrika answered with a smile. "But perhaps some warm milk with some fresh baked cookies will help console you, huh?"

"Oh," said Glynneth, "we brought you some gingerbread men."

"How kind," said Hendrika. "I will put them on a plate with the cookies. I will get the children the warm milk and warm some cider for us." She turned to her serving girl. "Mina, tell Gerd he may take a break from his lessons and have some cookies."

Glynneth liked Hendrika's cookies. In Ireland they called the little crunchy cakes biscuits, but they were not nearly as good as Hendrika's. Noel settled down to play with Skyla, and Meara greeted Gerhard when he scurried downstairs to enjoy an unexpected break from his studies. Once the children had their treats, Hendrika sat down beside Glynneth to enjoy a chat along with their mugs of warm cider. Mina joined them when Glynneth encouraged her saying, "Come, Mina, sit with us and bring your bright smile to help cheer me."

Mina giggled. "I have much to smile about today, Madame Fortier. Might I tell her Mevr. Kerstan?"

Hendrika smiled. "I see no reason why you should not."

Her face wreathed in a smile, her blue eyes dancing, Mina said, "Yesterday was my eighteenth birthday, and Dirk proposed to me. We are now betrothed. We plan to be married in June. You will of course be invited to the celebration."

"Oh, Mina, I am so happy for you. Your Meneer Cuyler seems a fine young man."

"He is," said Hendrika. "One more year with my husband, and he should qualify as a journeyman. Of course we hope both he and Mina will continue on in our employ."

"Indeed we plan to," said Mina. She turned back to Glynneth. "The Kerstans have said they will enlarge Dirk's room behind the boat shed so we can have our own private home."

"How grand," said Glynneth. "Your news has certainly cheered my day. Now all I need to completely cheer me is to learn of a tailor and a seamstress. My family will soon be in rags if we cannot find someone to clothe us."

Chuckling, Hendrika said, "Easily done. A month ago a Jacob Hey-

160

den arrived here. I understand he is a competent tailor. As to a seamstress, a friend of mine could use some added income. Her husband injured himself chopping wood and has been bedridden for a month. She does fine work. I think you will find her satisfactory. If you like, I could take you to meet her tomorrow. As to the tailor, I have no knowledge of his shop or residence, but no doubt your father-in-law can make inquiries."

"Hendrika, you are a blessing. How very glad I am to have you for my friend. Yes, please, let us go meet your friend tomorrow. And I will have Father Curtice search out Meneer Jacob Heyden. Now we will not have to go about in rags."

By the time Glynneth left the Kerstans', she was in much better spirits.

※ ※ ※ ※

Despite the harsh wind, Adler stood at the bow of the ship. He was chilled, but the cold was preferable to being below in the cramped quarters. He had told Latty he hoped to make this his last trade expedition. He meant to make this trip as profitable as possible, even if they had to be gone longer than previous outings, mayhap for as long as a year. He would miss seeing Glynneth and her family, but he needed to make enough to invest in a business. Once settled in New Amsterdam, he would have daily opportunities to see the Fortiers.

He felt more at ease about leaving Glynneth since she had developed a close friendship with Mevr. Kerstan. The competent Dutch woman had promised she would continue to keep an eye on Etienne. Adler did not like the way his friend looked. Etienne's bout with the ague seemed to have severely weakened him. Too often Adler had seen him double over in a coughing fit. He knew those signs too well.

His thoughts went back to his grandmother – her last days, confined to her bed, coughing up blood into a low pan. But she had been old. His sister had been but five when she succumbed to the dreaded consumption. Etienne's condition had improved so greatly since he had first met him aboard the ship bound from Dublin to Rotterdam that Adler believed Etienne might have licked the fatal disease, but now he was not feeling so confident about his friend's condition. Warmer weather would soon be arriving. That should help. Could Etienne but gain a little weight to help him ward off any other afflictions, mayhap he could again begin to recover.

Adler could not let himself think of what it would mean if Etienne should die. Etienne was his friend, and he cared deeply for him. More importantly, Glynneth loved Etienne, and Adler could never want her to suffer, not ever, not in anyway. Her heart would not only ache for the loss of her husband, but it would ache for her children who would be pained by the death of their father. No, dear God in Heaven he prayed, please let Etienne live.

❉ ❉ ❉ ❉

Snuggled down on a hard bunk in the Captain's cabin, Latimer pitied Adler up in the cold wind. His friend's fear of tight places was a mystery to him. Adler never seemed to want to talk about it. Latimer was glad he had no such primal fears. Truth was, the only two times he had ever been truly frightened was at the battle at Worcester, and when he and Adler arrived at Bold Crow's village to discover the Mohawks were set to torture and kill them.

Both times, he had known death could be imminent. Both times he survived. But what must it be like to know for months or even years that death was ever hovering, ready to take you away from those you loved and who loved you? That was what Etienne had faced for any number of years, but now, Latimer feared, death was getting ready to take his brave friend. Never had he heard Etienne complain of the fate he had been dealt. Never had Etienne gone about with a woe is me face. His humor and cheerfulness had ever been present. He welcomed into his home two men he had to know were in love with his wife. Yet Etienne had not cursed or reviled him or Adler. He offered them his friendship and placed his trust in their integrity and his wife's faithfulness and love for him. Etienne was a man to be admired.

Latimer would not be surprised if, when he and Adler next returned to New Amsterdam, they found Etienne was no longer with them. What that would mean to him or to Adler, he could not say. Glynneth would be a widow. A wealthy widow. Yet, could he win her love, Latimer could care less if she had naught a penny.

He glanced up at the lantern swinging from the ceiling, casting its dim glow about the cabin. He loved Glynneth, mayhap too much to marry her. He did not believe he would make her a good husband. He was nothing like Etienne. He had none of the same interests. His education, though not insubstantial, was limited in scope. It had only needed to be substantive enough for him to act as steward to the Drayehurst Barony which had once been his ancestral home, but since the time of Henry VII had been in the hands of the upstart Channings.

At age ten his father had sent him to Eton grammar school, then at sixteen he was sent to Oxford University where he met his sister Edythe's future husband, Hollis Burnham. The younger son of a wealthy yeoman, Hollis was landless, but his father was settling a tidy sum on him. In June of fifty-one, Hollis and Latimer's sister were married, and in August, Latimer, at the age of twenty-two, set off to join the King's army. Hollis could be the Channings' steward. Latimer knew he was destined for greater things. He would fight beside his King and be rewarded with a large land grant. He would no longer be subservient to anyone but the King.

Greater things. He chuckled. Look at him now – wearing leather breeches and a course linsey-woolsey shirt under a fringed leather jerkin with his flop-brimmed hat tossed on the table. Well, his day was yet to come. He would have his land. And here in New Netherland, he would not be subservient to any King. After this expedition, he would have enough money to purchase his first tract of land. Then nothing would stop him. No, not even his love for Glynneth.

He wondered if Adler would attempt to win Glynneth's hand. Adler would make her a good husband. Though his education had been minimal, he was quick to learn, and he had gobbled up everything Etienne taught him. Adler and Etienne shared many interest as well, from their love of myths and fables to their enjoyment of chess to their interest in history and relics of the past. Yes, Latimer had to admit, Adler would make Glynneth a far better husband than he would. And did Glynneth decide she wanted to return to Ireland, Adler, despite his fear of imprisonment was it discovered he had fought for the King – he would accompany her.

Latimer knew for himself, no matter what, he was never leaving New Netherland. His fate was here in this new world. Closing his eyes, he sighed and wondered how long before they would return to New Amsterdam.

Chapter 22

Glynneth sat beside her husband and held his limp hand. Tears streaked down her cheeks but she did not bother to brush them away. Etienne was dying. She knew it. He knew it. His father and brother knew it. So pale, so pale, his face had no color. He had coughed up so much blood in the past fortnight since he had been forced to return to his bed. He had no strength left to eat and barely enough to even take the little sips of cider she offered him.

The spring weather had finally arrived, flowers were blooming, trees were blossoming, the world was again magical, but Etienne would not see it. When his coughing was not racking his tired body, he mostly slept, his breathing ragged and breathy. For the past year, she had watched her husband's health slowly worsen. When they first arrived in New Amsterdam in late January of 1652, Etienne's health had improved. The clean air, the mild winter then a glorious spring left him more invigorated than he had been since the consumption first attacked him. Threat of the summer ague had chased them up the North River to Fort Orange. They had both enjoyed seeing the wilderness along the banks of the river. How different from anything they had experienced was this great new land.

The following autumn, Etienne continued to do well. He helped his father at his office and warehouses. But the bitter winter had been too much for him. Keeping the house warm for the children meant more smoke inside, and it had been too cold for Etienne to spend time outdoors. The ague had attacked him that January of fifty-three. She would have lost him then if not for Adler. Thanks to Adler and Hendrika, Etienne had survived – but in such a weakened state. He never fully recovered. Though they had enjoyed another summer in Beverwyck, by the time winter again descended upon them, they all knew they were losing him.

Glynneth was grateful Hendrika was keeping the children. Curtice had wanted them to stay with him, but she had convinced him that Jeanette had enough to do to care for Lothair. "She should not have to mind my little ones as well. Noel can play with Skyla, and Ignace and Gerd can study together and can help Meara with her reading lessons. And Hendrika will bake cookies for them. Please trust me, they will be happier with her."

Curtice must have realized Jeanette would not make a good mother substitute for he acquiesced to Glynneth's wishes. Hendrika brought Meara and Noel once a day to see their father. Glynneth would wake Etienne, and he would smile at his children, and promise them he would soon get well, but this time, they too seemed to know his illness was different. Neither child had any experience with death, discounting the numerous flies or mosquitoes, wasps or ants they swatted. They had never even seen the slaughter of animals that a child on a farm would have experienced. What she would say to them when the time came, she had not yet decided.

"My dear wife, how far away are your thoughts."

Glynneth jumped at the sound of her husband's soft but raspy voice. "Oh, Etienne, I thought you sleeping."

He smiled a weak smile. "I was. But I awoke to see your lovely face looking so peaceful. You looked as though you gazed into the heavens."

She bent and kissed his cheek. "Oh, my love, I wish I could see into the heavens. If I could, I would not have to be parted from you."

He smiled again. "Someday we will again be together, but now you must think of what future awaits you here on earth. You and the children. The children will need a father, and you, my dear one, you must have a husband."

She shook her head. "I cannot think in that direction, Etienne. Mayhap someday, but my thoughts rebel at the idea."

"You must think in that direction, Glynneth. In this new land, you need a helpmate. Yes, you might think to return to Ireland, but I would hate for you to take the children away from Father. They mean so much to him." He stopped talking as a cough shook his fragile frame.

Glynneth dabbed the blood from his lips, and he smiled weakly. Tears sprang to her eyes, and she whispered, "We will talk later. When you are stronger."

Etienne moved his head from side to side on his pillow, and drawing in a harsh breath, he said, "We must talk now. Even do you decide to go back to your family, even in Ireland, you will be happier with someone to love and to love you."

He paused and seemed to be summoning up strength to continue. Again he drew in a ragged breath then said, "Consider Adler, my dear one."

Glynneth looked at him in surprise. What did he know? Had he recognized the attraction she and Adler had for one another? They had done nothing improper, but the pull had been there.

She wondered what her face showed for he chuckled – then coughed, and she held the pan for him. More blood. Exhausted, eyes closed, he lay back against his pillows. She thought he had drifted into sleep, but in a moment, he spoke again. "Adler is a good man. And he loves you." He opened his eyes and looked up at her. "How could any man not love you."

Her heart pounding in her throat, she swallowed and tried to speak, but could think of nothing to say. She saw no accusations in his eyes. She saw nothing but his love for her.

He closed his eyes again, but added, "I will say no more except, you could look far and not find a more gentle and caring man for a husband." He heaved a sigh. "Now, I would rest."

She sat beside him listening to his shallow breathing and pondering his words. Would Adler make her a good husband? Did she wish to marry again? And if so, how long before she could contemplate taking any man other than Etienne to her bed? She wondered where Adler and Latty might be. They had been gone for over a year; had not returned to Fort Orange the previous summer when she took Etienne and the children north to escape the summer ague that plagued New Amsterdam. Even Jacques Chappell could not tell her exactly where they were – only that they were somewhere to the west and that their trade mission was most successful. The Mohawks were bringing in a continual supply of furs and skins.

Jacques assured her and Etienne they had no reason to worry about Adler and Latty. "They are now skilled woodsmen. They have good relations with the Mohawks. Rest easy." When winter approached, she had hoped they would return, but she received but a brief letter from them saying they had returned to Fort Orange for more trade samples, and planned to over winter with the Mohawks so they could get an early start come spring. She tried not to worry, but she missed her cheerful friends. Her children missed them, too. So did Etienne.

How long she sat detached, in a dream state, she had no idea. Dominique came and went, exchanged spent candles for new ones, bade her take a cup of cider then a bowl of stew. Curtice and Gaspard came as they did each evening before going home. They had little to say.

"Will he make it through the night?" Gaspard asked her quietly. "He is so pale."

She shook her head. "I know not."

Gaspard swallowed hard and tears welled in his eyes. "Should I stay?"

"I think not. You would but tire yourself, and he now does little but sleep. He has not eaten anything in near a week and has had but little to drink." She looked away from her brother-in-law and then back again. "I think when he sleeps, he is in no pain. I would not awaken him."

"No, no, you must not wake him." He looked over at Curtice. "We will return in the morning. God willing, he will still be with us."

With night, the air grew chilly and Dominique stoked the fire. "Would you have me sit with him awhile, Madame?" she asked.

Glenneth shook her head. "No, you go to bed."

"You will call if you need anything."

"Yes, now go on. You must be tired."

When Dominique left, Glynneth, gripping her hands about her waist, doubled over, the pain in her heart, her throat, her stomach, more than she could bare. A guttural groan was wretched from her throat and bitter bile assaulted her tongue. Why, oh, why? Etienne was such a good man. Why must his God take him? She was meant to end her days with him at her side. What a cruel fate they had been dealt.

She knew not how long she sat rocking back and forth, sobbing quietly, but eventually the room again grew chilly. Not bothering to do more than slip out of her shoes and bodice, she crawled into bed beside her husband. Snuggling up close to him, she wondered if this might be

168

the last time she would ever sleep by his side. She wrapped her arms around his slender body and closed her eyes. What would morning bring?

※ ※ ※ ※

Awakened by Lothair's happy chirping, Jeannette took her baby from his crib. Groggily, she put him to her breast, and he hungrily suckled his breakfast. She knew she should begin to wean him – he was a year and eight months, but she loved holding him next to heart, feeling his gentle tug on her breast. He was such a healthy baby, and so cute. Curtice was now paying more attention to him. He jiggled Lothair on his knee and proclaimed him as sturdy as an oak tree.

"Takes after his father," Curtice said. "Bright, too. You did your husband proud, Jeanette."

She beamed at her father-in-law's praise. His praise of her son was well deserved. Lothair was hardy and inquisitive. He was into anything and everything he could reach. She had to watch him constantly to keep him away from the fire. Toddling about on his chubby little legs, he seemed tireless. She but wished he would sleep a tad later.

Looking down at the babe at her breast, in the darkness, she could see naught but a dim shape, but it made her smile. Soon his tummy would be full, and he would go back to sleep until the morning sun awakened him. He would then be ready for another feeding, after that he would want to play, play, play. His little chuckle would warm her heart. How much she loved her son.

Gaspard loved him, too. And he was proud of him. He too beamed when his father praised Lothair. Every night when Gaspard came home from work, his first questions were about Lothair. What had his little mischief maker done this day? She loved watching her husband play with Lothair. She was always a bit frightened when Gaspard would toss the little boy up in the air, but Lothair would laugh with such glee, she could not bring herself to complain.

For the past fortnight, though, Gaspard had been too concerned about Etienne to pay much attention to Lothair. He still gave his son a hug and a kiss before the servant, Lina, put the babe to bed, but Gaspard had no heart to play with Lothair. Jeanette understood Gaspard's feelings. His brother was dying. Still, she hated to watch Lothair's attempts to get his father to play with him only to receive a vague pat to the top of his curly-haired head.

She wondered how much longer Etienne would linger. And how long after he died before Glynneth would take the first ship back to Ireland. How lovely life would be once Glynneth was gone. Gone far, far away. Yes, life would be perfect then. She and Lothair would hold the place they rightfully deserved in her father-in-law's eyes. And Gaspard would come to realize what a beautiful and loving wife he had.

Lothair started to squiggle, and she switched him to her other breast. That satisfied him, and he was soon feeding again. "Such a hungry little bunny you are," she whispered, careful not to awaken her husband. He had tossed and turned much of the night and had only drifted into a heavy slumber shortly after the clock downstairs struck one.

He and his father had come home that evening with the longest faces. Etienne had been sleeping, and Glynneth had not wanted to awaken him. They knew they might never speak to him again. Etienne could dye during the night. Then they would all be in mourning.

She had been priming herself to appear doleful, even grief-stricken, when in reality she would be jubilant. She had been waiting for Etienne's death for years. Well, no one would ever know her inner thoughts. She would give her husband love and sympathy. She would do all she could to console Glynneth – and then to help her pack. She would even suggest she and Gaspard host the obligatory gathering after the funeral. Her readiness to aid in any capacity should impress her husband and her father-in-law.

Smiling, she tucked her sleeping baby back in his crib. Yes, no one would guess her true sentiments. Everyone would think her the most gracious sister-in-law. She snuggled back in beside her husband, and listening to his even breathing, she drifted into sleep.

Chapter 23

Adler fell into line behind Latty. The two of them brought up the tail end of the Mohawk trading party. Kills Many was leading the party far to the west. The Mohawks were going to collect tribute from tribes they had subjugated, and to scout the strength of tribes they had yet to conquer. Adler and Latty were with them on this expedition because they wanted to encourage these tribes to trade with the Dutch rather than the French. Of course, the Mohawks expected to be the middlemen in most of these transactions. Though he admired much about the Mohawks and valued his friendship with Kills Many, Adler knew his friend and the other Mohawks could be ruthless in their conquests. They had become dependent on the goods the Dutch provided, and if it meant they had to go to war to gain access to furs from areas further afield, then so be it.

The party was up before the false dawn. Adler marveled at the Indians' eyesight. How they could stick to the path in the dark amazed him. Only hazy glimpses of figures ahead of him kept him on the trail. The last glittering moonbeams streaking through the foliage provided the only light. Traveling at a trot in single file down the narrow path, the Mohawks, toes pointing inward, moved soundlessly. Adler and Latty, matching their strides to the Mohawks' jog, kept pace, but Adler knew he and Latty were not slipping silently through the forest.

When the sun eventually crept over the horizon, and the forest awakened to shimmering rays of sunlight, Kills Many halted their trek. They would break their fast with water from a stream and the pemmican they carried in leather bags at their waists. Adler was hungry, but he was more interested in getting another tracking lesson from Kills Many. Stuffing down a couple of mouthfuls, he joined his friend.

His eyes alert, his head cocked as if listening, Kills Many squatted beside the stream. "We are now in territory of our sometimes enemies. We must be more cautious," Kills Many said. "The Eries are weakened, but not yet defeated. The Hurons come down from the north and attempt to retake lost territory. We first tried peaceful negotiations with the various tribes. They refused us and continued to barter with the Hurons and the French. Now they barter with us, and they pay us tribute." Smiling, he changed the subject. "You are ready for another lesson, I think."

Adler nodded. "I am amazed by how you seem able to see in the dark. Only now with the sun up can I clearly see the path."

Kills Many chuckled. "You must use all your senses, my brother, not just your eyes. When you track the deer, you have learned to look for his scat, for his prints in the soft earth or leaves, crumpled bushes where he lay, stripped branches where he foraged. These are all things you can see. But you must also listen. The snap of a branch, the rustle of the bushes, the sudden flight of a bird, or the scurry of the rabbit. Any of the sounds can mean your prey is near to hand. Then there are smells, dank earth recently disturbed, a raw wood smell when the barks been stripped off by a rutting buck. Even fear can have a scent if the deer knows it is being stalked."

Rising, Kills Many added, "As to seeing in the dark. It is a sense also. Your body must perceive your surroundings, the movement of the air, the swaying of the branches. It will come to you with time. Now we must go. To linger in one spot would not be good."

He gestured with his arm and immediately his troop fell in line, and they were off. Adler and Latty again brought up the rear. Adler tried to pay attention to the details Kills Many had mentioned. As the troop moved near soundlessly through the woods, he listened for bird calls, paid heed to the slight breeze that tickled the branches of the taller trees, listened for sounds other than the footfalls of his own and Latty's feet. He was concentrating so hard, before he knew it, the sun hung high in the sky. He chuckled to himself. Not being aware of the passing time could not be good. He guessed Kills Many would tell him he should always be aware of the time of day. The sun and the stars, when they could be seen, helped orient the tracker even in the densest of forests.

He was not tired, and he could not imagine the Indians were tired, yet they slowed their pace. The forest seemed so quiet. Was it too quiet?

His skin prickled and the hairs on his arms stood at attention. Something was amiss.

When a shrill cry sounded from behind him, he was not surprised. Other war whoops resounded all around from every direction. They were under attack. Even as he heard the cry, he turned to face his assailant. He saw naught but a blackened face and a raised tomahawk. Catching his foe by both his wrists then tucking into a rolling position, Adler fell backwards with the man, kneeing him in the groin in the process. His opponent yelped, and as they hit the ground, Adler threw him over his head. The impact caused the tomahawk to drop from the Indian's hand, but he still had a knife in his other hand. Adler was first to regain his feet, and he landed a hard, well-aimed kick to his foe's chin. The man was down, most likely his jaw broken. A benefit of boots over soft moccasins, Adler thought, as sensing movement behind him, he turned with raised arm to ward off a second attack. A glancing blow to his head, brought blood, but minimal pain.

Bare-chested, his skin painted in black and red stripes, his new opponent seemed little more than a boy. Adler suspected this could well be the youth's first war experience. It would also be his last. Pulling his knife from its sheath, Adler deftly shoved it into the boy's midsection. A look of surprise crossed his youthful opponent's face before it dissolved into pain. He crumpled at Adler's feet, but Adler had no time to feel remorse, Latty needed help.

His friend had managed to get off one shot when the attack began, but now he was reduced to using his gun as a club. Grabbing up the tomahawk his first opponent had wielded, Adler used it to dispatch one of the men trying to circle behind Latty. The other man turned when his comrade fell, and Latty bludgeoned him with the butt of his musket.

Adler found the close hand to hand combat not so different from the final frantic fighting at Worcester. Less smell of gun powder, but the scent of blood already hung heavy in the air. They were fighting in tight quarters, the trees hindered movement and hid opponents until they sprang from behind them or dropped down out of the dense foliage. Adler had no idea how large a war party they fought nor how long they had been fighting. It might have been moments, it might have been hours. He and Latty stood back to back and managed to kill or maim each assailant who came at them. Adler knew one thing for sure, he would die here in these woods before he would ever surrender. He had seen enough of the Indians' brutal torture. He had no intention of experiencing it firsthand.

Then, as suddenly as it had started, the battle ended. The attackers hoisted or dragged away the bodies of their fallen comrades and disappeared into the forest. Quiet again reigned except for an occasional groan. Wary, Adler and Latty remained back to back. Adler searched the woods, cocked his head to listen. Had they defeated their attackers, or were they regrouping for another assault? Not until Kills Many joined them did he minimally relax his guard.

"You fought well, my brother," Kills Many said. "I think I am glad I had not to fight you when we first met. You are skilled in combat."

"More instinct," Adler answered, his eyes still searching the woods.

"We have lost two braves and we have two lightly wounded and one seriously wounded. You and Laughs A Lot," he referred to Latty by the name the Mohawks had given him, "seem to have minimal wounds." Kills Many eyed the wound on Adler 's head.

Reaching up, Adler touched his head. His fingers came away sticky with his own blood. "Had I not lost my hat at the beginning of the battle, I would not have this wound." He turned to Latty. "You, my friend, seem not to have suffered even a bruise."

Latty laughed. "Thanks to you. Had you not come to my aid when you did, I would not now be standing here. I admit I thought my time had come to an end." He looked at Kills Many. "What now? What do we do? Will they attack again?"

Kills Many frowned. "But for a few Eries, they were Hurons. They now have dead and injured. My hope is they will want to take them back to their home to the north. My concern is that the last Erie village we visited may have set us up. We cannot return there to see to our injured. Nor can we continue to the next village. We cannot trust them either. We must make our way back to the Seneca village we left before entering Erie territory."

His eyes switched to Adler. "We need help from the Seneca. We could be attacked at any point along the way. You, Brother Bear," his name for Adler, "you and Laughs A Lot must go ahead of us and take

174

word to our Seneca brothers. The war chief, Strong Arm, must form a party and come to our aid." He raised his hand when Adler started to protest. "I cannot leave my warriors. We must depend on you. You can do this. You have learned much this past year. We will skirt the Erie village we left yesterday, then once we pick up the trail back to Strong Arm's village, you and Laughs A Lot will strike out ahead of us." He put his hand on Adler's shoulder. "Use all your senses, Brother Bear."

They had not the luxury of taking their dead with them. Adler feared they would be slowed enough by their injured members. They had been but a party of twelve, counting him and Latty, and had been on a peaceful mission. The attack had been unprovoked and a surprise to him. Kills Many had not seemed surprised. But he was alert to so many things. Adler wondered how he could make it back to Seneca territory without his blood brother's guidance.

After hoisting their dead into the trees to keep them from being prey to the forest animals, the party set off, but it was at a much slower pace. The skin on Adler's neck prickled, and his stomach tied itself in knots. Again, he and Latty brought up the rear. Once or twice, Latty looked back at him. His look seemed to ask, 'Are we going to make it this time?' Adler felt determination building in him. Yes, they were going to make it. He was not yet ready to die. Glynneth might have need of him, and he meant to be there for her. But he needed to concentrate on his surroundings, so he pushed Glynneth from his mind. He needed to look, to listen, and to feel, to be aware of everything around him, from bird chirps, to branches cracking. Yes, he would reach that Seneca village. All he had learned in the past two and a half years since becoming a woodsman would help him find his way to safety.

Chapter 24

Her eyes swollen from crying, Glynneth blinked back more tears and hugged her daughter close to her heart. "Oh, my dear little Meara. Cry my sweet child. It will help heal your soul. Remember though, your father is with his beloved God. He looks down on us and prays for us, and mayhap sheds some tears for our sorrow, but he is happy and no longer in pain."

In the two days since she awakened to find her husband had died peacefully in his sleep, Glynneth had known scarcely a moment to herself. She had had no time to reflect on her feelings, the pain that had stabbed her innards when she had touched Etienne's cold, lifeless body and realized she would never again feel his kiss, the gentle touch of his hand, or see his sweet smile or thrill to the sound of his loving voice. He was gone from her, yet people, a multitude of people, were now ever around her.

The bier for Etienne's body was set up in the family room. Gaspard refused to leave his brother. From the moment he arrived to find Etienne had died, he had done all he could to be of assistance. The temperature having warmed, Curtice and Gaspard determined the funeral would need to be on the third day after Etienne's death. They made all the arrangements, and Curtice insisted he would host the after funeral gathering at his house. Jeanette had volunteered to see they had plenty of food, and Gaspard would see to the ale.

So many people had been coming and going, expressing their sympathy. She had had no idea Etienne had known so many people. People who worked at the warehouses, people who had various business dealings with him, the people from the church he and his father and brother attended. Even Director-General Stuyvesant stopped by to pay his respect.

Now all the invited friends and family were waiting for her to tell them she was ready to take Etienne's remains to the cemetery. Well, she was not ready. She wanted to be alone with him one more time. She wanted to tell him again how much she loved him, wanted to place her cheek next to his. How could she give him up? When they first married, they had had such plans. Then had come the consumption. How hard Etienne had fought to live. What joy they had found when this new land gave him new life. At least they had had that first year of hope.

She clutched Meara tighter to her, then released her, and taking her hand, stood. "You and Noel go outside with Grandfather," she said. "I will be with you in but a moment."

Meara obeyed and Glynneth turned to Gaspard. "Please, clear everyone out for a few moments. I would have one last time alone with Etienne."

Gaspard's eyes filled with tears. He nodded and swallowed hard. "Of course," he said, and clearing his throat, he spoke in a loud voice asking the people, including the pall bearers to wait outside. "We will be ready to leave shortly." When everyone exited, he looked at Glynneth, gave her a wan smile, and excused himself.

At last alone with Etienne, Glynneth could scarce bear to pull back the pall. She could have that one last glimpse of him, yet she hesitated. At last, drawing in a deep breath and straightening her shoulders, she lifted the pall. Etienne was barely recognizable. His lively eyes closed forever, his lips bloodless, his face shrunken and an unreal white. Her hand shaking, she reached out and stroked his dark hair. How she had loved to wrap her fingers in his hair and pull his face to hers for a sweet kiss. "Oh, Etienne, what am I to do without you?" she rasped, tears choking her.

Touching his cheek with her palm, she whispered, "My dear, dear love. I so hope you are right about your God, and that you will be happy with him. But how we will miss you here on earth." Bending, she placed her cheek next to his. So cold, so dry but for the moist stain on his cheek left by her tears. "Good-bye, my love."

She straightened, wiped the tears from her eyes, and replaced the pall. She went to the door and opened it. Gaspard turned to her. "I am ready," she said.

He nodded, beckoned to the men who would be the pall bearers, and they slipped past her into the house. She stepped outside. The day was bright and sunny. Birds chirped in the trees. A slight breeze blew in off the river and set a stray strand of her hair to tickling her nose. She brushed it aside and turned to Hendrika. The Dutch woman gave her a hug, then took her hand. Together, following the pall bearers, they set off for the cemetery. Curtice, holding Meara's hand and carrying Noel, fell in behind her. A chapter in her life had ended, she thought. What awaited her, she chose not to contemplate. Such thoughts could wait for the morrow, or longer.

🌿 🌿 🌿 🌿

Adler heard a crack. He cocked his head. The snap of a branch? Mayhap. He motioned Latty to move off the trail into the brush. Quiet, nothing but quiet. No birds chirped. No squirrels chattered. Something moving through the woods frightened them. He waited, scarcely daring to breathe. Then he saw them. They moved silently, but they carried a deer between them, slung over their shoulders, so their pace was slow and the deer antlers brushed against low hanging branches. A branch cracked. The two Indians did not seem particularly wary. They were in their own territory, they had had a successful hunt, and they were returning home with their kill.

For a brief instant, Adler debated whether he and Latty should jump the two hunters. The sight of the deer set his empty stomach to rumbling. In his ears, it sounded like a cannon going off. Could the Indians have heard it. No. They never looked in his direction. To kill the hunters would be foolish. The two could easily have had nothing to do with the raid on Kills Many's trading party. They could be innocent. Yet he dare not reveal himself to them. They could as easily have been part of the raiding party. After all, he and Latty were not that far from the village Kills Many feared may have set them up for the attack that had taken two of their party's lives and had set him and Latty off on the greatest quest of their lives.

Two days it had taken their party to skirt the village that three nights earlier had offered them hospitality and feasting. He and Latty had displayed various goods that could be obtained if they traded with the

Dutch. They had given small token gifts to the chiefs. Now those display trade items lay scattered on the forest floor – unless the raiders returned and claimed them. In hopes of avoiding another attack, Kills Many had led them down deer paths that meandered round and about and at times disappeared only to reappear when they crawled through a thick layer of brush. Two of the injured warriors could walk or hobble, the third had to be carried in a litter. As long as the brave lived, Kills Many would not leave him behind.

Adler knew the man had to be in mortal pain. The bone of his calf protruded through his skin. His left shoulder was dislocated, and his left eye had been stabbed, leaving him with a gaping socket and blood drenched face, yet the brave seldom groaned. Those groans he did emit, he did his best to stifle. Adler had to admire his courage. He doubted he would exhibit such tenacity if so horribly injured.

Kills Many had two of his warriors acting as rear guardsmen. If they saw any signs they were being followed, they would fire a shot. Two other warriors were sent out to find food. Their pemmican had run low and needed to be saved as a last resort if no game could be killed. The first night the warriors returned with two rabbits and an opossum. Kills Many had been forced to risk a small fire to cook their meal. Not much of a meal split between ten people, but better than nothing. Adler had been so hungry, even the opossum without any seasoning tasted good. The next night they dined on raw fish. Kills Many said they were too near the village to risk a fire. Adler had more trouble getting down the raw fish, but hunger, he learned, made many things palatable. The following morning, they reached the main trail back to Seneca territory. That was when he and Latty left the party behind and set out on their own. Other than some berries, that was the last time they had had anything to eat.

Determining the hunters were far enough away he and Latty would not be heard emerging from their hiding place, Adler gave Latty a nod, and they were back on the trail, moving as swiftly and quietly as they could. Barring any unforeseen difficulties, by this time the next day, they should be back in Seneca territory and by nightfall, they should be in Strong Arm's village. The following morning, they would be leading

Strong Arm and his warriors back down the trail to help Kills Many and his party.

❁ ❁ ❁ ❁

Jeanette stood beside her husband and watched as dirt was shoveled into Etienne's grave. As was the practice of the Calvinist followers, few words were said over the dead. They wanted nothing that smacked of the Papist rituals they abhorred. But all attendees stood solemnly by until the grave was filled in.

Glancing out of the corners of her eyes at Glynneth, Jeanette wondered how her sister-in-law felt when the first spades of dirt fell onto Etienne's coffin. The sound of the dirt hitting the wood must surely have caused her pain. For a brief moment, Jeanette could almost feel sorry for Glynneth. She had no doubt Glynneth had loved Etienne deeply, had been devoted to him, but Jeanette could not afford to waste her sympathy on Glynneth. She needed to be rid of Glynneth. Needed her out of her life, and the sooner, the better. She had been shocked to overhear her father-in-law telling Gaspard that he meant to move Glynneth and her children, as well as the half-breed son of the Chappells into their home.

"Glynneth and the children cannot stay in that house alone," Curtice had said. "It is not safe. She needs to be in the company of those who love her and will see to her care."

Gaspard had quickly agreed with his father. Too quickly, to Jeanette's thinking. Her opinion had not been sought. Had it been, she would have assured them Glynneth was too independent. She would prefer to remain in her own home. To uproot her and her children would not be kind. She could not believe Glynneth would want to move into her father-in-law's home, but Curtice could at times be imperious. He might well leave Glynneth no choice.

To Jeanette's thinking, nothing could be more disastrous to her own peace of mind than to have Glynneth and her children in her home. Raising her eyes to heaven she said a silent prayer asking God to make Glynneth strong. Make her resist her father-in-law's pressure to turn her world upside down and inside out.

Chapter 25

Latimer stretched and yawned. How luxuriant it felt to have a full stomach, a thick bed of furs under him, and a soft and cuddly woman beside him. In one week's time, he had gone from fearing his life was at an end to being celebrated as a brave warrior and a hero. Of course, he knew much of his present good fortune, he owed to Adler. Somehow his friend had managed not only to get them safely to Strong Arm's village, he had unerringly led the Seneca warriors back to find Kills Many's party.

Warriors from another Seneca village had been visiting Strong Arm's village and had eagerly joined Strong Arm's war party. Their intent had been first to rescue their Mohawk brethren, then to teach the Eries a lesson. A healer had accompanied the war party, plus they carried food and blankets to aid the injured. Once Kills Many was found, some of the Seneca braves stayed with his party. After the Mohawks had been fed, and the healer had seen to the wounded, the Seneca helped them back to their village. The rest of the war party went on to the Erie village. Latimer and Adler, though invited to join the war party, made an easy decision – they chose to stay with Kills Many and help get him and his warriors to safety.

Having found wounded Hurons in the Erie village, the war party had proof the Erie had been behind the attack on their Mohawk brothers. In revenge for the unprovoked attack, they laid the village waste and returned to their village with a number of captives. Some, particularly the women and children, would be fortunate enough to be adopted into the tribe. Some not so fortunate warriors would be tortured and killed. The hideous torture was to begin after Latimer and Adler were honored and feasted. Kills Many made a long speech telling how bravely his white friends had fought, and how despite their lack of knowledge of the territory, they had brought the Seneca to his party's aid.

Latimer understood that the Indians found the torture of their enemies a form of entertainment, but he could not stomach it. Nor could Adler. They had snuck away when the victims' long night ordeal began. An appealing young squaw had been more than willing to accompany Latimer, and he readily accepted her company. Adler had been offered one of the captive women, but he had professed weariness and had gone off to his lone bed. Latimer wondered how many years his friend would continue to go without relations with a woman. He doubted many priests remained as celibate.

Having enjoyed his companion, Latimer drifted into sleep only to be startled awake by a pitiful scream. The woman beside him stirred a little and cuddled closer, but she seemed unconcerned by the anguished cries. Covering his ears, he finally drifted back into sleep, not to awaken until morning. Well rested, he again enjoyed himself with the pretty dark-skinned woman. Afterward, she left him but soon returned with food and drink. A bright path of sunlight lit the center walkway of the long house, and members of the house began to stir. What time they had come to bed, he had no idea. He but hoped the tortured captives had found a quick release from their torment, and that their ordeal had not lasted until dawn as he had seen happen in another instance. His stomach full, his body rested, his sexual lust satisfied, he just wanted to push away the memories of the previous night and start the day afresh. Where they would head next, he had no idea. He wished they were headed back to Fort Orange, but he had a feeling their journey was far from over.

❊   ❊   ❊   ❊

Glynneth looked around the house that had been her home for near a year and a half. For the moment, she was enjoying the Sunday afternoon quiet. Dominique had taken Ignace, Meara, and Noel to visit the Kerstans, so for the time being she had the house to herself. She had known much joy and much sorrow in this small abode. Daily, Curtice or Gaspard came by to urge her to move in with them, but she resisted their pleas. She liked being under her own roof, making her own decisions, but within a month, she would have to accept her father-in-law's invitation. The Chappells were returning to New Amsterdam and needed their house back.

Glancing down at the letter on the table, she wondered at the hand fate had dealt her. She would be pleased to have her friend, Capucine, back in New Amsterdam, but at the same time, she would miss her freedom. She had given some thought to returning to Ireland. But her grandmother had recently died, so if she returned to Ireland, she would have to live with her brother and his family. She would have no more freedom there than she would living under Curtice's roof. Mayhap less, her brother being sweet but rather domineering. Besides, she would hate to take the children away from Curtice. They meant so much to him. And the children loved their grandfather.

Still, the thought of moving in with Jeanette rankled. She imagined Jeanette would not be any more pleased about the arrangement than she was. She would have to make the best of it. Eventually, she would look to have her own home built, but in the meantime, she would have her morning walks, and in the afternoon, she would continue the children's lessons. She believed Etienne had worked so hard to prepare the lessons for the boys because he had known his time on earth was limited. She hoped she would be able to do justice to his efforts. No doubt, Capucine's older son, Guyon, would be joining her for his lessons. That would please Meara. She and Noel were excited they would soon be reunited with their playmates.

Flattening the letter on the table, she read again the section about Adler and Latty. The Chappells had no news of them. They but knew they meant to travel deep into the wilderness in an effort to encourage more tribes to trade with the Dutch rather than the French. When they might return, no one knew. For the first time since Etienne's death, Glynneth let her thoughts turn to Adler. Thoughts of him had popped up regularly, but she had pushed them to the recesses of her mind. Somehow, thinking about Adler seemed disloyal to Etienne's memory. But now she let the memories flow over her.

She pictured Adler as she had first seen him on the ship leaving Dublin for the Netherlands. Wary, ready for flight, he had been startled by her presence. She saw him at the bow of the ship, enjoying the wind in his face. Their walks around Rotterdam, cooking together in the tight

184

little foc's'le galley on the trip to New Amsterdam, seated across from Etienne at the chess board, holding Meara on his knee while telling her a story – each memory was so clear, and so cherished. But the memory she held most dear was the determined look on his face when he stood over Etienne's sick bed. He would not let Etienne die. He had given her another year with her husband.

A year she would always treasure. She had tucked so many little nothingness memories of Etienne into her heart. His smile, his laugh, the look on his face when he played with the children, his look of concentration as he made the lesson preparations, how he looked when Dominique fixed his favorite meal, venison roast and Yorkshire pudding. All were memories she would not now have if not for Adler.

She knew Adler loved her. Etienne had known Adler loved her. Question was, did she love Adler? Etienne thought Adler would make her a good husband, had recommended him. Adler was a kind and caring man. That she knew. And he aroused a passion in her she at times had trouble controlling. Was that love? Her feelings for Adler were so different than her feelings for Etienne. She had no doubt Adler would make a loving father to her children. And from the electricity that shot between them whenever they chanced to touch, she expected their love life would be fulfilling. But could he also stimulate her mind as Etienne had? Perhaps. At least he was ever eager to learn.

If she were to marry him, what would he do to support his family? She would not like him to continue going off into the wilderness. She wanted a husband who came home to his family every night. He could perhaps go to work for Curtice in the warehouse. A portion of the income from Curtice's import and export business was hers and her children's inheritance, but she could not imagine Adler would want to live off her income.

She smiled and chuckled to herself. She believed she had just decided she would marry Adler. Assuming he asked her to marry him. Not that she had any doubt but what he would. But he was such a considerate man, he would wait, thinking he needed to give her time to grieve. That was good. She needed time to let her soul heal. She supposed it was a good thing Adler was still off on his trading mission. Mayhap he would be back at Fort Orange when she and the children accompanied the Chappells up the river in July to escape the fevers that could be so rampant in the summer months in New Amsterdam.

The Chappells would have but a couple of months to settle back into their home before they returned for a brief sojourn to their house in Beverwyck. Hard to think Etienne had been so hopeful the previous summer when they sailed up the river. They had both been hopeful. Yet now he was gone from her life. She wondered if he had believed he was living on but borrowed time. If so, he had never let on to her. Always he had shown his cheerful face.

Tears sprang to her eyes. How long would these simple memories continue to bring such grief? Mayhap moving in with her father-in-law would be a good thing. She would not be expecting to see Etienne every time she turned around. She would not be cocking her head, thinking she heard his voice. It might be better for the children, too. She wanted them to remember their father, at the same time, she wanted them to be happy, to enjoy their childhood.

Slowly, she folded the letter. Could she ever have imagined when she was a child that she would be living in a faraway land? She hoped her children would have a less painful life than she had experienced. She had lost her mother and her father as well as two siblings. At least she had had her dear grandmother. She wiped away a tear that escaped her eye and trickled down her cheek. Her life had its sorrows, but she had also been blessed many times over. Though her time with Etienne had been limited, at least she had not missed the joy of knowing him, of being one with him, and of sharing a sweet and gentle love, if only for a few short years.

※　※　※　※

Adler said a heartfelt good-bye to Kills Many. His Indian brother was headed back to his own village. Due to the attack on his trading party, Kills Many considered the Mohawk to now be at war with the Eries. They were always at war with the Hurons. That was nothing new. Adler hoped his friend would survive the conflict. While Kills Many headed northeast, Adler and Latty, with two guides from Strong Arm's village, were headed southeast. They wanted to try their luck with the Indians along the Delaware River. They had hopes of drawing their trade away from the Swedes.

As they set off, Adler let his thoughts go to Glynneth. Was she well? How was Etienne? Had Etienne's health improved? When he and Latty finally returned to New Amsterdam, would they find Etienne well and hardy? Or would he be dead? For Glynneth sake, as well as for his friendship with Etienne, he hoped he would again have the pleasure of clasping his friend's hand.

When he did return to New Amsterdam, it would be to make it his home. He hoped the contacts they had made thus far, and the contacts he hoped to make among the Munsee and Delaware, would generate the income he would need to start a business with Bonifacius Kerstan. Their dealings with the Erie had been a bust, but the Iroquois tribes had all been receptive to his and Latty's trade agreements. If they followed through and took their furs and hides to Fort Orange, he and Latty would be well rewarded by the Chappells.

He was glad Latty, too, was ready to settle down. He was ready to start building his land holdings. He had been talking to Armand and Capucine about buying Capucine's property that they presently rented out. The sale of the land would provide Capucine's two daughters by her first husband with dowries, and would leave enough left over, when combined with Armand's savings, for Armand to purchase some land he had been eyeing to the north of New Amsterdam. A small settlement was growing up on the North River where, amongst the nestling rolling hills, farmers were producing bumper crops of wheat to sell to the residents of New Amsterdam. Like Latty, Armand wanted an estate he could leave to his sons.

Adler envied Armand his sons. And someday, Latty, too, would marry and have heirs for the vast estate he planned to build. Ironic, Adler thought, that he, the farmer, wanted a business, not land. And Armand and Latty both wanted land. At least Latty had experience with the needs of an estate. He had been educated to steward one. Armand on the other hand, had always been involved in the fur trade. His only property was his house in New Amsterdam. Capucine had been the wife of a farmer, so she would have some knowledge of the needs of keeping the property producing. He wondered if they would turn to the use of slaves. Capucine was set against slavery. But sometimes need overrode convictions. Glynneth disliked slavery, but she had needed a servant and none but slaves were available. So there was Dominique.

Personally, he was pleased Glynneth had Dominique to help her. Glynneth had not been reared to wash and iron clothes, to feed goats and hogs, or cook meals. She had been reared as a lady, and he saw no reason she should not continue doing the occupations suitable to a lady – light sewing, teaching the children, keeping the household running smoothly. Besides, Dominique was well treated, and she would eventually have her freedom.

Readjusting the pack on his back, Adler mentally thanked Strong Arm's warriors for bringing back the gifts and trade items they had found in the Erie village. Without those items, he and Latty would have had to return to Fort Orange much sooner than they planned, and poorer as well, he suspected. Now, when they might return, he could only guess. What they would encounter, he could not imagine, but he prayed he would not be in any more battles. He but needed to survive this last outing, and his fur trading days were over.

Chapter 26

Jeanette watched Glynneth leave for her walk with Meara and Noel. How she hated the woman. Why had Glynneth not gone back to Ireland when Etienne died? Jeanette had tried to encourage her to go, but Glynneth claimed Curtice was too attached to the children, and they to him. She said New Amsterdam was now their home. So at every meal, she had to look down the table at Glynneth's smiling face.

Why should she be smiling, her husband was dead? "How can you be so cheery when Etienne is gone? Do you not miss him?" Jeanette had demanded.

"Etienne would not like me to live in gloom," Glynneth answered. "You are sweet to be concerned, but I do my weeping at night. I have no wish to burden others with my grief. Especially not the children. They are resilient, and I could not wish them to see their mother with a constant woebegone face. It would not be good for them."

Jeanette wondered if Glynneth really thought her sweet or had she been mocking her. Glynneth was forever showing off her superior education. The discussions she engaged in with Gaspard and Curtice appeared unseemly to Jeanette. And for Glynneth to be teaching Greek and Latin seemed most inappropriate. Yet Gaspard and Curtice both applauded her. What Jeanette really hated was the way Gaspard was always eager to help her if she stumbled over one of the lessons Etienne had written out before he died. Oh yes, Gaspard was eager to help her with anything – including raising her children.

When she complained to her husband that he spent as much time with Meara and Noel as he did his own son, he frowned at her. "They are my dead brother's children. If I can be a father to them, I will. They must think of this house as their home. You, too, must help them adjust."

Jeanette wanted to help them adjust. She wanted to take a switch to Meara. That child was far too forward, and her mother and Curtice encouraged her self-assertive behavior. She always expected to be the center of attention, and Curtice doted on her. "Be easy, Jeanette," he said when she complained Meara was tiring him out with her games. "She amuses me. I can think of few things that give me more pleasure than hearing Meara laugh."

She could think of a lot more pleasant things. She wished she had some way of keeping Meara away from Lothair, but her son seemed as enraptured by the child as did Curtice. Was Meara around, Lothair was forever tagging after her or reaching out to her. One of his first words was Meara's name. But as irritating as Meara was, it was Noel Jeanette despised. He was a quiet boy, serious in many respects, especially for one so young. At three he was speaking in complete sentences, be it French, English, or Dutch. Strangely, Noel had a fascination with boats. Mayhap because he spent so much time at the Kerstans'. But it was of no matter. What mattered was the way Curtice lauded the boy.

Noel was perfect. He was bright, strong, well-behaved. He could do no wrong. Noel was going to make the family proud. He was a credit to his father and his mother. A credit to the Fortier name. Before Noel came to live in the house, Curtice bounced Lothair on his knee. Now he more often bounced Noel and proclaimed him the brightest little boy in the whole of New Netherland – nay, the whole new world. And Glynneth sat there and beamed before carting Noel off to bed.

Everything about Curtice's behavior since Glynneth and her children moved in rankled Jeanette. Curtice had even suggested Glynneth should sit at the end of the table in her spot. "Oh, no," Glynneth said, "Jeanette is the lady of the house. This is her home, and the seat at the end of the table is rightfully hers."

"This is your home now, too," said Curtice, "and as the older of my daughters-in-law, I think you should have the presiding seat."

"No, no." Glynneth shook her head and adamantly refused to usurp Jeanette's seat, but Jeanette's resentment had not lessened. It increased every time Curtice consulted Glynneth instead of her on issues concerning the house. Were the children getting enough milk? Should he buy another cow? "Another cow might benefit," Glynneth answered, thoughtfully. "It could mean more cheese and butter, as well, but it would also mean more grain would need be purchased to feed the additional cow. Mayhap Gaspard could figure the cost versus the merit."

"Gaspard, you heard Glynneth. Work up an accounting." To Jeanette's umbrage, Gaspard dutifully obliged. His figures showed a second cow would not adversely task their finances, and a cow was purchased. Curtice had also asked Glynneth if she thought they should invest in draperies or continue with the shutters for the parlor. "Well, they might brighten up the room and add some warmth in the winter," Glynneth said, "but they would collect a lot of soot. Your chimney draws well, but the smoke still escapes into the room."

"Yes, indeed," Curtice agreed. "Trying to keep them clean would prove an unnecessary expense. I can always count on your wise head, my dear."

Jeanette would have liked having draperies. Several of the Dutch homes she visited had draperies. They even hid their beds in the walls behind curtains. Strange customs the Dutch had. But for the most part, they were tidy and clean. She admired that. And New Amsterdam was improving in appearance, thanks to the new general assembly. Streets were being cobbled, the canal widened, and a wall had been built to protect the town from attacks by the English. The Dutch and the English were at war, and Director General Stuyvesant feared the English from the New England area might attack them. The thought of war coming to her home frightened Jeanette, but Glynneth seemed unconcerned.

"I cannot think the English in New England will leave their homes, their farms, their businesses to attack us. They must have better things to do, especially with harvest season soon upon us. Then comes winter, and with snow covering the ground, how could they make their way here. Next comes spring and time to plant. Surely the English are sensible people and have no wish to risk their lives in an uncertain war."

Curtice and Gaspard had, of course, agreed with Glynneth, though Gaspard said he had some fears the English might attack by sea. That had not soothed Jeanette's frayed nerves any, but several months had gone by and the English had not attacked so her fears eased. No matter, she had not broached the subject again. Gaspard would only chide her for her needless worrying. "Be more like Glynneth," he would say. "Be brave of heart."

More like Glynneth. She had no wish to be like Glynneth. She wanted her husband to love and appreciate who she was. She kept his home running smoothly. She kept up her appearance. She had given him a fine, healthy son, and she never refused his amorous desires. What made him look with such longing at Glynneth?

She had had enough of Glynneth and her children. But soon she would be rid of them. Soon.

❆ ❆ ❆ ❆

Glynneth strolled slowly along the river bank. She loved this part of her day. It helped ease the pain in her heart. Noel tripped along at her side, stopping to look at flowers or bugs or whatever caught his fancy. Meara, stopping occasionally to throw lose pebbles or small stones into the river, skipped ahead with her constant companion, the little exuberant dog, Lady Ann, bouncing beside her. This lazy autumn afternoon with the sun shining brightly above them, with birds chirping in nearby trees, and with seagulls calling out in their raucous cries then soaring off on the gentle breeze seemed near perfection. To Glynneth, these daily walks that got her out of the house and away from Jeanette's angry eyes were a respite for her soul.

Too soon, though, she would need to return to the house. Ignace and Guyon Chappell, Gerhard Kerstan, and Jan Lange, the son of Hendrika's seamstress friend who had made new clothes for Noel and Meara, as well as for Glynneth, and was presently employed in making clothes for Jeanette, would be arriving for their lessons.

Ignace, now living with Armand and Capucine, was enjoying getting to know his older half-brother better. His dark eyes gleaming, Ignace told Glynneth, "I often was allowed to go hunting with Armand, and we oft times took meals together, but adults were always present, and they spoke as adults. They seldom addressed me. Now in the evenings, when Armand is home from his journeys up and down the river with the trade items, he often talks with me. He has told me much about my father and about his youth and what it was like here in New Netherland in the early days of the settlements. He is very interesting."

Glynneth was pleased Ignace had settled in so comfortably with his brother's family. He had been in her care for a year and a half, and she had grown very fond of him. Did she not see him daily for his lessons, she would sorely miss him. She was also pleased with how willingly Ignace helped his nephew with his studies. Though he was but three years older than Guyon, he was considerably more earnest about his education. "Mother expects it," he said when she complimented him on how well he was doing. The boys did their studies in the morning, then came for their lessons in the afternoon.

Glynneth had Meara taking the same lessons as Guyon. "I see no reason you should not begin your Latin," Glynneth told her daughter. And to her delight, Meara was an apt pupil.

Later in the afternoon, Capucine's daughters, Raissa and Jolie, came to join Meara and the boys for lessons in Geography and Literature. Glynneth had them studying works by Homer, tying the stories in with the geography of Greece and Turkey. She was glad Curtice had such an extensive library. Not only had he brought a number of books with him when he left Ireland, he had ordered more once he was settled in his new home. A large beautifully bound book of maps was one of his most prized possessions, and Glynneth was grateful to him for allowing her to use it to teach the children.

Stopping to watch her son copy his big sister, she chuckled as the little boy tossed a stone at the water. The stone did not go very far, it hit the rocks forming the bulkhead, bounced off them, and finally landed in the fast moving water with a little plunk. That satisfied Noel. A laugh gurgled up out of his throat, and he stomped his feet in joy. Joining in his laughter, Glynneth said, "Very good young man."

He did not acknowledge the compliment, something else had caught his attention. A butterfly. Off he went to investigate the colorful creature that fluttered away from his small grasping hands. How much he looked like his father, Glynneth thought. Was there a God, she thanked him for that blessing. Through Noel, she would always have a piece of Etienne with her. For an instant she closed her eyes as the ache for her husband stabbed her. Had he really been dead for seven months? It seemed like yesterday – it seemed like years ago. He had been sick with the consumption for so long, she had almost grown used to it, but it had been painful to watch his suffering the last few weeks of his life. The hacking cough that drained away his strength. The lack of appetite, the coughing up of blood.

No, she pushed those thoughts away. They were too painful and the day was too lovely. She instead turned her thoughts to Adler. He had been gone for near a year and a half. He could not know of Etienne's death. If he knew, she had no doubt, he would drop all else and come to her. She could not say how she knew he would come, but she knew. The Chappells had not heard from him and Latty, but the furs and hides from the Iroquois territory to the west were pouring in. A constant stream of Indians came to trade with the Chappells on Adler's and Latty's promises of fair trade and reliable trade goods. Having spent the month of August in Beverwyck with Capucine and her family, Glynneth had firsthand knowledge of her friends' successes. But where the two were, no one seemed to know. They had learned the Iroquois and the Erie were immersed in a bloody war. She hoped Adler and Latty were not a part of it.

"Look at the pretty ship," Meara called to her and pointed out to the river. Glynneth glanced over her shoulder to see a ship with cream-colored sails fluttering moving slowly down the river with the tidal current.

"Yes, it is pretty, dear," Glynneth answered. She enjoyed the sights and sounds along the East River. Always some kind of activity going on. Boats ferrying goods or people back and forth across the river from Long Island. A number of English settlers had established homes on the island, but Etienne had told her they were loyal citizens of New Netherland. They were escapees from the tyrannical Puritans in England and New England. The tolerant Dutch offered them a home, and they made good citizens. Though Dutch was the official language, and most new comers learned to speak it, the number of other languages that could be heard about the town astounded her. Her children were growing up speaking three languages, English, French, and Dutch. It amused her the way they interwove the languages.

"Look at the boat," Noel said. "I like the boat."

Glynneth laughed. "Yes, you would. You like all boats." She looked at the single-masted boat her son pointed at. Its sails furled, it rocked gently in the water. A bit dangerous to have it tied up so close to the

194

rocks, she thought, but the two men next to the boat seemed to be doing some kind of repair work to it. Both men were slovenly dressed with unkempt hair and beards. One of them glanced in her direction then returned to his work. Could be pirates, she thought. People had been complaining about pirates stealing cows and horses and raiding lone farms of late. Gaspard said he believed the pirates were mostly men whose businesses had failed, and they were seeking a means to recoup their finances. The magistrates, on behalf of the settlers, had complained to Stuyvesant and were expecting him to act on the problem.

She decided she would hurry the children past the men. Not that she had any real fear, but something about the way the second man turned and looked at her made her anxious, and at the moment, no one else was close to hand should she need help. Taking Noel's hand, she sped up her pace, causing the little boy to trot beside her. Before she could make her way past the two men, one clambered up the rocks, and blocking the path, doffed his hat. "Be you Madame Fortier?" he said.

Surprised to be addressed by name, she stopped rather than push past him. That he spoke English not Dutch or French registered with her. Could he possibly be someone Adler or Latty knew. Might he have news of them. "I am," she answered.

A grin she found frightening spread across his face. Plopping his hat back on his head, he looked down at Noel. "That be your boy?" he asked.

Now she was frightened, and she tightened her grip on her son's hand. A noise to the rear startled her. In concentrating on the man in front of her, she had not noticed the second man had slipped up behind her. She turned to see what he was doing. At that moment the man in front grabbed Noel. His movement was so sudden, so unexpected, she stumbled forward as he pulled her son from her. Noel yelped as his little arm was jerked from her grasp, then before her horrified eyes the man tossed Noel out into the river. Reaching out in terror, she screeched. Her only thought was to get to her son, but as she took a step forward, the same man swung his fist and hit her in the jaw. She staggered backwards into the arms of the second man.

Dazed by the blow, her vision blurred, she thought she saw her son's head pop up above the water. An indistinct form flew through the air and splashed down near him. Lady Ann's little head could barely be seen above the water, then dog and boy were swept away by the current. Struggling in the man's arms, she heard Meara screaming, "Mother, Mother."

Her eyes sought her daughter. "Run, Meara, run home," she cried.

"What o' the girl," the first man asked, looking as though he meant to run after Meara.

"Let 'er go," the second man said. "We got paid t' dispatch the woman and the boy, she said naught about no girl."

"That is right," the first man said, nodding. He stooped and picked up a rock. "Shall I dispatch 'er now." He nodded at Glynneth.

Her head clearing, Glynneth realized they meant to kill her. Though knowing it was hopeless, she began struggling more violently. The second man chuckled, "Bit 'o a she-cat is this one. I likes the feel o' her. Bash her hard 'nough t' knock her out, but 'twould be a shame t' waste a morsel this tasty. She could bring a tidy sum at Fort Orange."

Glynneth saw the stone raised above her, but she could do nothing to stop the blow. She felt the rock hit the side of her head. Pain radiated out in all directions, then all went black.

Chapter 27

With each stroke of the paddle, Latimer felt his spirits rising. The tide was with them, carrying them rapidly down river. Soon they would be back in New Amsterdam. And he would be a property owner. He had been lucky to find Armand Chappell in Beverwyck. To Latimer's delight, Armand informed him his wife, Capucine, had agreed to sell the property she inherited from her first husband – on the condition the family leasing the farm land could continue their lease for another five years. That met with Latimer's approval. He preferred to have the rental income. He had no desire to farm the land himself. Not yet anyway.

Armand had just arrived from New Amsterdam with more trade goods. The Chappell commerce in hides and furs had never been better, Jacques proclaimed, and he made a substantial settlement on Latimer and Adler. The sum pleased Adler as much as it did Latimer. They had returned to the fort disheartened after the months they had spent trying to convince the Indians along the Delaware they would fare better trading at Fort Orange than with the Swedes. They had been completely unsuccessful. Every tribe they encountered, though friendly and welcoming, had shown no interest in switching loyalties. Add that bust to their disappointing adventure with the Eries, and they had not been expecting such a generous remuneration. However, the pelts brought by the Iroquois were proving such a lucrative trade, that keeping a good supply of goods on hand had the Chappells hopping.

Latimer believed Adler's friendship with Kills Many helped convince many of the Iroquois to trade with the Chappells. Jacques apparently thought so too. He tried to convince them to go out on one more trip, but as soon as Adler learned Etienne had died, Latimer knew they were headed back to New Amsterdam.

Glynneth was a widow. A wealthy widow. Had he any sense, Latimer thought, he would pursue her, try to win her hand. But he would not even make an attempt at courting her. He loved her too much, and he well knew he was not the right man for her. Adler was the man she should marry. Both he and Adler would miss Etienne, but they had known since they first met him that he could not live a long life. He had actually lived longer that Latimer had expected. And it had been a privilege to know the man. But now, though Etienne's memory might be cherished, it was time for Adler to win his lady's love.

Looking over his shoulder at Adler in the canoe stern, Latimer said. "We are home. And am I ready to get out and stretch my legs." In the three and a half days it had taken them to get down river, Adler had given them little time to sleep or eat. When the tide was with them, they made good time, but when the tide turned, they had been forced to do some strenuous paddling. Add in the various currents at the mouths of creeks, and it had not been an easy trip. They could have waited until Armand completed his business and returned on his fluyt, but Adler had not been willing to wait. He wanted to get back to Glynneth, though he never stated that was his intent. He but contended he had had enough of Fort Orange.

Adler pointed the bow of the canoe into shore. When it grated onto the beach, Latimer hopped out and pulled it further up. Adler then climbed out and helped pull the canoe clear of the water. "You go on and find Glynneth and give her our condolences," Latimer said. "I will see to the canoe then report in to Gaspard and Curtice. I have no mind to face Glynneth immediately. I would rather you deal with any weeping. I would not like to see her with tears in her eyes. And cry she will when she sees you. You and Etienne were close. That will tear at her heart. I will come later."

Adler straightened and looked at him. "By rights I should help you, Latty."

Latimer could tell his friend was longing to accept his offer, but Adler's sense of duty made him at least make a protest. "Nay," Latimer said. "Go on with you. I will see to things."

Adler nodded. "That I will then."

"You might want to stop by a tavern and spruce yourself up a tad. No doubt your scent is not much better than your appearance. I would not know as I am thinking I am no better and cannot know is it you or

198

I that I am smelling."

Adler chuckled. "Glynneth's seen us looking worse. Think how we looked when she first met us. After all those days in hiding, we were sorry specimens."

"Aye, you are right there," Latimer agreed with a smile. "Well, off with you."

"You will join us soon?"

"Aye. That I will."

Giving a nod, Adler turned and strode purposely off, and Latimer turned to securing the canoe. He doubted Adler would spend much time with his appearance. The man was too eager to see the woman he loved. The woman they both loved. Well, it was for the best. And Glynneth should have the best. He would always want naught but the best for her.

✻ ✻ ✻ ✻

Adler took his friend's advice and stopped by a tavern he knew had a room where a man could spruce himself up a bit. He could also do with a quick mug of ale. Not only was he thirsty, but he wanted to fortify himself before he saw Glynneth. He could not blame Latty for not wishing to see Glynneth cry. He dreaded the thought himself. He would want to take her in his arms, hold her close to his heart, and try to ease her pain. Yet he had no right to that luxury.

He was deeply sorry about Etienne's death. He would miss his friend. Yet he could not help wondering if he might stand a chance of winning Glynneth's hand. He could never expect to take Etienne's place in her heart, but he could offer her love and comfort. He could be a father to her children. Could he bring Etienne back for her, he would, but that was not possible.

His clothing and hat brushed, face and hands washed, and hair combed, he swilled down the rest of his ale, squared his shoulders, and set out for the Fortiers' house. They had learned from Armand that Glynneth was now living with her father-in-law. Adler wondered if she was happy with that arrangement. He could not think living with Jeanette could be very pleasant. The woman was the opposite of Glynneth. She seemed ever dissatisfied, never happy. Glynneth, on the other hand, was ever cheerful. She saw the sun even on gloomy days. Jeanette was a pretty woman, yet he never thought of her as pretty for her face always wore a frown. In a way he pitied Gaspard. Could not be easy having such a wife.

His knock on the Fortier door was answered by Dominique. She showed real pleasure when she saw him. "Ah, Monsieur Adler, how wonderful you are now returned. Madame will be most pleased. But she has not yet returned from her walk. She should be here very soon if you should like to wait. Her young students have already arrived and await her also."

Armand had told him and Latty that Glynneth was teaching not only Armand's son, Guyon, and Jacques's son, Ignace, but a couple of other youths as well. Adler admired her for continuing the boys' education. He knew Etienne would be proud of her. Passing on their knowledge had been a great pleasure to both Etienne and Glynneth. A joy they had shared. He would never be able to share that joy with her. She knew so much of the world – he so little. What could he offer her that could compensate for that lost compatibility.

An over whelming feeling of inadequacy overcame him, and he shook his head. "No, Dominique, I will come back later with Latty. I would not want to interfere with her lessons."

"Oh, but Madame will be so disappointed she missed you. Are you certain you will not stay? I expect her back any time now. She is actually a little late today."

Again he shook his head. "I will return later. Better I should clean up a bit anyway." Dominique tsked, but he turned and trod down the three front steps. His spirits could not be much lower. He had been so eager to return. He had needed to see Glynneth. Assure himself she was well. And more, he admitted, he had thought he might have a chance to win her love. But who was he to think he could make a fit husband for Glynneth. He was not in the same category as Etienne. He could expect to do little more than love Glynneth from afar as he had been doing.

"Adler, oh, Adler, Adler." Recognizing the little voice hailing him as he left the Fortier house, Adler turned to see Meara running toward him. Her hair disheveled, her breath coming in gasps, she clasped his coat to keep from falling and cried, "Oh, Adler, I am so glad you have come home. They took Mother, and they threw Noel in the river. You have to save them!"

Squatting on his haunches, he grasped the child by the shoulders. Her small body heaving convulsively, tears streaming down her face, she struggled to drawn in gulps of air. Something had her terribly upset. What had she said about her mother? "Where is your mother?" he demanded. "Why are you alone?"

Drawing in a deep breath, she repeated, "They took her. They threw her in a boat. Mother told me run, run home. I ran as fast as I could, but I got lost." She sniffled and swiped the back of her hand across her nose. "I was so scared. But you will find her, Adler? You will find her. You will not let them hit Mother again?"

He could not be more confused, but Meara's last words had him grasping her arms more tightly. "Someone hit your mother?"

She squiggled, and realizing he was hurting her, he released his hold and cupped her chin in his palm. "Look at me, Meara. Has someone hurt your mother?"

She nodded, her tiny chin rocking in his hand. "Yes, the two men. They threw Noel in the river, and they hit Mother. Then Mother told me to run."

He could not comprehend what he was hearing. "Two men hit your mother?"

Her eyes wide and brimming with tears, she answered, "Yes, and when she tried to get away, one hit her on the head with a stone. They threw her in their boat. You have to help her!"

Thoughts darting around everywhere, he rose and scooped Meara up in his arms. "I will, but we have to get you home." He shook his head. Could this be real? None of what Meara was saying made any sense. "Where, Meara, where did this happen?"

"On our walk along the East River."

He ran back up the steps to the Fortiers' house but stopped before knocking. "Meara, did you say they threw Noel in the river?"

Nodding, she sobbed, "Yes. One man grabbed him and flung him out into the river. And my Lady Ann jumped in after him. Now she is gone, too."

"Good God," Adler said. How could this be? Raising his hand, he pounded on the door.

Dominique again opened the door, and a look of shock crossed her face when she saw Meara in Adler's arms. "What is this?" she asked, trying to look around Adler as if seeking Glynneth. Then she stepped back to allow Adler to enter. "What is wrong with the child?"

As Dominique questioned him, he saw the four boys sitting around the dining room table, their books open, look up at him. He recognized Ignace and Guyon and the Kerstan boy, but another boy with straight blond hair and wide blue eyes was new to him.

Still holding Meara to his chest, Adler said, "Meara says someone has abducted her mother. She says two men hit her mother and threw her in a boat."

"What nonsense is the child spewing now?" a sharp voice quipped.

Adler looked over Dominique's shoulder to see Jeanette. An annoyed look on her face, her hands on her hips, she shook her head. "Meara is forever making up stories to get herself out of trouble. Give her to me." She started forward with her arms outstretched. "I will take her to her room, but she would be better served did I take a switch to her."

Clutching Meara closer, Adler shook his head. "Nay, I cannot think Meara lies. She is too upset. Something has happened to Glynneth. And Meara says the same two men who abducted Glynneth threw Noel in the river."

Jeanette stood in front of him, her arms reaching for Meara. "Now does that not tell you what utter nonsense she is spouting. Give her to me."

"Nay." He turned and headed for the door.

"Where are you going?" Jeanette snapped.

"I am taking her to Curtice, then I am going to find her mother."

Jeanette followed after him. "You must not bother the old man." Her voice sounded panicky. "You are being foolish, I tell you." She grasped his arm but he shook her off.

Dominique grabbed a wrap from a peg by the door. "I am going with you. I have never known Meara to make up lies. Something bad has happened. I feel it."

"You get back in the house, Dominique," Jeanette hissed.

202

Not bothering to look back, Dominique said, "I am not your slave."

"You will be, you nasty harridan. Get back in this house or I will make you sorry."

Adler stopped and looked around at Jeanette. Her face red with anger, and perhaps fear, she stood trembling in the doorway. "What did you say?" Had he heard her right? Had she said Dominique would be her slave? Why would she have said that? "What do you know of this, Jeanette?" he demanded.

She looked confused. Shaking her head, she stepped back into the house. "Nothing," she said, fluttering her hand. "Go, just go."

She turned from him and was nearly knocked over as the four boys erupted through the door. "We are going with you," said Ignace. "We know Meara. She would never tell such a lie. We want to help."

"Perhaps it would be better did you boys go home," Adler said, thinking the boys could be more nuisance than help. "Until we learn more, I am not sure what we are going to be doing."

"Nay," said Ignace. "We are going with you. We want to know what happened."

Not wanting to waste any more time getting to Curtice, Adler shrugged, and with Dominique and the boys trailing behind him, he hurried down the street to Curtice's office and warehouses. He hoped Glynneth's father-in-law would be at his office. He hoped Latty would still be there, not off searching for a bath then a woman to bed. They would need as much detail as they could get from Meara, then they would begin their search. Mayhap the boys would be of some use. Once they had a description of the boat, the boys could help look for it.

Luck was with him. When he burst into the Fortier office with his parade behind him, he found Curtice, Latty, and Gaspard sitting around with mugs of ale in their hands. Their initial greeting turned to surprise when they saw the tearstained Meara in his arms.

Curtice was on his feet immediately. "What is it my child, what ails you?" He reached out to take her into his arms and Adler reluctantly let him have her. She was his only contact with her mother, and he hated to be parted from her.

"She says someone – two men," he corrected himself, "have abducted Glynneth."

"What!" Latty and Gaspard were on their feet, their chairs toppling backwards in the process. "What do you say!" Latty demanded. "Glynneth abducted?"

Adler swiped a hand through his hair. "Meara says two men hit her mother and threw her in a boat." He shook his head and avoiding Curtice's eyes, he chocked out, "She says they threw Noel into the river."

"No," Curtice gasped, and Latty, grabbing him by the shoulders, guided him back onto his chair. "That cannot be," the old man said, his face sagging.

"And Lady Ann jumped in after Noel," Meara said, peering up at her grandfather. "Now they are both gone." She hiccupped. "And Mother's gone."

"We are going to get your mother back, Meara," Adler said, squatting down to turn her face to look at him. "Believe me we are." He would get her back did he have to search the whole world over. "But we need your help. You must remember everything. You must tell us what the men looked like. What the boat looked like. Anything the men said. Can you do that for us?"

Meara nodded, and amidst interspersed questions from the four men in the room, and one important question from Dominique, "In what language did they speak?" the tale was related.

"You say the men said they had been paid?" Latty asked, having pulled his chair over so he could be on a level with Meara.

Meara repeated her statement. "Yes, one asked should he chase me, and the other said, 'Nay, we got paid t' dispatch the woman an' the boy." Tilting her head, she asked, "What did he mean, dispatch?"

Latty looked up at Adler, and Adler widened his eyes. What could they tell the child?

"They were paid to take them away," Dominique said. "Now I think if you have no other questions for Meara, she needs to be put to bed with some hot milk. She has been through a lot."

Adler nodded. "Dominique is right, but I cannot say I trust Jeanette with her."

"What do you mean?" Gaspard said, sounding slightly incensed.

Adler had not wanted to mention Jeanette's attitude, but his concern for Meara outweighed his reluctance. "She said Meara was lying.
204

Would not believe her. Said she should take a switch to her." He looked at Curtice. "I think 'twould be best, sir, did you go with Dominique. Make sure Jeanette understands Meara is not lying." He shifted his eyes back to Gaspard. "We will need your help, Gaspard, to aid in our search."

Gaspard looked down and slowly shook his head. "At times I cannot understand Jeanette." He looked at his father. "I think he is right, Father. You should help see to Meara. I will help with the search. But I am thinking we must act quickly."

Adler could not help but feel sorry for the man with a wife like Jeanette.

"One other thing," Latty said, "we will want no scandal to touch Glynneth." He looked down at the four youths. "You boys can help in our search, but you must be careful what you say. What questions you ask. We must not have Madame Fortier's reputation besmirched."

The boys nodded. "We will be careful."

Adler understood what Latty was trying to avoid saying. If Glynneth was molested before they found her, she could be embarrassed to face people in the future. He had no doubt he would find Glynneth. He but wanted to find her before any more harm could come to her. He would not let himself think they might not find her or that she might be dead. He would be a blithering idiot who could accomplish nothing did he give in to such thoughts.

Squaring his shoulders, he said, "Curtice, you and Dominique should get Meara home." He bent and placed his hand on Meara's cheek. "We are going to bring your mother home, little one. I promise you that."

The little girl nodded. "I believe you, Adler. You will find my mother."

Curtice rose with the child and over her head, his eyes met Adler's. Sad eyes. Eyes that asked, should you make such a promise. Drawing a deep breath in through his nose, Adler firmed his lips and met the questioning gaze. He would find Glynneth. He would find her. Curtice nodded, turned, and with Dominique following him, left the room.

With Meara safely on her way home, Adler took charge. As no one objected to his assumption of command, he gave out the search assignments. "Gaspard, you and the boys go to the wharf. Spread out. Talk to the sailors, the wharf men, the vendors. Try to find anyone who knows that boat. Meara gave us a good description of it. Single mast, yet large enough to support a tarp cover in the bow. Number of crates and barrels in the belly. Sounds to be a boat large enough to go up and down the North River with ease. Mayhap 'tis owned by someone involved in carrying trade goods.

"You also have a description of the two men. English speaking, shabbily dressed, big floppy brimmed hats, grizzled faces. I know that could describe any number of men, but it gives us a place to start. Latty and I will visit the taverns. If the two men were paid for this deed, they may feel flush in the purse and could well be about spending their ill-gotten chink."

"We are on our way," Gaspard said, but as he headed for the door, Adler stopped Gerhard. "I have another thought. Gerd, you and your young friend here." He nodded to the boy he had yet to meet. "You two go tell your father what has happened. Describe the boat and the men. Mayhap he knows the men, or 'tis a boat he built. Then can he spare the time, could he go with you to the East River and question people who live in the area. Ask them if they saw anything untoward." He put his hand on Gerhard's shoulder. "But remember, boy, you must not divulge what has happened to Madame Fortier to anyone but your family."

His eyes wide, Gerhard nodded solemnly. "Yes, Meneer Hayward, Jan and I understand. And I know Father will help. As will his assistant, Dirk." He raised a small hand when Adler narrowed his eyes. "No fear, sir, Dirk can be trusted. He is like family."

"Good boy," Adler said. "All right. Let us all to our task. We will meet back here, and is luck with us, we will have the information we need to find Glynneth before the sun goes down." He wished he felt as hopeful as he tried to sound. But New Amsterdam was not that large. Surely someone would know the men.

Chapter 28

Adler and Latty started with the taverns closest to the waterfront. How to gain the information they needed without telling about Glynneth's abduction was a problem. They needed a story. They decided Latty should do the talking. He knew a number of the tavern owners. Was on good terms with them. He would tell them Adler's purse had been stolen, and they would describe the two men they thought might have taken it. Was anyone meeting their description suddenly spending big? Latty promised there would be a reward if the purse was found before it was emptied. The first three taverns they visited offered them nothing, but in the fourth tavern, the tavern keeper's hefty wife, Mevr. Smedt, cackled, and slanting her eyes at Latty, said, "I remember you, my dear. You have not been around for many a month. Are you back now for another tumble upstairs?"

Adler could swear his friend was blushing. And well he should be had he bedded the pasty-skinned, ill-kempt woman ogling him. "Not at present," Latty said, and the woman looked offended, so he hastily added, "Maybe later when our business is concluded."

The woman gave Latty a gape-toothed grin and leaned closer to him. Even from where he stood, Adler could smell her rotten breath, and he pulled back a little. Latty, however, had no choice but to humor the woman. "We are looking for a couple of men who we think stole my friend's purse," he said, giving a nod to Adler.

The woman cocked her head to one side and narrowed her eyes as she listened to Latty's description of the two men. "I might have seen one of them," she said after a moment.

"There is a reward," Adler said, leaning forward.

The woman eyed him for a moment then gave him the same lascivious grin she had given Latty. "Well now, poplet, what would that reward be?"

"If we find the man, we are talking two beaver pelts."

The woman straightened. Her face went blank. "Must be a hefty sum he stole from you."

Adler had been so eager to learn about the man, he had offered too much as the reward. The woman was now suspicious. "It is more than the money," he said. "I want to make sure he never steals from me again."

Tilting her head, she looked at him from under her pale, sparse eyelashes. "Maybe," she said. "Maybe you want to give him a beating – or maybe you have some other reason for wanting to find him." She grinned again. "However, it makes no difference to me if I get the pelts. His name is Keane, Welby Keane, and you are apt to find him right upstairs, fast asleep." She pointed to the stairs. "Second room on the left."

🌱 🌱 🌱 🌱

Latimer recognized the room. It was the same one where he had had his tryst with Mevr. Smedt. Somehow, now that Adler knew about his bedding Mevr. Smedt, it made him feel even more lewd. Opening the door, he peered into the dimly lit room. A half-naked man lay sprawled across the bed, his mouth wide open and emitting resounding snores. Latimer hoped the oaf was not in such a drunken state he could not be awakened. The crumpled clothing strewn upon the flooring, a floppy-brimmed hat upside down in a corner, the grizzled stubble on the man's face all fit Meara's description.

Adler pushed past Latimer, and grabbing a handful of the man's hair, yanked him up on the bed. The man gave a startled yelp, and groggily tugged at Adler's arm in an attempt to free himself. "You Welby Keane?" Adler demanded.

Opening bloodshot eyes, the man tried to focus on Adler. "Well, are you?" Adler demanded, giving a twist on the man's hair.

Realizing he could not escape the tightening grasp on his hair, the man wiped a meaty paw across his face, and narrowing his eyes, asked, "Who is wantin' t' know?

Adler glanced back at Latimer. "Make sure that door is closed. This may get unpleasant."

208

At Adler's words, a look of fear crossed the man's face. "Now wait a moment 'ere, bravo. I be a bit befuddled, but yeah, I be Welby Keane. What would you be wantin' with me?"

Latimer made sure no one was listening outside the door. He suspected Mevr. Smedt of being more than a little curious and would not have been surprised to find she had crept up the stairs in their wake, but the corridor was empty. He crossed to the bed. "You want to hit him first or would you give me the pleasure?"

"Now wait, wait," Keane cried, trying unsuccessfully to back up. "Whut be you a-wantin' with me. I cannot say I know either o' you. 'Cept you be English lack me." He gave a half-hearted chuckle. "Fellow Englishmen, eh, eh?"

"I plan to knock out what is left of his teeth," Adler said with a glance at Latimer, "then you can gouge out his eyes if you have a mind."

Keane squeezed his eyes shut. "Have pity, knaves. I... I can pay you. I have got coin, hard coin, not wampum. I know not whut I did t' ye, but I am that sorry, I swear I am."

"Coin," Adler said. "What is a chuff like you doing with coin?"

Keane warily opened his eyes. "A lady paid me t' do her a little favor."

Adler tightened his grip, and Keane winced. "Just a favor? Nothing else?" Adler said through clinched teeth.

Hedging, Keane said, "Yeah, yeah, a mere favor."

Jerking Keane's head back, Adler brought out his knife and pricked Keane under his chin. "What favor?" he demanded, easing up enough so Keane could talk. "Make it the truth or you are a dead man."

His eyes desperate, Keane said, "The lady needed t' be shut o' another lady an' the lady's son. She said t'other lady was plannin' t' run off with her husband. Said her husband meant t' maike t'other lady's son his heir 'stead o' her son. She paid me an' a co-mate, name o' Filmore, t' dispatch 'em."

"What did you do with them?" Adler asked, again pricking Keane and little droplets of blood stained his knife blade.

Keane gulped. "We tossed the boy in the East River. The woman, Filmore be taikin' t' Fort Orange. He has him a truepenny there what runs a brothel. Filmore figures his friend will pay him a good price for the woman. She is a toothsome wench."

Feeling a loathing he had never before experienced, Latimer took a fistful of Keane's hair and turned him to look at him. In a quiet voice he asked, "Then did you think nothing of tossing a little boy into the river?"

At his question, Latimer could see light dawning in Keane's eyes. The man was beginning to comprehend that they were not after his money, they were after him for the murder of Noel Fortier and abduction of Glynneth. His Adam's apple jumping up and down in his throat, Keane begged, "I thought I was helpin' the lady. Savin' her from desertion. Pretty lady – 'twas not right her husband should abandon her."

Before Latimer knew what was happening, Adler let go of Keane's hair and slammed his fist into the man's nose. Blood gushed out, and a handful of hair came lose in Latimer's fingers as the sudden blow knocked Keane backwards, and he still had a grip on Keane's hair. Keane grabbed for his nose and whimpered, but Adler jerked him to his feet.

"Get dressed, and be quick about it," Adler commanded, and Keane crawled around on the floor gathering up his breeches, waistcoat, and neck scarf.

"What are we to do with him?" Latimer asked. He was a little afraid Adler meant to kill the man. He had never seen his friend in such a quiet rage.

"We will take him back to the Fortier warehouse and lock him up. Then we will meet up with the others, tell them what we have learned, then we are off to Fort Orange."

Latimer nodded as he watched the sniveling Keane scramble into his clothes. "Hush your bawling, man. You are not dead yet. Do we find Madame Fortier alive, you may well live."

Adler grabbed a small bag from Keane's pocket and dumped several coins into his palm. He looked down at his palm then up at Keane. "You killed the boy for this?" he asked, looking at Keane with such malevolence that the man shrank in size.

"Let us get him out of here before I kill him," Adler said, and Latimer, slapping Keane's hat on his head to partially hide the man's busted nose, hurriedly opened the door. With Keane between them, they made their way down stairs to the main tavern room. The men at their tables stared, but none ventured to rise and ask what was amiss. Latimer guessed the look on Adler's face was enough to keep any man from challenging him. It did not stop Mevr. Smedt, though.

She waddled in front of them, blocking their exit. "I see you found your man."

Latimer nodded, but Mevr. Smedt looked past him to Adler. "What about my pelts?" she asked, hands on her hips.

"You will have them before the sun has set," Adler answered her, "and I owe you my deepest gratitude." He bowed to her, and she raised her eyebrows in surprise. She was not used to being treated so graciously.

Cackling, she stepped out of the way. "I will take you at your word."

The next instant they were out in the sunshine and were shepherding Keane toward the Fortiers' warehouse. What better place to hold the man and still keep Glynneth's plight a secret.

※ ※ ※ ※

They were in luck. They met up with Gaspard, the four boys, and Kerstan outside the warehouse. "You have one of the men?" Gaspard asked.

"Aye," Adler said, his anger barely under control, "and he has admitted to the crime."

"Looks like he needed a bit of persuading," Kerstan said.

Adler shrugged. "A little. We were headed to the warehouse with him. Thought we could find a safe place to lock him up until we return to Fort Orange."

"Ah, ha. So you have confirmed the second man is headed to Fort Orange?" Gaspard questioned.

"We have. And we know Glynneth is alive."

"Thank the Lord," Gaspard said.

"Would the second man be named Filmore?" Kerstan asked.

Adler cocked his head. "That would be correct."

Latty said, "Let us get off the street. We are attracting stares. Our questions and actions are apt to be talked about enough as it is. We can finish this in the office."

"He is right," Gaspard said and led the way into the warehouse.

Once inside the office, Adler pushed Keane into a corner. "Stay put and keep your mouth shut unless you are wanting more of the same."

"I can hardly draw breath," the man said, his chest heaving from the exertion of the hurried walk. "My nose, 'tis ... 'tis."

"I care not whether you can breathe or not," Adler growled. "Do you say another word I will punch your nose up into your skull."

Still gasping for air, Keane scrunched up into the corner his hands covering his nose, and Adler turned his back on him. Together, he and Latty informed the group what they had learned from Keane concerning Glynneth, and why they believed she was still alive, then Adler asked, "What have you learned?"

Kerstan spoke first. "When Gerd told me what happened and described the men and the boat, I had a feeling one of the men had to be Filmore, and that it was the boat I built for him. He still owes me several payments on the boat. Has owed me for over a year now. I thought I could find out more at the wharf than by speaking to people on the East River, but I sent Dirk to ask anyone there if they had seen or recognized the men or the boat. At the wharf Gerd, Jan, and I met up with Gaspard and the other two boys. Took but a couple of questions to some of the sailors I know, and we learned Filmore was headed to Fort Orange. Even learned his cargo – caskets of nails, whetstones, cakes of soap, barrels of birdlime, salt, pepper, and brandy."

Gaspard interrupted, "The good thing is, he stops at settlements along the way to deliver items to various customers. Thinking we hit on the right man, I ordered the readying of a fast little sloop. If we set out immediately the tide will still be with us for a while yet. I have hired three men, so two can be rowing constantly if the tide turns and the wind fails to cooperate."

"Good thinking Gaspard," Adler said. "We can set out as soon as we have secured Keane and tell your father what we are about." He looked around at the man he would like to slowly choke to death. He did not know if Keane understood what they had been saying. He was English, and they had been speaking in Dutch. He narrowed his eyes, and wide, frightened eyes looked back at him. He hoped the man was terrified out

212

of his mind. Hoped he was in abject pain. Never had he imagined he could hate any person the way he hated Keane.

"We have a small closet off the office here," Gaspard said. "We can tie him up and lock him in there. I will tell my warehouse steward to have a constant guard kept on him. As far as the men will know, Keane was caught stealing, and we are after the goods his comrade made off with. The men will believe it. Thefts are the primary reason Armand now accompanies our goods up and down the river."

Adler nodded. "Perfect. Now I wonder if you should stay here. Latty and I can head upriver, but you can be here for your father." His biggest concern was for Meara. He had no doubt the pretty lady who paid Keane and Filmore to kill Glynneth and Noel was Jeanette. Why she would do such a thing he could not imagine, but until he had Glynneth safely back, he had no wish to confront her. At the same time, he worried Jeanette might try to kill Meara. The woman had to be crazy.

"No way am I staying behind," Gaspard said. "I have ordered the boat, I am paying for it, and I am going. I want Glynneth safely back as much as either of you two." His lips firmed, his brows lowered, he presented a stubborn face to all in the room.

"As you wish. I was but concerned for your father," Adler said in a mollifying voice.

"Father will be fine. He will be better when we bring Glynneth home."

"Agreed," Latty said, "so let us get Keane secured and be on our way."

"You get him tied up and locked away," Gaspard said. "I will find my steward and have him set a guard outside the office door."

By the time Gaspard returned with his steward, Adler and Latty had Keane tightly bound, but they had to forgo a gag as the man, because of his busted nose, could only breathe through his mouth. "Could I have a wee drink afore you leave me," Keane begged. "My tongue be parched."

"It can dry up and drop off as far as I am concerned," Adler said, pushing Keane down into a corner. "We come back and you are not in that corner, consider yourself a dead man," he said, and turning on his heel, he stalked out of the tiny room stacked high with financial books and papers. Bound hand and foot, Adler doubted the man would be able to regain his feet even if he tried. The guard would need to be warned, though, did they hear him crying out for mercy, they were to ignore his pleas. Except perhaps to give him something to drink.

"No reason I cannot inform Monsieur Fortier of your plans" Kerstan said. "The sooner you are on your way, the better. I will go by the house and tell all."

"That would be splendid," Gaspard said. "And thank you for all your help," he added, pumping Kerstan's hand.

"Can we not go with you?" Ignace asked. "We want to help. We love Cousin Glynneth."

"Yes, we do," piped up Guyon.

"No," Gaspard stated in a hard, uncompromising voice, then in a more subdued voice, his mouth down-turned, he said, "Guyon, tell your mother what has happened. Maybe she could go sit with Father. He will need comforting. I fear my wife may not give him the care he needs."

"Ah, but we want to help," Guyon wheedled.

Latty squatted in front of him. "Do you truly want to help?"

Guyon and Ignace both nodded rapidly. "Then you must be here for Meara. Guyon, imagine how you would feel if you lost Pierre." The boy, his eyes wide, looked at Latty and blinked. "Meara has lost Noel, and she is worried about her mother. She will need you here with her. You are her dearest friend. She has need of you and Ignace. You must be here for her."

Tears coming to his eyes, the boy blinked several times. "I had near forgotten about Noel. I will stay to be with Meara. She will need me."

"Indeed she will," Latty said ruffling Guyon's hair. Rising, he directed his gaze at Ignace. "You are older. You have to know you are needed here."

Ignace nodded. "Yes, Latty. I will do what I can to help Meara and my Uncle Curtice."

"Good boy." He looked at Adler. "Let us be off."

Adler admired Latty's way with children. His friend seemed to understand their thought processes. He doubted he ever would. Shaking his head as the boys turned to leave, he laid a hand on Kerstan's arm, but his gaze locked on Latty. "You two go ahead and make sure all is ready. I need a word with Kerstan then I will quickly join you."

214

Latty's side-long glance and nod told Adler that Latty understand his need to talk to Kerstan. Meara would have to be protected from Jeanette. Telling the boys to wait outside, Adler explained to Kerstan what they had learned from Keane. "Though I cannot now take the time to prove it. I believe Jeanette was the woman who paid Keane and Filmore. I cannot think Meara safe with her. I need you to tell Dominique and Capucine Chappell that between them, they must make certain Meara is never left alone with Jeanette. At this time, I prefer not to tell Curtice what we have learned. There is always a small chance I am wrong in my assumption."

"I will see to it," Kerstan promised. "I will go first to the Fortier house, then I will go talk with Madame Chappell. By that time Ignace and Guyon will have had time to tell her what has transpired. Is there anything else you wish me to do."

"I can think of naught, but I thank you for all you have done." Catching himself, Adler said, "Yes, tell Curtice we owe Mevr. Smedt of the Smedt Tavern two beaver pelts. Without her help, we might not be on Filmore's trail. I would prefer those pelts were sent to her before the sun sets."

"I will see to it. Good luck," Kerstan said, and hurried off, herding the boys along with him. Leaving the steward to lock up the office and place the guard at the door, Adler made his way to the wharf. His heart was singing. Glynneth is alive, Glynneth is alive. She has not been killed. She is hurt and scared and sick over the loss of her son, but she is alive. He would find her and bring her home. He might well kill both Filmore and Keane. If ever any two men needed killing, they did. But for the time being, what mattered was Glynneth was alive.

Chapter 29

Glynneth groaned and tried to reach for her throbbing head only to find her hands were bound. Confused and dazed, she tugged again then realized her hands were tied to her ankles. What had happened? Why was she trussed in such a manner? "Wakin' up are ye, me pretty," came a voice she failed to recognize. "Keane hit ye a bit harder than I meant him to, but no matter, I needed to take advantage o' the tide afore I could be enjoyin' ye company."

Opening her eyes, Glynneth tried to focus them on the man speaking. Everything was blurry, and she blinked several times trying to clear her vision. A man sat at the aft of a boat, his hand on the rudder. A boat – she was on a boat. But why? She realized the man was chuckling. Why? Why was he laughing? She tried to concentrate.

"We will be comin' t' a nice inlet ere long. I can drop anchor, an' ye an' I can get better acquainted. I got t' say, ye are a comely thing. Goes agin me better judgment t' lay low one such as you. We will have us some fun on the way t' Fort Orange, then ye will bring me a tidy profit. Between what the laidy paid me for dispatching ye and the young'un', an' what Perkins will pay me, I will be able t' pay off that boat builder who keeps threatenin' t' taike me boat."

Little of what the man said was making any sense to Glynneth until he mentioned 'the young'un'. The words stirred thoughts of her son. Her son! God! They had thrown Noel in the river. "No!" she screamed and started thrashing about, pulling at her bonds.

"Hey, what is this. What are ye about. Stop that screamin'." He aimed a kick at her and caught her in the stomach. The blow knocked the breath from her, and she gasped for air. Her head pounded, and her wrists felt raw and burning.

"Now that is better. No more o' that wailin' less ye wants another knock t' the head," the hideous beast said.

216

What kind of a vile creature was he that he would throw a baby into the river? What of Meara? Had she made it home safely? Licking her dry lips, she again opened her eyes and looked at the man sitting there gloating over her misery. "My daughter?" she squeaked out, "what of my daughter? Did you kill her?"

"The chit?" He widened his smile. "Nay, no reason t' kill her. She was no' part o' the deal. That what all yer fuss was about? Ye worrying' 'bout the girl? Ye can rest easy 'bout her." He removed his floppy-brimmed hat and scratched his head. "Damn lice. Cannot seem t' be shut o' them." Cocking his head he leered at her. "Bet ye got no lice in yer pretty hair, have ye?"

Ignoring his question, she instead shut her eyes and turned as much away from him as possible, but she could not shut out the sound of his chuckling. She tried to piece together all the various things he had said, yet somehow most of it made no sense. Had he said someone had paid him to kill her and Noel? No, that could not be right, because he had not killed her. Did he say they were on their way to Fort Orange? Yes, she was certain he had said that. Did he mean to kill her there? Might she escape and make it to safety with Jacques and Simone? Gads, if her head would stop pounding so she could think.

"Here comes our inlet. We will put in here an' get acquainted." As he spoke, the boat turned, the sails flapped then went slack and the boat glided to a stop. The man dropped an anchor over the side. "We dare not stay here too long. Soon as the sun starts t' set, the bugs come out. Not near so many this time o' year, but enough t' maike it plenty unpleasant.

"Here now, I got t' untie yer feet. Hard fer ye t' spread yer legs with yer feet bound."

Glynneth opened her eyes to see him squatting at her feet, his grubby fingers working on the rope about her ankles. It was the first time she had a good look at him. Scraggly brown hair hanging down from under his hat, growth of stubble on his face, dark eyes under shaggy brows, and a lascivious grin that displayed a couple of missing teeth. As he untied the knotted rope, his words sank in to her. He meant to rape her. Her first instinct was to kick him the moment her feet were free, but that would only anger him, and tied up as she was, she would be no match for him. She had to somehow distract him. If he turned his back, maybe she could hit him over the head with something. She looked around, but saw no convenient objects she could wield. Still, she should try to stall him. If she could sit up, look around, mayhap she would spot something.

The rope untied and tossed aside, the man sat back on his haunches and peered down at her. "I been lookin' for'ard t' this e'er since ye was squigglin' 'bout in me arms. Let's see what ye got t' offer, huh?" he said and tossed up her skirt and petticoats.

Her hands no longer attached to her feet, Glynneth pushed the skirt back down. "I realize you mean to rape me," she said, trying to keep her voice from shaking. "But I do think it only right you should first give me something to drink. I am parched. And the deck of this boat is terribly hard. I wonder if we might have a blanket or two under us."

A guffaw broke from the man, and he nodded his head. "Ye be right. Where be me manners. We should have us a drink. An' let me introduce meself. Name is Filmore, Wallace Filmore. I will tell ye this frankly, I have ne'er had me a woman anywhere near as fine as ye be. A laidy ye be an' 'tis only fittin' I maike ye comfortable." Tilting his head, he glanced at her sideways. "Ye know, there be no reason this cannot be fun fer ye, too. Ye want t' be cooperative, I can maike it right nice for ye."

Swallowing, Glynneth said, "Yes. I would prefer this be as painless as possible. I already have a pounding headache."

"Now I bet ye do, an' I am right sorry 'bout that. Keane hit ye way too hard. But here let me he'p ye up. I will lay out a couple o' blankets t' pad yer arse, then I will pour us a little rum, an' we will have us a fine time."

He helped Glynneth into a sitting position, and while he went to the bow of the boat for blankets, she looked around. She was surprised to see the boat was not more than ten feet from the bank. The water looked calm and the bank slope gentle. She had no way of knowing how deep the water might be, and though she had never swum a stroke in her life, she had watched dogs swim. They just kept their heads up and paddled their front paws and hide legs. Surely she could do that, and it would not be for long.

She managed a smile for Filmore when he placed the blankets beside her. "Might you untie my hands so I can spread these out?" she asked.

"Sure, why not," he said, squatting in front of her. "I will be havin' t' retie ye, though, once we have our fun. Have t' gag ye, too, I am afeared. Settlement up the river a mite where I gots a delivery t' maike. Cannot have ye maikin' a fuss while we are there now can we."

He snorted and his breath near robbed her of hers. She pulled back and turned her head. She had to get away from this man. Even if she could not make it to shore, it would be preferable to drown rather than to let this inhuman beast touch her. She wondered if he could swim. Most likely not. If she could make it over the side of the boat, she would be free of him one way or another.

"There ye be," he said, rising and dropping the rope on the deck. "Ye spread out those blankets an' I will be gettin' us that rum."

When he turned his back she rose, ready to jump over board, but she realized she would have no chance to swim to shore with the heavy, sodden petticoats weighing her down. She had to get out of most of her clothes, and she had to delay him, keep him from getting the rum before she was ready to make her escape. "Would you help me please to get out of my skirt and petticoats?" she asked.

Jerking around, surprise on his face, he said, "Huh!"

"They are terribly binding, and the bodice is boned and is cutting into me." She knew she was taking a chance. He would be bound to fondle her as he helped her undress, but she could think of no other way to disrobe and keep him occupied at the same time. Mayhap if her head was not still aching she could have come up with a better plan, but that was not to be.

Filmore was eager to help her shed her garments. And his hands roamed over her in a fashion that near had her retching. When she had slipped out of the petticoats and bodice, and was down to naught but her shift, she said, "Now how about you get us that drink while I remove my shoes and hosiery." She had no intention of removing her shoes. She would need them once she reached shore. She would not be able to travel far on bare feet. She but hoped the shoes would stay on in the river.

He stood leering at her, and for a moment she feared he meant to forego the drink and take her right then, but grabbing his crotch, he massaged his member, and licking his lips, said, "Ye are right. A mite o' rum will maike this the better fer the both o' us."

As soon as he turned his back and took a step away from her, she backed up to the railing. When he bent and reached for his jug of rum, she sat on the railing, whirled around, and dropped into the water. The boat rocked, the water splashed, Filmore yelped, and the cold of the river took the air from her lungs. She sank under the water, but she kicked her feet, paddled with her hands, and was quickly up again, and gasping for air.

Glancing up, she saw Filmore leaning over the side of the boat looking down at her. "How did ye manage t' fall in?" he asked, reaching down a hand to her. "Here, grab me hand an' I will pull ye in afore ye drown."

Desperately paddling and kicking the way she had seen dogs swim, she managed to turn herself and head for the shore. "Here now, what are ye about? Come back here," Filmore called. "Crazy woman, ye will die alone in them woods. The bugs will eat ye alive. Come back here!"

Her arms and legs were quickly tired by her efforts, but in the next instant, one foot kicked the bottom, then the other foot hit bottom, and she was able to start walking the rest of the way to the embankment. Filmore was still yelling at her, but he was not coming after her. He had not followed her into the water. She had made good her escape. Struggling up the bank on her hands and knees, she began to shiver. Her exertion in the water had warmed her a bit, but as soon as the late afternoon autumn air hit her, the cold returned. And small insects rose from the leafy bank to attack her exposed flesh.

Not looking around as Filmore continued his threats and dire warnings, she headed into the woods. Not until she was hidden by the trees did she look back. Filmore had stopped calling to her, but he still stood at the railing. Fearful he might find some way to land his boat and come after her, she decided she had best leave the area. Then, too, she needed to escape the biting flies, needed to keep moving to warm herself. How she would keep warm during the night, she had no idea, but for the moment her only thought was to get as far away from Filmore as possible.

Jeanette inwardly fumed. Ever since Curtice returned with the quietly sobbing Meara in his arms, she had been reproved, rebuked, and reprimanded. And in front of the servants. Curtice had told her to keep her peace when she had offered to help with Meara. "Dominique will see to the child," he said, handing Meara into the servant's waiting arms. He brushed his hand over Meara's hair. "I will be up to see you when you are tucked into your bed, my little one."

Curtice then turned and chastised Jeanette, his French for the first time ever, harsh on her ears. "That you should have been so unkind to the child does you no credit, Jeanette. Where is your woman's heart?"

Indignant, Jeanette bristled. "I could not credit her story, Father Curtice. Surely you can understand that? Who would think someone would harm Noel or Glynneth?"

Ignoring her speech, he said, "We can only thank the Lord that Adler and Latty returned today. With luck they will find the men who abducted Glynneth." Tears welled in his eyes. "But we will never get our Noel back." Shaking his head, he said, "The brightest little star, and now he is gone. How will my poor heart survive this. First my son, now my beloved grandson."

"At least you still have Lothair," Jeanette said, and Curtice snorted. He snorted!

"Yes, Lothair," he said sadly. "Lothair is a good little boy, but he will never be Noel."

Never be Noel! How dare he dismiss her son in such a fashion. Well, Noel was no more. And Glynneth – why was she still alive? Curtice said she had been abducted, but that could not be right. Why would the men who threw Noel in the river abduct Glynneth? It made no sense. Seething she watched the old man trod slowly up the stairs. She hoped his heart did give out on him, then maybe she and Gaspard and Lothair could leave this terrible land with its wretched cold and horrid heat and biting flies and return to Ireland.

She had finished feeding Lothair and given him over to Lina when she heard voices downstairs. Tidying herself, she hurried down to see who had called and was surprised to find Meneer Kerstan. His news could not have been more devastating. They had found one of the men involved in the abduction and according to Meneer Kerstan, her husband and Adler and Latty had hired a sloep and gone chasing up the river after the second man. They believed Glynneth could still be alive. But why? Why?

And was it not just like her husband to have hired the sloep to go after Glynneth. Always Glynneth. God how she hated the woman. Pray God they would not find her. If they brought her back alive, Jeanette feared she could well go crazy. Especially after thinking she was finally rid of her nemesis. Curtice was, of course, jubilant. But they could do naught now but wait. It was going to be a long night for both of them – but for different reasons.

🌿 🌿 🌿 🌿

Adler cursed the tide. It now flowed against them. At least they still had the wind at their stern, and if necessary, two of the men Gaspard had hired, could take to the oars. Darkness was approaching much too rapidly. In all likelihood, Filmore would be putting in some place for the night. They could keep going up river despite nightfall. They had lanterns, but they might pass Filmore by, never see him tied up in some cove. The thought of Glynneth in Filmore's clutches sent chills up Adler's spine. They had to find them before Filmore could molest Glynneth. Did the man touch her, Adler swore he would kill him with his bare hands. His gut in knots, his eyes aching from the constant strain of watching the shore and the river ahead, he felt a sudden lightness when he spied a small settlement.

He recognized the thriving Dutch settlement. Farmers, fishermen, and a few trappers called it their home. It would be a good place for Filmore to put up for the night. A couple of small craft rocked gently near the shore. "Let's put in," he said, turning to Gaspard. "Could be Filmore is here or may have stopped here."

"I think we should keep going while we still have the light," Gaspard said. "We may yet catch them. Filmore cannot know we are after him."

Adler shook his head. "Something tells me we need to stop here. If Filmore carries various goods up and down the river, this could easily be one of his stops."

"You both have good points," Latty said, "but in this instance, I think we should go with Adler's gut instinct. By God, if it has not served us well in many a situation."

"All right, but we must be quick," Gaspard said, and turning to the man at the rudder, he ordered him to head for the settlement. A small dock had been extended out into the river, and Adler was out on it the moment the boat pulled up beside it. Leaving the boatmen to secure their craft, Adler, with Latty and Gaspard in his wake, sprinted toward a beckoning tavern.

Bursting in through the door, they startled a couple of customers, and the tavern keeper looked up in some alarm. "We are looking for a man." Adler addressed the room in the Dutch tongue. "There is a reward do we find him," he added. At his announcement, the men looked wary but interested. "The man's name is Filmore. He carries goods up and down the river."

"Oh, now, you just missed him," said a man who looked to be a farmer, his dress plain, his hair bobbed. "Mad as hell he was. Seems some indentured servant of his escaped him and fled into the woods."

"What!" Adler said. "She escaped!" She escaped, she escaped. It sang in his heart.

The man looked at him curiously. "How did you know his servant was a she?"

"We know because she is no servant. She is my sister-in-law, and Filmore abducted her" Gaspard blurted out and Adler cringed. All their effort to keep Glynneth's identity concealed was in jeopardy.

"We are attempting to rescue her," Gaspard added.

"Well, that may take some doing," said a second man. He scratched at the side of his bristled face. "Seems in a cove a short ways back, she jumped into the river and made it to shore. But how she will survive in the woods on her own, is a good question. Filmore did say should she wander out of the woods, we should hold her until he returns. He said she was apt to make up any kind of wild story, but we should not believe her."

"Filmore is the one who lies," Adler snapped, "and does he stop here again, tell him if he shows his face in New Amsterdam, he is a dead man. We will not suffer such behavior to go unpunished." He would love nothing better than to get his hands around Filmore's throat.

The first man spoke up again. "Cannot say I ever thought that much of Filmore. You can be sure we will do all we can for the woman does she make her way into the settlement."

"Come morning, we can even put together a search party," said the second man.

"Indeed," agreed the tavern owner. "Now can I offer you some ale? Not much to do now with the sun near to setting."

"Nay," Adler said. "I saw a canoe down at the river. If you can tell me who it belongs to, I mean to purchase it."

"Belongs to me," said a man from the corner of the room. Hidden in the shadows, Adler had not noticed him until he spoke.

Adler was at the man's table in three long strides. "As I said, I mean to purchase your canoe. Name your price."

"Not planning on selling it," the man said, his voice quiet and slightly accented.

The man's hat was pulled low over his brow so Adler could not see his face, but he meant to have that canoe whether the man was willing to sell it or not. He was going after Glynneth. She would not be spending the night alone in the woods. He meant to find her. But he needed the canoe to get him back to the small cove where she had made it to shore. He had to pick up her tracks before the night closed around them.

Before Adler could make any threats, the man pushed the hat up on the crown of his head and said, "Mean on making you a loan of the canoe. I will be wanting it back."

The anger that had been boiling up quickly evaporated, and Adler grasped the man's hand. Though he had never seen the man before, he liked the openness of his face, wide eyes, winsome grin. He appreciated the man's generosity, however, he had no time to reflect on it. Time was racing away. "Thank you. We will get it back to you in good condition." Turning to Latty, he said, "Let us go."

Latty needed no second bidding. He was out the door on Adler's heels.

"Why do we not take the sleop?" Gaspard asked, hurrying after Adler and Latty.

"Winds in the wrong direction. We would have to tack back and forth across the river. We have not the time. But the tide is in our favor, and we can hang in close to the bank. The canoe will be much faster. We must reach that cove before the light is gone. I have to find Glynneth's trail."

"But it will be pitch dark in less than an hour," Gaspard said. "Even do you find the trail, how can you hope to follow it?"

"He will follow it," Latty said. "The man is uncanny."

Back at the boat Adler said, "Latty, ready the canoe, I need to get a few supplies." He gathered up two blankets, some bread and cheese Gaspard had had the good sense to pack when he commissioned the boat, a tin cup, and a lantern. When he found Glynneth, and he would find her, she would be cold and hungry.

"What am I to do?" Gaspard asked.

"Best you wait here," Adler said. "If by some chance Glynneth does find her way out of the woods to the settlement, 'twould mean a lot to find family awaiting her."

Gaspard nodded. "Do I not hear from you, I will start a search party in the morning."

"Good." Adler clasped Gaspard on the shoulder. "Your forethought in having this boat readied made all the difference." He started off, but paused and looked back. "I will find her. Never fear," he added before hurrying off to the canoe.

He found Latty talking to the man who was lending them his canoe. "He figured we would be needing these," Latty said, holding up two paddles.

"Cannot thank you enough," Adler said, taking his paddle and stepping gingerly into the bow of the canoe. Latty sank into the aft and their benefactor pushed them off. Looking back over his shoulder, Adler called, "I have not your name."

"Name's Spangler, Lambert Spangler. Good hunting, sir."

Chapter 30

"This has to be it," Adler said as they paddled into a cove. "Keep as close to the shore as you can." While Latty paddled, Adler searched the bank. Glynneth's trail should be easy to spot. There it was! Leaves strewn about, grass matted, and yes, hand and foot prints. "This is it," he cried. "Nudge the canoe into the bank."

Latty did as bid, and Adler hopped out and pulled the canoe up the gently sloping bank. A swarm of mosquitoes and flies rose up to greet him, but he had spent enough time in the woods to be used to the annoying creatures. Latty swatted his neck before scrambling from the canoe. "A plague on these pesky little devils," he snapped. "Let us get this canoe secured and get away from here."

"I am with you," Adler said.

They soon had the canoe hidden, the supplies bundled, and with the last bit of light, Adler picked up Glynneth's trail. "She is going to be easy to follow," he said.

"While there is still a light, but the sun has set. We have not but the afterglow, and that will soon be gone," Latty said.

"Aye, but look above your head, Latty. What do you see?"

Latty looked up. "A lot of tree branches."

"Right again. Naught but branches. Most of the leaves have fallen, and there is a big harvest moon on the rise. Many is the time I worked beside my father and brother to bring in the wheat by the light of the moon. Its beams will shine right down through the branches and light up every broken twig and branch, every scuffed patch of leaves." He knelt and brushed aside a few leaves to show Latty a slight indentation of a heel. "Glynneth is not trying to hide her trail. She is but fleeing. As fast as she can by the looks of it. And should we need it, we have the lantern." As he spoke, he pulled his hatchet from his belt and notched a tree.

226

"Why do you do that?" Latty asked. "I cannot think you will have any trouble finding your way back to the river."

Adler chuckled. "Nay, I will not, but you may."

"Me?"

"Aye. Depending on what condition Glynneth is in when we find her, she may not be able to return to the canoe tonight. You may need to make your way back on your own. Someone will have to tell Gaspard so he can bring the sloep down to pick us up come morning. And Spangler's canoe must be returned."

"You are saying I should be that someone."

"I am," Adler answered, but gave Latty no explanation. They both knew why. Adler was the better woodsman. He could take better care of Glynneth. There was no knowing what condition she would be in when they found her. He but hoped they would soon find her.

Darkness overcame them, and the moon had yet to fully rise. They had no choice but to stop. "We will have us a wee bite," Adler said, taking the bundle from his back. "My stomachs been gnawing since before we reached the settlement. Do you realize we have had naught to eat and little to drink since this morning?"

"Aye. I thought I would be sitting down to a nice supper with the Fortiers this evening. Never dreamed we would be on the river again. I could sure do with a mug of ale right now."

"Well, let us eat. Soon the moon will be beaming down on us, and we can pick up Glynneth's trail again."

"Pick it up! You have not lost it?" Latty's voice rose in consternation.

"Nay. She is following a deer path. Easy for her. Easy for us. My guess is it will lead us to a nice brook where we can wash down this bread and cheese. But until the moon is up, I will not take a chance. She might veer off the path. I have got to be alert to that possibility."

"Right you are," Latty said, accepting a hunk of bread and a piece of cheese.

They ate in silence, often looking up. Adler hated having to wait on the moon, but he had no choice. The longer they had to wait, the longer Glynneth was alone and cold and hungry, and probably scared. And dear God, to have seen her son killed. She had to be heartbroken. How she must be feeling he could scarcely imagine. It had to be the way he would feel had Glynneth been killed. That was too horrid to contemplate.

At last the moon was high enough for its beams to penetrate the woods. "Be near bright as day before much longer," Adler said, rising. "We go."

Latty was instantly on his feet, and they were back on the path. Adler continued to mark trees along the way. Did they not find Glynneth soon, he worried about sending Latty back on his own. The man was a master shot, and he could walk all day and never tire, but his other woodsmen skills were sorely lacking. The two of them had made a good team, but that was soon to end. Latty would pursue his dream of owning a vast estate, and he would hopefully go into business with Kerstan. And mayhap, someday he would win Glynneth's love.

"Ah ha," he said. "Just as I thought. You can hear the brook ahead."

In a matter of moments, the deer path they had been following, and that Glynneth had followed, ended at a bubbling stream. The spot was lovely with the moon shining down. It was easy to see Glynneth had taken some time there. She had knelt beside the brook to drink her fill. She had lain down for a bit to rest. Leaves had been bunched to make a little bed. Mayhap she had used the leaves to warm herself. She had to be chilled after swimming to shore. Swimming. She constantly amazed him. He would never have dreamed she could swim.

"Our Glynneth is a smart one, Latty," he said. "Look, she is following the stream. I told her once that one of the first things Armand taught us was to follow a stream if we got lost. It would keep us from going in circles and would lead to the river or a settlement. And that is what she is doing. She is following this stream. Means you can head back to the canoe now."

"What!" Latty looked at him in surprise.

"Glynneth will not stray from the stream. Now I know I will soon find her. With night, she is bound to have found a place to bed down. She is no doubt very weary. So if you head back now, you can be back in the settlement for the night. Then meet us at the cove tomorrow."

Latty cocked his head. "You feel certain you will find her?"

"Not a doubt."

"Then I shall go back. Though should you be wrong, Gaspard's and my disappointment will be great."

Adler clamped his hand on his friend's shoulder. "I am not wrong. I know our Glynneth. Now off with you. You should have no trouble finding your way back. I marked the trail well, but do you think you need the lantern, you may take it."

Latty shook his head. "Nay. You keep it." He thinned his lips and Adler wondered if he meant to say more, but he but gave a nod and headed off down the path. Adler watched him until he disappeared, then he took off after Glynneth. Soon he would find her, and he could assure himself she was safe. For the moment, little else mattered.

❉ ❉ ❉ ❉

Shivering, Glynneth snuggled up closer to the mossy fallen tree. She pulled more leaves up around her, and pushed others about to better pillow her head. She knew she had been asleep, and was not certain what had awakened her. The cold, her hungry stomach, the ache in her heart, the fear she would starve to death before she again reached any kind of civilization? She knew she had cried herself to sleep, but then she had been crying on and off ever since she had escaped Filmore. Would the memory of that vile man ever leave her?

A number of times sounds in the woods had frightened her. What if she came across a bear or a wolf? What would she do? But each time the noise had been caused by a squirrel or a bird. When dark settled over the woods, she sought a place to sleep. Now as she gazed up through the branches, she was surprised at the amount of light shining down. Such a bright moon. Everything seemed to glow.

What was that sound? She raised her head. A strange sound, but it was the sound that had awakened her. She was certain of it. She heard it again. It sounded like someone calling her name. It definitely sounded like a human voice, not some noise made by an animal. Could it be Filmore? Might he be following her? Fear clamped around her heart. The voice was coming closer. Yes, the voice called her name. But it sounded like a voice she should know. A voice she should not fear.

Then it came clearly to her. "Glynneth, it is Adler. Be not afraid." She sat up. Was she dreaming? Hallucinating? There it came again, closer. "It is Adler." But how, how could it be Adler? Peering into the woods, she saw a bobbing light, like a lantern. It was a trick. It had to be Filmore pretending to be Adler. But no, Filmore would not even know Adler.

"Glynneth, be not afraid, dear one," came the voice.

Filmore would never call her 'dear one'. It had to be Adler. Somehow, as impossible as it seemed, he had come for her. "Adler," she called out. "I am here, I am here."

"Glynneth," he called. "At last I have found you." The little light danced along until the man carrying it appeared out of the forest. He dropped the lantern to the ground as Glynneth raced into his arms.

"Oh, Adler, Adler. Am I but dreaming. Are you for real? Are you truly here?"

His arms closed about her, and he pressed her to his chest. "Thank the Lord you are safe," he said, and as she wept, his hand went up to stroke her hair. "You need have no fear now. You are safe, and tomorrow we will take you home."

She heard the thudding of his heart, and it helped calm her. "How came you to be here? How did you find me? How did you know I was abducted? How did you know I escaped?"

"Here," he said, "you are shivering. I have blankets. I have food. Let me but get you warm and get a fire going and some food in your stomach and I will then tell you all."

She was afraid to release him, afraid if she let go of him she would awake and find he was naught but a dream. Finally at his gentle urging, she let go of him with one hand, but with the other she continued to grip his coat sleeve. Despite her hold on him, he managed to untie the pack on his back. It dropped to the ground, and he scooped up a blanket and draped it about her shoulders. Warmth. The warmth was real. At least she was pretty certain it was real. Could it be she was not dreaming? Adler next handed her a kerchief wrapped around a hunk of bread and wedge of cheese. She tentatively took a bit of the cheese. It tasted real. She swallowed. Her stomach reacted with jubilant appreciation. Tentatively releasing Adler, she concentrated on the meal he provided her.

"Come now," he said. "It looks like you selected a good location for us to bed down for the night. You sit on that log while I get us a fire going. We have a nice clear sky so we have no need to worry about rain. That means the second blanket I brought can be used for your bedding. Are you warming up some?"

She nodded in the affirmative, but thought he might not have seen her. Swallowing a piece of bread, she said, "Yes, I am getting warmer."

"Good. Let me but get a fire started then I will heat you up some water. That will help warm you from the inside. Sorry I have no ale."

"You need be sorry about nothing. I still think I am dreaming. I am afraid I will awaken and find you are naught but a dream."

He stopped his fire preparations and dropped to one knee in front of her. "Nay, my dearest Glynneth. Have no such fear. I am real. You are safe. Trust me."

She touched his face. Felt the several days' stubble on her palm. Oh, he was real. He was very real, and she did trust him. "Yes, my dear friend, I believe you. My noble knight, please rise." The image of a knight that sprang to her mind made her think of her daughter. How Meara loved the stories of King Arthur and his court. Tears came to her eyes. "Do you know aught of my daughter, Adler? Is she safe?"

Adler rose and sat beside her on the log. He took her in his arms and brought the top of her head to his cheek. "Meara is safe and well. And she is a very brave and bright little girl. 'Tis thanks to her that we were able to find you. Right now she is asleep in her bed with Dominique or Capucine at side. I have much to tell you, but I must get us a fire going."

She thanked him, and he rose to finish setting up their camp. Pushing away leaves, he cleared a spot, dug a pit for the fire, lined the pit with rocks from the stream, gathered wood, and soon had a fire glowing. He set a tin cup of water near the fire to warm while he bunched up a bed of leaves and moss next to the log. Throwing a blanket over the leaves, he invited Glynneth to join him on the couch he had made. She slid down beside him and together they shared the bread and cheese and the warm water. The lantern oil having burned low, Adler extinguished the flame, but with the firelight and the silvery moon glow, they had no trouble seeing each other.

As relief of her own predicament washed over her, Glynneth's thoughts turned to her son. "Noel," she whispered. "My baby." A lump formed in her throat. "Oh, Adler, those horrid men threw Noel in the river. Why? Why?" She could not stop the tears that started to flow.

Adler's arms encircled her, and he drew her close. "Go ahead and cry, dearest Glynneth. 'Twill help heal the pain. I cannot say why, but I fear...," he hesitated.

Still crying, she peeked up at him.

He sighed. "I should not say anything yet. But...," again he halted and gnawed his lip.

"What do you know, Adler, that you are not telling me?" she stared up at him, the tears momentarily stopping.

He sadly shook his head. "Let me start at the beginning." He patted her shoulder and stared at the fire. "Latty and I arrived in New Amsterdam shortly after the dinner hour. Latty said he would check in with Gaspard, and he told me I should find you and apprise you of our arrival. We had returned to Fort Orange and learned of Etienne's death." He stopped and looked down at her. "Glynneth, I am so sorry. Was there any way I could bring him back, I would."

She nodded against his chest. "I know that, Adler. I know you cherished your friendship with Etienne, and he prized yours. That dreadful winter when you brought down his fever, you saved his life, and you gave me another year with him. I can never thank you enough for that."

"You owe me no thanks. He was my friend." Before she could say anything else, he renewed his tale. "After learning from Dominique that you were not to home, I started to leave. That is when I heard Meara calling to me. I expected to see you, but Meara raced into my arms with a story about you being abducted. She was frightened, but coherent. I at first thought to take her home, but Jeanette would not believe the child, so I took her to the office. There, Meara gave us a complete description of the men, the boat, and all that had befallen you."

She pulled away a little that she could better see his face. "'Twas but chance then that you returned this very day in time to come and find me?"

"'Twas but good fortune," he said slowly. "I shudder to think had we delayed even a day. Or had we arrived even a little later, I would not have encountered Meara. She would have told her tale to Jeanette and would not have been believed." He stopped, looked down at her, then looked away again. "Or even had she been believed, Jeanette would

232

have hidden the truth."

Glynneth cocked her head and tried to catch his eyes, but he was staring into the woods. "Why do you say that about Jeanette."

Frowning he again looked down at her. "Latty and I found one of the men who accosted you. With a little persuading, he told us where Filmore was taking you. Gaspard hired a boat and was ready to sail in short order."

Glynneth could imagine the persuasion administered to the man, and she silently thanked her two friends for their persuasive efforts.

"Glynneth, I know no easy way to tell you this, but the man said a woman paid him and Filmore to kill you and Noel. Fearing that woman might be Jeanette, to make sure Meara is safe, I left instructions either Dominique or Capucine should be with her at all times."

Glynneth gave a little shake to her head. Had she heard Adler right? A woman had paid to have her and Noel killed? Surely that woman could not be Jeanette. Surely Jeanette could not hate her that much. And why would she want to kill Noel? No one could hate Noel. But what woman would want her dead?

Realizing Adler was unaware of the thoughts tumbling about in her head, she returned her focus to him as he continued, "We put in at a settlement just up river from the cove where you escaped Filmore. 'Twas there we learned of your escape." Shaking his head, he looked down at her. She could read admiration in his eyes and felt warmed by it. "God, Glynneth, you cannot imagine the relief we felt. Latty and I borrowed a canoe and went back to the cove, found your trail, and followed it to the brook." He smiled. "I knew you would stay with the brook, so I sent Latty back to tell Gaspard. They will meet us at the cove in the morning. By tomorrow afternoon, you will be home with your daughter. But how? How did you escape Filmore."

She took a moment to digest all he had told her. Fate had brought Adler back in time to come to her rescue. But fate had been cruel as well. It had taken her son. Her link to Etienne. Sitting beside Adler, snug and safe in his arms, she felt she had found a refuge from the horrors she had been dealt. She had no doubt of Adler's love for her. She believed he loved her far more than she could ever love herself. Few women would ever know such selfless devotion.

Shifting slightly to snuggle closer to Adler, she told her tale, from the attack, to waking up on Filmore's boat, to her escape strategy, and its successful conclusion. First came her joy of being safe, later came her fear and the numbing cold, the hunger, and the terrible pain in her heart. As she struggled through her account, Adler stroked her hair, made appropriate comments from soothing umms to angry snarls. He wiped a tear from her cheek, and she was certain he planted a kiss on the top of her head. She shifted again, and raising her chin, brought her lips close to his.

His eyes held hers, then ever so tentatively his lips met hers. Sweet and gentle was his kiss. So light, she could almost believe she was imaging it. Reaching up, she cupped her hand at the back of his head and brought his lips more forcefully to hers. She needed him. Needed him to love her. Needed him to take the pain, the incredible, numbing pain from her heart. He answered her need, pulling her closer to him, so close she could feel his heart hammering against her breast. His lips firmed, and he deepened the kiss. She responded with a fervor she had thought she would never feel again.

This man was not Etienne, but he loved her, and he stirred in her a passion that need no longer be denied. Did she love him? Yes. She loved his strength, his honesty, and yes, his intelligence. He might not have been educated like Etienne. He might not be able to discuss the histories of the ancients or the literature or art of the great masters, but he had found her in this great wilderness, and he had seen her daughter would be kept safe until their return. He was a good judge of human nature. And he enjoyed learning. They could have a good life together.

Giving free rein to her ardor, she encouraged his kisses and his gentle caresses. His touch sent thrilling shivers coursing through her body. She helped him struggle out of his coat, waistcoat, and breeches, and they both laughed a little self-consciously at the awkwardness. Then he removed his shirt, and she placed her hand on his broad chest, feeling the muscles. She stroked his arms and finally lowered her gaze to his manhood. He was ready for her, and raising her arms, she let him slip her shift off over her head.

He pulled her to him and the feel of his bare skin on hers set every nerve in her body to tingling. Again their lips met, and he entwined his

234

fingers in her hair. Slowly he urged her down on the blanket, and they stretched out together, their bodies melding. "My dear Glynneth, I love you so very dearly. Are you certain you want this? I would not want to take advantage of you. You have been through so much."

"Hush." She stroked his cheek. "Did I not want this, did I not know you love me, I would not be lying with you." She again found his lips, and with a groan, Adler entered her. They moved together as if they had been lovers for many years. Neither of them felt a need to rush their first intimacy. They were as one, in sync with time yet beyond time. When at last he slipped his fingers between them and caressed her, she exploded in a molten deluge, and he followed after her. Never had she soared to such a height. Never had her release been so all encompassing. From head to toe, she pulsated with a pinnacle of fulfillment.

When at last she came back down to earth, replete and flush with a blissful euphoria, she ran her fingertips down Adler's back. "Oh, my," she whispered. "I never knew love making could be so transporting. I believe I visited a whole new world amongst the stars."

"You were not there alone, Glynneth," Adler said, rolling onto his side, and carrying her with him in his strong embrace. "We climbed to those stars together. You filled all my senses and possessed my soul. How I wish I had the words to make you know how much I love you. How much I need you. But I do swear to you, my love, could I bring Etienne back to you, I would do so without the slightest hesitation."

"I know you would, Adler. I have never doubted your love for him."

"I would never wish to take his place in your heart," he said, stroking her hair, "but if someday, you would consider marrying me, I could know no greater happiness. 'Tis too soon to be asking for your hand, but I need you to know I would wait for you forever."

Chapter 31

"I think I would not like to wait forever, Adler. I think I would not like to wait even a full month, but I suppose we must, for you will have to find us a place to live."

Adler blinked his eyes. Could he have heard Glynneth correctly? Had she said she would marry him? Surely he must be dreaming. He had experienced the most glorious moment of his life. He had become one with the only woman he had ever loved, would ever love, so his mind could well be fogged.

Rising to a sitting position, he stared down at Glynneth. "My dear love, did you say you would marry me?"

She reached up her arms to him. "Yes, Adler, I wish to marry you, the sooner the better. But come back to me, 'tis cold without you."

Sliding down beside her, he pulled the blanket up around them then gathered her into his arms. "I cannot but think I must be dreaming. No man on earth could be happier than I am." He kissed her, a long sweet, soft kiss, then pulled back to see her face. "I have loved you, Glynneth, since that first night we met. Wrongfully so, I know that. You were a happily married woman with two lovely children. But I could not help my love for you. You saved my life. You brought peace to my grieving soul. You gave me hope that life could still hold some meaning for me.

"I immediately came to love Etienne, as well. Loved and honored and respected him. I cannot think I have ever known a finer man. That he called me friend is as great an honor as anyone has ever bestowed on me. Had he been a well man, hale and hardy as is Gaspard, I would never have sailed with you to this new land. I knew my love for you was wrong."

Glynneth started to protest, but he put his finger to her lips. "No, my dear, loving you, a married woman, was sinfully wrong, but I feared for your safety. Etienne was not well, Curtice is old. I wanted to be to hand

236

to protect you, if 'twas needed. I had to sail with you."

"And so you have protected me, my dear Adler. Protected me, my husband, and my children." Tears welled in her eyes. "Except now I have lost my little Noel ...," she coughed and looked down. "My poor baby ... he was so fond of you and of Latty. You were the strong fathers Etienne could not be for him." She looked back up. Her lips quivered. "Oh, Adler," her voice cracked, "how could anyone want to kill that dear little boy?"

His heart bursting for Glynneth, Adler gathered her into his arms. Her wet cheek rested against his, and her body shook with her sobs. He held her close, stroked her back, murmured softly, and let her cry. She needed to cry. Could he take her pain from her and give it to himself, he would do so gladly, but he could do naught but wait for the tears to subside. She would be drained and ready to sleep. Sleep would give her a respite from the pain.

Slowly the sobs weakened. Her body relaxed, but she still clung to him. "Thank you, Adler. As always, you are ever my shield." She rubbed her cheek against his. He wished he had shaved more recently, but she seemed not to notice his prickly face, for she did not pull away. "I do love you," she whispered. "Not in the same way I loved Etienne. Differently, very differently, but equally. In some ways you are much like Etienne. In other ways, so opposite."

She sighed and gave him a half smile. "Tonight when we made love, I felt as one with you. We seemed to have been made for each other. I believe 'twas fate we were to meet and bond there on that Dutch ship. Both of us bound for new lives. Both of us attempting to escape our fears. My fear was that I would lose my husband. I knew Etienne was dying, but I could not let him go. Was there any chance he might improve here in this new land, I had to take that chance. And I think I had over two extra years with him because we moved here."

She looked thoughtful, and Adler waited, not wanting to interrupt her rumination. He was joyful she said she loved him. His heart had soared at her admission. But his joy was tinged with sorrow for her for the loss of her beloved husband.

Glancing away from him then back, she at last spoke again. "You, Adler, your fear is of being closed in. You hate small tight places, or at least any place you cannot leave when you wish. You left your home and family behind because you feared prison, not death. Would it pain you greatly to tell me of this fear of yours?"

He met her gaze. She had agreed to marry him. She had a right to know any and all his secrets. He nodded. "I will tell you of my fear. A shameful fear it is, but I cannot escape it."

"Nay," she declared. "'Tis nothing shameful about it. You are no coward, dear Adler. We all have our fears. I wish to know more of yours only that I may know you better."

Again he nodded. "So you shall hear all, but first I must replenish our fire. And here, your shift has been warmed by the fire. Don it, the air grows more chill. I will be but a few moments." He slipped into his shirt and boots, and busied himself collecting wood. The ground was strewn with dried twigs and branches, and the harvest moon, casting its glow over the woods, made finding them easy. Soon he had the fire again blazing and had enough wood to see them through the night. Glynneth had remade their bed, and sat crossed-legged on it, the extra blanket wrapped around her. He settled back down beside her, and she slipped a portion of the blanket around him.

"Are you warm enough?" he asked.

"I am, and I am quite comfortable."

He heaved a sigh. "Very well. I shall tell you my tale."

Staring at the fire, he let his memory take him back to the family farm he had loved so dearly. He saw the well-maintained ditch that kept heavy rains from flooding the croft. The stone house with its neatly thatched roof, the barn, the chicken coop, the pig sty, and the household garden plot – the well – all came into view.

Slowly, painfully that frightful day that had nearly cost him his life resurfaced. "I was nine, I think." He paused, wiped his hand across his brow, felt the sweat. Forcing himself to continue, he said, "My mother was not well. She was recovering from a miscarriage. She was weak. My six year old brother, Caleb, was sick with the measles. I helped my father tend the sheep, make sure the lambs were all up on their feet. The night before there had been a late spring frost. All were fine, so Father was off to help a neighbor dig a new ditch around his croft, and he sent me home to help Mother.

238

"On the way to the house, I stopped at the well to draw water." He glanced at Glynneth then looked back at the fire. "This was a job my father usually did, but I felt grown up. Was I not there to help my mother. Our well rim was low, the well deep, the water cool and clear. I dropped the bucket in. It was a heavy wooden bucket. Well caulked to hold the water. The rope was of a strong hemp." He shivered.

Glynneth touched his hand. "Mayhap I ask too much of you. Another time, perhaps."

He patted her hand that rested gently on his, but not looking at her, he said, "Nay, you faced your fears, I must face mine." He drew in a deep breath and continued. "I started pulling up the bucket. It felt leaden. The rope tore at my hands, but I was determined. I would get that bucket of water for my mother. I imagined her surprise and her praise. I had the bucket nearly to the top. A wee bit more and I could grab it, pull it over the rim. I was feeling proud of myself."

Turning to Glynneth, he shook his head. Answering his half smile with one of her own, she said nothing, but she kept her comforting hand on his. "Chickens, pigs, goats had free run about the croft during the day. As I grabbed the handle of the bucket with one hand and was reaching with my other hand, a squealing pig darted between my legs." He swallowed and squeezed his eyes shut. "I lost my balance. Into the well I went, right after the bucket. I bumped against the side of the well on the way down and grazed my arm." He rubbed his arm as if he could again feel the scraping. Opening his eyes, he said, "Luckily for me, the bucket tumped over on the way down, so when it hit the water, it floated. I landed on the bucket. Hurt my ribs something fierce, but I grabbed hold of that bucket and clung to it, knowing it was all that kept me from drowning. As soon as I regained my voice, I started calling for help. My voice bounced off the walls of the well, but it was too young a voice to make it to the top of the well and beyond. Too weak for my mother in the house to hear me."

"Oh, my poor Adler," Glynneth said, resting her head against his shoulder.

Appreciating her sympathy, he kissed the top of her head. Worried his tale might lead her to think of Noel, thrown into the fast moving river, but with no bucket to cling to, he hurried on. "I spent near the entire day in that well. My father, since he was helping the neighbor, was having dinner with him. Both Mother and Caleb were housebound. I was scared, miserable, and numb with cold, but I also felt terrible guilt. My father had sent me home to give aid to my mother, and I was no help to her at all. I pictured her, sick, but trying to comfort my brother. I imagined both of them hungry and no one there to fill their porridge bowls or cut them chunks of bread. Mother, weak as she was, would have to drag herself out of her bed to fix their meal."

Glynneth shook her head against his arm. "I can think of few people in your frightful position who would be feeling guilt at such a time. Only you, you dear man, would be more concerned about the needs of others than of your own dreadful situation."

"'Twas pride, Glynneth, pride that had me in that situation. Pride and pride alone."

Glynneth placed her palm on his cheek and turned his face until he looked at her. "Pride is not always bad, Adler," she said. "To be proud of your work, to be proud of your home and family. To try your best to do a man's job is not wrong."

He kissed her creased forehead. "My dear love, how kind are your words." Gazing deep into those eyes he loved so dearly, those eyes that gave him so much comfort, he resumed. "I hollered until I no longer had a voice. Looking up from my hole, I watched the sky. A piece of the sun appeared, then it was a round globe directly overhead. I watched it disappear, watched clouds come and go. My arms grew so tired from holding onto that bucket, and I was so cold. I thought about letting go. I wondered what it would be like to drown. Would it hurt? Then I thought how my father needed my help. Mother needed my help. They would think me a coward if I gave up, so I continued to cling to that bucket. At some point I fell asleep, lost my grip on the bucket, and found myself swallowing water. I panicked. It was dark in the well, but as I lashed out, my hand hit the bucket. I grabbed it and pulled it to me.

"I realized the sky had grown dark. Then I heard my name being called. My father was calling me. I tried to call back, but I could barely hear myself. How was my father to hear me? I think I was more scared then than at any time. I knew I could never make it through the night. My father had to find me."

His voice grew soft, his eyes glazed over, and he was back in the well. The numbing cold, the terrifying feeling that he would die there in that well. The walls closed in on him.

"Adler, Adler," he could hear his father calling.

Then he saw a light, a lantern light. His father held it over the well. He could see his father above him trying to peer down into the dark depths. He called up to him in the loudest voice he could muster. "Here I am. I am here, Father." His voice was little more than a squeak, but somehow his father heard him. "

"Hold on boy," he said. "Hold on to the bucket. I will pull you out."

The rope grew taunt, and he and the bucket started to rise, but as he left the water, his tired arms could not hold onto to the bucket. With a little screech, he dropped back into the water. For an instant he thrashed madly about in the cold water before the bucket splashed back down beside him. He grabbed it, clutched it to him as desperate tears filled his eyes.

His father called to him again. "That is all right son. I will get another rope. Hang on."

When his father disappeared, fear gripped Adler's heart, but in a few moments, his father returned with a large log that he pushed across the opening of the well. He tied a loop in a rope and lowered the looped end down into the well.

"Slip the loop under your arms and pull it tight," his father said.

Adler tried to do as directed, but his fingers and hands were numb, and he was afraid to turn loose of the bucket. "I cannot manage it, Father," he whimpered.

"Yes you can, Adler. Get one arm in, then get the other. You can do it."

Somehow, the firmness, the confidence in his father's voice gave him the courage to try. With stiff fingers he grasped the bucket with one hand and managed to get the loop over then under one arm. Breathlessly, he switched hands on the bucket. Floundering in the water, he struggled to get the rope over and under his other arm. The bucket escaped him as he fought with the rope. Panic again seized him, but the rope tightened around him, and before he knew it, he was being pulled slowly up out of the water.

"Hold onto the rope, Adler," his father's voice came to him, and he obeyed, his stiff fingers gripping the rough hemp. He heard his father's grunts as he pulled on the rope, heard the rope scraping against the log his father used for leverage, then hands gripped his soggy shirt, another set of hands grabbed at his breeches, and he was pulled over onto the rim of the well.

"Hold onto him," his father said while securing the rope to the log. Then he was there, lifting Adler into his arms and clutching him to his chest.

"My son, my son," his father cried.

Adler was crying too, crying from so many emotions he could not put names to them. He felt other hands patting him and heard his mother's voice. "Oh, my poor Adler, my poor little love." His mother had left her sick bed. And Caleb was there. They helped pull him to safety.

"My poor love," he heard again, but it was not his mother speaking. It was Glynneth. "How very dreadful for you."

Slowly he came back to the present. He shook his head to clear his thoughts. "I was back in that well again. And whenever I am in any small closed space from which I cannot leave when I wish, the fear returns. I am back in the well, and I panic." He swiped his forearm across his brow and felt the sweat. "I am sorry. I know I must seem a coward. Letting a long ago childhood memory put me in such a trance."

"Oh, nay, Adler. I can only think what a very brave little boy you were. That the memory still haunts you is not surprising, nor is it anything that should shame you." Bringing his head down to hers, she softly kissed him. "And 'tis no wonder you so hated to leave your home. Much love was shared by you and your family."

"Aye, but had I not left them, I would not have found you. And you, Glynneth, are more dear to me than life itself." He returned her kiss, then his kiss became more passionate. He had bared his soul to her, and she had not rejected him. Responding to his passion, she slipped her arms around his neck.

The knot in his stomach lessened. The fear receded and his whole being became immersed in loving the woman in his arms. He wanted to ease her pain as she eased his. For as long as he lived, he meant to do all in his power to make her happy, to make her life complete and com-

242

fortable. She might not love him as she had loved Etienne, but that she loved him at all was to him as great a miracle as had ever transpired. He could not ask for more.

Their love making was slow and sweet, and when they again reached for the stars, they met in a sublime passion that left them breathless but replete. They lay together for a while, then Adler stirred himself to replenish the fire. Snuggling together under the blanket, he felt more content than he had ever felt, and with Glynneth's head resting on his shoulder, her soft breath on his neck, he fell asleep.

Chapter 32

Latimer leaned back against a tree and watched Gaspard pace back and forth. Swatting at a tiny black fly, he frowned. "Gaspard, if you must pace, go further into the woods. Leave off stomping about the marsh there." He looked at the muddy ground where the tiny skiff from their sloep was tied up. The hungry little bugs should be sleeping this time of day, the sun was near directly overhead, but instead, Gaspard kept them stirred up.

Sweeping about, Gaspard asked, "Are you certain this is the right cove?"

Latimer chuckled. "I may not be the woodsman Adler is, but I know my waterways."

"Then why are they not here? What could be keeping them? Could he have been wrong about finding Glynneth's trail?"

"Nay." Latimer shook his head. "Glynneth's trail was clear even to me. Mayhap she continued further than Adler thought she would, but rest assured, he never stopped until he found her. No doubt they will be here soon."

Gaspard resumed his pacing, but when he neared the marshy area, he halted and stood looking out at the river a moment before whipping about on his heel and stalking into the woods. Latimer watched him and sighed. Poor man. Saddled with a wife like Jeanette when he was madly in love with Glynneth. Latimer knew how Gaspard felt. Knew the desperate longing that would never be satisfied. But for Gaspard it had to be worse. All those years of wishing he could be his brother. No doubt envying his brother and hating himself for that envy, especially when Etienne grew more ill, then died. He could but imagine the guilt that resided in Gaspard's heart.

Pacing back to the water's edge but stopping short of the marsh, Gaspard barked, "How can you just sit there? Should we not go after them?"

"And end up lost in the woods and have to have Adler come find us? Nay, let us not."

"Did you learn nothing in all your traipsing about in the woods?" Gaspard snapped.

"Aye, I learned a most important lesson. I learned never to let Adler out of my sight." Gaspard started to retort, but Latimer hopped up and pointed into the forest. "They come," he said, starting off through the trees.

Gaspard was on his heels as he hurried forward to greet his friends. Latimer needed but one look at Glynneth and then at Adler to know the two had become lovers. They both glowed. For a moment a sharp pain stabbed at his heart. Glynneth would never be his. Despite the keen ache, he knew 'twas for the best. Adler was the right man for Glynneth.

Clasping Glynneth in a tight embrace, he whispered in her ear, "I have ne'er been so glad to see anyone in my life."

"Oh, Latty," she cried, tears filling her eyes, "how pleased I am to see you, dear friend."

Latimer released her that Gaspard might embrace her. Tears in his eyes, Gaspard could do nothing more than croak out a greeting to her.

Glynneth patted his back. "Yes, Gaspard, I am fine. Adler took good care of me. I had food to eat, blankets and a nice fire to keep me warm. And look how he fashioned me this dress." She pulled away from Gaspard to display the blanket adorning her. Adler had cut holes for her arms and had used a swath of rope to tie the blanket about her waist. Her hair a tousled mess, she, to Latimer's eyes, looked like a pagan goddess. And she was safe. Nothing else mattered.

Standing back he made out to be admiring her costume. "Aye, Madame Fortier, your gown is becoming, but the gown I have awaiting you on the sloep is perhaps a bit more suitable for your trek through New Amsterdam.

"Latty found a woman willing to part with her Sunday best petticoat and jump," Gaspard said. "I think 'twill fit you and look well enough no one will take undue note when you return."

"Cost Gaspard a hefty price, I might add," Latimer said, "but he came with plump pockets, so all is well. We thought it best your abduction not become public knowledge."

Glynneth grabbed Latimer's hand and reached for Gaspard's. "Thank you both so much. How lucky I am to have such dear friends."

Gaspard reddened and looked to Latimer. "'Twas Latty who thought of your need. I did naught but supply the coin."

"Both are worthy of my most heartfelt thanks," Glynneth said. "But now, I am most eager to get home to my daughter."

"Right you are," Latimer said. "The skiff is small. It will accommodate but two. I mean to take Gaspard back first, then you, and last Adler. I have no reason to distrust our sailors, but I prefer one of us be at your side until you are safely home."

"Aye," Adler said. "Good thinking Latty. So heave off that we may head for home."

Latimer thought it best not to leave Gaspard alone with Glynneth. It would be too hard on the man. He might say something foolish that he would not be able to take back. With the skiff flitting back to the sloep, he glanced over Gaspard's shoulder at Adler and Glynneth. The two were lost in each other. That was good.

※　※　※　※

Glynneth stood between Adler and Gaspard at the bow of the sloep. In the small cabin, she had washed as best she could before donning the clothing Latty had found for her. She then tucked her tousled hair up under a lappet cap Latty also had the good sense to purchase. He was a good and caring man. She knew he thought himself in love with her, but his love was not the kind Adler felt for her. Latty's was but an infatuation. She somehow fit an image of a woman he had conjured up in his mind, most likely in his youth, and he was yet unwilling to part with that imagery. But someday he would – when he found the right woman.

Her concern now was with Gaspard. He seemed unwilling to be parted from her. He kept touching her as if he was afraid she might vanish. She would like to enjoy time with Adler on the way home, to stand with him as they had on the voyage from Rotterdam, both reveling in the feel of the wind and the spray in their faces, fingertips occasionally touching and shooting sparks between them. But Gaspard would not leave her. He prattled on, telling her about all the efforts involved in finding her. He made no mention of Jeanette, though. Mayhap he had no knowledge of his wife's possible malefaction. Adler had not said if he mentioned his suspicion to Gaspard.

She tried to make appropriate answers, to offer praise for the ingenuity of all those involved in her rescue. Much Gaspard was telling her, she had learned from Adler. She would have far preferred some quiet time to gather her thoughts. She could not keep a niggling worry about Meara from rising. Adler could have calmed her fears, but he could do naught but stand by silently as Gaspard, often repeating things he had previously told her, continued his monologue.

Hearing footsteps, she turned slightly as Latty joined them at the bow. Grasping Gaspard's elbow, Latty said, "I have need of your advice, Gaspard. I wonder would you grant me some of your time. I must make an important decision and make it soon."

Gaspard looked confused. "A decision? What kind of decision? I am talking with Glynneth, telling her of all who helped solve the mystery of her abduction and then set about her rescue. Can we not speak on the morrow."

"Nay," Latty said, pulling Gaspard more forcefully. "I must make the decision this evening. Concerns a deal with Spangler, and I can think of no one who could give me better advice. Come let us get out of this wind and go somewhere that we may speak privately."

"But....," Gaspard protested, looking over his shoulder at Glynneth as Latty drew him away. "I have not finished...."

"Adler can finish telling her all about how wonderful we all are. Come now." Latty, too, looked over his shoulder at her. He winked.

Dear man, she thought, and smiling, she fluttered her hand. "You go ahead, Gaspard. Help Latty. I wish to stand here and feel the wind in my face. A little quiet will do me good. Go on. Latty has need of you."

As the two men disappeared, she turned to look up at Adler and said, "How kind of Latty. Somehow he knew I needed time alone with you. Do you think he knows about us?"

Adler smiled and nodded. "He knows. When he rowed me over from shore, he said, 'So you have won her, have you?' I could not help but admit you have agreed to marry me." His forehead creased. "I hope my telling him has not upset you."

"Why should it upset me, my dear love?" She patted his hand. "Who better to be the first to know of our betrothal than our dear friend. I but find it amusing that he should have guessed."

"He says we glow."

"Do we?" She tilted her head. "Mayhap we do. I know I never thought to feel this way again. My heart is so heavy at the loss of Noel, yet my love for you, and your love for me help me face the painful burden."

Gazing down at her, his love for her in his eyes, he said, "I would I could take every pain you must feel into my own heart and relieve you of it." He glanced over his shoulder. "I wish I could hold you close, but 'twould not yet be right. Not until our betrothal has been announced. I would have nothing besmirch your reputation."

She nodded. She would have liked to lean against Adler and rest her head on his strong shoulder, but for her family's sake, she knew they must be circumspect. "'Tis hard to wait. Tonight we will tell Meara and Father Curtice, and of course, Gaspard. Tomorrow, we will make our announcement public."

"The day I call you my wife will be the happiest day of my life."

"Let us hope it will be soon, and yet, we have talked but little of your plans." Over their breakfast of dry bread, crumbling cheese, and water at their campsite that morning, Adler told her his days in the wilderness were finished. He had no intention of leaving her. He briefly outlined his hopes of entering the boat building business.

She liked his idea. "I think 'twould be good, do you and Meneer Kerstan form a partnership. He is a good man. But what do you know of boats, Adler?"

He chuckled. "Very little, but I see the need for more boats. I have the investment money to expand Kerstan's shop and to hire and train more workers. Of course, all depends on whether Kerstan wishes to expand. Though I think he may. He wants a promising future for his children. That is why he wishes to see them educated beyond the basics."

"I hope you may be right. I like the Kerstans. They are honest, caring people, and Hendrika has become a cherished friend."

"They are good people," he agreed. "Kerstan's apprentice seems a fine lad, too. He will be able to help train new workers."

248

"We have much to look forward to, my love," she said, deliberately touching her fingertips to his and feeling the physical rush that always accompanied that small intimacy. "But do bear in mind, I have my dower and inheritance from Etienne to contribute."

Adler shook his head. "Nay, sweet love. That will go to Meara. I will provide for us."

"Do you use your earnings to buy us a house, you will have less to invest with Meneer Kerstan. Do I use my dower to buy the house, the house can still someday go to Meara as her dower." She held up a hand as he started to protest. "When your business is successful, do you then choose to provide us with a new house, all to the good. But let us not handicap our future by using your earnings in a way that is not to our best interest. Surely when your brother married his love, he accepted a dowry."

Smiling half-sheepishly, Adler admitted his brother's wife had brought a substantial dowry to their marriage. "Aye. As our land abutted the Yardleys', Sidonie's father tendered a prime grazing mead-ow and ten cows to the contract."

She smiled, knowing she had won the debate. "And does your brother use that meadow and those cows?"

Adler laughed out loud. "He does indeed. Your point is taken. But look you," he said pointing ahead. "New Amsterdam comes into view."

She turned to look. Soon she would be safe at home. Soon she would hold her daughter in her arms, but never again her dear little son. Tears filled her eyes, and she blinked. Life could be so full of joys and yet deal out such incredible pain. But she would not be facing the pain alone. The man standing beside her would be her bulwark. And her love.

Chapter 33

Jeanette paced back and forth in her room. She knew she looked a fright. She had not slept the entire night. Her stomach was twisted in knots. Lothair must have recognized her distress for he had been more cranky than was his usual. She was actually glad when Capucine returned with her two boys and Meara so Lothair had the children to keep him amused and out from under her feet. She had been surprised the previous evening when Curtice allowed Capucine to cart Meara off to her house for the night.

"Poor little one," Capucine had said. "Does she have the boys to comfort her, 'twill help keep her from worrying so about her mother."

"Yes, yes, you are right" Curtice answered, his head bowed. "Best she stay the night with you. I would be poor comfort to the child this night."

Jeanette had started to suggest she would care for Meara, but Curtice had already chastised her for not believing Meara when the girl came with her story of her mother being abducted. His tongue had been sharp, biting. She had decided it best not to draw attention to herself. Relieved he had not joined her for supper, she had but picked at her meal before slipping off to bed without disturbing him. In the morning, when she emerged from her room and went downstairs to break her fast, she found him sitting slumped in the same chair she had seen him in before she had gone off to her own restless repose. She did not think he had been to bed all night.

Unable to eat more than a few bites, she watched Dominique coax Curtice to drink some ale and nibble on some dry toast. "Never fear, Monsieur Fortier," the maid said in her lilting French, "Monsieur Adler will find Madame. He will bring her safely home."

Answering her in French, the old man had slowly nodded. "Yes, I must trust he will, but my poor Noel is gone from me forever."

250

"He is lost to us, yes, but he is with his dear father. His father has him by his hand."

Curtice looked up. "Yes, Etienne has him in his care." Dominique's words seemed to have lightened his heart enough that he took the mug of ale and drank a few sips.

Jeanette sneered. She had grown to hate Dominique. Once she had envied Glynneth her cheerful maid, but the woman was too haughty. Glynneth should have taught the maid to mind her place. Well, with Glynneth gone, Dominique would soon know a firm hand. And Glynneth had to be gone. Surely they would not find her. Surely Filmore would kill her as she had paid him to do. Her thoughts went back to the day she first encountered the slovenly dressed Englishman, Keane. He accosted her outside the van der Berg's Mercantile Shop.

"Here now, Mevr. Might you be speaking English?"

Eager to return home to feed Lothair, she had left her maid, Lina, to gather up her purchases, and had exited the shop unattended. Disgusted by the man's appearance as well as his smell, yet a little fearful, she demanded, "What do you want?"

"Ah, you do speak English. 'Tis me lucky day. A job, Mevr. I am in dire need. I would be willin' t' do whate'er ye might need doin'."

Distracted, her mind on the argument she had had with Gaspard over his defense of Glynneth and the way Glynneth let her children enter into adult conversation, she had snapped, "Out of my way. The only thing I need is to be rid of my sister-in-law."

To her dismay, the man had stepped closer, his foul breath nearly taking hers away. "That I can be doin' Mevr. For the right sum, o' course."

For a moment she stared wide-eyed at him. What had he said? Get rid of Glynneth? Might it be possible? He must have noticed her hesitation because he persisted. "Taken care o' right an' tight, an' no one the wiser."

Confused by both the man's offer and her disturbing desire to actually be rid of Glynneth, she raised her chin haughtily and again snapped, "Out of my way." This time he did step back but to her own surprise, she took but a couple of steps before turning back to him. "Meet me outside the almshouse this time tomorrow," she said and hurried off.

Above the tap of her shoes on the cobble stones, she heard him answer. "I will be there."

Stumbling home, her wits in a fog, she contemplated her brazen behavior. Such a flurry of thoughts rushed through her head. Be rid of Glynneth. How glorious that had sounded. Then the almshouse had popped into her head as if by magic. Where else might she address such a creature and not be noticed. Able-bodied beggars were always hanging about the exterior, hoping for some kind of handout. And she could disguise herself. No one need be the wiser.

But what had the man meant when he said he could get rid of Glynneth? Did he mean kill her? Surely not. Yet what else could he mean? Did she want Glynneth dead? She wanted her out of the house. But dead? No. Kill Glynneth? That was impossible. It was wrong. She would not meet the man. She would not go out at all the next day. Would not risk encountering him. Her mind had been made up – at least until that evening.

She sat at the supper table, nibbling a piece of cheese, taking an occasional sip of a thin beef gruel, and watching Gaspard, his eyes alight, as he told Glynneth about an amusing encounter he had at work with a Herr Mogens who had arrived on the same French ship that had brought all the Jews from Brazil. Jeanette had waited – never once had her husband included her in the conversation. How Gaspard glowed when Glynneth laughed at his description of the little man and his eagerness to invest a goodly sum in some recently arrived merchandise. How he puffed his chest out when she praised his bartering skills.

Later that evening, Lothair, wobbling on his little chubby legs, toddled over to Glynneth. Jeanette hated that her son was drawn to Glynneth, but gritting her teeth, she smiled sweetly as Glynneth scooped Lothair up in her arms and gave him a big kiss.

Her insides burned, though, when Curtice criticized the little boy, saying, "Lothair is not near as stable on his feet as Noel was at that age." As always the old man compared Lothair to his older cousin, and he always found Lothair lacking, and Noel perfect. Jeanette realized she hated Noel. Was he not around, Lothair would again be the center of his grandfather's attention.

Defending Lothair, Glynneth said, "Nay, Father Curtice, Lothair is such a plump, healthy little babe, he but waddles a bit. He will soon

252

outgrow that."

Jeanette wished she, not Glynneth, had defended Lothair, but Curtice would not have heeded her. Continuing to darn a rent in her husband's hose, she seethed as Gaspard knelt beside Glynneth to tickle his son. But he was not looking at Lothair. He was looking at Glynneth's lips, and she could see the longing in his eyes. She had known then – she would meet Keane.

Wearing an old gown that she never wore outside the house, and with every strand of her hair tucked into a head rail, she snuck out of the house. She had fed Lothair early and put him down for his nap. She then sent Lina on a minor errand that should have her back to care for Lothair should he awaken and start to cry. Hoping she would be gone such a short time no one would notice her absence, Jeanette hurried down the street. Would the man be there? He was, but he had brought another man with him. The two men introduced themselves, then the one named Filmore suggested they leave separately but meet in a less trafficked area.

"We are not apt t' be seen behind the Squat Dog tavern," Filmore said. "Would not do t' have anyone taike note o' us." A degree less disgusting than Keane, Filmore had shrewd dark eyes under scraggly eyebrows. The way he looked at her frightened her, and she wished Keane had not brought the man with him. She considered not meeting them, hurrying home instead, but the memory of the way Gaspard looked at Glynneth, the thought of Curtice forever finding fault with Lothair while praising Noel resurfaced, and she hastened to the pre-scribed rendezvous.

"Keane tells me ye be needin' t' be rid o' yer sister-in-law. Ye got good reason fer it?" Filmore asked, his head slightly tilted.

Did she need a reason? "She means to take my husband from me. Means to make her son instead of mine his heir," she blurted out.

"Good enough fer me," Keane said.

Filmore nodded, and in short order, they determined the East River would be the best place for the deed to be done. A price was set, and arrangements made for Jeanette to pay them. They would again meet in front of the almshouse, and she would pass Keane the fee as though she was handing him a charitable donation. At the last moment, she decided she wanted to be rid of Noel as well. With naught but a shrug, the men agreed to it, asking for but two extra guilders.

Dazed by her own temerity, she raced away. Had she really agreed to pay the two men to kill Glynneth and Noel? Keeping her head down, avoiding any eye contact, she made it home without encountering anyone she knew. She slipped into the house by the back entrance. No one was about. She made it to her room, closed the door behind her, and leaned against it.

What had she done? What had she done? She straightened, stiffening her spine. She had done what she had to do to save her marriage. But would God condemn her? Nay! She shook her head. Glynneth was a non-believer, no different than the savages in this frightful land. Glynneth had turned her back on Christ. Her children would copy their mother. Better Noel should die young than that he should later forsake God and end in hell. Etienne had seen him baptized. She was actually saving him from everlasting damnation. As for Glynneth, for all she knew, Glynneth could well be a witch – the way she enchanted men was not normal. She could be casting spells on them. Why else would so many men be bewitched by her? Witch or no, she was evil, and life would be far better once Glynneth was no longer in it.

Finding the money to pay Keane and Filmore presented a bit of a challenge, but she could manage it. Curtice kept a large bag of coins in a strong box in his room. The box had a sturdy lock on it, but she knew where he hid the key. He would eventually notice the missing money, but the servants could be blamed. Dominique could be blamed. Who better, the haughty doxy. Several times she had seen Dominique coquetting with a man. She had little doubt they were having relations. Shameful. Well, she would soon put a stop to Dominique's sinful behavior.

Soon, very soon all would be right in her world.

※　※　※　※

Loud voices sounded from downstairs, and Jeanette abruptly returned to the present. What could be going on? Taking a quick glance in her looking glass, she tucked a stray hair back under her lappet cap and hurried to the stairs. She stopped at the top. Her breath caught in her throat, her heart pounded in her ears, her knees near buckled under her.

Glynneth had returned. Alive. No! It was not right! She had paid Keane and Filmore. Glynneth should be dead. Yet there she knelt, tears streaming down her cheeks, her arms wrapped around Meara. Beaming, Curtice awaited his turn to embrace Glynneth.

The hall was filled with people. Holding Lothair, Capucine stood to one side with her two boys. All three servants were there, Dominique, Lina, and Gusta. Jeanette's eyes shifted to her husband. He looked like the conquering hero, his chin stuck out, a proud grin on his face. He had rescued the fair damsel and returned her to her throne. Behind him were Adler Hayward and Latimer Draye. No doubt they were the ones who had truly rescued Glynneth. It was their fault Glynneth was alive. Their fault Filmore had not killed her as he promised. She had trusted the man. Fool. What a fool she had been. What a waste of good money.

She would have to join the fracas. Have to pretend she was pleased by Glynneth's safe return. She wanted to scream, to swear, but she forced a smile to her face and hoped it was not a grimace. As she started down the stairs, a shrill, sharp barking pierced the air, and she stopped midway down. A small yellow dog darted in the door. She recognized the dog. It was Meara's. According to Meara, the dog had jumped in the river after Noel. So what was it now doing here?

"Lady Ann, Lady Ann," cried Meara, releasing her mother to grasp the dog that was jumping all over her, its tail wagging so fast it seemed a blur. "How are you here?" the little girl sobbed. "I thought you dead."

"Excuse us," came a voice at the door. All eyes turned from the dog to the man standing at the threshold. "I am thinkin' as the wee dog seems so happy; we would be at the Fortier home." He looked like a farmer, big floppy brimmed hat, loose jerkin, skirt like breeches. He spoke English. More and more English settlers were moving to New Netherland. Fleeing the Puritans in England and the even stricter Puritans in the colonies to the north. They sought sanctuary amidst the Dutch renowned tolerance. Many were taking up residence across the East River on Long Island, in an area the Dutch called Breuckelen. Gaspard and Curtice welcomed them. More customers for the goods they imported. Could this man be one of their customers? He should know not to come to their home. Still, she was pleased by the diversion. It gave her more time to compose herself.

Gaspard stepped to the door. "Aye. I am Gaspard Fortier. How may I help you."

The man turned slightly to his left, and Jeanette saw a woman come up the steps. A sugar-loaf hat with a huge brim shielded her face, all but a broad smile. What did she have in her arms? "I believe this belongs to you," the man said, taking the large bundle from the woman.

"Mother, mother," cried the bundle when the man deposited it on the floor.

Jeanette gasped. She heard Glynneth scream. Other screams, grunts, and oaths resounded in her ears as she watched Noel Fortier run into his mother's arms.

"No," she said, then again louder. "No! No! No!" She heard herself screaming. "No. He cannot be alive. He is dead. They threw him in the river! He and Glynneth should both be dead! This is all wrong!"

Everyone was staring at her. She glanced at her husband. A look of disbelief on his face, he started to step toward her but stopped. She put her hands to her mouth. What had she done? She looked around at all the faces. Glynneth still knelt on the floor, her arms around both her children and that barky little dog, but her glistening gaze was unblinking. Capucine still held Lothair. Holding to their mother's skirt, Capucine's boys, with eyes large as saucers, looked slightly frightened. Adler Hayward and Latimer Draye, their faces impassive, showed no surprise in their eyes. They knew. They knew what she had done. At last she looked at Curtice. His dark eyes, sunken in his face, looked up at her with such malevolence, she shuttered. Gathering her skirt in her fists, she fled to her room.

Chapter 34

Adler had been surprised by Jeanette's outburst. Surprised she would give herself away, but his suspicions that she had planned the attack on Glynneth and Noel, were now confirmed. That was good, he would not have to bring Keane to the house to identify her. But Jeanette's reaction left them in an awkward situation with the couple at the door who had miraculously returned Noel alive and well. They looked confused, wary. He doubted they understood Jeanette's outburst, it had been in French, still, seeing the stunned look on Gaspard's face, Adler thought it best he take over as host and welcome Noel's saviors into the house.

"Do come in, please," he said, speaking in English. "I am Adler Hayward, friend of the family. We cannot express deeply enough our debt to you for saving the boy. We will want to hear all about it. But first we must see to some refreshments for you."

The couple hesitated, but as he continued to stand with outstretched arm, welcoming them inside, they slowly stepped over the threshold. Adler turned to Dominique, and as over the years, she had learned English, he used his native tongue, and said, "Some of the best ale and a platter of cheese and meats for the …" He stopped and looked back at the couple. "I am sorry. I have failed to catch your names."

"Dower," the man said, "Ernest Dower." He reached out a hand to the woman behind him. "My wife," he added.

"So pleased to meet you. So pleased," Adler said then looked again at Dominique. "A repast for the Dowers, please, Dominique."

As Dominique and Gusta scurried away, Mister Dower protested, "You need go to no trouble on our account. We but meant to bring the boy home."

"Nay," said Adler you must let us show you our gratitude.

"Aye," agreed Latty stepping forward, his hand outstretched. "Latimer Draye," he said, "and may I say I have ne'er been so pleased to shake anyone's hand as I am to shake yours, sir. Let me introduce the rest of the household." He gestured to Gaspard. "You met the boy's uncle. The woman on the floor who cannot stop hugging Noel is his mother. The older gentleman, who has no business being on his knees on the floor, is his grandfather." He nodded to Capucine. "His cousin, Madame Chappell, and her two sons. You must know, we all thought the boy drowned."

As he spoke, Latty directed the couple to the two best chairs in the hall. When the Dowers were seated, he continued. "Two men attacked Noel's mother. During the struggle, the boy ended up in the water. Madame Fortier escaped, but too late to be of any help to her son."

Adler recognized Latty's glossing over of the events. The Dowers need not know Glynneth had been abducted. 'Twas so easy to besmirch a woman's reputation. A word to the wrong person, an unguarded sentence. Did everyone follow Latty's lead, the Dowers would never be the wiser. There would be no tale to tell.

At last Glynneth released her hold on Noel and let his grandfather take him in his arms. Adler was there to help her to her feet. "Mister and Mistress Dower." She reached out to the couple. "I am totally beholden to you. You have given me the most precious gift any mother could ever want, the return of a child she thought lost to her forever. The torment I have known these past two days ..." Her voice choking, she stopped and shook her head. She cleared her throat and wiped away a large tear that spilled down her cheek. "My heart now is breaking, but it is from the joy I cannot describe. Please, I beg you, do tell me how you saved my son."

"Oh, you poor dear," said Mistress Dower, rising to take Glynneth's outstretched hand. "Come, sit beside me, and we will tell you all. You do have a most remarkable little boy," she added as Adler hastily pulled over a chair that Glynneth might sit.

Rising with aid from Gaspard, and with Noel still clutched in his arms, Curtice said, "We must have zee sherry for zee Dowers. In zee glass goblets, Gaspard." He turned to Lina, and in Dutch, as that was hers and Gusta's tongue, he said, "The tilt table, girl, fetch the tilt table that they may have a place to set their food and drink."

"Ja, Meneer," Lina said, hurrying to set up a drop leaf table between

258

the two high back chairs with their thick gold cushions and leather padded backs.

"You need not go to so much trouble," said Dower, but Gaspard, pulling up a chair for his father, said, "Indeed, we cannot do enough for you. We all owe you our deepest gratitude."

Pleased Gaspard had recovered his composure and his hospitality, Adler helped Latty spin a bench from the meal table around that they and Capucine might have a seat. Capucine's boys and Lothair joined Meara and Lady Ann on the floor, and Noel, snuggling contentedly on his grandfather's lap, watched their play. Gaspard busied himself pouring sherry for the Dowers before taking up a position behind Glynneth's chair.

At Curtice's urging, Mistress Dower took a sip of the sherry. "Oh, this is very nice," she proclaimed and took a second sip. Mister Dower downed his serving in one gulp, and Gaspard hastened to refill the goblet.

"Now that is a fine drink," Mister Dower said, smacking his lips, but sipping his second serving more slowly. "I must say, I did have me a thirst built up after rowin' over here."

"I will see you get a case of zee sherry," Curtice said, and shook his head when the Dowers protested. "Zat eez only zee very least I can do. I will do more, I promise you zat."

"You live across the East River?" Glynneth interrupted.

"Aye," Dower answered, turning from Curtice to Glynneth. "We have a goodly sized farm. Two cows, two oxen, sundry other animals. House that meets our needs. All we are lackin' is a family. Lord ne'er saw fit to bless us in that way."

"We have my nephew," Mistress Dower said. "He is a good lad. Bit weak in the mind since he received that knock to his head, but he is still a hard worker."

Dower nodded. "Aye, that he is. A hard worker, I mean. Sweet tempered, too. Lad worked long side his father shoein' horses till one up and kicked him. His father havin' two other sons, and us havin' none, well he thought it best Wally come live with us after that."

"And a blessin' he has been," interposed Mistress Dower, and turning to Glynneth, she patted her hand. "'Twas Wally what spotted yer little yeller dog swimmin' in the river."

Glynneth griped the woman's hand. "Oh, do please tell me all."

Before Mistress Dower could begin, Lothair let out a loud angry screech. His lips set in a determined line, he tugged at a popgun Capucine's youngest son, Pierre, seemed equally determined to keep. Speaking in French, Capucine said, "Please forgive my interrupting, but I do think Lothair is hungry." She looked at the servant girl again hovering by the stairs, and switching to Dutch said, "Lina, would you please take Lothair up to his mother."

The slender young woman, her dark eyes lowered, her face a mask, bobbed a curtsy and hurried to pick up the little boy. He squiggled in Lina's arms and let out another shriek, but holding him fast, she lithely ascended the stairs.

Capucine again apologized for interrupting and was assured by Gaspard she had done the correct thing. Adler wondered how much of the Dowers' speech Capucine could understand. The capable woman spoke French and Dutch, but he doubted she had ever had any need to learn English. Making a mental note to explain all to her later, he returned his attention to Mistress Dower who took another sip of the sherry, settled back in her chair, and resumed her tale.

"As I said, 'twas Wally saw the little dog in the river. Nothin' would do but we must save the dog." She glanced at her husband. "Ernest was not of a mind to row against the current to rescue the whelp, but Wally took to caterwaulin' so, that to quiet him, Ernest agreed to save the dog." She looked at Glynneth. "Earnest was worried did we get too close to the rocks and the current sweep us into the rocks, we could damage the boat."

"Not our boat," chimed in Dower. "We rented it to take our turnips and apples to market. Better price for them do we sell them ourselves and not to a wholesaler."

"You shall have your own boat. I shall see it ordered on the morrow," declared Curtice.

Both Dowers looked at him in surprise, but Glynneth placed her hand on Mistress Dower's and urged, "Do please continue."

Mistress Dower gave her head a little shake and glanced once more at Curtice before turning back to Glynneth. "There is a bit of land juts out

260

into the river. Bit rocky. That is where the dog was swimmin' about. No sooner do we draw up close, and Wally leans out to grab the dog, than the dog climbs up on a rock, starts prancin' about and barkin'. Ernest was mad as all get out, puttin' the boat to risk for a dog that needed no rescue, but that is when I spotted the boy." She looked over at Noel, cuddled in his grandfather's arms, and smiled at him.

"Wonder she saw him," Dower said. "All I could do to keep the boat off the rocks. An' lack she says, I was hoppin' mad."

"I cannot say what made me look down at the log stuck between two rocks. Mayhap I feared it would come loose and strike the boat." She shook her head slowly. "I tell you, my heart stopped dead in my chest when I saw that babe hangin' onto that log. I blinked and blinked. Could not at first believe me own eyes, but there he was. Those big brown eyes lookin' up at me. 'Ernest, Ernest,' I says, 'there is a babe a-clingin' to that log. We got to save him.' And Ernest looked 'round where I pointed and near fell out of the boat."

Dower took up the story when his wife paused to wipe her brow. "Naught I could do but get the boat close as I could to the log and pray the current would not knock me into the boy. Wally, with Hannah holdin' on to his coat tail, reached way out and snagged the boy. When he got the boy in the boat, the cur jumped back in the water, and Wally pulled her in, too."

Noel must have been paying heed to the Dowers for he piped up, "I was very brave, Mother. I never let go of that log until Wally grabbed me."

"Oh, my darling, yes you were brave," Glynneth said, her hand going to her heart.

"Now that is what I mean," said Mistress Dower. "The boy tells us he is but three, yet he speaks as well as any adult."

"Better'n some I know," said Dower.

Ignoring her husband, Mistress Dower continued. "The little tike was shiverin' so I feared he would die of the cold afore we could warm him up. I got his sodden clothes off him and Wally undid his waistcoat and pulled up his shirt and tucked the little fellow up against his warm chest and stomach. I do think that is what saved him. Anyway, his teeth stopped chatterin', and once we landed the boat, I wrapped him in my shawl to cart him home to bed. I got him all tucked in and asked him did he know his name." She chuckled. "He perked right up and said, 'My name is Noel Fortier, and I live with my mother and grandfather in New Amsterdam.' Him speakin' up so clear like that near knocked me over."

Glynneth nodded. "Yes, he is a very astute child. His grandfather says his father was much the same."

"Exactly zee same," Curtice asserted.

"You a widow then?" Mistress Dower asked, again patting Glynneth's hand.

"I am," Glynneth said. "Noel's father died seven months ago."

"Right sorry to hear that," said Dower. "Boy's father would be powerful proud of him."

"Another thing that surprised us," said Mistress Dower, "is Noel said a man threw him in the river. We found that hard to believe, but as Mister Draye explained you were attacked, it makes more sense."

Scrambling down from his grandfather's lap to trot over to his mother, Noel interposed, "He was a mean man."

"Yes he was, my dear," Glynneth agreed, planting a kiss on the top of Noel's head.

"Lucky you escaped him," Dower said. "Think you he was a pirate? I hear they have been mighty brazen of late. Even raidin' farms what lie close to the shore."

Glynneth shrugged and shook her head. "I could not say. I but know I will not walk unescorted along the East River ever again."

"Most likely wise," stated Mistress Dower. She looked ready to comment further, but at that moment, Dominique and Gusta arrived with platters piled high with an assortment of cheeses, meats, bread, tarts, and cookies. After setting the platters on the table, Dominique said they would be right back with the mugs and ale.

The Dowers seemed overwhelmed by the bounty spread before them, but at Gaspard's urging, Mister Dower picked up a roasted chicken leg and bit into the crisp, brown skin. Soon he was gnawing the leg with relish, and Mistress Dower was "oohing" over a plump apple tart. After mugs of ale were poured for the adults, the children were given milk and cookies. Noel, joining his sister and cousins on the floor, seemed

262

his usual cheery self, but Adler had no doubt Glynneth would keep him close to her side for the next few days to make certain he suffered no serious trauma. That the boy had survived seemed an incredible miracle.

When Dower finally sat back in the chair, patted his stomach, and declared he could not eat another bite, Mistress Dower looked down sheepishly, then looked up at Curtice and said, "I could tell by Noel's clothing that he come from a good home. We would have brought the tike back, though, were he rich or poor, but seein' as we had to rent the boat again to bring him over, we were thinkin' you might have the coin to reimburse us."

"Woman, what can you be thinkin' after this goodly repast." Dower shook his head and looked at Curtice. "You have treated us most kindly. We will not be askin' for more."

"Nonsense," declared Curtice. "Gaspard, bring me one of zee bags from zee strong box. You know where I keep zee key." He looked at Dower. "I will pay zee rent on zee boat for today and for yesterday. And I will do much more. You will see. And zis nephew of yours." He looked at Mistress Dower. "I would reward him as well. He eez not with you today?"

"Oh, yes, he came with us, but he is mindin' the boat," Mistress Dower answered. "Too easy for someone to make off with it."

"From now on, whenever you come across zee river, you must dock at my wharf. Your boat will be safe zere. I will see to zat." He turned to Lina who had taken up her place near the stairs, and again speaking in Dutch, said, "Lina, have Gusta package up some of the foodstuffs for the Dowers to take to Wally."

"Ja, Meneer," Lina said and began carting a couple of platters back to the kitchen. Dominique began helping her, and soon the table was cleared. Dominique brought out wet, warm napkins for everyone that they might clean their hands, and Gusta brought out more ale. Adler smiled. He had to think the Dowers would go home feeling they had been royally treated.

He was a bit curious about the expression on Gaspard's face when he returned and placed a bag of coins on his father's lap. He whispered something to Curtice, and the old man's eyes widened, but he said nothing. Loosening the strings on the bag, he pulled out several guilders. These he handed to Gaspard, telling him to give them to the Dowers.

When Gaspard plunked the coins into Dower's hand, the farmer did naught but stare at them for a moment, then he showed them to Mistress Dower. She gasped. "Oh, my," she said. "Such a lot. 'Tis most kind Monsieur Fortier."

Curtice waved his hand. "Zat eez naught compared to what you have given me, given Glynneth. When Noel seemed lost to me forever, especially so soon after losing my son, I zink I had little desire to keep living. You have given me back my life. Zere are no words to zank you enough, but however else I may be of aid to you. Please allow me to do so."

"Sir, we thank you for your hospitality, but now we must be leavin'. The days grow shorter, and we have no wish to be crossin' the river in the dark."

"Naturellement," Curtice said rising and extending his hand. "We will be seeing you again soon, I hope. And remember, from now on you dock at zee Fortier wharf. Gaspard will tell our men to look to your boat."

"Thank you, thank you," Dower said, bobbing his head. "You have been most kind."

"And thank you for the wonderful food," Mistress Dower said, as Dominique handed her a large package wrapped up in a couple of napkins.

"Noel, the Dowers are leaving," said Glynneth. "Do you give them a farewell?"

The little boy sprang to his feet and rushed over to Mistress Dower and wrapped his arms around her legs. She laughed and leaned down to embrace him with her free arm. "What a fine lad you are. Did I have a son, I would want him to be just like you."

"Thank you for saving me," Noel said, looking up at Mistress Dower before directing his gaze to Mister Dower. "Please tell Wally good-bye for me. He is fun."

Dower ruffled Noel's hair. "That we will young fellow, that we will."

With many more good wishes and expressions of gratitude, the Dowers exited and Dominique at last closed the door behind them. "Will there be anything else?" Dominique asked in French. She could speak and understand Dutch and English, but being from the French Indies, she seemed to prefer the French tongue.

Curtice shook his head. Also speaking in French, he said, "Do take the children upstairs to Noel and Meara's room. You and Lina mind them until time for supper."

"Wee, Monsieur," she answered, and calling to Lina, the two soon had the children bundled off.

"We must talk," Curtice said, continuing in French. He looked to Gaspard. "My son, this pains me, for my love for you is deep, but I cannot have your wife spend another night under my roof. With her vitriolic outpouring, she as much as admitted she paid the two men to kill Noel and abduct Glynneth. And from the missing guilders from the strong box, it would seem she paid them with my money. Why she would do such a thing I cannot imagine, but I will not suffer her to abide in my home another night."

"But Father, where shall I take her? And Lothair, what of my son?"

"They may stay with us, Gaspard, until you find a home for your family," said Capucine.

Gaspard thanked her, but she looked sad. "Meneer Kerstan warned me of Adler's suspicions concerning Jeanette. That is why Adler wanted me to keep Meara close until he returned. He feared for her. She could, after all, identify the man who attacked them." She looked at Adler. He but shook his head. What could he say. "I prayed all night that his suspicions were wrong," she continued. "Jeanette's sweet son bears none of the blame. And it would not be right to deprive him of his mother."

"She is correct," said Curtice. "Lothair must not be made to pay for his mother's sins. I pray the day will not come that we have to tell him why his mother is not allowed to step foot under my roof. Why his mother is an outcast in our family, but I fear someday he will question you, my son, and what you will tell him, I can but leave to your invention. In the meantime, I will allow you to take Lina with you to help care for the child. You will have what monies you may need to purchase a house." His face drooping, he shuddered. "This event must remain within the family. I will not have the Fortier name bandied about." He looked at Glynneth. "I will not have Etienne's wife shamed."

Everyone nodded in understanding, and Adler glanced at Glynneth. She looked so sad. She should be joyous. Her son had been returned to her. Yet he knew she would never be able to forgive the woman who tried to kill her and her child. He knew it pained her.

"Adler," Curtice said, and Adler looked back at the sad old man whose life had been so assaulted in his old age when he might well expect to be living in peace.

"Yes, Monsieur Fortier," he answered.

"I will trust you and Latty to make sure all zose involved in helping to rescue Glynneth will be made aware of our curtailed story. Zere will be no mention of Glynneth's abduction."

"Have no fear. Gaspard has seen to the sloep's crew. They have been well paid to hold their tongues. They have also been promised shipping jobs, so I think we need have no fear they will spread any tales. Meneer Kerstan and his wife are both trustworthy. That I can guarantee, and I will speak with all the boys. They will understand. I have no doubt we can trust them."

"Splendid. Now I find I am exhausted. I never went to bed last night. However, before I budge from this room, Gaspard, I wish you to remove your wife from my house."

Chapter 35

Gaspard at first looked shocked by his father's pronouncement, then he nodded sadly. "As you wish, Father," he said and disappeared up the stairs. Latimer could almost feel his pain. Gaspard would have to live with the woman who had tried to kill the woman he loved.

Capucine rose. "I will get Guyon and Pierre and start home. I will have to prepare the house for our guests. And I must tell Ignace what has transpired. I left him at home with his books. He was so worried about Glynneth, he slept little last night, and this morning, he did naught but pace the floor. Most likely he has napped and will be ready for his supper and for the joyous news about Glynneth and Noel."

"She is a good woman," Latimer said, watching Capucine ascend the stairs. "Armand was a lucky man when he won her heart." He wondered if he would ever be able to find as fine a woman to take to wife. A woman with land, beauty, and a kind soul. He looked at Glynneth. Because of his love for her, he would never be able to offer any woman the kind of love Armand gave Capucine, but he believed he could still make some woman a good husband.

"Latty." Adler brought his attention around to him. "We have a little matter in the Fortiers' office closet that we have yet to deal with."

Curtice's head snapped up. "Zee malfeasant?" he asked returning to English as Adler had been speaking in English. Latimer half chuckled. Adler still had not become competent in the French tongue.

"Yes," Adler said. "We have to decide what to do with him. I would like to kill him, but that we cannot do. We want no trial, but we must be rid of the man. I am thinking Latty and I can put enough fear in him that he will leave and never return."

"Zat is good," said Curtice, then jerked upright when a guttural shriek came from above.

Capucine, on the stairs with her sons, looked upward, then gave Guy-

267

on a nudge and hurried the boys to the door. She stopped beside Glynneth. "Dear friend, I know I will not see you in my home until Gaspard finds a home for his family, but I will visit you soon. I am so thrilled to have you and Noel home, both of you safe and well."

Glynneth gave her a hug. "You are kind to take Jeanette in. Had not Father Curtice insisted she must leave the house, I would be the one staying with you."

Capucine gave her a peck on the cheek. "I would prefer you were again staying with me. Such jolly times we have together, huh? Well, I must hurry."

Glynneth had just closed the door after Capucine when Jeanette appeared on the stairs. Following her, a portmanteau in each hand, Gaspard looked stone-faced. Lina with Lothair in her arms brought up the rear. Jeanette stopped at the bottom step and looked at each person in the room. Her gaze settled on Curtice.

"So, you choose to drive me from my home. You think I am too evil to stay under the same roof with your sainted Glynneth."

"Jeanette, that will be enough," growled Gaspard, but she turned on him.

"No, my fine husband. That is not enough. You wonder that I would want Glynneth dead? Want her son dead?" She looked back at Curtice, and Latimer thought he had never seen such malice in anyone's eyes. Nay, not even in the eyes of the savages that had attacked and tried to kill him and Adler and Kills Many and his men.

Jeanette raised her chin. "You, Father Curtice, you always had praise for Noel, never for my Lothair. In fact you found fault with my sweet babe. He could never measure up to Noel. And always you had praise for your dear Glynneth. She could do no wrong, while anything I might say or wish you thought silly, lacking in intelligence."

She swept her arm out over the room, her gaze glancing off Latimer and Adler to return to her husband. "All of you are in love with Glynneth. Even my husband. He made love to me, but he dreamed of her. He coveted his brother's wife." She spit it out, her upper lipped curled disdainfully. "Coveted her so much, he even ignored his own son to play with her son."

"Jeanette!" Gaspard dropped a portmanteau on the step and reached

268

for his wife, but she shook off his hand.

"Deny it! Swear to God on the holy Bible that you are not in love with her. Swear it! You cannot." She again looked out over the room. "None of you can deny it. You all had to go racing off to rescue her. And my husband had to lead the way, hire the boat."

Latimer pitied Gaspard. The man was blushing furiously, whether because his wife's statements were true, which Latimer doubted not they were, or because he was embarrassed by her behavior, Latimer could not know, but he saw Curtice blanch under his daughter-in-law's vicious attack on him and his son.

Finally Jeanette looked at Glynneth. "And you! Why did you not return to Ireland? Had you but had the sense to leave after Etienne died, all would have been well. Father Curtice would have given Lothair the love he deserves. My husband would have forgotten you and come to love me. But no. You had to stay. Had to move in. Had to mesmerize my husband." She returned her gaze to Curtice, but pointing a finger at Glynneth she cried, "She is the evil one, not me. She is a witch! She bewitches men." Dropping her arm, she hunched her shoulders dropped her gaze. "She bewitches men," she said again quietly.

Latimer could almost feel sorry for her. She looked exhausted. Her defiance had fled.

"I am ready to go," she said. Not looking at her husband, she started for the door.

Adler stepped to Glynneth's side to shield her from Jeanette, but her sister-in-law never even glanced in Glynneth's direction. At the door, a little of her defiance returned for she flung open the door, looked back at the room and spat out, "Good riddance!" Then she was gone, into the darkening afternoon.

Gaspard ushered Lina with Lothair out the door then stopped. "I will return to collect any other necessities we may have forgotten, Father." He bowed his head. "I apologize to all of you. Especially to you Glynneth." Before anyone could answer him, he closed the door behind him.

"Oh my," Glynneth said. "I had no idea such thoughts were raging through her head. She must be sick to have such thoughts. She is so disturbed. I wish I could forgive her. Had her attack been against me alone, I think I could forgive her." She shook her head. "But I can never, never forgive her for what she did to Noel."

Latimer knew he could never forgive Jeanette for what she had done. Had she succeeded in killing Glynneth, he would have killed her – at the very least, seen her hang. The woman had a sickness in her head, but that did not excuse her infamous behavior. She was correct, though, Glynneth did bewitch men – and women and children and the elderly – near everyone she came in contact with. But not by casting evil spells. She bewitched them with the sparkle in her eyes, the joyous lilt in her voice, her warming smile, her caring heart, her loving soul. What man would not delight in such a woman? She offered peace and hope to saddened hearts, and fun and laughter to happy hearts. She was good for the soul.

Why Jeanette could not see Glynneth's splendor baffled him. He had noted Glynneth's radiant spirit the first time he ever set eyes on her. She loved life and her genial manner lightened the very air around her. In a matter of days, he had fallen in love with her and that love had grown with each passing week, month, and year. Yet he knew he would not be the right man for her. As much as he loved her, his dream of building an estate as large or larger than the one his family had once been masters of in England, still came first.

Adler was the right man for her. No man could love her more. Adler would devote his every waking moment to making Glynneth happy. He would protect her. See that no harm ever again threatened her or her loved ones. Adler was a capable man, resourceful, brave, and generous. Latimer knew he owed his life several times over to Adler – from their first encounter with the Mohawks, to the attack by the Hurons, to the numerous times Adler safely guided them through the wilderness. He doubted he would have survived even his first trek into the woods had he not partnered with Adler. Dearer to him than any member of his family, Adler embodied all he could want in a friend. Or in a husband for Glynneth. They would suit.

A hand slapped on his shoulder told him Adler was ready to depart. They had business with Keane. How he would like to turn the man over to the Mohawks. Let them slowly deprive him of his life. Instead, they would set Keane free. "I am ready," he said, looking past Adler to Glynneth. "We will see you on the morrow. Have sweet dreams. All is

270

now right in your world."

She smiled at him. "Thank you, Latty. I shall never be able to repay you for all you have done. You are a true friend."

He gave her a little wave and exited.

🌿 🌿 🌿 🌿

Keane was in sorry shape when they opened the door to find him huddled in the corner where they had left him. The smell emanating from him made Adler want to gag. "I gave him some ale last evening," the guard said, "and Vogel gave him some this morning. Other than that, he has had naught to eat or drink." The guard made a face, his upper lip curling derisively. "Any man who would try to steal from Monsieur Fortier deserves no better than he gets."

"So right you are," said Adler. "We thank you and Vogel for keeping such close watch on him. Monsieur Fortier says you will each have a bonus for your effort."

The man grinned. "Will there be aught else, Monsieur Hayward?"

"Nay, we will deal with him now."

"Good evening to you then," the guard said, and left the office.

Latty held the lantern high and took a step toward Keane. "What you goin' t' do now?" Keane sniveled, cowering closer to the wall. A pitiable sight, his breeches soiled, his lips dry and cracked, face and nose caked with blood, he drew in ragged breaths and belched out foul air.

"We mean to set you free," Adler said, waiting for his words to register.

At first Keane but stared at him, then he stuttered, "L...let m...me go?"

"Aye," said Latty. "Unless you would rather stay tied up here."

Keane's gaze jumped to Latty, but he blinked when he looked into the lantern light. "Nay," he said, but his eyes narrowed. "You not plannin' t' kill me when I leave?"

Adler shook his head. "Not if you leave New Amsterdam, better yet, New Netherland and never return. Because do either of us ever see you again, we will kill you."

Keane started nodding his head. "Aye, aye, I will be leavin' this very night." He scrunched up his face. "But how, how am I t' go? Where am I t' go?"

"That would be your problem," said Latty. "Did I have my way, you would be at the bottom of the East River just as you tried to do to the boy, but Hayward here is more forgiving than I am. He is willing to let you live."

Keane looked at Latty when he started talking, but his eyes darted back to Adler. "I thank you, Mister Hayward. I will find a way t' leave. Leave right away, I will."

"Good. There is one more thing. You are never to mention to anyone Madame Fortier's name. And do you ever encounter Filmore again, let him know we are looking for him and do we find him, we intend to see him dead."

Keane bobbed his head up and down. "I have forgotten the laidy's name a'ready. An' do I see Filmore, I will be givin' him your message."

Adler frowned. The man was so disgusting, he hated to even touch him, but as Latty had the lantern, he supposed he would have to be the one to untie him. He decided instead to cut the ropes, but when he pulled out his knife, Keane let out a yelp. Adler shook his head. "I but mean to cut your bides."

Still looking wary, Keane struggled up and turned to the wall. Adler slashed the ropes, and Keane stomped his feet and brought his hands around to his front and rubbed his wrists. "I can go now," he asked.

"Aye," Adler said, "but try not to touch anything on your way out. You reek."

Shaky on his legs, Keane staggered to the door. He looked back over his shoulder for an instant, then disappeared into the darkness.

"Think we can trust him to leave the island?" Latty asked.

"Aye," Adler said. "He may hide out for a day or two while he thinks of where to go, but I doubt we will ever see him again. He was that scared and miserable. He will not want to chance another meeting with us."

"Most likely you are right" Latty agreed, looking around the office. He set the lantern down on a table. "So, what do we do now?"

"We will go by and see the Kerstans. Give them the news and stress with their lad the need to watch his tongue. Then it is back to the Fortiers. I had thought we would be staying with Capucine, but that option is no longer available, so Glynneth told me she will see beds are made up for us at Curtice's home."

"Most likely she has already had Dominique make up the beds. But speaking of Dominique, that does bring about a bit of a dilemma."

Adler cocked his head and narrowed his eyes. "Why do you say that?"

"Well, I learned why I ne'er had a chance at winning a night's snuggle with the pretty Dominique. She has a beau."

"Does she? And how do you know this?"

"Her beau told me." Latty paused, his mouth twisting wryly before he added, "Her beau is Lambert Spangler."

Adler stared at him a moment then asked, "The man we borrowed the canoe from?"

"Aye. He bought a large estate not far from the settlement where we met him. He says he has little but trees and a stream on the land, but he means to settle there. He has been courting Dominique for over a year. He wanted to buy her from the Fortiers, but Dominique said she would not leave Glynneth, not when Glynneth has need of her and has been so good to her. He wants to marry Dominique." Latty glanced down then back up to meet Adler's eyes. "We, Glynneth and we – we owe him much. Without the use of his canoe, we would have never found Glynneth's trail by nightfall. The next day, you would have picked up her trail, but I shudder to think if something had befallen her, or that she would have spent the night alone and frightened, cold and hungry."

Adler nodded. He had the same thoughts that Latty had expressed. Spangler had been most generous in offering his canoe. He hated to think of Glynneth not having a suitable servant, but were Dominique and Spangler in love, he doubted Glynneth would want to keep them apart.

"I will speak with Glynneth on the matter," he said. "But for now, let us be off to the Kerstans. Most likely they will offer us some ale. I could do with it after dealing with Keane."

Agreeing, Latty extinguished the light in the lantern, and they exited, slipping the heavy lock onto the door's thick metal latch.

Chapter 36

Adler slipped his arms into his new coat, or rather, his peacock blue, high-waisted, loose-fitting doublet. He carefully buttoned the row of buttons and attached the white broad-lace falling band around the collar. He bent and tied the long-legged breeches below his knees with ribbon sashes. Never had he dreamed, that he a farmer, a woodsman, would be wearing such trappings. Straightening, he turned to Latty.

"Well, do I look as ridiculous in these duds as I feel?"

Latty guffawed. "Nay, my friend. Your bride will find you entirely enticing."

Adler shook his head. "I can scarce believe this day is truly here. I am soon to marry the only woman I have ever loved. Can it be true?"

"'Tis true. I can think of no one who more deserves the lady. Glynneth is a treasure, and I know you will make her happy."

Adler clasped Latty's hand. "I will do my best. I want nothing but her happiness."

"I know that. So, are you ready?"

"I am ready," Adler answered, though his head was spinning. So much had happened in but two short months. He and Kerstan had formed a business partnership. With Adler's savings, they were building a large workshop on the East River outside the new wall that stretched across the island. Three men had been hired, and Kerstan and his apprentice, Cuyler, had begun training them. Adler's job was to find the buyers and provide the needed materials. He already had a backup of orders, and Latty would be supplying the wood.

Latty had entered into an agreement with Spangler to provide the timber for the boats. Latty would help Spangler cut the wood, he would arrange for the logs to be shipped down river, and the two would split the profit. Spangler would get his land cleared, his home and barn built, and Latty would add to his savings.

274

Glynneth had given Dominique her freedom, but Dominique would continue to work for her until Spangler had a proper home and furnishings to offer her. Once all was ready, the two would be married. Adler hoped Glynneth would have a replacement for Dominique by the time Spangler had his estate in order. Glynneth had written to her brother in Dublin asking him to try to find her a couple of Irish girls to come as bond servants to work for her. Both she and Adler had determined they were not comfortable owning slaves.

He and Glynneth were not completely comfortable with their house arrangement either. Curtice had insisted they take his house. "What need have I for such a large house now," Curtice said. "I will move back to Jacques's house. It suits me well. Jacques has no use for it. He and Simone prefer living in Beverwyck."

Curtice's house was larger and more grandiose than either Glynneth or Adler believed they needed. "It will require more labor to keep it up," Adler said when he and Glynneth discussed the situation. "That will mean more of your dowry, your children's inheritance, going to pay for various sundries. Everything from the men who care for the garden and animals, to more wood and coal to keep the place warm. Of course, I suppose I could take care of the animals. I certainly did for much of my life."

"Nay," said Glynneth. "You will be busy enough with your business. We will manage. I was very happy in Capucine's comfortable home." She glanced off to the side and her voice softened. "Etienne and I never had a large place. We liked cozy." She brightened. "But you and I are apt to add to our family. With this house, we will have room for a large family. And we can keep any rooms not in use closed off. We will also have room for guests. With Curtice moving back to Jacques's house, do Jacques and Simone come to visit, they can stay with us."

He loved the way Glynneth always found the bright side to things. And the thought of increasing the family thrilled him. He loved Noel and Meara, but he would also like to have children of his own blood – his and Glynneth's.

"You dawdle, Adler. What ails you?" Latty asked.

Adler blinked. "Nothing. I was but thinking what an incredibly lucky man I am."

"That you are, but you would not wish to keep your bride waiting."

"Indeed, you are right," Adler said, heading out the door to the stairs. They had been staying in the house that was soon to be his. Curtice had moved most of his belongings to Jacques's house, and would be completely moved out after the wedding. Latty would be leaving, too. Gaspard having found a home for his family, Latty would stay the night with Armand and Capucine then would head up the river to continue his lumbering.

"I am getting skilled at this logging," he had said. "Much better than I am at tracking." He looked at his hands. "Hands are hardening up. Back breaking work, though. Glad it is not what I intend to do for the rest of my life."

The wedding was being held in Curtice's home – no, it was not Curtice's home, Adler thought, 'twas his and Glynneth's. The magistrate performing the ceremony had done business with Curtice over the years and was pleased to officiate. Adler was relieved Curtice so readily accepted the news he and Glynneth had decided to marry. He immediately gave them his blessing, and later confided to Adler that he had feared Glynneth might take the children and return to Ireland. Her marriage to Adler meant she had decided to make her home in New Netherland permanent. He would not have to fear the loss of his adored grandchildren.

Gaspard had looked shocked when he learned of their marriage plans but quickly recovered and offered them his heartfelt solicitations. He was there for their ceremony with Lothair at his side, but of course, Jeanette was not in attendance. Neither Adler nor Glynneth had seen her since she left Curtice's house. Adler hoped Glynneth would never have to see the woman again. Jeanette's evil hatred was not something he could understand, but Gaspard had tried to apologize for her. Had tried placing some of the blame on himself. He had not realized his wife thought his devotion to his brother's wife was more than a general wish to see Etienne's family receive the care and comfort they needed.

The other guests were Capucine and Armand with their children and Ignace, the Kerstans and the Cuylers, the Langes, and the Fortiers' warehouse steward and his wife. Dominique and Gusta were also in attendance. After the ceremony, they would serve the wedding breakfast.

Meara and Noel, dressed in their best, looked up eagerly when Adler and Latty descended the stairs. Lady Ann, at Meara's side, had a bright red bow around her neck. The little dog had been treated as the heroine she was. For the past two months, she had been lavished with love and attention, and had been given free rein throughout the house.

After the celebration, Meara and Noel would go home with the Kerstans for the night. Adler and Glynneth would have the house to themselves but for Dominique and Gusta who would keep to their rooms once they had cleaned up after the guests. Adler was both eager and nervous at the thought of again bedding Glynneth. They had not had intimate relations since that magical night in the woods. In the past two months, they had kissed and embraced, but an opportunity for more intimacy had not presented itself. Adler shared a room with Latty; Glynneth, wanting to be certain her children had no nightmares after their traumatic experiences, slept with them rather than relegating them to the nursery; and Curtice, for proprieties' sake, remained in the house with no plan to vacate his room until after the wedding. The fourth bedroom had yet to be furnished so was being used for storage and as a sewing room for Mevr. Lange who made the gowns for Glynneth, Meara, and Capucine, who proclaimed, since the age of twelve, she had never worn anything she had not made for herself. Glynneth insisted on gifting the gown to Capucine to show her gratitude for all Capucine had done for her over the years since she had first arrived in New Amsterdam, but especially for keeping Meara safe during Glynneth's travails.

Greeted by the joyful guests, Adler looked around the hall. Glynneth and Dominique, with help from Capucine and Hendrika Kerstan, had done a masterful job of decorating the room. A warm fire blazed in the hearth adding light to the flickering candles gracing every flat surface in the room. The hall fairly glowed. Holly and various sweet smelling greenery hanging about the room enlivened the white-washed walls. The chairs and benches had been pushed against the walls to create maximum space in the room. After the ceremony, they would all adjourn to the large dining chamber for a breakfast of rolls, boiled eggs, cold meats, roasted lobster, onion pie, corn custard, and at Meara's suggestion, ginger bread men.

"You look stunning," said Hendrika. "December is a lovely month for a wedding. It is a month of celebration for us. We Dutch enjoy our feasting and gifting as we settle in to await Christmas, the new year, and then spring. I know the Calvinists frown on celebrating saints' feast days, but we are Lutheran, and though Director General Stuyvesant may disapprove of us, we do enjoy our celebrations. The children particularly enjoy the treats left to them by Saint Nicholas."

"Yes, Meara and Noel both questioned why Saint Nicholas failed to visit them," Adler said with a chuckle.

Hendrika started to respond but then pointed to the stairs. "Look, your bride descends."

Adler looked up. His heart jumped into his throat before returning to his chest to beat a rapid tattoo against his ribs. Glynneth looked incredibly beautiful. Her gown of royal blue satin had a high-waisted bodice, but the décolletage was cut low in the front partially baring her shoulders which were covered by a white lace bordered collar. Wide laced edged sleeves extended to her elbows and the gown's full skirt hung in loose folds. Her hair was entwined with a blue ribbon that perfectly matched her gown. But it was the glow in her eyes that held him breathless. Those entrancing gray-blue eyes that gave life to his soul. Glynneth was to be his wife. He could know no greater joy.

❧ ❧ ❧ ❧

Jeanette stared into the fire and wrapped the blanket more tightly about her. Cold, so very cold. How she hated this disreputable edifice Gaspard was forcing her to live in. It seemed unnecessarily cruel. The two weeks they had lived with Capucine had at least been bearable. Capucine kept a clean home, and though Jeanette knew Capucine bore her no love, she had always been civil. Her son, Guyon, and young brother-in-law, Ignace, had not been as courteous. They knew what she had done, and they hated her, but they were usually either studying or with Glynneth for their lessons. They, like all males, were bewitched by Glynneth.

Before moving her to the house, Gaspard told her, "It is more cottage, than house, but it is all that is available, and I will not continue to impose on the Chappells' generosity. I will ask Father to let Gusta help Lina clean it. Because it is small, we will not need much in the way of furnishings."

Small was an understatement. Jeanette had collapsed into tears when Gaspard moved them into their new home. It was little more than a two room shanty with a tiny loft. Lina had to sleep on a cot in the main room. Lothair, too, seemed bemused. He had been happy enough at Capucine's with Pierre to play with, but he had constantly asked when he would be going home. Jeanette told him to ask his father. Gaspard told him as soon as he could find them a home, but of course, Lothair had no idea what that meant. He resumed his questioning when his father settled them into their new abode.

"This is our home," Gaspard told him, and the little boy turned a woebegone face up to his father and cried, "No. Want Meara and Noel and Grandfather." At but two and a half, he could not understand why he had been separated from the people he loved. Her poor little boy, she thought. She had tried to make life better for him, but because Keane and Filmore had not done as they had promised, as they had been paid to do, she and her son were being punished. And here was Glynneth, marrying Adler Hayward. Had Glynneth told her she meant to marry Adler, she would not have had to seek other means to be rid of Glynneth.

Adler Hayward. How she hated him. Had he not come back when he did, Glynneth would not have been found. She would be gone from her life forever. Instead, Adler and Glynneth were living in her house. Jeanette ground her teeth. How could life be so unfair? And as she sat shivering, Gaspard and Lothair were attending Glynneth's wedding. The only thing that gave Jeanette the hint of a smile was thinking about how jealous Gaspard must be of Adler. How envious. After lusting after his brother's wife for all those years and then to have to watch her marry another man. Must be torture.

Well, it had been torture for her for years, knowing her husband was finding his release with her, while wishing he was rutting with Glynneth. Jeanette frowned. She had always been the dutiful wife. Had always complied with her husband's wishes, but not now. Until he provided her with a decent home, she had no intention of coupling with him. Not that he had made any advances in the past two months. They slept in the same bed, but they both tried their best never to touch. Sometimes, as the nights grew colder, she missed being able to snuggle up next to him, but she knew he would repel her. He seemed to hate to look at her, to talk to her, to sit down to a meal with her. He never said he hated her, yet she believed he must. Neither of them spoke of her attempt to have Glynneth and Noel killed. But her malfeasance lay there between them. To Gaspard, she had committed an unpardonable offence.

Dear God, Jeanette thought, how she hated Glynneth. And why not? Glynneth had destroyed her marriage, her life, her son's life. She cocked her head and caught the sudden patter of rain on the roof. A bucket catching a leak sat near the door. She had sent Lina to the baker's for some fresh bread. She supposed the slave would be drenched by the time she returned, and the bread could well be soggy. She wished the rain had started sooner. She would have liked everyone going to Glynneth's wedding to be soaked. She gasped. No! Lothair would have gotten wet. In this winter weather, and in this chilly house, she worried her son might catch a cold, or worse, the whooping cough.

She had not wanted Lothair to go to the wedding, but Gaspard had insisted. "Lina, dress him in his best gown. My son will not be exiled from his family," he declared, narrowing his eyes and glaring at Jeanette.

She stared right back at him. She could not prevent her husband from taking Lothair to the wedding, but she would let him know of her disapproval. He seemed not to care. He turned from her and went into their bed chamber to ready himself for the event. When he left, the clouds were lowering, but the rain had not yet started. She hoped Lina could get to the baker's and back before the rain started, but the girl was not to be so lucky. At least she had a warm woolen cape with a hood to protect her. Curtice had made sure his slaves had suitable attire.

Curtice! Hateful old man! To kick her and her son out of his house. And to give his house to Glynneth. Had he been as good to Lothair as he was to Noel and Meara, she would never have attempted to have Noel killed. Curtice was to blame for her need to rid her home of Glynneth's son. Her anger rising, she dug her nails into her hands. He should

280

be made to pay. They all should be made to pay. Glynneth, Adler, Curtice, even Gaspard, they should all have to suffer as she and her son were suffering.

A sound made her whirl about. Could Lina be back already? The shadowy figure of a man stood in her doorway. "I been knockin', Mistress."

Still clutching her blanket, she rose from her chair. A tickle of fear shot up her spine. Who was he? He spoke English, not Dutch or French. "What do you want?" she demanded.

The man stepped further into the room and removed his hat. A gust of wind and rain swept in the doorway behind him, and he hurriedly turned to close the door. She was alone in the house with a strange man. She backed up a little, keeping her chair between them. "Who are you?" she snapped. "How dare you come in my house uninvited!"

He stepped a little closer. Water dripped off him onto the roughhewn flooring. "Do you not recognize me, Mistress? 'Tis me, Welby Keane."

"Keane!" she spat out his name. The light in the room was dim, but she doubted she would have recognized him even in the bright sunlight. His nose looked to be mashed to one side of his face, he appeared to be skin and bones, his ragged clothing hanging on him, and his eyes, sunken in their sockets, had a desperate look to them.

"I seen your husband leave, then your servant. I waited a bit t' be certain you was alone."

"I am asking you again. What do you want?" He had tried to catch her alone. Why? Did he mean to rape her? To kill her? She stepped back a little further, and her grasping fingers found the fire poker.

"I need your help, Mistress," he said. "I need some money to book passage to the Virginia colony. I been warned t' stay out o' Manhattan by the louts what done this to my face." He pointed to his crooked nose. "They said do they see me, they will kill me. I been hidin' out on a farm north o' here, but now the harvest is in, the farmer says he cannot afford t' keep me on. Paid me next t' nothin' an' fed me even less. I slunk back into town an' down t' the wharf an' I found me a cull what will slip me aboard his ship do I give him ten guilders. I spotted your slave yesterday and followed her here. That is how I learned where you live." He wiped a grubby hand across his forehead. "Now, I figure you can afford me the coins. So's I will not be talkin' t' your husband 'bout what you paid us t' do."

Speechless, she stared at the man. He had not done the job she had paid him to do, and now he was wanting her to give him more money. When she thought back to all that had happened to her since he first accosted her outside the mercantile shop, she realized he was the one to blame for all her misery. She would still be in her lovely home. She would be attending Glynneth's wedding, playing the gracious hostess, happy in the knowledge she would no longer have to live under the same roof as the woman who so beguiled her husband. Her cherished son would be living in the kind of home he deserved, not this blighted hovel.

Red hot anger gripped her. How dare he come slinking around, threatening her. Drawing in a deep breath, she felt her nostrils flare. She reached behind her with her other hand to get a better grip on the poker. She smelled an acrid scent in the air but ignored it. She would not give Keane any money. She would instead give him the beating he so deserved.

He made a sudden move toward her, a look of alarm on his face. "Mistress!" he cried, pointing at her. "The fire, the fire!"

Paying no heed to his words, she sprang at him. Wielding the poker with both hands, she took a swipe at his head and caught him on the ear. He yelped and backed up. "Mistress, the fire," he cried again, and she realized the blanket that slipped from her shoulders had caught fire. A blaze could quickly spread. Well what care she if the decrepit house burned down. At the moment, all she wanted to do was smite the man who was the cause of all her pain and suffering.

She continued swinging, and he, arms raised to ward off the blows, continued backing up. When he turned to jerk open the door, she jabbed the pointed end of the poker into his back. Blood spurted out and began streaming down his worn coat. Groaning, he staggered out the door. Following after him, she applied blow after blow to his head. Not until he fell face down in the muddy street did she feel a scorching heat on her legs and buttocks, but even then she could not stop whacking at the prostrate form at her feet.

She heard someone screaming, "She's on fire, she's on fire."

Heat singed her hands, and looking down, she saw her gown was on fire. Dropping the poker, she tried batting at her flaming skirt. Pain brought an agonized scream to her throat. Panicking, she realized her entire gown was burning. God help her, her hair had caught fire. She pounded on her head, then suddenly, she was knocked to the ground and rolled around in the puddled street. People all around her were shouting. Smoke filled the air. She realized she was no longer on fire, but oh, the pain, the pain.

Chapter 37

Latimer popped an egg into his mouth and munched happily. The wedding, the breakfast feast, the beauty of the bride, all were perfect. The large dining chamber accommodated the adult guests. The children had been relegated to the smaller family dining chamber. They seemed pleased to be considered responsible enough to need no adult supervision. He heard occasional bursts of giggles come from the nearby room, but no squabbles. Of course, Raissa and Jolie were old enough to keep the younger children from getting too effusive.

Raissa Gervais was turning into a pretty young woman, he thought. Soon young men would be pounding on the Chappells' door asking to court her. She had a softness to her, a gentleness. He doubted she would ever match her sister's beauty or vivaciousness, but she had a steadiness he found admirable. When he teased her, she would look up at him with her large innocent brown eyes and proclaim she knew he was full of flummery, and she would not believe a word of his prevarications. He would hoot with laughter, and she would smile sweetly like a fond mother enjoying the pranks of her child. Yes, she would make some lucky man a very good wife. A sensible, loving wife.

Turning to answer a question Hendrika Kerstan put to him, he stopped in mid-sentence when the Fortiers' slave, Lina, burst into the room. Her wide and frightened eyes searched the table and landed on Gaspard. Wringing her hands she cried, "Oh, Meneer, Meneer, you must come at once! Mevrouw! And the house! A fire! Oh, you must come quickly."

Gaspard and every other man at the table sprang to their feet, but Latimer raised his voice, and in a harsh Dutch that could be heard over the exclamations that ratcheted around the room, demanded, "Is there a fire spreading and are all men needed to help put it out?"

Lina's gaze leapt to him. She shook her head. "No. No. The fire is

284

out, but Mevrouw…" She looked back at Gaspard. "Mevrouw, she is burned."

Gaspard started around the table, and Adler looked to join him, but Latimer was quicker. Putting a firm hand on Adler's shoulder, he said, "No, 'tis your wedding day. You stay here with your bride. I will go with Gaspard."

As Gaspard headed out the door behind Lina, Armand said, "I will go with you, Latty, but let us get our coats and Gaspard's as well."

"Indeed. We will need them," Latimer agreed.

"Should I come?" Capucine asked.

Latimer shook his head. "Nay, are you needed, I will come for you. For now, resume your meal. This may not be as bad as Lina would have us think."

But it was. Latimer had to look away when he first got a glimpse of Jeanette. She had been carried into a neighbor's house and placed on a low cot. A couple of women were in the process of stripping her burned clothing off her. With each tug, each movement, Jeanette let out an agonized groan or a shriek.

Stiff and looking dazed, Gaspard stood inside the doorway. A woman with thin, graying hair straggling from beneath her cap stepped over to him. "Near every part of her body is burned." She looked down and shook her head. "I fear she may not survive this."

Gaspard stared blankly at the woman for a moment then went to kneel at his wife's head. His brow furrowed, he attempted to hush her moaning, saying, "I am here, Jeanette, I am here," but if she heard him, she gave no indication. A hefty woman who seemed to be in charge began spreading a smelly grease over her.

"May help ease the burning sensation," the woman said, but Gaspard made no answer. He but gazed with hopeless eyes at his wife.

"Do you know what happened?" Latimer asked the thin woman.

Swiping a lock of her hair off her brow, she said, "Not exactly. We think the man she killed must have tried to attack her, and she beat him off. How she caught fire, I know not."

"She killed a man!" Latimer could not have been more astounded. "Where is he?"

"I think he is still lying out there in front of her house where he fell.

Beat him with a poker, she did. The men are awaiting the constable to know where to move him."

Good lord. Turning to Armand, he saw his friend looked as surprised as he felt. "Let us have a look," Latimer said.

The constable had arrived and was in the process of turning the body over when Latimer and Armand approached. "Anyone know him?" the constable asked.

No one answered. Like the other men, Latimer shook his head, but he knew the man. It was Keane. But why admit to knowing Keane. Better if no one knew the Fortiers were in any way connected with the villain. A heavy-set man standing nearby kicked something lying in the mud with the toe of his heavy shoe. "She came out of the house beating the wretch with this poker. She was all ablaze, but I cannot think she knew it. At least not until the beggar dropped." He swiped his hand across his brow. "Then she looked down, saw she was afire and started swatting at her gown. When her hair caught fire, that is when I thought to knock her down and roll her through the puddles to stop her from burning." He looked toward the house. "Inside of the house is pretty burned, but the roof being wet, it failed to catch fire. Fire mostly crept along the floor." He pointed to several other men standing around. "We put it out by throwing mud in on it. Would not think it is livable in there, though."

"Do you know who owns the house?" the constable asked.

"I know him," said Latimer, stepping closer. "His name is Gaspard Fortier. He is currently with his wife, two houses down. He was at a wedding when this happened. His wife was not with him because she had been feeling poorly." He had no trouble lying. No need to start tongues wagging. No one need know of the rift in the family. He wanted nothing to cast any shame on Glynneth.

"They have lived in the house less than two months," said the heavy-set man in his thick Dutch. "French they are. The Monsieur, he is a friendly sort. Always gave a cheery good day to the neighbors. Never saw his wife though. Not sure anyone saw her. Saw the maid, that slave over there." He pointed to Lina standing at the door, staring into the burned house. "They have a little boy, but there was no sign of him in the house."

"He was at the wedding celebration," Latimer interjected, looking at

286

the constable who had risen and was brushing off his hands. "The boy is being cared for. There need be no concern for him. But if you have no objection, we would like a look inside the house." Clamping a hand on Armand's shoulder, he added, "This is Monsieur Chappell, Monsieur Fortier's cousin."

"Ah, yes, Monsieur Chappell. We have met before."

Armand agreed. "We have met. Agreeable times until now." He shook his head. "If I may, I would see what is left of my cousin's belongings. I will move him and his wife back to our house. This was a temporary home for them while they decided where they wanted to build their new home. I dread thinking what my poor cousin will do. He was devoted to his wife."

Latimer appreciated the tale Armand fed the constable. No reason anyone should suspect the Fortiers were not a happily married couple. The fact that few had seen Jeanette played well into the lie that she was not well.

The constable nodded then asked, "Neither of you know this man?"

"No," said Armand. "I feel certain I have never seen him before."

Latimer shook his head and asked, "About the house?"

"Of course, go ahead. Check it out, but be careful. Roof seems secure, but walls may not be sound. Whole thing could crash down around you."

"We will be careful," Armand said, "and thank you." They left the constable calling to a couple of men to help him cart Keane off the street. But he would be back, and he would want to question Gaspard. They would need to make certain Gaspard was aware of the information they had given the constable. He would want to protect his wife's and his family's name.

"What should I do?" Lina asked when Latimer and Armand joined her at the door.

"Help us salvage what we can," said Latimer, "and we will take it to the Chappells'. But be careful not to trip over anything."

Filtered light seeping in the doorway provided their only light, but it was enough to see the damage, mud, thick on the floor and burned furnishings. They found next to nothing to salvage in the main room. Lina's possessions were either ashes or too burned to ever be used again, but the bed chamber, though smoky, had not been reached by the fire. Most of what was in the room could be saved. Armand requested a couple of the men who were still milling about outside to help him and Lina cart the personal items and few furnishings that had fit in the small room to his home. Latimer went to talk to Gaspard. He would then go get Capucine. What a way to end the happy wedding celebration. Well, no need for Glynneth and Adler to know the whole of it. They would find out soon enough.

Chapter 38

The last of the guests had departed. Gusta was clearing the remaining mugs and goblets from the hall, and Dominique and Hendrika were upstairs with Glynneth preparing her for her bridal bed. Adler paced restlessly back and forth, his mood vacillating between heavenly bliss and gnawing anger. Again Jeanette. She had to do her best to destroy Glynneth's peace. What had started as such a happy day despite the rain, had been turned into a tragedy.

Latty had returned to tell them Jeanette had indeed been burned. Gaspard was taking her to the Chappells' home, and Capucine would be needed to care for her. Poor woman. He saw Capucine rub her work hardened hands over the soft woolen skirt of the gown Glynneth had insisted be made for her. How seldom were the chances to get to wear such a gown. In the middle of the festivities, Capucine had to leave.

Adler knew he should pity Jeanette. Latty had pulled him aside and had privately admitted Jeanette had been badly burned, but Adler could find little empathy for the woman who had tried to have Glynneth and her son killed. Latty also told Curtice that he would need to take Guyon, Pierre, Ignace, and Lothair home with him. Raissa and Jolie could stop by their home and pick up anything they and the boys might need, but Armand wanted all of them out of the house while Jeanette was there. Adler knew on the morrow, he and Glynneth would be obliged to help with the children. Perhaps move them all in with them.

Latty had also informed him that Keane had somehow been involved in the mishap and was now dead. Unless Jeanette recovered, they might never know what truly transpired. To be honest, Adler cared little about what happened. If Keane was dead, that was a good thing. He could wish the same on Filmore. But all he was truly concerned with was making Glynneth happy.

Footsteps on the stairs brought him around. Dominique and Hendrika were descending. Both had wide smiles on their faces. "Your bride awaits you," said Hendrika. "As beautiful a bride as ever there was." She gave him a pat on the arm. "Go to her."

Dominique stopped in front of him. "I think I should go see if I can help Madame Chappell if you have no objection, Monsieur Adler. Gusta can finish what needs doing here."

Adler nodded. "Yes, go help her. But remind Gusta we are not to be disturbed before morning. No visitors, no messages unless one of the children becomes ill."

Answering for Dominique, Hendrika said, "The children will be fine. No doubt Mina has them busy with a game of spin the top or some such. You push all thoughts out of your mind except thoughts of your wife." She smiled and patted him again. "I bid you good afternoon."

Adler started up the stairs as Dominique closed the door behind Hendrika and headed out to the kitchen. Trying to keep his step light, not heavy like his heart, he entered the bed chamber that had once been Jeanette's and Armand's. Curtice had changed the furnishings and had the room freshly whitewashed. Any traces of its former inhabitants were gone, yet Adler could almost feel Jeanette's woeful presence. At least until he gazed upon his wife.

She sat in the middle of the bed, pillows piled around her. She wore a night rail of soft pink with silver ribbons tied up in bows. Her hair, floating about her shoulders, glistened under the candle light. His breath caught in his throat. How often he had dreamed of this moment yet had never believed it would actually happen. His heart swelling with his love for her, he advanced slowly into the room.

"You are so beautiful," he said. "That you would give yourself to me is more than I deserve, but I will treasure you and do all in my power to make you happy."

She held out her arms. "Then come to me. I am lonesome in this bed on my own. Come be one with me."

He needed no second invitation. Quickly disrobing down to his shirt, he padded about the cold floor on his bare feet putting out the candles. His eyes adjusting to naught but the dim light coming from the glow in the hearth, he crawled into bed with his bride. "Should I draw the bed curtains about us," he said.

She shook her head. "Nay, 'twould then be too dark for me to see you. I want to see you as I did when we were in the woods. I want to see the love in your eyes when you look at me."

"Then so it shall be," he said. In an instant he had his shirt off over his head and tossed it to the floor. Turning to Glynneth, he began untying all the little bows on her shift. As he worked, she reached out to touch his chest. Her fingers crawling across his skin sent tremors throughout his body. He wanted this bedding on the day of their marriage to be special. He would hurry nothing. He wanted to savor everything. Wanted Glynneth to savor everything.

When at last he had the ribbons undone, he helped Glynneth slip the soft garment off over her head. Her breasts, at last exposed to his view, were so lovely so enticing. Slowly, gently he touched her, caressed her as she had been caressing him. Bending forward, his lips met hers. So soft, so sweet. Tender and warm, her lips responded to his. Shifting her down onto the pillows, he entwined his fingers in her hair while caressing her body with his other hand. He nearly lost his good intentions to keep his lovemaking slow when she cupped his buttocks with her hands and pulled him closer. But though his member throbbed, he would not be rushed. This was her night. He wanted her to experience every delight imaginable.

His experience with women was not great. He feared he was no great lover, but he meant to pleasure Glynneth in every way he could think of. They would float to heaven together and enter paradise in a breathless euphoria wrapped in each other's arms.

※ ※ ※ ※

Glynneth had always enjoyed her lovemaking with Etienne, but she had never felt the wild, heady passion she experienced with Adler. He sent her head spiraling into the heavens, set her pulse racing, her heart cavorting in utter abandonment. Every inch of her body thrilled to his touch, longed for his kisses. She craved him with a fervor that left her gasping for air. Oblivious of time or reality, she let all thoughts of past or future depart and simply reveled in the present, in her surrender to his fervent capture of her soul.

When at last they melded and became one, she drew him deep inside her, arching upward to possess all of him. Then together they moved in amorous bliss until they climaxed with a fiery burst of brilliance that sent them shooting through the sky like a red hot comet. Coming back to earth, she clasped him tightly to her. This man who had been her dear friend for the past three years, and was now her husband, had won her heart and soul. She was his.

"God, I love you, Glynneth," he whispered, giving her a soft kiss on the cheek.

"No more than I love you, my dear husband. From this moment, we are ever bound as one. Never shall I love another."

"Ah, Glynneth," he whispered and claimed her lips.

She responded with eager delight, her passion rising as his kiss deepened. She was more than ready for another ride on a comet.

※ ※ ※ ※

Adler knew not how long they had been immersed in each other, but he noted the room had chilled and the fire had grown dim. Glancing at the hearth, he saw naught but a few glowing embers. Did he mean to stir them into a fire in the morning, he had best bank them. Glenneth's head was pillowed on his shoulder, and he hated to disturb her though he knew she was not sleeping. Giving her soft hair a kiss, he said, "I best tend the fire."

Shifting, she turned enough to offer him a kiss. "I suppose you must, but hurry back, we have things we must speak of."

"What would that be?" he asked, surprised.

"First, bank the embers. I feel I am going to be a spoiled wife. I have not had bedchamber embers banked by aught but me in many a year."

"I intend to do all in my power to make you a very spoiled wife," he said, giving the top of her head a kiss before rising.

When he returned to bed, Glynneth embraced him, warmed his toes with hers, and soon had him toasty and his member again rising to attention. However, her first question deflated his amorous intentions.

"Tell me about Jeanette. I saw Latty talking with you. You cannot deny knowing what has transpired. What caused the fire? Is Jeanette badly burned?"

"Would this not better wait for morning?" He wanted nothing to destroy the beauty of their time together.

"It cannot wait. I must need know. I know not why. I but know I need you to tell me what has happened. I would not wish evil to befall Jeanette, and yet in my heart, I cannot forgive her. I try, but over and over again, I see my little boy tossed into the river. I see him clinging to that log. I cannot bear to think of what would have been his fate had Lady Ann not jumped in after him." She reached up and touched Adler's face. "I can never thank you enough for giving them the dog. I still have an image of you – how you looked with that tiny puppy in your pocket. You were so hopeful you had done something good not wrong. I think perhaps I fell in love with you then, though I knew it not."

Turning from him, she continued, "I wish I could forgive Jeanette, but I cannot. Still, I must need know if she is badly injured."

"You have no need to forgive her. Nor have I, but I cannot tell you how badly she is burned. Latty chose not to tell me. However, I fear she could well die ere the night is through. I allowed Dominique to go to the Chappells' to help Capucine. I can tell you that Jeanette is badly enough burned that Armand wanted all the children to stay with Curtice. And I can tell you, the house is burned enough they cannot again live in it." Cupping her face, he turned her chin up so despite the dark that now pervaded the room, he could see the whites of her eyes. "I will tell you this. Keane, the man who tossed Noel into the river is dead. Apparently, Jeanette killed him."

"What!" Glynneth sat up. "How? Why?"

"We have no answers to any of those questions. And unless Jeanette lives, we may never have the answers." He slipped an arm around her waist. "Lie back down beside me. This whole thing has upset you. That is why I wanted to wait until morning to tell you about it."

"Perhaps I should not have asked," she said, snuggling back down beside him. She tilted her face up to his. "Kiss me, my dear husband, and make me forget all but my love for you."

He readily obliged her and soon they were again immersed in fervent lovemaking. He could not have imagined he could have such stamina. But then he had been well over three years without bedding a woman.

Once he had fallen in love with Glynneth, he would have felt sullied had he had relations with any other woman. To be honest, he had never even been tempted.

Their passions once again quenched, they lay curled in each other's arms. He was determined he would not go to sleep until he knew Glynneth slept. He would not have her wakeful and thinking about the tragedy that had marred their wedding day. He intended to be alert to her needs. His wait was brief. Glynneth cuddled closer, gave him a little kiss, and in a matter of moments, he felt soft puffs of air on his cheek. She slept.

What the morrow would bring, he had no way of knowing, he but knew all his dreams had been fulfilled. He could ask for nothing more miraculous.

Chapter 39

Thanks to Capucine's and Dominique's care, Jeanette survived. At least she lived, but the physician said she would never walk again, would never have more children. She would be bed ridden for the rest of her life and would need a constant care taker. Almost her entire body had been burned. Only her feet and her beautiful face had remained unscathed.

Latimer could not help but feel sorry for her. He tried to be of assistance to Gaspard and the Chappells. He again took up residence in the Chappells' loft as he had done on and off since first arriving in New Amsterdam. With winter upon them, he had no need to continue his wood harvesting. It would be spring before more logs could be floated down river from Spangler's property. Jeanette's earsplitting wails during the first days after the fire had been hard to endure, and he well understood why Armand wanted the children out of the house.

They were all presently living with Glynneth, and he knew she loved having them. During the day, they continued their education, and at night, Adler told them stories. From time to time, Latimer slipped away to join them in the evenings. Just being near Glynneth was always a treat, but seeing her so happy with Adler helped him sleep at night. The two people he loved most in the world had found a joy few people were ever lucky enough to know. He could not think he would ever know such joy, but he had hopes he would someday find a woman who could make him feel content.

The weeks passed, and Jeanette's body began to heal, but Latimer feared her mind had been affected. Though she could not explain why Keane had been at her house, she was proud of herself for having killed him. She seemed to think that fact absolved her of guilt. She seemingly had no memory of paying Keane and Filmore to kill Glynneth and Noel. The constable, satisfied Keane had meant to rob or maybe rape

Jeanette, decided she had been justified in killing Keane. That ended that. Latimer learned Filmore had returned to New Amsterdam, but only long enough to dispose of his wares, and to purchase supplies he would need for his planned move to Virginia. No one outside the family need ever know what transpired that day. Glynneth's reputation was safe and that was all that mattered to Latimer.

As she healed, Jeanette begged Gaspard to have Curtice come to see her, and the old man reluctantly agreed. Latimer had been present when, with dragging steps, Curtice entered the Chappells' home. He stopped at the door to Jeanette's bedchamber, took a deep breath, and drawing himself up, he entered the room. At first glance, seeing naught but Jeanette's face, he could not have thought her bad off, but as soon as she reached out a red, scarred hand to him, his face changed. He blanched, and Latimer stepped to his side to steady him.

"Ah, Father Curtice, you are so kind to come to see me. Please sit beside me," she said, waving her deformed hand at a chair next to her bed. Her voice sounded little different than it ever had, perhaps a bit raspy. Capucine had her propped up against her pillows. Her back finally healed enough she no longer had to spend all her days on her stomach.

Curtice slowly took the chair, and the little hand Jeanette held out to him, but he seemed repelled by her touch. Whether it was still because he hated her for her attempt on his grandson's life or because the hand was so grotesque in contrast to Jeanette's pretty face. A large red welt on her neck was not completely concealed by her bed gown, and Latimer saw Curtice glance at it then look away. Curtice could not know that most of Jeanette's body looked far worse. Latimer had seen the disfigured body numerous times when he had helped Capucine and Dominique apply emollient poultices of absorbent powders and oily fluids to her wounds when they changed her bandages. Fortunately, they had a good supply of laudanum to help ease her pain. As she slowly healed, they reduced the daytime doses so she was fairly cognizant, but her night time doses remained heavy enough to allow her to sleep through the night.

"You asked to see me," Curtice said stiffly.

"Yes, dear Father Curtice. You must know... surely Gaspard has told you... that I killed the horrid man who tried to kill Noel. Now that he is

296

dead, may Gaspard and Lothair and I move back into your house with you? I cannot bear to go back to that shanty we were living in, and we cannot stay with Capucine forever, though I will say she has been most kind. Still, I would like to return to my home." She cocked her head and looked dazed. "You know, I cannot remember whatever possessed me to leave it." She brightened. "Oh, yes, I had to kill Keane. That is what it was. He was to blame for all my suffering. But now he is dead." She looked directly at Curtice. "So may we come home?"

Curtice looked up at Latimer, then over at Capucine who stood in the doorway. His eyes asked the question – is her mind gone?

Capucine crossed over to stand at the foot of the bed. "Now, Jeanette, you must not think of going anywhere. You are not yet well enough."

Jeanette stuck out her lower lip. "You and Gaspard keep saying that. And when will you let me see my baby? I have not seen Lothair in … in…?" She shook her head. "Well it has been a long time."

"Soon. You shall see him soon. I promise you. Now I think you should rest," Capucine said

"Yes, I am tired." She looked directly at Curtice. "Thank you for coming." She again held out her hand.

Curtice took her hand and looked down at her. "I will consider your request, Jeanette. I will talk with Gaspard. We will see."

She smiled, and Latimer thought he saw a glint in her eyes. Was she really mentally confused, or was she but fooling them all? He wondered.

§   §   §   §

Jeanette breathed a soft sigh as her new maid adjusted the pillows behind her. Claudine, black as night and with large brown eyes and a bright smile, was the newest addition to the Fortier household. Her sole job was to tend to Jeanette's needs. Curtice had relented, and for Gaspard and Lothair's sake, had allowed Jeanette to move back into his home – under the condition he never had to see her. She wondered if he never wanted to see her because of her hideous disfigurement. Why else did he wish to avoid her? Sometimes she seemed close to having an answer, but then it would vanish as her pain increased, and Claudine gave her another dose of laudanum.

When Curtice went to work, Jeanette could be carried downstairs, but she must be back in her room before he returned. She was not allowed to dine with the family on any occasions. Curtice said he could never forgive her, but he believed God had delivered a harsh enough punishment on her, and he would not add to it. What she had done that Curtice could not forgive her or that God should visit such painful punishment upon her escaped her. It must be something evil, but what? She had asked Gaspard, and he had but stared at her. Then he shook his head and said he had no wish to speak on the subject.

Jeanette believed it had something to do with Glynneth and Noel, but she had killed the man who tried to kill them. So what? What had she done?

"Madame, would you have me sing to you to help you sleep?" asked Claudine.

Jeanette nodded. Claudine had a low, melodic voice, and her songs from her mother's African homeland, though Jeanette could not understand the words, were soothing and helped her fall asleep as the laudanum took over. Curtice had personally seen to the purchase of Claudine. She came from the French Indies and spoke only French, but Gusta was attempting to teach her Dutch. Jeanette liked Claudine's youth, her cheerfulness and her strength – she was a burly young woman. She clucked over Jeanette, worried about making sure she was comfortable, and always made certain Jeanette's gloves were on and her arms and neck were covered whenever Lothair was brought in to visit his mother. Jeanette agreed with Gaspard that her son was too young to see her disfigurement. Such a sight might give him nightmares.

Gaspard no longer shared Jeanette's bed, not even her bedchamber. Claudine slept on a cot to be handy should Jeanette need her at any time during the night. Sometimes Jeanette missed Gaspard, missed snuggling close to him when the night grew cold, but now, was she cold, she had Claudine stir up the fire or add another blanket to the bed. And soon, warmer nights would be returning. Spring was advancing. She was glad her bed was situated at an angle where she could look out a window. See the trees leafing out. Claudine assured her when the weather was warm enough, she and Gusta would carry her downstairs and let her sit under a tree until time for Curtice to return for his dinner.

Jeanette hated Curtice but was not certain why. Was it because he had forced her out of her home and made her live in that terrible shanty? But why he had done so was another one of those mysteries. She knew it all centered around Keane. Keane had tried to kill Glynneth and Noel. And she had needed to kill Keane. She could not remember why. At times she thought these questions would drive her crazy. It often angered her that Gaspard would not explain things to her, but then the never ending pain would become unbearable, and all she wanted was another dose of laudanum.

Gaspard visited her every evening but he seldom stayed long. He never gave any indication he missed their coupling. But she knew he must. He had been very lustful. She wondered if he would find himself a paramour. Mayhap Lina. The maid was attractive enough. Besides helping tend the needs of the house, she was in charge of looking after Lothair. But not after the babe was put to bed. And Curtice retired early. Who would be the wiser did Gaspard couple with the slave?

Jeanette wished she could see Lothair more often, but she knew her dazed condition made that impossible. She saw him in the morning before Lina took him to Glynneth's, and in the evening before Lina put him to bed. Lothair was yet too young to be learning his letters, but he enjoyed being with the other children at Glynneth's house. Jeanette hated that Glynneth got to enjoy Lothair, while she, his mother, had such brief moments with him. And what, when he visited her, must Lothair talk about in his bubbly little voice, but his Auntie Glynneth and his cousins, Meara and Noel.

Jeanette was slightly surprised neither Glynneth nor Adler had been to see her. They bore her no love, and she bore them no love, though she could not remember why. Still, she thought Glynneth might visit and thank her for killing Keane, the man who tried to kill Noel. Glynneth should be grateful, yet she showed no appreciation. Jeanette wondered a bit at that.

She knew Glynneth and Adler were presently living in Jacques Chappell's house while they were having a home built outside the wall that crossed the island. Gaspard told her it was close by the boat building shop Adler had invested in. She was not particularly interested in where they might live except for the fact, she wanted to know where Lothair would be each day. She wanted to be able to picture him toddling about, laughing his adorable little chuckle, giggling when anyone tickled him. God how she missed her child.

With Claudine's voice falling pleasantly on her ears, Jeanette became more and more drowsy. How greatly her life had changed. She had been young and beautiful and had married the handsome Gaspard. They had lived in a fine home in Dublin, and she had been the consummate hostess. Then Curtice forced them all to move to this horrid new world.

She tilted her head to one side and opened her eyes a fraction. Was that why she hated him? Certainly that would be a good enough reason, but somehow it did not seem like the whole reason. She closed her eyes again. She had little in her life now that offered her any solace. There was but one fact that never failed to give her a smile. Her mind reached back to a day she should want to forget, but instead cherished. She had been lying on her stomach, enduring abject pain from her burns, when Gaspard had knelt beside her. Through her pain-blurred eyes, she thought she read concern on his face.

Concern? It near choked her. She would not have been in that misery if not for him. If he had loved her as he should have. Loved her as she loved him. Had he loved her and not Glynneth, she would never have needed to kill Keane. She would never have been living in that horrid shanty. Would never have caught on fire. Would not be suffering so abominably. Concern indeed! Red hot anger as hot as the burns tormenting her body invaded her heart.

She managed a semblance of a smile and whispered, "Come closer, Gaspard."

He obeyed, positioning his ear near her mouth.

"Did Glynneth marry Adler Hayward?" She managed to croak out the question.

He drew back enough to look at her. "They are married. Yes," he said.

Again she forced what she hoped was a smile. "Good. Do you know why I say good, my husband?" she asked.

He but stared at her, so she continued, "Because now I know that even if I die, you will never have Glynneth. She will always be beyond your grasp."

He jerked back. Stared at her a moment longer, then rose and left the room. She would never forget the look on his face. She had seen the pang of despair, his acknowledgement that she spoke the truth. Over and over he had stabbed a knife into her heart. She at last took her revenge. Adler Hayward was strong and virile, not apt to die like Etienne. Gaspard would go to his grave ever loving another man's wife. Never able to have his dreams fulfilled. He would live a life as tormented as her own.

"Are you feeling more at ease, Madame?" asked Claudine. "I do believe I see a little smile on your lips."

"Yes, Claudine, I am more at ease, but very sleepy. Keep singing, and I know I shall soon be asleep."

Claudine resumed the soft crooning, and Jeanette let her mind drift. Drift back to Dublin where she was hosting a fine dinner. Her parents were there, and Glynneth and Etienne. Everyone dressed in their finest. How handsome Gaspard looked. How lovely the table looked. White cloth, bayberry candles, pewter polished until it glowed. The scent of roasted pheasant and lamb stew wafting on the air. Ah, how delightful life was, how very delightful.

Chapter 40

Adler clasped Latty in an embrace and patted his back. "I shall miss you, dear friend. Glynneth and I and the children — we will all miss you." Spring was upon them and the river had thawed. Armand was headed back to Fort Orange with a boatload of trade goods, and Latty was headed back to Spangler's to continue his logging. Dirk Cuyler, Bonifacius Kerstan's young assistant, was going with him. Cuyler would select special trees, mostly white oaks and pines for the boats, but also trees with the natural curve between trunk and branch that were needed for the keel and sternpost. Cuyler would mark the trees, then return to help Kerstan. Latty's job was to log the trees and get them down river to Adler's and Kerstan's boat building shop, which Adler was pleased to say was prospering. They had hired several additional workers, including, Wally, the Dowers' nephew who had been instrumental in saving Noel.

Whenever the Dowers had come over to New Amsterdam to sell their produce, they allowed Wally to visit Noel. Wally was no longer needed to guard the boat since they could tie up their new boat that Curtice purchased for them at the Fortier wharf. In an attempt to thank Wally for her son's life, Glynneth gave Wally reading lessons and taught him to sign his name. The youth, though he had some trouble speaking, or making his thoughts clear, was incredibly adept at carving. Glynneth discovered his ability when he carved a small boat for Noel. Kerstan saw the boat carving and immediately wanted to hire Wally. For the smaller details needed for the boats, Wally was a natural.

Since Wally could not row across the East river every day to work, arrangements were made for him to live with the Kerstans — they had an extra room since Mina and Dirk were married. Wally could then go safely to and from work with Kerstan. He was a strapping youth, but because he was so gentle with his large puppy dog eyes and sweet

302

smile, Glynneth worried some of the rougher sort about the water's edge might try to bully him was he not with Kerstan.

Wally liked working on the boats, and he liked attending lessons with Glynneth. "I like to read," he told Glynneth. "I think I used to read before the horse kicked me, but then I forgot." He came for lessons every other day. One day he worked, the next day he studied. Glynneth felt the variety was best for him. The Dowers appreciated all they were doing for Wally, but they missed his help on their farm. Curtice solved that problem for them. The Dutch government had sent more than forty orphans to New Netherland that spring to work as indentured servants. Curtice purchased two young boys' indentures for the Dowers.

When the Dowers protested they could not accept such largesse, Curtice said, "In no way can I ever repay you and Wally for saving zee life of my grandson. No token will ever be enough. If Wally eez happy working on zee boats, zen I am happy. And I know you to be kind and caring people. Could zeez two young boys have better masters zan you two?" So the matter was settled. The Dowers had the help they needed, and Wally had a new more fulfilling life.

"You will have a care, will you not?" Adler said, returning his thoughts to Latty's departure. Latty and Cuyler were traveling upriver with Armand as far as the growing village of Tarrytown where Spangler lived and where Armand had purchased some property. Once Latty finished his work on Spangler's property, he and Spangler would begin logging Armand's property. Of course, Spangler hoped to have his house finished and his barn up so he could marry Dominique by the beginning of the summer. Adler hoped by that time Glynneth's brother would have found her two Irish maids willing to come to New Netherland. He and Glynneth had determined they would have no more slaves.

"Have no fear for me," Latty said. "I will not go too deep into any woods without marking a trail so I can find my way back. I will miss the lot of you, but I will see you when I bring the next bunch of logs down river."

Gaspard joined them just before the fluyt was ready to set sail. The tide had turned, and a strong breeze was blowing. They should make good time going up river. "Our best to your father and Simone," Gaspard said, gripping Armand's hand. "I cannot think we will be seeing them this summer. Jeanette will not be able to travel. Mayhap, does Glynneth go to Beverwyck, Lothair may go with her."

Adler nodded in agreement. "Aye, most likely Glynneth will wish to escape the sultry summer heat and the biting flies. Do please give our best to Jacques and Simone as well, and tell them Ignace is becoming a brilliant scholar."

After a final good-bye, Armand and Latty traipsed up the gangplank, and soon the fluyt, laden with a variety of goods for trade with the Indians and for the inhabitants of the growing Beverwyck settlement, swung out into the current. Her sails fluttered then billowed out. The ship shot away. Adler and Gaspard watched it for a bit, then Adler turned to Gaspard. "I am expecting our house to be finished and ready for us to move into it in less than a fortnight." He smiled. "With Glynneth in the family way, we will be needing more room."

Gaspard smiled. "I am happy for you both. Glynneth is so good with children." He looked back out at the river. "Lothair adores her."

Adler clasped his hand on Gaspard's shoulder. "Lothair is a fine little boy. You can be proud of him. Soon he will be learning his numbers and letters."

"Yes, yes. I am very proud of him. He is a good boy. I am glad he will have Glynneth to teach him."

Adler frowned. "Glynneth is concerned that she may not be giving the boys the education they should be getting. Especially Ignace. He has completed all the lessons Etienne wrote out for him in both Latin and Greek. Glynneth says she can continue his Latin lessons, but she fears she has not the expertise needed in the Greek. I think she means to ask Jacques if he wants to send Ignace to Amsterdam to complete his studies."

Gaspard shook his head. "She should have come to me. I was never the scholar Etienne was, but I can provide her with some additional lessons in Greek."

Adler brightened. "Could you. I told her she might ask you, but she feared you were so busy with your work and with your care of Jeanette, that it would be too much to ask of you."

"Nonsense. I would welcome the challenge. Jeanette mostly sleeps,

304

and Claudine gives her the best of care. Often in the evenings after Father retires, I am left with naught but a book."

"Ah, that will please Glynneth greatly. Why not have supper with us tonight, and afterward, you and Glynneth can thrash out what she needs."

Gaspard nodded. "I will do that."

"This evening then," Adler said, and headed off for a meeting he had with a newly arrived French Huguenot. The young man said he had worked as a shipwright, and Adler and Kerstan were considering expanding their trade from just boat building to ship building. A friend of Kerstan's was planning to open a rope making shop. Enough hemp was being grown to make the business possible. A ready supply of rope was needed before they could contemplate ship building. They would need a blacksmith, caulkers, sailmakers. They had much planning to do, but Adler and Kerstan both wanted to have a prosperous business to leave to their sons.

Adler smiled. He was a lucky man. Good friends, promising future, and the most wonderful wife any man could ever wish for.

☙ ☙ ☙ ☙

Glynneth gave Meara a kiss and Lady Ann a pat on the head and turned to tuck the blankets more closely around Noel. "Sleep well, my little love," she said, and picking up the candle, headed out the bedchamber door.

"Good night, Mother," her two children chimed in unison.

Smiling, she drew the door partially closed so the light from the family room would not keep the children awake. They had been allowed to stay up later than usual because their Uncle Gaspard had come for supper. It had been a jolly meal, then Alder had entertained Meara and Noel with a story about his brother's lively, headstrong sister-in-law, Arcadia, while Glynneth and Gaspard discussed Glynneth's needs for lessons in Greek for Ignace.

When they were done, Gaspard gave each child a small decorative marzipan. "Now you must save them for after your dinner tomorrow," he told them, no doubt knowing the sweets would be devoured before he was long out the door.

It had been a relaxing and fruitful evening. Glynneth thought Gaspard looked more at ease than he had in months. When she asked after Jeanette, he but said, "She dotes on Lothair, and she sleeps. She does little else. I think her pain is less. Claudine and Gusta have had her downstairs a couple of times, but Gusta says she never wishes to stay very long." He shrugged. "We have all adjusted to the life God saw fit to give us."

Glynneth nodded. He knew she had no belief in his God, but if it helped him – made his life more acceptable – she was glad he had his God.

Walking over to Adler, she wrapped her arms around his neck and sat down on his lap. His arms immediately encircled her.

"How do you feel, my love?" he asked.

She touched her forehead to his. "I feel wonderful. A new life is growing inside me. A little brother or sister for Meara and Noel. I could not be any happier."

He kissed her. "If you are happy, then I am happy. Nothing means more to me."

Sitting up straight, she brushed his hair off his forehead. "I have a letter from Nolan."

"Your brother! Is it good news? Did he find us a couple of maids?"

"He did. He was arranging for their passage when he sent this letter." She waggled her head. "I am guessing they could be here by next month. One girl is rather young. She is but twelve and a bit small for her age, being under nourished, he says, but he thinks she will be a good and faithful worker. The other is twenty and is married. Her husband will be coming with her." She ran a finger down the side of Adler's cheek. "He thought we might need a man to see to our gardens."

"Hmmm," Adler thinned his lips, then said, "'Twill make housing them a bit more complicated, but having a man for the heavier chores, and to see to the animals. That is good."

"I agree. We have Noam and Heloise while here in Jacques and Simone's house, but we cannot take them with us. Besides, we cannot condone lifetime enslavement. Anyway, we will need a man's hand about so that you feel free to work on your projects. If need be, we can put the

306

young girl in with Meara and give the servant room over to the married couple. We will work it out." She looked over at the low glowing fire in the hearth. "I would think Dominque will soon be leaving us. How I will miss her. Not just her service, but her companionship."

"Aye. She has been more than a servant, she has been a devoted friend. I hope she will be happy with Spangler. He seems a good man."

Glynneth nodded. "He does. And Dominique beams when she is with him. We must think of something truly remarkable to give them as a wedding gift."

"True, but now, with you sitting here on my lap, I have no mind to be thinking of gifts."

She giggled and rose. "Well then, my husband, do bank the fire, and lets us off to bed." They had allowed Noam, Heloise, and Dominique to retire after the supper dishes had been cleared and cleaned.

Adler apparently needed no second invitation. He soon had the fire in the family room and the one in their room banked. She blew out all the candles but one beside the bed, and slipped into her night rail while he shed his boots and clothing. He placed his clothing neatly on a chair where they would be handy for him to don come morning, or should any emergency arise during the night. Fires were a never ending threat in this burgeoning town. Adler had learned to be ever on the alert during his days in the woods. She liked his readiness. His concern for her and her children made her feel blessed.

When he crawled into bed beside her, she placed her hand on his chest. She could feel the pounding of his heart. He wanted her, and she wanted him, but tonight would be a night of slow lovemaking. They would revel in each other. She loved the feel of his hard body pressed against hers. Loved his soft kisses, his gentle caresses. Loved that he was hers.

She was a most fortunate woman. She had been lucky enough to have two wonderful husbands. Etienne would always have a place in her heart, but she loved Adler with equal, perhaps more, fervor. He had such a courageous, yet generous heart. Like the knights of Camelot. Could be he came from a long line of Celtic knights. After all, he had that half of a torque. She hoped they would have a son to inherit the torque. She wished she knew some way to discover its meaning, but she doubted she would ever know how it came to be in Adler's family. Well, it was an entertaining mystery, a piece of the man she loved.

Adler nuzzled her, and she turned her attention back to him, her sweet and loving knight. Her lips met his, and she surrendered to her desire.

The End

Look for my Next Novel!

Excerpt from

A Bewitching Dilemma

Chapter One

Salem, Massachusetts 1692

The sharp wind biting the back of his neck, Garrett D'Arcy hunched his shoulders as the skiff grated onto the pebbled beach. Thick leather boots protected his legs from the cold ocean waves as he stepped from the boat and splashed ashore. Too long in confinement, he savored the crunch of the graveled shore under foot and the call of the seagulls as he marched up the slight incline to get a better view of the nearby borough. It was a gray day and a gray town, but a surprisingly bustling town for so early in the morning. The sun was not yet over the horizon.

"I would not have expected so much to-do before the sun breaks," D'Arcy said, glancing over his shoulder at his first mate.

Sefton Ridgely nodded. "Aye, Salem is a busy port, but no doubt 'tis the hanging what has brought more folk out."

"Hanging!" D'Arcy whipped about, near colliding with his first mate. An unbidden shiver coursed down his spine, but his jaw tightened when Ridgely asked, "Are you sure you are well enough tae be about, Captain? 'Tis a mite nippy for mid-October."

"I am well enough," D'Arcy growled, "but curse this damn plague and curse those damn islands." He had first contracted the ague three years earlier in the West Indies. It had nearly killed him then, and he still suffered from periodic chills that left him shaking in his bunk, often at most inopportune times. The trade of goods in this flourishing seaport had been conducted by Sefton Ridgely. Not that he failed to have complete faith in his first mate's ability to bargain profitably – he just hated being helpless. Helpless and vulnerable whenever the chills attacked. Even more he hated being dependent on his crew – loyal though his hand-picked men might be.

He brushed aside Ridgely's concern and demanded, "What is this about a hanging?"

"They mean tae hang a witch taeday."

"A witch!" D'Arcy knew his voice sounded choked as his throat tightened.

Ridgely raised an eyebrow, "Aye, Captain, a comely one, too, so I have been told."

D'Arcy's skin prickled as he met his first mate's level gaze. "In truth?"

"Aye," Ridgely acknowledged with a grunt, and he gripped D'Arcy's shoulder in a patent attempt to propel him toward the town. "Come, let us be getting you out o' this wind. I will take you tae meet Breakwaite, and he can tell you the whole o' it. He holds no countenance wi' it, I warn you. Seems, o'er the past few months, they have hanged several others, including a minister. I have been told that throughout the colony, over a hundred souls are in prisons awaiting their trials."

D'Arcy jerked free and again faced his first mate. "Lord, Seff, what manner of people are these Puritans?" He knew little of the Puritans' faith, only that they shunned the feast day celebrations and opulent trappings of the Church of England.

"Fearful ones, I would say. Ones we want no' tae have much truck wi'. I am more than ready to be rid o' this town. Breakwaite's a decent sort, but most o' the others be much tae God fearing for my taste. They have half a dozen rum distilleries, and alehouses abound, but none o' the women, be they plain nor pretty, would dare be seen so much as talking wi' any o' the crew. I tell you, the men are sorely tried. So let us step lively and we will soon be putting these Puritans behind us."

After skirting the teeming activity around the warehouses and

312

wharves where fishing vessels were putting out to sea and trading ships awaited their turn to dock, D'Arcy allowed his first mate to pilot him through the town proper. He chose to ignore Ridgely's nudge to his ribs as the young women of Salem turned to stare. Aware of the passions he stirred in the breasts of women, he readily used them to gratify his own desires. The women of Salem might pay no heed to his men, but they were as susceptible to his charms as any other females. Tall and broad shouldered, D'Arcy knew he cut an impressive figure. Having lost little weight with this recent fever, his muscular legs needed no false padding. He believed himself fortunate to be as well-favored in face as in form. His strong chin, narrow high-bridged nose, and high cheek-bones gave testament to his Norman ancestry, but he thanked his Celtic heritage for his most striking features, his mane of burnished red hair and his sea green eyes. Most women found the combination mesmerizing.

Wide-eyed chits, willing to risk their mother's ire, flitted about in obvious attempts to attract his attention. That is, were they able to overcome their bemused numbness and close their gaping mouths. He noted even the town matrons could scarce resist casting sly glances in his direction. But today, as he brushed past their simpering faces, he did little more than touch his fingers to the brim of his hat. His earlier buoyancy deflated by Ridgely's revelation, he simply wanted to finish his business in this unsettling township and set sail with the outgoing tide.

҂   ҂   ҂   ҂

Tempest Winslowe pulled her worn cloak more snuggly around her, tugging it tight about her throat as the harsh chill crept through the cracks between the slats of the dismal prison. She was grateful her trial date had been speedy. She feared she could not have borne many more days in these pinched dirty quarters. The cold dirt floor, strewn with filthy straw, crawled with all manner of insect life, and closing her eyes, she willed her skin not to itch. Her legs were cramped and her back ached as the heavy iron fetters and manacles on her ankles and wrists were shackled together and prevented her from either lying down or standing up straight.

The jail, made of rough-hewn slats crudely slapped together, was secure enough to keep the prisoners in, but not the weather elements out. When it rained, the prisoners had no choice but to sit in the mud and muck. Two leaky wooden buckets also occupied the small interior. One was supposed to hold drinking water, the other was to be used for personal necessities. Neither was filled nor emptied with any regularity, and on still days, a sour-sweet stench hung in the air.

Tempest's days were filled with the moans, bickering, and sorrowful prayers of the other prisoners. But to her, nothing was worse than the rats. They came at night. Their scuffling noises and the occasional gleam of small beady eyes caught by a glint of moonlight announced their presence. Scrunched into a corner, her knees drawn up to her chest, Tempest shivered each time one of the hideous creatures scampered across her feet or brushed against her hips. Other prisoners squealed or cursed when accosted. Tempest supposed the rats were after food scraps, though there were few or none of those. A bread crust at morning, another at evening, was all the town provided. If not for Serenity Norcross, Tempest was certain she must have starved to death.

Dear Serenity. Every morning with the sun, Serenity appeared. She brought fresh water that Tempest might bathe her hands and face and nourishing morsels to tempt her waning appetite. To oblige her friend, Tempest managed to consume each tidbit and even to drink a little ale. Serenity often brought treats for the other prisoners, and Tempest credited her friend's generosity with the kindly treatment she received from the other inmates.

The once soft woolen blanket now caked with mud and straw, which she tucked about her legs and feet, also came from Serenity. The nights were cold, and she cherished the meager warmth the blanket provided. Even with the blanket, she often awakened from her fitful and fleeting sleep with numb hands and feet. At least she had warmed up on clear days when the afternoon sunrays pierced through slits between the boards of the prison walls. Nonetheless, for the past few days she had been feverish, and her throat was so sore she hated to swallow. Her throat would soon be getting a lot sorer, she thought, as she peeked through the cracks at the shimmery dawn.

Tempest knew she should feel frightened or angry or both, but the past fortnight's injustices had melded with her mounting despair to consume her passions till all she could dredge up out of the pit of her stomach was a sense of nausea. She could see the crowd gathering. Almost time for the show. How many of the God-fearing populace of Salem, who had known her all her life, would be there to watch her hang? Shaftbury would certainly be there. Right up front, no doubt.

Against her will, her thoughts drifted back to nigh a year earlier when Elder Hiram Shaftbury had appeared on her doorstep. She had been amazed that the lean, sallow-faced man should come courting her. He was near old enough to be her father. Add to that, his wife had scarce been in her grave a month. Her stepmother thought she should feel honored. "After all, Tempest, he is a church elder and an important man in our community. And he is well off by most standards."

"That he may be Mother Eden, but I have no need of his wealth or his prestige." Tempest's eyes met her stepmother's stone-gray eyes. "I have the rent from my dowry house that Father left me, and I am content here. I want naught to do with the man."

Despite all she had done to dissuade Shaftbury – from refusing to accept the little gifts he brought her, to hiding out in the barn when he came calling – he continued to pay her court. She had believed herself fortunate her stepmother had not encouraged his suit as no doubt her father would have. But Eden had never encouraged any of her suitors. Why should she? Tempest knew that having her about to help care for the younger children and to clean and cook saved her stepmother the cost of a servant. And Eden was ever the frugal one.

But Shaftbury was a shrewd charlatan. One day Tempest had come in from milking the cows to find Eden and Shaftbury deep in conversation. She turned to leave after depositing the milk buckets by the door, but Eden called to her. "Tempest, do you not see you have a visitor?"

"I have other chores to finish," she replied and almost had the door closed behind her when her stepmother's raised voice stopped her.

"Tempest, come back this instant. You are being rude."

How well she remembered that spring day. Blue forget-me-nots dotted the fields and white blossoms on the apple and cherry trees scented the air. From that day forward, her stepmother had made her life a misery. She could not sit down to a meal without having Elder Shaftbury's virtues extolled or her own inadequacies deplored. Her stepmother would awaken her in the middle of the night to lecture her about her duties as a good Puritan to marry and reproduce for the glory of God. The next day, while Eden napped, she had her chores to tend.

And nothing she did was done correctly. Her butter was too salty, her bread too hard, her wash not clean enough. The socks she darned, the tears she patched, the hems she mended were shoddy and Eden insisted she redo them. Worst of all was sitting through Shaftbury's visits. She hated his self-righteous discourses, his ogling stares, and she cringed any time he touched her.

For near a month, she had been at a loss to why her stepmother had become Shaftbury's champion. Then she overheard Eden tell a friend that once Tempest married Shaftbury, he would allow Eden to collect the income from Tempest's dowry house. Tempest knew her stepmother had been angry that Tempest's father had bequeathed Tempest the house he had built in Salem when he, her mother, and she, but a wee babe, had first settled there. Even though Tempest gave half the rent to Eden for her bed and keep, Eden had not been satisfied. She wanted it all.

Jolted back to the present by a sharp shout of laughter, Tempest stiffened as dull thuds sounded against the planks near her head. Another thud and a shower of dirt sprinkled through the cracks. Peering out, she could see several young boys throwing dirt clods at the jail as they taunted, "Die, witch, die!" She knew all of the boys. One she had helped nurse through a fever only last spring. Another she had helped to find a wayward calf. Now they were ready to believe she was a witch who would do them harm. In their little hearts they hated her.

She closed her eyes and covered her ears with her hands to block out their hurtful gibes. She must not brood upon her fast-approaching fate. She must not let the chilling images cowering in the recesses of her mind surface. With a shudder, she channeled her thoughts back to her family.

The images of her young half brothers, Abel and Jacob, and her half sister, five-year-old Ruthie, brought tears to her eyes. They would miss her. She had been their bulwark against their mother. Eden Shipton

Winslowe, a severe and exacting woman, had little use for endearments or hugs. She had raised her two sons by her first marriage with a rigid discipline. Tempest doubted Noah and Ira Shipton had ever known a gentle caress or soothing word until she entered their lives. Their father had died six months before Tempest's mother. Though the Widow Shipton had been entertaining several suitors, she wasted no time letting Tempest's father know, even before Tempest's mother was in the ground, that he would be her choice for a new mate.

"In the harsh environment of this new world, surviving without a helpmate is a severe handicap. No man or woman is expected to mourn a lost spouse for long," Tempest's father explained the night before he married Eden. "Women are in great demand in this burgeoning colony of ours, especially strong and fertile women. Eden Shipton has proven to be both."

Large-boned and square-jawed, Eden could not be considered a beauty, but her commanding presence lent her a certain attractiveness. Still, Tempest suspected the fact that Eden Shipton had inherited from her husband a productive farm, which included a substantial house and barn and two indentured laborers, might also have influenced her father. The widow Shipton had been considered a prize, and Tempest's father had shown no reluctance in hastily forming an alliance.

Even in his middle years, Uriah Winslowe, tall and of moderate girth and with a full head of wavy brown hair, had been an attractive man. In later years, Tempest learned from Serenity, her mother's, as well as her own dearest friend, that no one had been surprised by Eden's partiality. "Your father could have had his pick of the single women in Salem," Serenity declared. "Women younger than Eden Shipton. Prize or no, the Widow Shipton wanted to quickly snare her prey."

Tempest allowed that Uriah and Eden had been well suited. Both being robust, miserly, and self-disciplined, they lived together in relative harmony until Uriah's sudden death five years past. During their six-year marriage, Eden had given Uriah two healthy sons and another daughter. Something Tempest's mother had been unable to do, though she had died trying. Every child after Tempest had been stillborn at birth or had not reached term. Uriah had blamed Tempest for this. She had been a difficult birth and had put too much strain on her mother.

"Sheer twaddle," Serenity, her dark eyes gleaming, asserted upon learning of Uriah's recriminations. "Your mother suffered far more from the difficult sea crossing than from your birthing. Should anyone be blamed for your mother's debility, 'twould be your father for taking her on the voyage when she was large with child."

Tempest still mourned her mother though she had been dead near twelve years. At times she could almost hear her tinkling laugh or feel her light touch upon her shoulder. Never a strong woman, the petit Deborah Maddock had not the stamina of her Celtic ancestors who prevailed against Roman, Saxon, and Norman invaders and clung to their homeland in the fens of Cambridgeshire. She had been proud of her heritage and had thrilled Tempest with tales of old.

Dark haired, and with wide-set delft-blue eyes and a generous mouth, Tempest favored her mother in appearance, but she had her father's height, vigor, and tenacity. With the hanging gibbet mere heartbeats away, she wished she had had more of her mother's docility and less of her father's obstinacy.

Chapter Two

D'Arcy found Benjamin Breakwaite's house substantial, if unassuming. Its clapboard sides and shingled roof were grayed with weathering, as were the various out-buildings, but the grounds were neat and well kept. Donning his coat, Breakwaite met them at the door. Though of finely woven wool, the coat was unadorned and of a somber hue, as were his breeches and stockings, but his waistcoat of emerald green, embroidered with perpendicular stripes of gold worsted braid, rivaled D'Arcy's own richly embellished scarlet damask waistcoat and quilted velvet full-skirted frock coat. A jovial man with a round face and firm handshake, he boomed a welcome, drawing first D'Arcy and then Ridgely into his home. "Good to see you again Mister Ridgely. I trust your good captain here finds all in order."

"I do find all in order and have but come by to pay my respects and to apologize for being unable to meet with you sooner," said D'Arcy, sweeping off his hat once his hand was released.

"Ah, Captain, you have no need to apologize. At times we are all laid low, though I trust you do not blame your illness on a spell cast by some witch. We have had a plenitude of such accusations here in Salem over this past year." No smile accompanied Breakwaite's banter.

D'Arcy squared his jaw. "No spell, naught but the misfortune to have visited the West Indies. I know not how any Englishman with good sense can live in that sweltering, stinking climate. Nary a soul can long escape the fevers that seem to breed there. But here now, what is this about witches and spells? Do you truly hang a witch today?"

Breakwaite's heavy brows drew together. "Tempest Winslowe is no witch. I have known the girl since she were a babe. Willful she may be, but as caring as she is willful. This hanging is a grievous wrong, a mockery of justice. Witches! The very idea is monstrous. A bunch of young girls with too much time on their hands have made fools of their elders and are responsible for the deaths of twenty innocent people. They claim they are bewitched. They see witches hanging from the rafters, tempting them. Mind you, no one else can see these spectacles." An angry red stained Breakwaite's face and his eyes swept from D'Arcy to Ridgely and back to D'Arcy. "Did their elders take a switch to their bottoms when all this started, we would have had the truth. Instead we have neighbors telling tales on one another because of some past spite, or to save his own skin because he has been accused of witchcraft. Witchcraft! Can you believe it! And now this! A man's cow dies, most like of old age. And a beautiful young girl is to be hanged."

D'Arcy had not meant to rile Breakwaite. He glanced at Ridgely who answered with a near imperceptible shrug. Breakwaite, noticing the exchange between his guests, drew a big hand across his face. He shook his head. "Forgive me. This past year has been trying. In ninety-one we lost our charter and became a royal colony with an appointed governor. Then all these witch trials started. Forgive my yammering. Have you broken your fast? Would that you might partake of some sustenance with me. I have some fine ale and happen to have a round of Dutch cheese off your own ship to go with some fresh baked bread. Join me, please," he urged.

D'Arcy felt he could hardly refuse. According to Ridgely, Breakwaite was a good man, and though he bargained shrewdly, he had been honest in his dealings. D'Arcy admitted, he was hungry. He had had little more than fish or chicken broth to eat since he had first become ill.

"You honor us," he said, pleased to see the big round face again wreathed in a smile.

"Good, good." Breakwaite rubbed the palms of his hands together. "I will get my wife to slice up the bread and cheese while I pour the ale. Please, be seated. Take the chairs. I will pull up a stool. Do get thee comfortable."

Breakwaite vanished into a back room, and D'Arcy pulled up one of the chairs Breakwaite had indicated at the trestle table. Ridgely sat at the opposite end. Breakwaite's booming voice could still be heard, though less distinctly, as he set those in his kitchen to preparing their meal.

The glowing remains of a fire in the massive central hearth, combined with low ceilings and small shuttered windows, made the front room stifling after the briskness of the outdoors. D'Arcy loosened the linen stock at his neck. Still wrestling with the baneful mood he had fallen into upon hearing about the hanging, he looked around the room, "Our host seems prosperous."

"Indeed," Ridgely answered, untying his fleece-lined jerkin. "The door behind you leads tae his office where we transacted our business. Breakwaite's a busy merchant wi' a finger in many pies. A number o' townsmen were in and out on various errands whilst I dealt wi' him."

"Good solid furniture, too," D'Arcy observed, hoping he did not sound as melancholy as he felt. He gestured to a tall hutch displaying pewter platters and mugs and to a low boy topped by a large Bible bound in delicately tooled leather. "More color and artistry than I might have expected."

Ridgely stroked his honey-brown beard and nodded. "Aye", he agreed, his vivid blue eyes alight in an appraisal of the room's furnishings. "Mind the red panels trimmed in green wi' gold scrolls about the borders on the hutch, the low boy, and the settle next the hearth. These Puritans know quality. They are no' apt tae buy a chair what will break apart after tae or three years o' service."

Breakwaite's wife, a round, pink-cheeked woman, bustled into the room with a wooden trencher heaped high with chunks of cheese and dark rye bread. Her garments were somber but of rich fabric. Her lace edged cambric overskirt, looped to reveal a brown woolen petticoat, was protected by a white linen apron. Her hair was hidden under a neat lappet cap. Though she greeted them cordially, her eyes looked red-rimmed as though she had been crying.

A homely young woman, the pox having marked her, entered behind Mistress Breakwaite. She might have been a daughter, but D'Arcy guessed her a servant, her clothing being plainer. And Breakwaite, carrying three brimming mugs of ale, made no attempt to introduce her.

The girl placed two smaller trenchers, one with smoked cod, the other with thick slices of sausages, on the table. D'Arcy could feel the girl's eyes upon him. She continued staring until Mistress Breakwaite admonished her and sent her scurrying back to the kitchen. He and Ridgely had risen when Mistress Breakwaite entered the room, but she urged them to resume their seats. Her husband introduced her, and she bade them welcome and encouraged them to eat hardy. She then retreated to the kitchen, but not, D'Arcy noted, without a glance over her shoulder at him.

After setting the mugs of ale on the laden table, the hefty Breakwaite pulled a sturdy stool up to the table and joined his guests. He bowed his head and began offering a lengthy blessing for the food set out before them. D'Arcy looked at Ridgely. Their eyes met then Ridgely bowed his head. D'Arcy followed suit. Breakwaite concluded with a plea to God to accept the soul of Tempest Winslowe, whom he knew to be no witch but a good God-fearing Christian.

"Now my friends," Breakwaite entreated them as he pulled out his knife to stab a sausage and put it on a chunk of bread along with some cheese, "help yourselves, and enjoy. Enjoy!"

His immediate hunger assuaged, D'Arcy sipped his ale and peered over the mug's rim at his host. He had no wish to nettle Breakwaite. And he knew his first mate would chide him for delving into an affair that did not concern him, but he could not restrain his curiosity about the accused witch Breakwaite so readily defended. He set down the mug. "Would I be impertinent to ask why they mean to hang this girl, Master Breakwaite? Why do they think her a witch?"

Breakwaite chewed his food and washed it down with a swig of ale. He eyed D'Arcy before he spoke. "I have to struggle to keep my choler in check on this. As I mentioned, Tempest is a caring girl. Sat with my wife when she had the fever last spring. Ne'er left her side afore she could sit up in bed and feed herself. A good girl Tempest is. And pretty, far prettier than most."

Breakwaite paused, and D'Arcy, his jaw muscles tightening, watched Breakwaite's liver-spotted hands absently stroke his mug. "Her father, when he died, left to her the home he built when first he moved to Salem. It brings a tidy rent and 'twas to be her dowry. No need to say she had plenty of young men offering her marriage, but she seemed to fancy none of them."

Breakwaite lifted his mug but set it down as a thoughtful expression crossed his face. "Tempest's mother was ever a gentle soul, but ill-starred. She died when Tempest was but a young chit, no more than ten,

322

I would hazard. Tempest's father was hearty enough, but never a mild man. I do believe 'twas his spleen what done him in."

"Better way tae go than some." Ridgely spoke from his end of the table, but D'Arcy waved him to silence as he pushed away thoughts of his own parents long since departed. He had no wish to flush out buried memories.

Their host drew himself up and puffed a sigh out through his nose. "Well, along comes Shaftbury. His wife not a month in her grave, and he sets out to court Tempest. She refused him as she had all the others. This embarrassed Shaftbury. He is an elder in our congregation and a man of no small amount of influence. Despite a twenty year age difference, he considered himself a desirable match for Tempest." Breakwaite made a face as if he smelled something unpleasant. He leaned forward and whispered, "Myself, I see him as a lecherous old man looking to a pretty young girl when by rights, 'twas to her stepmother he should have plied his court."

D'Arcy admired the girl's fortitude. At the same time a rank bitterness swept over him. For an instant his mind flew to England, to a meadow draped in clover, and to a pair of silver blue eyes brimming with desire. Then Ridgley's voice drew him back.

"So what has the old man's lechery to do with this... this girl being hanged as a witch?"

Ridgely was not one to mince words D'Arcy thought, glancing down the table at him before returning his attention to Breakwaite. His host, brow furrowed, rocked back and forth on his stool before responding. "'Twas early September. Late afternoon. The weather was almost balmy, the briskness of autumn yet to be felt in the air. Tempest, on her way home from taking a crock of broth to an ailing neighbor, stopped by a field to admire the sunset. Shaftbury happened along and spotted Tempest leaning on a gate railing. He admonished her for loitering, told her, was she his wife, he would soon have her doing God's work instead of dawdling about."

Breakwaite shifted on his stool and narrowed his eyes. His voice grew steely. "This, you understand, is what came out in the trial." D'Arcy felt their host meant to assure his listeners of his accuracy as he regarded first him and then Ridgely. At their nods, he continued, "Tempest responded that, indeed, she would never be his wife and would sooner marry the devil. Enraged, Shaftbury stormed off. The next day a cow, which had been grazing in the field where Tempest paused, died. Shaftbury learned of this and went to the magistrates who hold these witch trials. He told them he believed Tempest to be a witch. She had caused the cow to die. He said he feared for his own life and repeated what Tempest said about preferring to marry the devil."

"On that they mean to hang the girl!" D'Arcy protested. His agitation was rising while the food in his stomach seemed to be settling in a lump.

Breakwaite shook his head. "Not on that alone. Tempest's stepmother testified that she too believed Tempest a witch. Said she had feared her for years. Said she believed Tempest responsible for her mother's death to prevent her having other children. And for her father's death, once she had been willed the dowry house. Widow Winslowe swore the night before Tempest's father died, she awakened to find Tempest in their room, staring at her father. When Tempest saw her stepmother was awake, she left, but the next morning her father had the apoplexy and died."

"And the judges believed her?" D'Arcy's voice rose. He knew he was daft to be disturbed over this girl's hanging. Some girl he had never met. Yet the fact remained, he was. His hand went involuntarily to his throat. He could feel the rope burning his neck, his breath being cut off. The desperate struggle, the pain returned. His heart pounded. His eyes latched onto Ridgely. His first mate's calm gaze helped slow his racing heart, and he dragged in a raspy breath.

Breakwaite seemed not to notice his consternation. "Fools that they are, yes, they believed her. But 'tis certain, I am, the widow was after Tempest's dowry house. I said as much at the trial, but nary a soul would listen. Not judge nor juryman would believe the widow would perjure herself and thereby condemn her immortal soul to everlasting torment in hell."

Breakwaite twisted his mouth to one side. "Tempest denied the accusations, except the statement about preferring to marry the devil. That hurt her. Then others came forward. Girls who are not as pretty, boys rejected in their suit. Envy or wounded pride drove them. Suddenly

324

they remembered some incident of evil they were certain happened after Tempest visited their homes, a beloved pet dying, a poor fish harvest, even bread that failed to rise. The usual spectral evidence from the squirming, screeching girls who started these trials was scarce needed."

D'Arcy lifted his mug to his lips, but he did not feel like drinking. His throat tightened. He set his mug back on the table and let out a breath he had not noticed he had been holding. "And besides you, did no one stand up in her defense?"

"Her friend, Goody Norcross, and Goody Simon, a neighbor who has oft' been helped by Tempest. No doubt others would have liked to but were too afraid. Afraid they would be the next to be accused of witchcraft. As indeed happened with some who have criticized these trials."

"So the judges deemed Mistress Winslowe tae be a witch," said Ridgely.

"They did," said Breakwaite, anger staining his cheeks. "They determined she was a witch, and she is to be hanged this very morning."

D'Arcy numbly thrust a thick slice of sausage into his mouth then wondered if he would be able to swallow it. He wished he had never asked Breakwaite about Tempest Winslowe. Wished he had listened to Ridgely and had stayed aboard his ship.

"Well, 'tis glad I am I ate my fill afore you concluded your tale," Ridgely said. "My appetite might have suffered otherwise."

"I think mine has," D'Arcy said, managing to down the sausage. He doubted Ridgely would have found his appetite spoiled. Nothing seemed to disrupt the man's equilibrium.

Breakwaite shook his head, "Ah, good Captain, an empty belly serves no man well when the day's chores still need tending. Better to face the day's trials on a full belly. Our fasting will not halt the hanging."

Irritated by his discomposure, D'Arcy scraped back his chair and stood. "We thank you, Master Breakwaite, for this generous repast, but we must be getting back to the ship. The tide will have turned and, with luck, the wind will still be up. You have been most gracious."

"You are indeed welcome, Captain D'Arcy. I hope we may do business again someday."

"Cannot say for certain. 'Tis seldom we get up this way, but should we, you will be the man we contact," D'Arcy assured Breakwaite and extended him his hand.

Breakwaite answered with a hardy handshake to both D'Arcy and Ridgely. He wished them God's speed and a safe journey home before escorting them to his door.

As D'Arcy and Ridgely made their way back to their skiff, D'Arcy noticed the populace moving toward a hill outside the town's perimeter. The air seemed fraught with electricity, as though a storm brewed, but looking up, he saw the dark gray clouds of the early morning were no longer in evidence. The high clouds hastening along in the stiff breeze were white and wispy.

"Must be near time for the hanging," Ridgely said.

D'Arcy nodded but voiced no answer. He had been listening to snippets of conversation whirling about as they merged with the crowd. No words of sympathy, just spiteful twittering. Memories flooded back, a throng pressing forward eager to see and smell the fear of the victim. Eager to hear a last desperate plea for mercy. Eager to watch the death dance at the end of the rope. He shivered.

Biography

Celia Martin is a former Social Studies/English teacher. Her love of history dates back to her earliest memories when she sat enthralled as her grandparents recounted tales of their past, As a child, she delighted in the make-believe games that she played with her siblings and friends, but as she grew up and had to put aside the games, she found she could not set aside her imagination. So, Celia took up writing stories for her own entertainment.

She is an avid reader. She loves getting lost in a romance, but also enjoys good mysteries, exciting adventure stories, and fact-loaded historical documentaries. When her husband retired and they moved from California to the glorious Kitsap Peninsula in the state of Washington, she was able to begin a full-fledged writing career. And has never been happier.

When not engaged in writing, Celia enjoys travel, keeping fit, and listening to a variety of different music styles.

Visit my web site at:
cmartinbooks.kitsappublishing.com